Praise for the BONE DOLL'S TWIN

"*The Bone Doll's Twin* is a thoroughly engrossing new fantasy. It got its hooks into me on the first page, and didn't let loose until the last. I am already looking forward to the next instalment."
—GEORGE R R MARTIN

"Lynn Flewelling's *The Bone Doll's Twin* outshines even the gleaming promise shown in her earlier three books. The story pulled me under and carried me off with it in a relentless tale that examines whether the ends can ever completely justify the means."
—ROBIN HOBB

"A fascinating read, both intellectual and haunting."
—BARBARA HAMBLY

Voyager

HIDDEN WARRIOR

Book Two of the Tamír Triad

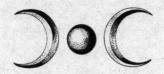

Lynn Flewelling

HarperCollinsPublishers

Voyager
An Imprint of HarperCollins*Publishers*
77–85 Fulham Palace Road,
Hammersmith, London W6 8JB

www.voyager-books.com

A Paperback Original 2003
2

Copyright © Lynn Flewelling 2003

The Author asserts the moral right to
be identified as the author of this work

A catalogue record for this book
is available from the British Library

ISBN 0 00 711310 2

Set in Goudy

Printed and bound in Great Britain by
Clays Limited, St Ives plc

For my father

Acknowledgments

Thanks, as always, to Doug, Matt, Tim, Thelma, Win and Fran for their continuing love and patience. To Lucienne Diver and Anne Groell, the best agent and editor a writer could wish for. To Nancy Jeffers, Laurie "Eirual" Beal, Pat York, Thelma White, and Doug Flewelling for reading, commenting, and urging me on. To Helen Brown and the good folks on the Flewelling newsgroup at Yahoo, for knowing my work better than I do. To Ron Gefaller, for getting the kinks out. To Horacio C. and Barbara R.—they know why. To all my friends on SFF.NET, for being there, in particular to Doranna Durgin and Jennifer Roberson for that last minute horse-related advice; any errors are mine for not asking.

The Skalan Year

I. WINTER SOLSTICE—Mourning Night and Festival of Sakor; observance of the longest night and celebration of the lengthening of days to come.

1. Sarisin: Calving
2. Dostin: Hedges and ditches seen to. Peas and beans sown for cattle food.
3. Klesin: Sowing of oats, wheat, barley (for malting), rye. Beginning of fishing season. Open water sailing resumes.

II. VERNAL EQUINOX—Festival of the Flowers in Mycena. Preparation for planting, celebration of fertility.

4. Lithion: Butter and cheese making (sheep's milk pref.) Hemp and flax sown.
5. Nythin: Fallow ground ploughed.
6. Gorathin: Corn weeded. Sheep washed and sheared.

III. SUMMER SOLSTICE

7. Shemin: Beginning of the month—hay mowing. End and into Lenthin—grain harvest in full swing.
8. Lenthin: Grain harvest.
9. Rhythin: Harvest brought in. Fields plowed and planted with winter wheat or rye.

IV. Harvest Home—finish of harvest, time of thankfulness.

10. Erasin: Pigs turned out into the woods to forage for acorns and beechnuts.
11. Kemmin: More plowing for spring. Oxen and other meat animals slaughtered and cured. End of the fishing season. Storms make open water sailing dangerous.
12. Cinrin: Indoor work, including threshing.

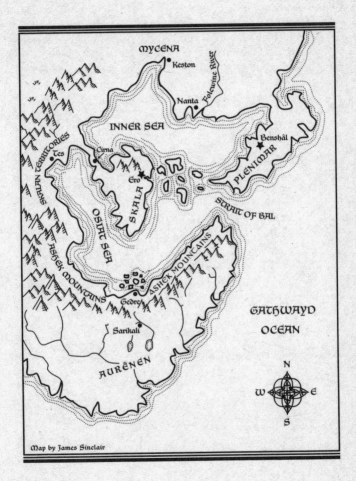

Map by James Sinclair

THE INNER SEA

Skalan Territories

Cirna

Colath • Atyion
• Ilear
★ Ero
Alestun •
Volchi •

Ylani

OSIAT SEA

Afra

Erind

· SKALA ·

Map by James Sinclair

Hidden Warrior

PART I

I ran away from Ero a frightened boy and returned knowing that I was a girl in a borrowed skin.

Brother's skin.

After Lhel showed me the bits of bone inside my mother's old cloth doll, and a glimpse of my true face, I wore my body like a mask. My true form stayed hidden beneath a thin veil of flesh.

What happened after that has never been clear in my mind. I remember reaching Lhel's camp. I remember looking into her spring with Arkoniel and seeing that frightened girl looking back at us.

When I woke, feverish and aching, in my own room at the keep, I remembered only the tug of her silver needle in my skin and a few scattered fragments of a dream.

But I was glad still to have a boy's shape. For a long time after I was grateful. Yet even then, when I was so young and unwilling to grasp the truth, I saw Brother's face looking back at me from my mirror. Only my eyes were my own—and the wine-colored birthmark on my arm. By those I held the memory of the true face Lhel had shown me, reflected in the gently roiling surface of the spring—the face that I could not yet accept or reveal.

It was with this borrowed face that I would first greet the man who'd unwittingly determined my fate and Brother's, Ki's, even Arkoniel's, long before any of us were born.

Chapter 1

Still caught at the edge of dark dreams, Tobin slowly became aware of the smell of beef broth and a soft, indistinct flow of voices nearby. They cut through the darkness like a beacon, drawing him awake. That was Nari's voice. What was his nurse doing in Ero?

Tobin opened his eyes and saw with a mix of relief and confusion that he was in his old room at the keep. A brazier stood near the open window, casting a pattern of red light through its pierced brass lid. The little night lamp cast a brighter glow, making shadows dance around the rafters. The bed linens and his nightshirt smelled of lavender and fresh air. The door was closed, but he could still hear Nari talking quietly to someone outside.

Sleep-fuddled, he let his gaze wander around the room, content for the moment just to be home. A few of his wax sculptures stood on the windowsill, and the wooden practice swords leaned in the corner by the door. The spiders had been busy among the ceiling beams; cobwebs large and fine as a lady's veil stirred gently in a current of air.

A bowl was on the table beside his bed, with a horn spoon laid out ready beside it. It was the spoon Nari had always fed him with when he was sick.

Am I sick?

Had Ero been nothing but a fever dream? he wondered drowsily. And his father's death, and his mother's, too? He ached a little, and the middle of his chest hurt, but he felt more hungry than ill. As he reached for the bowl, he caught sight of something that shattered his sleepy fantasies.

The ugly old rag doll lay in plain view on the clothes chest across the room. Even from here, he could make out the fresh white thread stitching up the doll's dingy side.

Tobin clutched at the comforter as fragments of images flooded back. The last thing he remembered clearly was lying in Lhel's oak tree house in the woods above the keep. The witch had cut the doll open and shown him bits of infant bones—Brother's bones—hidden in the stuffing. Hidden by his mother when she'd made the thing. Using a fragment of bone instead of skin, Lhel had bound Brother's soul to Tobin's again.

Tobin reached into the neck of his nightshirt with trembling fingers and felt gingerly at the sore place on his chest. Yes, there it was; a narrow ridge of raised skin running down the center of his breastbone where Lhel had sewn him up like a torn shirt. He could feel the tiny ridges of the stitches, but no blood. The wound was nearly healed already, not raw like the one on Brother's chest. Tobin prodded at it, finding the hard little lump the piece of bone made under his skin. He could wiggle it like a tiny loose tooth.

Skin strong, but bone stronger, Lhel had said.

Tucking his chin, Tobin looked down and saw that neither the bump nor the stitching was visible. Just like before, no one could see what she'd done to him.

A wave of dizziness rolled over him as he remembered how Brother had looked, floating facedown just above him while Lhel worked. The ghost's face was twisted with pain; tears of blood fell from his black eyes and the unhealed wound on his breast.

Dead can't be hurt, keesa, Lhel told him, but she was wrong.

Tobin curled up against the pillow and stared miserably at the doll. All those years of hiding it, all the fear and worry, and here it lay for anyone to see.

But how had it gotten here? He'd left it behind when he'd run away from the city.

Suddenly scared without knowing why, he almost cried out for Nari, but shame choked him. He was a Royal Companion, far too old to be needing a nurse.

And what would she say about the doll? Surely she'd seen it by now. Brother showed him a vision once of how people would react if they knew, their looks of disgust. Only girls wanted dolls . . .

Tears filled his eyes, transforming the lamp flame into a shifting yellow star. "I'm not a girl!" he whispered.

"Yes, you are."

And there was Brother beside the bed, even though Tobin hadn't spoken the summoning words. The ghost's chill presence rolled over him in waves.

"No!" Tobin covered his ears. "I know who I am."

"I'm the boy!" Brother hissed. Then, with a mean leer, "Sister."

"No!" Tobin shuddered and buried his face in the pillow. *No no no no!*

Gentle hands lifted him. Nari held him tight, stroking his head. "What is it, pet? What's wrong?" She was still dressed for the day, but her brown hair was unbound over her shoulders. Brother was still there, but she didn't seem to notice him.

Tobin clung to her for a moment, hiding his face against her shoulder the way he used to, before pride made him pull back.

"You knew," he whispered, remembering. "Lhel told me. You always knew! Why didn't you tell me?"

"Because I told her not to." Iya stepped partway into the little circle of light. It left half her square, wrinkled face in shadow, but he knew her by her worn traveling gown and the thin, iron-grey braid that hung over one shoulder to her waist.

Brother knew her, too. He disappeared, but an instant later the doll flew off the chest and struck the old woman in the face. The wooden swords followed, clacking like a crane's bill as she fended them off with an upraised hand.

Then the heavy wardrobe began to shake ominously, grating across the floor in Iya's direction.

"Stop it!" cried Tobin.

The wardrobe stopped moving and Brother reappeared by the bed, hatred crackling in the air around him as he glared at the old wizard. Iya flinched, but did not back away.

"You can see him?" asked Tobin.

"Yes. He's been with you ever since Lhel completed the new binding."

"Can you see him, Nari?"

She shivered. "No, thank the Light. But I can feel him."

Tobin turned back to the wizard. "Lhel said *you* told her to do it! She said you wanted me to look like my brother."

"I did what Illior required of me." Iya settled at the foot of the bed. The light struck her full on now. She looked tired and old, yet there was hardness in her eyes that made him glad Nari was still beside him.

"It was Illior's will," Iya said again. "What was done was done for Skala's sake, as much as for you. The day is coming when you must rule, Tobin, as your mother should have ruled."

"I don't want to!"

"I shouldn't wonder, child." Iya sighed and some of the hardness left her face. "You were never meant to find out the truth so young. It must have been a terrible shock, especially the way you found out."

Tobin looked away, mortified. He'd thought the blood seeping between his legs had been the first sign of the plague. The truth had been worse.

"Even Lhel was taken by surprise. Arkoniel tells me she showed you your true face before she wove the new magic."

"This is my true face!"

"My face!" Brother snarled.

Nari jumped and Tobin guessed even she'd heard that.

He took a closer look at Brother; the ghost looked more solid than he had for a long time, almost real. It occurred to Tobin that he'd been hearing his twin's voice out loud, too, not just a whisper in his mind like before.

"He's rather distracting," said Iya. "Could you send him away, please? And ask him not to make a fuss around the place this time?"

Tobin was tempted to refuse, but for Nari's sake he whispered the words Lhel had taught him. "Blood, my blood. Flesh, my flesh. Bone, my bone." Brother vanished like a snuffed candle and the room felt warmer.

"That's better!" Taking up the bowl, Nari went to the brazier and dipped up the broth she had warming in a pot on the coals. "Here, get some of this into you. You've hardly eaten in days."

Ignoring the spoon, Tobin took the bowl and drank from it. This was Cook's special sickroom broth, rich with beef marrow, parsley, wine, and milk, along with the healing herbs.

He drained the bowl and Nari refilled it. Iya leaned over and retrieved the fallen doll. Propping it on her lap, she arranged its uneven arms and legs and looked down pensively at the crudely drawn face.

Tobin's throat went tight and he lowered the bowl. How many times had he watched his mother sit just like that? Fresh tears filled his eyes. She'd made the doll to keep Brother's spirit close to her. It had been Brother she'd seen when she looked at it, Brother she'd held and rocked and crooned to and carried with her everywhere until the day she threw herself out of the tower window.

Always Brother.

Never Tobin.

Was her angry ghost still up there?

Nari saw him shiver and hugged him close again. This time he let her.

"Illior really told you to do this to me?" he whispered.

Iya nodded sadly. "The Lightbearer spoke to me through the Oracle at Afra. You know what that is, don't you?"

"The same Oracle that told King Thelátimos to make his daughter the first queen."

"That's right. And now Skala needs a queen again, one of the true blood to heal and defend the land. I promise you, one day you will understand all this."

Nari hugged him and kissed the top of his head. "It was all to keep you safe, pet."

The thought of her complicity stung him. Wiggling free, he scooted back against the bolsters on the far side of the bed and pulled his legs—long, sharp-shinned boy legs—up under his shirt. "But why?" He touched the scar, then broke off with a gasp of dismay. "Father's seal and my mother's ring! I had them on a chain . . ."

"I have them right here, pet. I kept them safe for you." Nari took the chain from her apron pocket and held it out to him.

Tobin cradled the talismans in his hand. The seal, a black stone set high in a gold ring, bore the deep-carved oak tree insignia of Atyion, the great holding Tobin now owned but had never seen.

The other ring had been his mother's bride gift from his father. The golden mounting was delicate, a circlet of tiny leaves holding an amethyst carved with a relief of his parents' youthful profiles. He'd spent hours gazing at the portrait; he'd never seen his parents happy together, the way they looked here.

"Where did you find that?" the wizard asked softly.

"In a hole under a tree."

"What tree?"

"A dead chestnut in the back courtyard of my mother's house in Ero." Tobin looked up to find her watching him closely. "The one near the summer kitchen."

"Ah yes. That's where Arkoniel buried your brother."

And where my mother and Lhel dug him up again, he

thought. *Perhaps she lost the ring then.* "Did my parents know what you did to me?"

He caught the quick, sharp look Iya shot at Nari before she answered. "Yes. They knew."

Tobin's heart sank. "They *let* you?"

"Before you were born, your father asked me to protect you. He understood the Oracle's words and obeyed without question. I'm sure he taught you the prophecy the Oracle gave to King Thelátimos."

"Yes."

Iya was quiet for a moment. "It was different for your mother. She wasn't a strong person and the birthing was very difficult. And she never got over your brother's death."

Tobin had to swallow hard before he could ask, "Is that why she hated me?"

"She never hated you, pet. Never!" Nari pressed a hand to her heart. "She wasn't right in her mind, that's all."

"That's enough for now," said Iya. "Tobin, you've been very ill and slept the last two days away."

"Two?" Tobin looked out the window. A slim crescent moon had guided him here; now it had waxed nearly to half. "What day is it?"

"The twenty-first of Erasin, pet. Your name day came and went while you slept," said Nari. "I'll tell Cook to make the honey cakes for tomorrow's supper."

Tobin shook his head in bewilderment, still staring at the moon. "I—I was in the forest. Who brought me to the house?"

"Tharin showed up out of nowhere with you in his arms, and Arkoniel behind him with poor Ki," said Nari. "Scared me almost to death, just like that day your father brought your—"

"Ki?" Tobin's head reeled as another memory struggled to the surface. In his fevered dreams Tobin had floated up into the air over Lhel's oak and found himself looking down from a great height. He'd seen something in the

woods just beyond the spring, lying on the dead leaves—
"No, Ki's safe in Ero. I was careful!"

But a cold knot of fear took root in his belly, pressing
on his heart. In his dream it *had* been Ki lying on the
ground, and Arkoniel was weeping beside him. "He
brought the doll, didn't he? That's why he followed me."

"Yes, pet."

"Then it wasn't a dream." But why had Arkoniel been
weeping?

It was a moment before he realized that people were
still speaking to him. Nari was shaking him by the shoulder, looking alarmed. "Tobin, what is it? You've gone
white!"

"Where's Ki?" he whispered, gripping his knees hard
as he braced for the answer.

"I was just telling you," Nari said, her round face lined
with new concern. "He's asleep in your old toy room next
door. With you so ill and thrashing about in your sleep,
and him hurt so bad, I thought you'd rest easier apart."

Tobin clambered across the bed, not waiting to hear
more.

Iya caught him by the arm. "Wait. He's still very ill,
Tobin. He fell and hit his head. Arkoniel and Tharin have
been tending him."

He tried to pull free, but she held on. "Let him rest.
Tharin has been frantic, going back and forth between
your rooms like a sorrowful hound all this time. He was
asleep by Ki's bed when I passed."

"Let me go. I promise I won't wake them, but please, I
have to see Ki!"

"Stay a moment and listen to me." Iya was grave now.
"Listen well, little prince, for what I tell you is worth your
life, and theirs."

Trembling, Tobin sank back on the edge of the bed.

Iya released him and folded her hands across the doll
in her lap. "As I said, you were never meant to bear this
burden so young, but here we are. Listen well and seal

these words in your heart. Ki and Tharin don't know, and they *mustn't* know, about this secret of ours. Except for Arkoniel, only Lhel and Nari know the truth, and so it must remain until the time comes for you to claim your birthright."

"Tharin doesn't know?" Tobin's first reaction was relief. It was Tharin, as much as his father, who'd taught him how to be a warrior.

"It was one of the great sorrows of your father's life. He loved Tharin just as you love Ki. It broke his heart to keep such a secret from his friend, and it made the burden all that much harder to bear. But now you must do the same."

"They'd never betray me."

"Not willingly, of course. They're both stubborn and stouthearted as Sakor's bull. But wizards like your uncle's man Niryn have ways of finding out things. Magical ways, Tobin. They don't need torture to read a person's innermost thoughts. If Niryn ever suspected who you really are, he'd know just whose heads to look into for the proof."

Tobin went cold. "I think he did something like that to me the first time I met him." He held out his left arm, showing her the birthmark. "He touched this and I got a bad, crawly feeling inside."

Iya frowned. "Yes, that sounds right."

"Then he knows!"

"No, Tobin, for you didn't know yourself. Until a few days ago, all anyone would find inside your head were the thoughts of a young prince, concerned only with hawks and horses and swords. That was our intent from the start, to protect you."

"But Brother. The doll. He would have seen that."

"Lhel's magic protects those thoughts. Niryn could only find them if he knew to look for them. So far, it would seem he doesn't."

"But now I *do* know. When I go back, what then?"

"You must make certain he finds no reason to touch

your thoughts again. Keep the doll a secret, just as you have, and avoid Niryn as much as you can. Arkoniel and I will do whatever we can to protect you. In fact, I think it may be time for me to be seen with my patron's son again."

"You'll come back to Ero with me?"

She smiled and patted his shoulder. "Yes. Now go see your friends."

The corridor was cold but Tobin hardly noticed. Ki's door stood slightly ajar, casting a thin sliver of light out across the rushes. Tobin slipped inside.

Ki was asleep in an old high-sided bed, tucked up to the chin with counterpanes and quilts. His eyes were closed and even in the warm glow of the night lamp, he looked very pale. There were dark circles around his eyes and a linen bandage wrapped around his head.

Tharin was asleep in an armchair beside the bed, wrapped in his long riding cloak. His long, grey-blond hair fell in untidy tangles over his shoulders and a week's worth of stubble shadowed the hollows of his cheeks above his short beard. Just the sight of him made Tobin feel a little better; he always felt safer with Tharin nearby.

Hard on that thought, however, came the echo of Iya's warning. Here were the two people he loved and trusted above all others, and now it lay with him to protect them. A wild, rebellious love welled up in his heart as he thought again of Niryn's prying brown eyes. He'd kill the man himself if the wizard tried to hurt his friends.

Tobin tiptoed toward the bed as carefully as he could, but Tharin's pale eyes snapped open before he reached it.

"Tobin? Thank the Light!" he exclaimed softly, pulling the boy into his lap and hugging him so hard it hurt. "By the Four, we've been so worried! You slept and slept. How are you, lad?"

"Better." Embarrassed, Tobin gently freed himself and stood up.

Tharin's smile faded. "Nari says you thought you'd caught the Red and Black Death. You should have come to me instead of running off like that! Anything could have happened to you boys alone on the road. The whole ride out here we expected to find your bodies in a ditch."

"We? Who came with you?" For one awful moment Tobin feared that his guardian had come looking for him, too.

"Koni and the other guardsmen, of course. Don't go trying to change the subject. It wasn't much better finding the two of you like this." He glanced at Ki, and Tobin knew he was still worried about him. "You should have stayed in the city. Poor Arkoniel and the others have had a time of it. They're ready to drop in their tracks." But there was no anger in his eyes as he gazed earnestly up at Tobin. "You gave us all a bad scare."

Tobin's chin quivered and he hung his head. "I'm sorry."

Tharin gathered him in again, patting his shoulder. "Well, then," he said, voice rough with emotion. "We're all here now."

"Ki's going to be all right, isn't he?" Tharin didn't answer and Tobin saw tears glazing the warrior's eyes. "Tharin, he will be well?"

The man nodded, but doubt was plain in his face. "Arkoniel says he'll probably wake up soon."

Tobin's knees went wobbly and he sank down on the arm of Tharin's chair. "Probably?"

"He must have caught the same fever you had, and with the knock in the head—" He reached to smooth Ki's dark hair back from the bandage. A yellowish stain had seeped through. "That needs changing."

"Iya said he fell."

"Yes. Struck his head quite a blow, too. Arkoniel thinks—Well, it looks like that demon of yours might have had a hand in it."

A shard of ice seemed to lodge itself in Tobin's stomach. "Bro—The *ghost* hurt him?"

"He thinks it tricked Ki into carrying that doll of yours out here for it."

Tobin's breath hitched tight in his chest. If this were true, he'd never, ever call Brother again. Brother could starve, for all he cared.

"You—you saw it? The doll, I mean?"

"Yes." Tharin gave him a puzzled look. "Your father thought it fell with your mother that day and got carried away by the river. He even sent some of the men out looking for it. But you had it all this time, didn't you? What made you keep it hidden like that?"

Did Tharin know about Lhel, too? Unsure, Tobin could only offer a partial truth. "I thought you and Father would be ashamed of me. Dolls are for girls."

Tharin let out a sad little laugh. "No one would have begrudged you that one. It's a shame that's the only one she left you. If you like, I could probably find you one of the pretty ones she made before her illness. Half the nobles in Ero have them."

There had been a time when Tobin had wanted one so badly it hurt. But he'd wanted it from her hands, proof that she loved him, or at least acknowledged him as much as she did Brother. That had never happened. He shook his head. "No, I don't want any others."

Perhaps Tharin understood, for he said nothing more about it. They sat together for a while, watching Ki's chest rise and fall beneath the quilts. Tobin yearned to crawl in beside him, but Ki looked so fragile and ill that he didn't dare. Too miserable to sit still, he finally went back to his own room so Tharin could sleep. Iya and Nari were gone and he was glad; he didn't want to talk to either of them just now.

The doll lay on the bed where the wizard had been sitting. As Tobin stared down at it, trying to take in what had happened, anger like nothing he'd ever felt gripped him, so strong he could hardly breathe.

I'll never call him again. Never!

Snatching it up, he thrust the hated thing into the clothes chest and slammed the lid down. "You can stay here forever!"

He felt a little better after that. Let Brother haunt the keep if he wanted; he could have the place for all Tobin cared, but he wasn't going back to Ero.

He found his clothes folded neatly on a shelf in the wardrobe. Little bags of dried lavender and mint fell out of the folds of his tunic when he picked it up. He pressed the wool to his face and inhaled, knowing that Nari had tucked the herbs there after she'd washed and mended his clothes. She'd probably sat by the bed as she worked, watching over him.

The thought dissolved his anger at her. No matter what she'd done all those years ago, he knew she loved him, and he still loved her. Dressing quickly, he made his way quietly upstairs.

A few lamps burned in niches along the third floor corridor, and moonlight streamed in at the rosette windows overhead, but the passage was still shadowy and cold. Arkoniel's rooms lay at the far end and Tobin couldn't help keeping one eye on the heavy locked door across from the workroom, the door to the tower.

If he went to it, he wondered, would he still feel his mother's angry spirit there, just on the other side? He kept close to the right-hand wall.

There was no answer at Arkoniel's bedchamber, but light showed underneath the workroom door next to it. Tobin lifted the latch and went in.

Lamps burned everywhere inside, banishing the shadows and filling the large chamber with light. Arkoniel was at the table under the windows, head propped on one hand as he studied a parchment. He started nervously as Tobin entered, then rose to greet him.

Tobin was surprised at how worn the young wizard looked. There were dark hollows under his cheekbones and his face had a pinched look, as if he'd been sick. His curly black hair, always unruly, stuck out in clumps about his head, and his tunic was rumpled and stained with dirt and ink.

"Awake at last," he said, attempting to sound hearty and failing miserably. "Has Iya spoken with you yet?"

"Yes. She told me not to tell anyone about this." Tobin touched his chest, unwilling to give voice to the hated secret.

Arkoniel sighed deeply and looked distractedly around the room. "It was a terrible way for you to find out, Tobin. By the Light, I'm sorry. None of us suspected, not even Lhel. I'm so very sorry . . ." He trailed off, still not looking at Tobin. "It shouldn't have happened as it did. None of it."

Tobin had never seen the young wizard look so dismayed. At least Arkoniel had tried to be his friend. Not like Iya, who only showed up when it suited her.

"Thank you for helping Ki," he said, as the silence drew out uncomfortably between them.

Arkoniel jerked as if Tobin had slapped him, then let out a hollow laugh. "You're most welcome, my prince. How could I do otherwise? Is there any change?"

"He's still asleep."

"Asleep." Arkoniel wandered back to the table, touching things, picking them up and putting them down without looking at them.

Tobin's fear crept back. "*Will* Ki be all right? There wasn't really any fever. Why hasn't he woken up yet?"

Arkoniel fiddled with a wooden rod. "It takes time, such a wound."

"Tharin said you think Brother hurt him."

"Brother was with him. Perhaps he knew we'd need the doll—I don't know. He may have hurt Ki. I don't know if he meant to." He began picking at things on the table again, as if he'd forgotten that Tobin was still there. At last he took up the document he'd been reading, holding it up for Tobin to see. The seals and florid looping handwriting were unmistakable. It was the work of Lord Orun's scribe.

"Iya thought I should be the one to tell you," Arkoniel said despondently. "This arrived yesterday. You're to go back to Ero as soon as you're fit to travel. Orun is furious, of course. He's threatening to write to the king again, demanding that you take a different squire."

Tobin sank down on a stool by the table. Orun had been trying to replace Ki since their first day in Ero. "But why? It wasn't Ki's fault!"

"I'm sure he doesn't care about that. He sees an opportunity to get what he's always wanted—someone who'll keep a closer eye on you." Arkoniel rubbed at his eyes and ran his fingers back through his hair, leaving it more disheveled than ever. "Of one thing you can be certain. He'll never let you run off like that again. You're going to have to be terribly careful now. Never give Orun or Niryn or anyone else any reason to suspect you're more than the king's orphaned nephew."

"Iya explained about that already. I don't see much of Niryn anyway if I can help it. He scares me."

"Me too," Arkoniel admitted, but he looked a bit more like his old self. "Before you go back, there are a few things I can teach you, ways to shroud your thoughts." He managed the ghost of a smile. "Don't worry, it's just a matter of concentration. I know you don't care much for magic."

Tobin shrugged. "I can't seem to get away from it, though, can I?" He picked unhappily at a callus on his thumb. "Korin told me how I'm the next heir after him, until he has an heir of his own. Is that why Lord Orun wants to control me?"

"Ultimately, yes. But for now he has control of Atyion—in your name, of course, but control all the same. He's an ambitious man, our Orun. If anything were to happen to Prince Korin before he marries . . ." He shook his head sharply. "We must keep a close eye on him. And don't worry too much about Ki. Orun doesn't have final say on that, no matter how much he blusters. Only the king can decide that. I'm sure it will all get sorted out when you get back."

"Iya's going to Ero with me. I wish you'd come, instead."

Arkoniel smiled and this time it was his real smile, all kind and awkward and well-meaning. "I wish I could, but for now it's best that I stay hidden here. The Harriers already know Iya, but not about me. Tharin will be with you, and Ki."

Seeing Tobin's crestfallen look, he knelt beside him and took him by the shoulders. "I'm not abandoning you, Tobin. I know it must feel that way, but I'm not. I never will. If ever you need me, you can be certain I'll find my way to you. Once Orun calms down, perhaps you can convince him to let you visit here more often. I'm sure Prince Korin will take your side in that."

That was little comfort to him now, but Tobin nodded. "I want to see Lhel. Will you take me? Nari will never let me go out alone and Tharin still doesn't know about her, does he?"

"No, though I wish more than ever now that he did." Arkoniel rose. "I'll take you to her first thing tomorrow, all right?"

"But I want to go now."

"Now?" Arkoniel glanced at the dark window. "It's after midnight. You should go back to bed . . ."

"I've slept for days! I'm not tired."

Arkoniel smiled again. "But I am, and Lhel will be sleeping, too. Tomorrow, all right? We can go as early as you like, as soon as it's light. Come on, I'll walk down with you and see how Ki's doing." He pointed to the lamps in turn, snuffing all but the one at his elbow. Then, to Tobin's surprise, he shuddered and hugged himself. "It's gloomy up here at night."

Tobin couldn't help glancing nervously toward the tower door as they went out, and was sure he saw the wizard do the same.

Chapter 2

Tobin woke up in the armchair with the sun in his face and Tharin's cloak tucked around him. He stretched, then leaned forward to see if Ki looked any different.

His friend hadn't moved, but Tobin thought there was more color in his cheeks than there had been the night before. He reached under the blankets and found Ki's hand. It was warm, another encouraging sign.

"Can you hear me? Ki, you've been sleeping forever. It's a good day for a ride. Wake up. Please?"

"Let him sleep, keesa."

"Lhel?" Tobin turned, expecting to find the door open.

Instead, the witch floated just behind him in an oval of strange light. He could see trees around her, firs and bare oaks dusted with snow. As he watched, big lacy flakes fell, catching in her dark curls and on the rough fabric of her dress. It was like looking at her through a window. Just beyond the oval the room looked exactly as it should, but she seemed to be standing in her camp.

Amazed, Tobin reached out to her, but the strange apparition shrank back and in on itself until he could see nothing but her face.

"No! No touch," she warned. "Arkoniel bring you. Let Ki rest."

She vanished, and left Tobin gaping at the place she'd been. He didn't understand what he'd just seen, but he took her at her word. "I'll be back soon," he told Ki and, on impulse, bent and kissed him lightly on his bandaged forehead. Blushing at his own foolishness, he hurried out and took the stairs to Arkoniel's room two at a time.

*   *   *

In daylight the corridor looked safe and ordinary, and the tower door nothing but another door. The workroom door stood open and he could hear Iya and Arkoniel talking inside.

Arkoniel was weaving a pattern of light above the table as Tobin entered. Something struck the wall close to Tobin's head and skittered across the floor. Startled, he looked down and saw it was only a speckled dry bean.

"And that's as far as I've gotten with it," said Arkoniel, sounding frustrated. He still looked tired and when he caught sight of Tobin the worry lines deepened around his mouth. "What is it? Is Ki—?"

"He's asleep. I want to go see Lhel now. She said I should come. You said you'd take me."

"She said—?" Arkoniel exchanged a look with Iya, then nodded. "Yes, I'll take you."

It was snowing outside, just as it had been in his vision of Lhel. The fat, wet flakes melted as they touched the ground, but they stayed on the tree boughs like sugar on a cake and he could see his breath on the air. The road behind the keep was covered with fallen leaves, a faded carpet of yellow and red that whispered under Gosi's hooves. Ahead, the peaks glistened white against the dull grey sky.

He tried to explain the strange visitation to Arkoniel as they rode.

"Yes, she calls that her window spell," said the wizard, not sounding the least surprised.

Before Tobin could question him further, the witch stepped from the trees to meet them. She always knew when they were coming.

Dirty and gap-toothed, dressed in a shapeless brown dress decorated with polished deer teeth, she looked more beggar than witch. Squinting up at them, she shook her head and grinned. "You keesas has no breakfast. Come, I feed you."

As if it were just another day and nothing strange had ever happened between them, she turned and walked back into the trees. Tobin and Arkoniel tethered their horses and hurried after her on foot. Another of the witch's peculiar magics guarded her camp. In all the time Tobin had known her, she had never used the same path twice, and he and Ki had never been able to find their way to her on their own. He wondered if Arkoniel knew how.

After many twists and turns, they came out in the clearing where her oak house stood. He'd forgotten how huge it was. Grandmother oak, Lhel called it. The trunk was as wide as a small cottage, and a natural split had hollowed a great space inside the trunk without killing it. A few leathery, copper-colored leaves still fluttered on the upper branches, and the ground around it was strewn with acorns. A fire crackled near the low opening that served as Lhel's door. She disappeared inside for a moment, returning with a bowl of dried meat strips and a few wrinkled pippins.

Tobin wasn't interested in food, but Lhel put the bowl in his hands and wouldn't say another word until he and Arkoniel had done as they were told.

"You come now," she said, going back to the oak. Arkoniel rose to follow, but she forestalled him with a look.

Inside, another small fire burned in a pit at the center of the packed-earth floor. Lhel pulled the deerskin door flap down and sat on the pelt-covered pallet beside the fire, patting the place beside her. When Tobin joined her, she turned his face to the light and studied him a moment, then opened the neck of his tunic to inspect the scar.

"Is good," she said, then pointed down at his lap. "You see more blood?"

Tobin blushed and shook his head. "That won't happen again, will it?"

"Someday later. But you may feel moontide in the belly."

Tobin remembered the ache between his hipbones that had driven him here. "I don't like that. It hurts."

Lhel chuckled. "No girl like that."

Tobin shivered at the word, but Lhel didn't seem to notice. Reaching into the shadows behind her, she handed him a small pouch containing dried bluish green leaves. "*Akosh*. If pains come, you make tea with just this much, no more." She showed him a generous pinch of leaves and mimed crumbling them into a cup.

Tobin stuck the bag inside his tunic, then stared down at his clasped hands. "I don't want this, Lhel. I don't want to be a girl. And I don't want to be—queen." He could hardly get the word out.

"You not change your fate, keesa."

"Fate? You did this. You and the wizards!"

"Goddess Mother and your Lightbearer tell it must be so. That make fate."

Tobin looked up to find her watching him with wise, sad eyes. She pointed skyward. "The gods be cruel, no? To you and Brother."

"Brother! Did Arkoniel tell you what he did? I'm never going to call him again. Never! I'll bring you the doll. You keep him."

"No, you will. You must. Souls tied tight." Lhel locked her hands together.

Tobin's hands curled to white-knuckled fists on his knees. "I hate him!"

"You need him." Lhel took his hands and spoke in his mind without words, the way she always did when she wanted to be clear. "You and he must be together for the magic to hold. He is cruel. What else could he be, angry and alone all the time and seeing you live the life denied him? Perhaps you can understand a little, now that you know the truth?"

Tobin didn't want to understand, or to forgive but her words struck home all the same. "You hurt him, when you sewed the bone into my chest. He cried blood."

Lhel grimaced. "He was not meant to be, child. I've done all I could for him, but he's been the burden of my heart since you were born."

"Your burden?" Tobin sputtered. "You weren't there when he was hurting me, hurting my mother and father and driving servants away— And he almost killed Ki!" The fire blurred before him as tears welled up. "Have you seen Ki? He won't wake up!"

"He will. And you will keep the doll and care for Brother."

Tobin wiped angrily at his eyes. "It's not fair!"

"Hush, keesa!" she snapped, pulling her hands away from his. "What gods care for 'fair'? Fair I stay here, far from my people? Live in tree? For you, I do this. For you we all suffer."

Tobin shrank back as if he'd been slapped. She'd never spoken to him like that; no one had.

"You *be* queen for Skala. That your fate! Would you abandon your people?" She stopped and shook her head, gentle again. "You young, keesa. Too young. This will end. When you take off Brother skin, you both be free then."

"But *when*?"

"I no see. Illior tell you, maybe." She stroked his cheek, then took his hand and pressed it to her right breast. It was soft and heavy under the coarse wool. "You will be a woman one day, keesa." Her voice was a dark caress in his mind. "I see the fear in your heart, fear you'll lose your power. Women have power, too. Why do you think your moon god made queens for Skala? They were all warriors, your ancestors. Never forget that. Women carry the moon in their blood tide, too, and in their heart blood."

She touched the inside of her wrist where the fine blue veins showed through. A thin cresecent moon appeared there, etched in fine black lines. "That you now—sliver moon, most of you dark." She moved her finger and a circle appeared, just touching the outer curve of the crescent.

"But when you grown like belly moon, you will know your power."

With the eye of an artist, Tobin knew there must be more to balance the design—a waning moon—but she didn't show him or speak of it. Instead, she touched his flat belly. "Here you will make great queens." Her eyes met his and Tobin saw respect there. "Teach them about my people, Tobin. Teach your wizards, too."

"Iya and Arkoniel know. They went to you when they needed help."

Lhel let out a snort and sat back. "Not many like them," she said aloud. Drawing the silver knife from her belt, she pricked her left thumb and squeezed out a drop of blood. With it she drew a crescent on Tobin's brow, then enclosed it in a circle. "Mother protect you, keesa." She kissed the mark she'd made. "You go back now."

As Tobin left the clearing with Arkoniel he paused at the spring, wanting to see what the blood mark looked like. There was no sign of it; perhaps it had vanished when she kissed him. He looked for that other face, too, and was glad when he saw only his own.

Tobin spent the rest of the day with Ki, watching Cook and Nari gently spooning broth between his lips and changing the thick woolen pads underneath him when he soiled himself. It hurt to see his friend so helpless. Ki was thirteen, and wouldn't think much of being treated like a baby.

Tobin wanted nothing more than to be alone, but everyone seemed determined to look after him. Tharin brought modeling wax and sat with him. Sergeant Laris and some of the other men came up, too, offering to play bakshi and knucklebones, but Tobin didn't want to. They all tried to cheer him up, joking and talking to Ki as if he could hear them, but that only made Tobin feel worse. He didn't want to talk about horses or hunting, not even with Tharin. It seemed like lying, to speak of such ordinary things. Lhel's words haunted him, making him feel like a stranger in his own skin. His new secrets lodged like caneberry seeds between his teeth, threatening to work loose and fly out at any moment if he wasn't careful.

"Now look, you've tired poor Tobin out!" Nari exclaimed, coming in with a stack of fresh linen. "He's only just up out of his own sickbed himself. Go on now and let him have some peace."

She shooed the soldiers out, but Tharin hung back. "Would you like me to stay, Tobin?"

For once, he didn't. "I'm sorry, I guess I'm just tired."

"You should go back to bed," said Nari. "I'll fetch you some broth and a warm brick for the foot of your bed."

"No, please. Just let me sit with him."

"He can sleep here if he needs to. That chair is good for napping." With a final wink over his shoulder at Tobin, Tharin gently guided Nari out of the room before she could fuss over Tobin any more.

Tobin curled up in the armchair and watched Ki's chest rise and fall for a while. Then he stared at his friend's closed lids, willing them to open. At last he gave that up and picked up the wax Tharin had brought. Breaking off a bit, he rolled it between his palms to soften it. The familiar feel and sweet smell calmed him as it always had and he began shaping a little horse for Ki; those were his favorites. Tobin had given him a little wooden horse charm soon after Ki came to the keep and he still wore it on a cord around his neck. Tobin's skill had improved since then and he'd offered to make him a better one, but Ki wouldn't hear of it.

Tobin had just finished marking the mane with his fingernail when he sensed someone in the doorway. Iya smiled at him when he looked up and he guessed she'd been standing there for some time.

"May I join you?"

Tobin shrugged. Taking that as an invitation, Iya drew

up a stool and leaned in to see the horse. "You're very good at that. Is it a votive?"

Tobin nodded; he should make an offering at the house shrine. The horse's head was too long, though. Pinching off a bit of the nose, he reshaped it, but now it was too small. Giving up, he rolled the whole thing into a ball.

"I just want to stay as I am!" he whispered.

"And so you shall, for a good while longer."

Tobin touched his face, tracing its familiar contours. The face Lhel had shown him was softer, rounder through the cheeks, as if a sculptor had added a little wax and smoothed it in with his thumbs. But the eyes—those had still been his own. And the crescent-shaped scar on his chin.

"Does it—can you see—her?" He couldn't bring himself to say "me." His fingers found the wax again and he pinched at it nervously.

Iya chuckled. "No, you're quite safe."

Tobin knew she meant safe from King Erius and his wizards, but they weren't whom he meant. What would Korin and the other boys say if they found out? No girls were allowed to serve as Companions.

Iya rose to go, then stopped and looked down at the new horse taking shape in his hands. Reaching into a pouch at her belt, she took out a few soft buff-and-brown feathers and gave them to him.

"Owl," said Tobin, recognizing the pattern. "A saw what."

"Yes. For Illior. You might consider making offerings to the Lightbearer now and then. Just lay them on the fire."

Tobin said nothing, but when she'd gone he went down to the hall, filled a small brass offering basin with embers from the main hearth, and set it on the shelf of the house shrine. Whispering a prayer to Sakor to make Ki strong again, he laid the wax horse on the embers and blew on them until the wax melted. Every bit of the little votive was consumed, a sign that the god had been listening. Taking out one of the owl feathers, he twirled it between his fingers, wondering what prayer was proper. He hadn't thought to ask. Laying it on the coals, he whispered, "Lightbearer, help me! Help Ki, too."

The feather smoldered for a second, sending up a thread of acrid smoke, then caught fire and disappeared in a flash of green flame. A sudden shiver seized Tobin, leaving his knees a little shaky. This was a more dramatic answer than Sakor had ever sent. More scared than reassured, Tobin dumped the coals back into the hearth and hurried upstairs.

The following day was much the same and passed even more slowly. Ki slept on, and to Tobin's worried eye, he was looking paler even though Nari said otherwise. Tobin made twenty-three horses, watched from the window as Laris drilled the men in the barracks yard, dozed in the chair. He even played idly with the little boats and wooden people in the toy city, though he was much too old for it now and got up hurriedly whenever he heard anyone coming.

Tharin brought supper on a tray and stayed to eat with him. Tobin still didn't feel much like talking but was glad for the company. After supper they played bakshi on the floor.

They were in the middle of a toss when the faint stir of bedclothes caught Tobin's attention. Jumping to his feet, he bent over Ki and took his hand. "Are you awake, Ki? Can you hear me?"

His heart leaped when Ki's dark lashes fluttered against his cheek. "Tob?"

"And me," Tharin said, smoothing Ki's hair back from his brow. His hand was shaking, but he was smiling.

Ki looked around blearily. "Master Porion . . . tell him . . . too tired to run today."

"You're at the keep, remember?" Tobin had to stop

himself from squeezing Ki's hand too tightly. "You followed me out here."

"What? Why would . . ." He stirred against the pillow, struggling to stay awake. "Oh, yes. The doll." His eyes widened. "Brother! Tobin, I saw him."

"I know. I'm sorry he—" Tobin broke off. Tharin was right there, overhearing everything. How was he going to keep Ki from blurting out more?

But Ki was fading again. "What happened? Why—why does my head hurt?"

"You don't remember?" asked Tharin.

"I the doll . . . I remember riding . . ." Ki trailed off again and for a moment Tobin thought he'd gone back to sleep. Then, eyes still closed, he whispered, "Did I find you, Tob? I don't remember anything after I got to Alestun. Did you get the doll?"

Tharin pressed the back of his hand to Ki's cheek and frowned. "He's a bit warm."

"Hungry," Ki mumbled peevishly.

"Well, that's a good sign." Tharin straightened up. "I'll fetch you some cider."

"Meat."

"We'll start with cider and see how you do with it."

"I'm sorry," Ki rasped as soon as Tharin was gone. "I shouldn't have said anything about—*him.*"

"It's all right. Forget it." Tobin sat on the edge of the bed and took Ki's hand again. "Did Brother hurt you?"

Ki's eyes went vague. "I—I don't know. I don't remember . . ." Then, abruptly, "How come you never told me?"

For one awful moment Tobin thought Ki had seen him with Lhel and Arkoniel, after all, and guessed his secret. He'd have blurted out the truth if Ki hadn't spoken first.

"I wouldn't have laughed, you know. I know it was your mother's. But even if it was just some old doll, I'd never have laughed at you," Ki whispered, eyes sad and full of questions.

Tobin stared down at their interlaced fingers. "The

night Iya first brought you here, Brother showed me a vision. I saw the way people would look at me if they knew I had it." He gestured helplessly. "I saw you and you—I was afraid you'd think badly of me if you knew."

Ki let out a weak snort. "Don't know that I'd believe anything *he* showed." He looked around, as if fearing that Brother was listening, then whispered, "He's a nasty thing, isn't he? I mean, he's your twin and all, but there's something missing in him." His fingers tightened on Tobin's. "I didn't understand why he wanted me to bring it before, but now—He thought it would make trouble between us, Tob. He's always hated me."

Tobin couldn't deny that, especially after what had happened.

"I'd have come after you anyway, though," Ki said, and a deep hurt crept into his voice. "Why'd you run off without me like that?"

Tobin clasped Ki's hand with both of his. "It wasn't like that! I thought I had plague. I was afraid I'd give it to you and Tharin and the others. All the way out here I was so scared it was already too late, that the deathbirds would nail you all up in the palace and—"

Tobin broke off in alarm as a tear trickled down Ki's cheek.

"If you had been sick . . . If you'd gone off and died somewhere alone on the road . . . I couldn't have stood it!" Ki whispered, voice quavering. "I'd just as soon die as live with the thought of it!" He clutched at Tobin's hand. "Don't you ever— Don't!"

"I'm sorry, Ki. I won't."

"Swear it, Tob. Where you go, I go, no matter what. Swear it by the Four."

Tobin shifted their right hands into the warrior's clasp. "I swear it by the Four."

Brother was wrong, he thought angrily. *Or he lied to me, just for spite.*

"Good. That's settled." Ki tried to turn his head and dry

his cheek but couldn't quite manage it. Tobin used the edge of the sheet to finish the job.

"Thanks," Ki said, embarrassed. "So what *did* happen?"

Tobin told him what he could, though he had no idea how Ki had found his way to Lhel's camp, and Ki still didn't remember.

"Wonder what Old Slack Guts will have to say about all this?"

"Don't worry, I'll explain what happened. It wasn't your fault." Ki wasn't strong enough yet to hear about the letter.

Satisfied for now, Ki closed his eyes. Tobin sat with him until he was certain his friend was asleep. When he tried to let go of his hand, however, Ki's fingers closed tighter around his.

"I'd never a'made fun, Tob," he mumbled, more asleep than awake. "Never would." Another tear seeped out from under his lashes and trickled down toward his ear.

Tobin wiped it away with his finger. "I know."

"Don't feel so good. Cold . . . Climb in, would you?"

Tobin kicked off his shoes and climbed under the covers, trying not to jostle him. Ki muttered softly and turned his face Tobin's way.

Tobin watched him sleep until his own eyes grew heavy. If Tharin did come back with the cider, Tobin didn't hear him.

Arkoniel and Iya met Tharin in the hall and heard the good news. Arkoniel nearly wept with relief, both that Ki was awake at last and that he recalled nothing that would endanger his life. Whether that was thanks to Brother or Lhel, he didn't care, so long as Ki was safe.

"I think I'll sleep in Tobin's bed tonight," Tharin said, kneading his lower back ruefully. "I've had enough of chairs, and it's certain Tobin won't leave Ki."

"You've earned a decent rest," said Iya. "I believe I'll do the same. Are you coming up, Arkoniel?"

"I'll sit up awhile."

"He'll be fine," she told him, giving him a reassuring smile. "Come up soon, won't you?"

Tharin started after her toward the stairs, then turned to Arkoniel. "Do you know of anyone the boys call 'Brother'?"

Arkoniel's heart seemed to stop in his chest. "Where did you hear that name?"

"Just something Ki said as he came around. Something about someone's brother giving him that doll. No?" He yawned mightily and ran his hand over his chin. "Well, he was still pretty groggy. His mind must have been wandering."

"I'm sure you're right," Iya said, slipping her arm through his and leading him to the stairs. "Or perhaps you heard wrong? Come along now, before we have to carry you up."

Arkoniel waited until the household was asleep, then stole in to see the boys. Tobin had crawled into bed with Ki. Even asleep he looked sad and depleted, but Ki was smiling. As Arkoniel watched, Tobin stirred and groped for his friend's shoulder, as if to assure himself that he was still there.

Arkoniel sank into the chair, not trusting his legs to hold him up. It was always worse at night, the memory of what he had done. And what he'd nearly done.

He'd relived that awful moment in the forest a hundred times over the past few days. Tossing on his bed at night, he saw Ki coming toward them through the trees, breaking into that ready smile of his as he caught sight of Tobin huddled over the spring, revealed in her true form. Ki raised his hand, waving to—who? Had he seen her, recognized her, or had it been Arkoniel he was greeting? Lhel had thrown a fur robe over Tobin, but had she been quick enough?

He'd clung to that crumb of doubt, even as he lifted his

hand to keep the vow he'd made to Iya and Rhius the day they'd agreed to let another child come to the keep. He himself had told Iya the new companion should be a child no one would miss.

Yes, he'd meant to keep that vow and kill Ki, but his heart had betrayed him and marred the spell; he'd tried to change it to a blinding at the last moment and instead released an unfocused blast that had knocked Ki through the air as if he weighed no more than a handful of chaff. It would have killed him if Lhel hadn't been there to coax his heart back to life. She'd claimed to take away whatever memories Ki might have had of seeing Tobin, too, weaving in their place vague memories of illness. If Arkoniel and Iya had only known such a thing were possible . . .

If only they hadn't been too arrogant to ask.

Glad as he was that Ki lived, Arkoniel could not escape the truth; he'd failed in his duty by not killing Ki, just as he'd betrayed the boy by trying.

For years he'd told himself he was different than Iya and Lhel. Now it seemed his supposed compassion was instead simply weakness.

Ashamed, he slipped away to his lonely chamber, leaving the two innocents to a peace he might never know again.

Chapter 3

Ki was still too weak and dizzy to get up the next day, so Cook served Tobin's belated name day cakes to them in the sickroom. Everyone crowded in and ate their portion standing. Nari presented Tobin with a new sweater and stockings she'd knitted, and Koni, their fletcher, gave him six fine new arrows. Laris had carved bone hunting whistles for him and Ki and Arkoniel shyly offered him a special pouch for carrying firechips.

"I'm afraid my gift for you is still in Ero," Tharin told him.

"And mine," said Ki around a mouthful of cake. His head was still mending but his appetite had recovered.

For the first time in a long time things began to feel safe and normal again. Tobin's heart swelled as he looked around at the others laughing and talking. Except for Iya's presence, it could have been any name day party he'd ever had.

By the next day Ki was well enough to be restless, but Nari wouldn't hear of letting him out of the sickroom. He sulked and complained so much that she took his clothes away with her, just in case.

As soon as she was gone Ki climbed out of bed and wrapped himself in a blanket.

"There, at least I'm up," he muttered. After a moment he began to feel sick again, but wouldn't admit that Nari had been right. Fighting down nausea, he insisted on playing bakshi. After a few tosses, however, he began to see two of everything and let Tobin help him back into bed.

"Don't tell her, will you?" he pleaded, closing his eyes. Trying to make the two Tobins frowning down at him join back into one made his head hurt.

"I won't, but maybe you should listen to her." Ki heard him settle in the chair by the bed. "You're still looking peaked."

"I'll be all right tomorrow," Ki said, willing it to be true.

The weather grew colder. Small sharp flakes drifted down from a hazy sky and the dead grass in the meadow sparkled with thick frost each morning.

Ki wolfed down all the broth and custard and baked apples Cook sent up, and was soon demanding meat. He continued to grumble at being shut in and made light of his condition, but Tobin knew he was far from his old self yet. He got tired suddenly, and his eyes still bothered him sometimes.

They grew bored with games long before Ki was strong enough to play at swords or go downstairs. Anxious to keep him quiet, Tobin arranged a nest of bolsters and blankets from him beside the toy city and they made a new game of tracing familiar routes through the city streets and trying to guess what the other Companions might be up to there.

Ki lifted off the roof of the box that served as the Old Palace and took the little golden tablet from its frame by the wood block throne. Tilting it to catch the light, he squinted at the tiny inscription there. "My eyes must be getting better. I can read this. 'So long as a daughter of Thelátimos' line defends and rules, Skala shall never be subjugated.' You know, that's the first time I've really looked at this since Arkoniel taught us to read." His dark brows drew together as he frowned. "Did you ever think maybe it wouldn't do you any good if your uncle knew about this? The one in the real throne room is gone, remember? My father claimed Erius melted it down when he destroyed all the stone copies that used to stand at crossroads."

"You're right." In fact, Tobin had never considered the risk before; now the idea took on a more dire cast than it would have a month earlier. He looked around, wondering where he should put it for safekeeping. Dangerous it might be, but it was still a gift from his father.

And not just a gift, but a message. For the first time it occurred to him that the toy city had not been simply a child's diversion; his father had been teaching him, readying him for the day—

"Tob, you all right?"

Tobin closed his hand around the tablet and stood up. "Yes, I was just thinking of my father." He looked around again, then inspiration struck. "I know just the place."

Ki followed him as he hurried back to his own room and threw open the clothes chest. He hadn't touched the doll since he'd hidden it here, but fetched it out now and found a seam in its side with stitches long enough to slide the tiny tablet through. He pushed it in deep, then shook it to make certain it slipped down inside. When he'd finished he buried it again and grinned at Ki. "There. I'm used to hiding *this* already."

*T*he sound of hooves on the frozen Alestun road broke the winter quiet the following afternoon. Ki left off his bakshi toss and the boys hurried to the window.

"Another messenger from Lord Orun," Tobin said, frowning at the yellow-liveried rider approaching the bridge. Sefus and Kadmen met him at the outer gate.

Ki turned to stare at him. "Another one? What did the last one want? Tobin?"

Tobin picked at a spot of lichen on the stone sill. "He wants me back in Ero, but Tharin sent word I was too sick to ride."

"That's all?"

"No," Tobin admitted. "Orun said he was writing to the king again."

"About me."

Tobin nodded grimly.

Ki said nothing, just looked back out the window, but Tobin saw the worry in his eyes.

Tharin brought the news up to them. "The same as before. Your guardian is impatient for your return."

"And to get rid of me," said Ki.

"I'm afraid so."

Ki hung his head. "This is my fault, isn't it, Tharin? I gave him a reason. I should have gone to you as soon as I knew Tobin was missing. I don't know why I listened—" He rubbed absently at the discolored lump on his forehead and gave Tobin a sorrowful look. "All I could think of was catching up with you. Now look what I've done!"

"I won't let him send you away. What did this letter say, exactly?"

Tharin handed Tobin the folded parchment and he scanned it quickly. "He wants me to start back today! Ki can't ride yet."

Tharin gave him a humorless smile. "I doubt that's of much concern to Lord Orun. Don't worry, though. Nari's down there explaining to the messenger how your fever is still too high for you to travel. You'd better keep to your room until he leaves. I wouldn't put it past Orun to have sent us a spy."

"Nor would I," said Iya, looking in at the door. "Before you go into hiding, though, would you come upstairs? I've something to show you. Privately," she added, as Ki started after him.

Tobin threw his friend an apologetic look as he followed her out.

"What is it?" he asked as soon as they were in the corridor.

"There are things we must speak of while there is still time." She paused. "Bring the doll, please."

Tobin did as she asked and they continued upstairs. Arkoniel met them in the workroom and to Tobin's surprise, he was not alone. Lhel sat at the long table just behind him. Everyone looked very serious, but he was glad to see her, all the same.

"You have call Brother?" asked Lhel, and he guessed that she already knew the answer.

"No," Tobin admitted.

"Call now."

Tobin hesitated, then spoke the words in a nervous rush.

Brother appeared in the corner farthest from the door. He was thin and ragged, but Tobin could feel the cold power of his presence from across the room.

"Well, what do you think?" asked Iya.

Lhel squinted hard at Brother, then shrugged. "I tell you the binding stronger now. So he stronger, too."

"I wonder if Ki is still able to see him?" murmured Arkoniel.

"I won't have him around Ki." Tobin turned angrily on the ghost. "I won't call you at all, ever, unless you promise never to hurt him again! I don't care what Lhel says!" He shook the doll at Brother. "Promise, or you can stay away and starve."

Tobin saw a flicker of hatred in the ghost's black eyes, but it was directed at the wizards, not at him.

"No one saw him in Tobin's sickroom," Iya was saying, as if she hadn't noticed his outburst.

"Those have the eye see him more now," said Lhel. "And he make others see when he wants."

Tobin looked at Brother again, noting how the lamplight seemed to touch him the same way it did the rest of them; it never had before. "He looks more—real, somehow."

"Be harder to put you apart, comes the time, but must be so."

For a moment curiosity overcame his anger. "Come here," he told the ghost. Tobin reached to touch him; but as always, his hand found only colder air. Brother grinned at him. He looked more like an animal baring its teeth.

"Go away!" Tobin ordered, and was relieved when the spiteful ghost obeyed. "Can I go now?"

"A moment more, if you please," said Arkoniel. "You remember how I promised to teach you to guard your thoughts? It's time we had that lesson."

"But it's not magic. You said so, remember?"

"Why do you fear magic so, Tobin?" asked Iya. "It's protected you all these years. And wonderful things can be done with it! You've seen that for yourself. With a wave of my hand, I can make fire where there is no wood, or food in the wilderness. Why do you fear it?"

Because magic meant surprises and fear, sorrow and danger, Tobin thought. But he couldn't tell them that; he didn't want them to know what power they had over him. So he just shrugged.

"Many magics, keesa," Lhel said softly, and he caught a flicker of the secret symbols on her cheeks. "You wise to be respecting. Some magic good, some evil. But we do no evil with you, keesa. Make you safe."

"And this isn't real magic, just a protection against it," Arkoniel assured him. "All you have to do is imagine something very clearly, make a picture in your head. Can you imagine the sea for me?"

Tobin thought of the harbor at Ero at dawn, with the great trading ships riding at anchor and the small fishing boats bobbing around them like skimmer beetles.

He felt the briefest cool touch on his brow, but no one had moved.

Iya chuckled. "That was very good."

"I tell you," Lhel said.

Tobin opened his eyes. "That's all?"

"That's a beginning, and a very good one," Arkoniel

replied. "But you must practice as often as you can, and do it whenever Niryn or any of the Harriers notice you. The real trick is to not look like you're thinking of something else."

"Arkoniel used to screw his face up like he had a cramp," Iya said, looking at him fondly, the way Nari looked at Tobin sometimes. "But you can't always think of the same thing. It's safest if you focus on something you've just been doing. For instance, if you've been hawking, think of jesses or wing markings, or the sound of the bells."

Tobin tried again, thinking of the game he and Ki had been playing.

"Well done again!" Arkoniel said. "Just remember, though, that your best defense against Niryn and his kind lies in never giving them a reason to look into your head."

*T*obin's apologies were carried back to Ero the following day. The boys watched from Ki's window, sticking their tongues out at the retreating horseman.

Ki was finally well enough to escape Nari's strictures and they spent the day wandering around the keep and visiting at the barracks. Ki wanted to visit Arkoniel, but the wizard didn't answer his door.

Ki looked back over his shoulder as they walked away. The sight of that closed door left him oddly depressed. "Where do you suppose he could be?"

"He's around," Tobin said with a shrug. "What's wrong? I just saw him yesterday."

"I haven't seen him since your name day party," Ki reminded him. "I'm starting to think he's avoiding me."

Tobin punched him lightly on the shoulder. "Now why would he do that?"

*K*i was surprised at how quickly his newfound energy deserted him. By midafternoon he was feeling weak again, and having spells of double vision. That frightened him, for Iya had assured him they would pass. The thought that she might be wrong was too frightening to contemplate. What good would a blind squire be to anyone?

As always, Tobin seemed to sense without being told how Ki felt and asked for an early supper upstairs.

That night they slept in Tobin's room. Ki sighed happily as he sank back against the soft bolsters. Even if it was only for a few nights more, it was good to have things as they used to be. He hadn't thought about Ero or his enemies among the Companions in days.

*T*obin's thoughts were running along similar lines as he watched the candle shadows dance overhead. Part of him missed Korin and the others, and the excitement of palace life. But Orun's angry letters tainted all that. Not for the first time, he wished things were the way they used to be.

"This damn thing itches," Ki grumbled, rubbing at his forehead. He turned his face for Tobin to see. "How does it look?"

Tobin pushed Ki's soft brown hair back for a better look. A swollen, crusted gash two inches long still stood out over Ki's right eye, just below the hairline. The lump was fading from purple to a nasty mottled green. "You must have hit a rock or something when you fell. Does it still hurt?"

Ki laughed up at him. "Don't *you* start fussing over me! I'm worse off from being kept indoors so long. My old dad would never have stood for it, I can tell you." He dropped back into the country accent he used to have. " 'Less you got a broke leg or guts hanging out, you can damn well get out and tend to yer chores."

"Do you still miss your family?"

Ki folded his hands across his chest. "Some of 'em, I guess. Ahra, and a couple brothers."

"After we get things settled in Ero, we could go visit them," Tobin offered. "I'd like to see where you come from."

Ki glanced away. "No, you wouldn't."

"Why not?"

"You just wouldn't." He gave Tobin a quick grin. "Bilairy's balls, I don't want to go back there. Why would you?"

Tobin let it go; why shouldn't Ki have a few secrets of his own and, anyway, that was all a long time ago. He pushed his fingers back through Ki's hair, pretending to take a closer look at the wound. "Anyway, it should leave a good scar."

"Not one to brag of, though," Ki grumbled. "Think the girls would believe me if I said we met with Plenimaran raiders on the road, or bandits, maybe? I bet Una and Marilli would believe me."

Tobin chuckled, but at the same time felt a familiar twinge of jealousy. He'd heard enough stories about his friend's hot-blooded kin, and Ki already had an eye for anything in skirts.

Tobin's own bashfulness in that regard had earned him his share of teasing among the Companions. Even Ki wasn't above the occasional good-natured jibe. Everyone—including Tobin himself—had always put it down to his youth and natural shyness.

Until now.

Now, fingers still twined in Ki's warm hair, Tobin had his first inkling of what that angry little knot in his belly might mean. He took his hand away and lay back, pulling the covers up under his chin.

I don't like girls that way because I—

He threw an arm across his face to hide the rising blush burning his cheeks and used Arkoniel's trick. He thought of Gosi's rough winter coat, the feel of cold rain down his neck, the bite of his hawk's talons on his fist—anything but the guilty heat coursing through him. Anything but the way his fingers remembered the weight of his friend's soft hair.

I'm a boy! Ki would never—

Ki had gone quiet, and when Tobin dared lift his arm he found him frowning up at the rafters. After a moment he let out a long sigh.

"What about Orun? What if he *does* get your uncle to send me away this time?"

"I told you, I won't let him."

"Oh, I know." Ki's buck-toothed grin flashed as he caught Tobin's hand in his, but he was worried. "I'll tell you this, Tob; whatever happens, I'll always stand by you, even if it's only as a soldier in your guard." He was dead serious now. "No matter what happens, Tobin, I'm your man."

"I know that," Tobin managed, caught between gratitude and guilt. "And I'm yours. Go to sleep now, before Nari comes in and makes you sleep next door."

Orun countered with another messenger the next day and, without thinking, Tobin went to get the news. Tharin was with the man in the hall and looked up in surprise as Tobin clattered down the stairs. He was too distracted for the moment to register what that look meant.

Their visitor turned out to be a most unlikely courier. It was Orun's own valet, Bisir. He was a meek, quiet fellow, pretty in the way that all the young men in Orun's household were. With his big, dark eyes and soft, nervous hands, Bisir had always reminded Tobin of a hare. He was one of the few people in that household who was always pleasant to him and, more importantly, the only one who was polite to Ki.

"A letter for you from my lord Orun, Prince Tobin," Bisir said, looking apologetic as he handed Tobin the sealed parchment. "And may I say, my prince, that it's good to see you looking so well. Captain Tharin's last letter gave my master to believe that your health might be in some danger."

Too late Tobin realized his mistake. It would be no use writing back of ill health now. He opened the letter and saw it made no difference, anyway. Orun was threatening to bring him home by cart, if need be.

It's all right," Ki said, as Tobin fretted in their room. "I can ride now, really."

Iya wasn't so certain, however, and they went to bed that night in low spirits. Unable to sleep, Tobin sent up a half-formed plea to Sakor and Illior, then wondered if the gods ever heard a petition without the offering smoke to carry it.

When he woke the following morning the first thing he noticed was something white on the floor. It was snow. A shutter had come open and a little drift of it had piled on the rushes under the window. More was blowing in. Jumping out of bed, he dashed to the window and leaned out, laughing as the driven flakes peppered his cheeks.

The meadow was gone, lost behind thick, shifting curtains of white. He could just make out the angle of the barracks roof but the bridge was nothing but a dark blur beyond it.

He scooped up a handful of snow and tossed it at Ki to wake him. Evidently the gods had been feeling generous.

The blizzard lasted for three days, heaping snow halfway up the doorposts and trapping Bisir in with them. This presented certain complications. Iya had made herself known, but Arkoniel had to stay hidden upstairs in case Bisir decided to wander where he wasn't wanted.

The young valet was awkward and ill at ease at first, clearly feeling out of place in this rude country household. There was nothing for him to do here, no one to serve. The women didn't want him underfoot in the hall, so Koni and some of the younger guardsmen took charge of him and dragged him off to the barracks. Ki and Tobin watched from the top of the stairs as they all but carried him out. Surrounded by rough, coarse-spoken soldiers, Bisir looked like he was on his way to be hanged.

They didn't see him again until breakfast the next day. Though uncharacteristically rumpled, he was actually laughing with Koni and the others, something Tobin had never seen the timid fellow do.

Even after the storm ended the roads were so choked with snow that for the present there was no question of travel. For three golden weeks they lived as if they'd never gone to Ero.

The snow kept them from riding, but they spent hours shooting, fighting snowball battles against the guardsmen, building whole squadrons of snowmen, and practicing their swordplay in the barracks. Koni somehow pulled Bisir into these pastimes, but the valet proved to be no warrior.

On those rare occasions when Ki and Tobin did manage to slip away unattended, they looked for Lhel at the edge of the forest, but the witch was either snowed in or refusing to show herself.

Ki grew strong again, but still had trouble seeing clearly sometimes when he was shooting. He thought about going to Tharin but instead ended up at Iya's door one night after Tobin was asleep. Once there, fear made it hard to tell her what the matter was. Iya was kind, seating him by her fire and giving him spiced wine. When he finally blurted out what the matter was, she seemed relieved.

"You eyes, is it? Well, let's see what I can do." Iya bent over him and pressed a hand to his brow. She said nothing for a few minutes, just stood there with her eyes half-closed, as if she was listening inside his head. Ki felt a tingling coldness against his skin; it tickled a little, but it felt good, too.

"You never told me you were a healer."

"Oh, I know a thing or two," she murmured.

Whatever she was doing, she soon seemed satisfied. "I

wouldn't fret about it. That knock on the head is still
mending. I'm sure this will pass."

"I hope so. When we get back—"

"You'll have to prove your worthiness all over again,"
she guessed, wise as always. "Your worth is known to your
friends, and you won't change the minds of your enemies
no matter what you do."

"My friends," Ki murmured, thinking of Arkoniel. No
matter what Tobin or anyone else said, Arkoniel was
avoiding him. He'd done no more than peek in at the
doorway when Ki lay sick, and they'd hardly seen each
other since. It hurt. Ki had always liked the wizard, even
when he was forcing him to learn reading and writing. This
sudden, unexplained coolness between them was hard to
bear.

He had not dared ask Tharin about it, scared of what
the answer might be. But now he couldn't hold back any
longer. Iya knew Arkoniel better than anyone else. "Is
Arkoniel angry with me for letting Tobin run off?"

Iya arched an eyebrow at him. "Angry? Why would
you think that? You know he can't risk being seen by our
houseguest."

"He was avoiding me before Bisir got here."

"He asks after you all the time."

Ki blinked. "He does?"

"Certainly."

"But I never see him."

Iya smoothed her hands down the front of her robe.
"He's been busy with some spell he's working on. That
takes up much of his time."

Ki sighed. That hadn't stopped Arkoniel from sending
for Tobin, just not for him.

Iya must have seen the doubt in his eyes, or maybe
she touched his mind to read it, for she smiled. "Don't
worry about this, my dear. Your illness frightened him
more than he likes to admit. Perhaps he has an odd way

of showing it, but he cares for you a great deal. I'll speak to him."

Ki rose and gave her a grateful bow. He was still too much in awe of her to hug her. "Thank you, Mistress. I'd be awfully sad if he didn't like me anymore."

Iya surprised him with a soft touch on his cheek. "You mustn't ever think that, child."

Chapter 4

It amused Niryn greatly to watch Orun fume and fret over Prince Tobin's absence. He'd suspected from the start that the Lord Chancellor had engineered the guardianship for himself, hoping to cement his connection to the royal family through Tobin. If the child had been a girl, no doubt he'd even have gone so far as to ask for a betrothal. He was powerful, it was true, and his oily loyalty to the king's mother had gained him both wealth and status; Erius might have considered such a match.

Instead, here was this skinny, skittish little boy, heir to the richest estates in the land, and Orun held the purse strings. Niryn's own hold on the king was secure enough, but it irked him to see such a plum fall into the lap of the most odious man in Ero. So he bided his time and kept spies in the house to see if Orun would trip himself up. Orun's penchant for young boys was no secret, though he'd wisely limited himself to servants and whores who could be counted on not to tattle. But if he should forget himself with Tobin? Well, that would certainly be a bit of luck. The wizard had even considered helping the matter along.

It was all moot anyway, though. Anytime the king chose—and here Niryn did have some influence—Erius could with impunity seize Tobin's estates, his lands, and treasuries. Tobin was young and virtually friendless among the nobles; with his parents dead, such a child was not worth anyone's loyalty.

If Ariani's daughter had lived, rather than this sprat, it would have been a different matter. As the plagues and droughts worsened and the peasants turned to Illior, it had not been terribly difficult to make the king see that any female of the blood posed a threat to his line. If the Illiorans had their way, any one of these pretenders could claim to be a "daughter of Thelátimos" and raise an army against him. The solution was the usual time-honored one.

Niryn had made a near-fatal error, however, when he pointed out obliquely that the king's sister, Ariani, posed the greatest threat of all. Erius had very nearly ordered Niryn's execution; that had been the first time Niryn used magic against the king.

The incident passed and Niryn was glad when it became apparent that the king's forbearance did not extend to his sister's children. They'd both taken it as an auspicious sign when Ariani's daughter was stillborn. Later, the princess' descent into madness had done Niryn's work for him. Not even the most fanatical Illiorans would want another mad queen on the throne. No one would back Ariani, or her demon-cursed son.

Yet that still left others. A girl, any girl, who could claim even tangentially to be a "daughter of Thelátimos" might find that the Prophecy of Afra had not been forgotten, no matter how many priests and wizards the king burned. It was a fact Niryn counted on.

No one had noticed when Niryn began paying monthly visits to Ilear. He dressed as a wealthy merchant and added a spell to fuddle the minds of any who might recognize him. In this way he'd come and gone as he pleased all these years. Who would dare spy on the leader of the Harriers?

Riding into the market town that misty winter afternoon, he reveled as always in his anonymity. It was poulterers' day, and the crowing, quacking, and honking of the birds in their pens echoed loudly inside the walled marketplace. Niryn smiled to himself as he guided his mount through the crowd. Who among them guessed that the horseman they jostled or muttered at or smiled upon had the power to end their lives with a word?

Leaving the markets behind, he rode up the hill to the most affluent neighborhood and the fine stone house he owned there. A young page answered, and Vena, the half-blind old nurse, met him in the hall.

"She's been fretting at her window since morning, Master," she scolded, taking his cloak.

"Is that him?" a girl called from upstairs.

"Yes, Nalia, my dear, it's me!" Niryn replied.

Nalia hurried down the stairs and kissed him on both cheeks. "You're a whole day late, you know!"

Niryn kissed her back, then held her at arm's length to admire her. A year older than Prince Korin, she had her kinsman's black hair and eyes, but none of his handsome looks. She was a homely girl, made homelier by a weak chin and the irregular pink birthmark that ran like spilled wine down her left cheek and shoulder. It made her shy, and she shunned society of any sort. This had served him well, making it a simple matter to keep her hidden away in this remote backwater town.

Her mother, a second cousin to the king on the matrilineal side, had been even uglier, but somehow managed to find a husband and whelp a pair of girls. Her good fortune had been Niryn's. He'd seen to the murders himself, stopping the father's heart as he opened the door to the wizard and killing the mother in the birthing bed. That had been in the early days of Erius' massacres, when Niryn still saw to such things personally.

Nalia's twin had been a pretty little thing, untouched by the unkind fate that had marred her mother and sister. She would have grown up a beauty, and beauty was hard to hide. Or control.

Niryn had meant to kill all of them, but as he'd lifted the second squalling infant from her dead mother's side he'd had the vision—the one that had guided his every action since. From that moment on, he knew he was no longer merely the king's coursing hound, but the master of Skala's future.

Other wizards glimpsed her in their own visions, and some of the Illioran priests, too. Preying on the king's fears for Korin, Niryn had wrested the power and the means to crush others before they could see clearly and reveal his sweet, tractable little Nalia. No one but he must bring this future queen forward when the time was right. No one but he must control her when she reached the throne.

He controlled Erius, but knew he would never be able to control headstrong young Korin. The boy had too much of his mother's blood in him and no hint of madness. He would rule long, while plague and ill fortune grew on the land until Skala gave way to her enemies like a rotten beam.

Mad Agnalain and her brood had tainted the crown; no one would argue that. His Nalia could trace her lineage back to Thelátimos on both sides. Niryn could prove it, when the time came. He, and only he, would restore the Sword of Ghërilain to a woman's hand when the Light-bearer gave the sign. In the meantime, she had grown up safely anonymous, unknown even to herself. She knew only that she was an orphan, and Niryn was her kindly benefactor and guardian. Allowed no other male companions, she doted on him and missed him terribly when he was away—as she believed—attending to his shipping business in the capital.

"It's very cruel of you to make me wait so long," she said, still chiding, though he saw the flush rising in her unblemished cheek as she drew him by the hand to his chair in the sitting room. Settling happily on his lap, she kissed him again and gave his beard a playful tug.

Despite her disfigured face, she'd grown into a shapely young woman. Niryn circled her slender waist with one arm and ran a hand lovingly over the generous swell of her breasts as he kissed her. At night in their unlit bedchamber, she was as beautiful as any mistress he'd ever taken, and the most abjectly devoted.

Let Orun have his little stick figure prince for now. Without Duke Rhius' power behind him—and Niryn had helped that demise along, too—the son of Ariani was just another male usurper to the throne, and a cursed one at that. He'd be easy enough to deal with when the time came.

Chapter 5

A warm wind from the south ended Tobin's exile in early Cinrin. Midwinter rains melted the drifts like sugar loaves. The snow forts crumbled and their army of snowmen lay like scattered pockmarked corpses, felled by the plague of mild weather.

Two days later a royal courier arrived with a letter from Korin and another sharp summons from Lord Orun.

"That's it, then," said Ki after Tobin read it out to Tharin and the others around the hearth fire.

Bisir had grown ruddy and rather cheerful during his unintended stay, but he had that frightened rabbit look again now. "Does he say anything about me?"

"Don't worry about Orun," said Tobin. "It wasn't your fault you got snowed in. He can't hold the weather against you."

Bisir shook his head. "But he will."

"We'll head back at first light tomorrow," said Tharin, looking no more pleased than the valet did. "Nari, see that their things are packed."

"Of course I will!" Nari snapped, offended, but Tobin saw her dab at her eyes with a corner of her apron as she went up the stairs.

Cook prepared a fine farewell supper that night, but no one was very hungry.

"You are still coming with me, aren't you, Iya?" Tobin asked, pushing a bit of lamb around his bowl.

"Maybe you could be Tobin's court wizard," Ki offered.

"I doubt the king would approve of that," Iya replied.

"But I'll come for a little stay, just to see how the wind's blowing."

Tobin's heart was heavy as he and Ki dressed by candle-light the next morning. He had no appetite for breakfast; there was a lump in his throat, and another heavy as a stone in his belly. Ki was quieter than usual, and made his good-byes hastily when the time came to leave. Bisir looked downright grim.

The day dawned rainy and cold as they passed through Alestun. The roads were churned to thick, sucking mud and made for slow riding. The rain came in squalls as they descended through the wooded hills to the rolling open country beyond. Dusk came on early so late in the year. They spent the night in a wayside inn and came in sight of the coast at noon the next day. The sky was the color of iron, the sea and the distant river black against the winter brown fields. Even Ero looked like a city of ash on her high hill.

They kicked their horses into a gallop over the last few miles and the sharp tang of the sea blew in to greet them. That and the excitement of galloping with his own men at his back lifted Tobin's spirits a little. By the time they reached the broad stone span of Beggar's Bridge, he felt ready to face his guardian. Even the slums between the bridge and the city wall did not dampen his spirits. He emptied his purse of coppers and silver, tossing the coins to the beggars who lined the way. Tobin and his warriors saluted the crescent and flame carved on the great stone arch of the south gate, touching hearts and hilts to honor the city's patron deities. Tharin announced Tobin's arrival and the pikemen bowed to him as he rode by. Iya reined aside to show the silver badge she wore and one of the guards marked something down on a wax tally board. The wizard's lips were pressed in a hard angry line as she caught up with Tobin. Tobin knew about the badges the Harriers made the free wizards wear, had seen the one Iya wore. Only now did he begin to understand what they really meant.

The narrow streets seemed all the more dark and filthy to Tobin after weeks in the mountains. This was a poor quarter and the faces he saw peering out from windows and doorways were pinched and pale as ghosts.

"Stinking Ero," he muttered, wrinkling his nose.

Iya gave him an odd look from under her hood, but said nothing.

"Guess we were gone long enough to get the smell out of our noses," said Ki.

Urging their mounts on at a gallop, they clattered up the steep, twisting streets to the walled Palatine. The streets grew marginally cleaner in the upper precincts, and in some the woven ropes of evergreen boughs and wheat had already been hung over some doorways in preparation for the Festival of Sakor.

The captain of the Palatine Guard greeted Tharin at the gates. "Prince Korin left word for Prince Tobin, my lord," he said, bowing low. "He bids his cousin come to the feasting hall as soon as he arrives."

"Did Lord Orun leave any message?" asked Tobin.

"No, my prince."

"That's good, anyway," muttered Ki.

Tobin turned reluctantly to Bisir. "I suppose you'd better take your master the news."

The young man bowed in the saddle and rode on ahead without a word.

The branches of the ancient, winter-bare elms lining the avenue formed a netted tunnel over them as they cantered on.

Tobin paused by the Royal Tomb and saluted the remains of his parents, which lay in the catacombs below. Through the age-blackened wooden pillars that supported the flat tile roof, Tobin could see the light of the altar fire flickering over the faces of the queens' effigies.

"Do you want to go in?" Tharin asked.

Tobin shook his head and rode on.

The New Palace gardens were a palette of grey and black. Lights twinkled from windows everywhere in the maze of fine houses that crowned Ero's high hill, like a flock of fireflies in winter.

At the Old Palace Iya went on with Laris and the others to quarters at the villa that had been Ariani's. Tharin stayed with the boys and accompanied them into the Companions' wing. Uncertain of his welcome, Tobin was glad of his company and Ki's as they made their way along the faded corridors.

The messroom was empty but sounds of merriment led them on to Korin's feasting chamber. The double doors stood open and light and music spilled out to greet the prodigals. Hundreds of lamps lit the room and the chamber felt stifling after the day's cold ride.

Korin and the other noble Companions sat at the high table, accompanied by a few select friends and favorite girls. The squires were busy serving. Garol stood ready with his wine pitcher behind Korin's chair and Tanil was busy carving on his left. The only person who seemed to be missing from the usual gathering was Swordmaster Porion. He was nowhere to be seen. As much as Tobin liked the gruff old veteran, he was in no hurry to hear what the man had to say about his absence from training.

Scores of guests of every age sat at two long tables below. Looking around, Tobin saw the usual collection of entertainers, as well. At the moment, a company of Mycenian acrobats were throwing each other into the air.

Korin hadn't noticed their arrival. Aliya was sitting on his lap, laughing and blushing over something he was whispering in her ear as he played with one of her braids. As Tobin approached the table, he saw with little surprise that his cousin was flushed with wine, despite the early hour.

Near the end of the table, Tobin's friends Nikides and

Lutha were talking with dark-haired Lady Una, though they looked more earnest than flirtatious.

Lutha was the first to notice them. His narrow face lit up as he elbowed Nikides, and shouted, "Look, Prince Korin, your wayward cousin is home at last!"

"Come here, coz!" Korin exclaimed, throwing his arms wide. "And you, too, Ki. So you finally dug yourselves out, did you? We've missed you. And missed your name day, as well."

"I've had my old seat back for a while," Caliel said, laughing. Giving up his place of honor at Korin's right, he shouldered in next to red-bearded Zusthra.

Ki went to join the other squires serving at table. Tharin was given a seat of honor among Korin's older friends at the right-hand table. Tobin looked around uneasily for his guardian; Orun inserted himself into Korin's doings whenever he could manage it. But not this time, Tobin noted with relief.

Ki had seemed welcome enough, too. Perhaps Orun hadn't done anything, after all. Down the table, however, he caught sight of their old nemesis, Moriel the Toad. The pale, sharp-faced boy was watching his rival with open dislike; if Orun had had his way, Tobin would be sharing chambers with him instead of Ki.

As he looked around to see if Ki had noticed, he was caught by a pair of dark eyes. Lady Una gave him a shy wave. Her open regard had always discomforted Tobin. Now, with his new secret lodged like a splinter in his heart, he had to look away quickly. How could he ever face her again?

"Ah, someone's glad to see you home," Caliel observed, misinterpreting Tobin's sudden blush.

"Mazer, butler, a welcoming cup for my cousin!" Korin cried. Lynx brought Tobin a golden mazer and Garol, none too sober himself, slopped wine into it.

Korin leaned forward, peering into Tobin's face. "You

seem no worse for your illness. Thought you had plague, did you?"

Korin was drunker than he'd thought, and reeked of wine. All the same, the welcome was genuine, if a little slurred, and Tobin was glad of it.

"I didn't want the deathbirds nailing up the palace," he explained.

"Speaking of birds, your hawk's been pining for you," Arengil called down the table, his Aurënfaie accent giving the words a graceful lilt. "I've kept her in trim, but she misses her master."

Tobin raised his cup to his friend.

Korin swayed to his feet and banged a spoon against a platter of goose bones. The minstrels ceased and the tumblers scurried away. When he had everyone's attention, Korin raised his cup to Tobin. "Let us pour libations for my cousin, for his name day's sake." With an unsteady hand, he tipped half the contents onto the stained tablecloth, then downed the rest as the others sprinkled the required drops. Wiping his mouth on his sleeve, Korin proclaimed grandly, "Twelve years old, my cousin is, and twelve kisses he'll get from every girl at the table to speed him on to manhood. And one extra, too, for the month that's passed since. Aliya, you first."

There was no point in arguing, for Korin would have his way. Tobin tried not to flinch as Aliya draped herself around him and delivered the required dozen all over his face. Korin was welcome to his opinion of her, but Tobin had always found her sharp-tongued and mean. For the last kiss, she pressed her mouth hard to his, then flounced away laughing. Half a dozen more girls crowded forward, probably more anxious for Korin's approval than Tobin's. When Una's turn came, she shyly brushed his cheek, eyes squeezed shut. Over her shoulder, Tobin could see black-haired Alben laughing with Zusthra and Quirion, clearly relishing his embarrassment.

When the ordeal was over, Ki set a parsley bread trencher and a finger bowl down before him. Tobin saw that he was tight-lipped with anger.

"It's just in fun," Tobin whispered, but it wasn't the kissing that had upset his friend.

Still glowering, Ki took the platter away. A moment later Tobin heard the clatter of dishes and Ki's muffled curse. Turning, he saw Mago and Arius laughing as Ki scooped greasy scraps back onto the platter he'd dropped. From the look Ki shot them, Tobin guessed those two had lost no time resuming their old tricks.

Tobin hadn't forgiven Mago for goading Ki into a fight that had gotten him a beating on the temple steps. He was halfway out of his chair when Korin's squire, Tanil, stepped in beside him to place several cuts of roast lamb in his trencher.

"I'll deal with them," he murmured.

Tobin grudgingly settled back in his chair. As usual, Korin took no notice. "What will you have for a present, coz?" he demanded. "Name anything you like. A gold-chased corselet, perhaps, to replace that battered old turtle shell of yours? A peregrine or a fine new Aurënfaie horse? I know—a sword! There's a new smith in Hammer Street, you've never seen the like—"

Tobin chewed slowly, considering the offer. He had no desire to replace his horse or his sword—both gifts from his father—and his old armor suited him just fine, though perhaps it was getting a little small. The fact was, he'd been given so many gifts since he'd come to court that he couldn't think of a thing to ask for, except one. And he didn't dare bring up Ki's possible banishment here. He wasn't even certain if it was in his cousin's power to decide the matter and wouldn't risk embarrassing Ki in front of the others.

"I can't think of anything," he admitted at last.

This was greeted with good-natured hoots and catcalls, but he overheard Urmanis' sister Lilyan whispering meanly to Aliya, "Always has to play the simple rustic lord, doesn't he?"

"Perhaps the prince would rather have a different sort of gift," Tharin suggested. "A journey, perhaps?"

Korin grinned. "A journey? Now there's a gift we could all share in. Where would you like to go, Tobin? Afra, perhaps, or down to Erind. You won't get better fried eels anywhere and the whores there are said to be the finest in Skala."

Caliel threw an arm around his friend's neck, trying to stem the drunken ramble. "He's a little young for that, don't you think?"

He gave Tobin a sympathetic wink over Korin's shoulder. Caliel and Tanil were the only ones who could steer Korin when he was this deep in his cups.

Still at a loss, Tobin looked back at Tharin. The man smiled and raised a hand to his breast, almost as if he were pointing at something.

Tobin understood at once. Touching the lump his father's seal ring made under his tunic, he said, "I'd like to see my estate at Atyion."

"Only that far?" Korin regarded him with bleary disappointment.

"I've never seen it," Tobin reminded him.

"Well then, to Atyion it is! I could use a new horse and the herds there are the best this side of the Osiat."

Everyone cheered again. Warmed by his little triumph, Tobin allowed himself a deep swallow of wine. Lord Orun had always found some excuse for Tobin not to go. In this, at least, Korin had the final say.

Well, well. Look who's back," Mago sneered as Ki helped collect the scraps for Ruan's alms basket.

"Yes, look who's here," Arius, Mago's shadow and echo, chimed in, jostling Ki's arm. "Our grass knight has come home. I hear Lord Orun's been fuming mad at you, letting the prince run off like that."

"Master Porion isn't too happy with you, either," Mago gloated. "How do you fancy kneeling on the temple steps again? How many lashes do you suppose he'll have your prince give you this time?"

For an answer, Ki stuck his foot out and sent Mago sprawling with the platter of roast lamb he'd been carrying.

"Tripping over your own feet again, Mago?" Tanil chuckled as he passed. "You'd better get that cleaned up before Chylnir catches you."

Mago scrambled to his feet, his fine tunic covered in grease. "Think you're pretty clever, don't you?" he spat at Ki. Then, to Tanil, "If I'm so clumsy, maybe Sir Kirothius here should finish the job by himself." He stalked off toward the kitchen with the empty platter. Arius shot Ki a dangerous look as he trotted off after Mago.

"No need to get yourself in trouble over me," Ki mumbled as he gathered the scraps. It embarrassed him that Tanil had heard the other boys' taunts.

But the head squire's eyes were bright with suppressed laughter. "Not your fault that he can't keep his feet, now, is it? That was a nice little move. Will you teach me?"

It was after midnight when Tharin and Caliel accompanied the princes to their bedchambers. Korin was blind drunk, and after several attempts to fall on his nose, Tharin picked the prince up and carried him to his door.

"Good night, sweet coz. Sweet, sweet coz," Korin warbled, as Tanil and Caliel took charge of him. "Sweet dreams to you and welcome home! Caliel, I think I'm going to puke."

His friends hurried him inside, but from the sounds that followed, they weren't quick enough getting him to a basin.

Tharin shook his head in disgust.

"He's not always like that," Tobin told him, always quick to defend his cousin.

"Too often for my taste, or his father's, I'd say," Tharin growled.

"Mine, too," muttered Ki, lifting the latch at their door.

The door fetched against something as he tried to open it. There was a grunt of surprise from the other side, then their page, Baldus, swung it wide, grinning at Tobin with sleepy delight. "Welcome home, my prince! And Lord Tharin, it's good to see you again."

Tapers had been left burning and the room was sweet with the welcoming scents of beeswax and the pines outside the balcony.

Baldus hurried to pull back the heavy black-and-gold bed hangings and turn down the covers for them. "I'll fetch a warming pan, my prince. Molay and I were so glad to hear you were coming back at last! Sir Ki, the baggage is in the dressing room. I've left it for you to unpack, like always." He stifled a huge yawn. "Oh, and there's a letter from your guardian, Prince Tobin. Molay left it there on the writing table, I think."

So Old Slack Guts wasted no time, after all, thought Tobin, picking up the folded parchment. Judging by the way that Baldus was looking anywhere but at Ki, his squire's precarious situation was no secret.

"Go sleep in the kitchen where it's warmer," Tobin told the boy, not wanting an audience. "And tell Molay I don't require him tonight. I just want to go to sleep."

Baldus bowed and dragged his pallet out with him.

Bracing himself, Tobin broke the seal and read the few brief lines.

"What does it say?" Ki demanded softly.

"Just that he'll summon me tomorrow and I'm to come alone."

Tharin read it for himself, scowling. "Alone, eh? Sounds like the Lord Chancellor needs reminding who he's dealing with. I'll have an honor guard waiting. Send word when you need us." He clapped them both on the shoulder. "No long faces, boys. Worrying yourselves sick tonight won't help. Get some sleep and whatever happens tomorrow, we'll deal with it then."

Tobin wanted to take Tharin's advice, but neither he nor Ki could find much to say as they got ready for bed. They lay in silence for a long time, listening to the embers tinkling on the hearth as they cooled.

Finally, Ki nudged Tobin's foot with his own and gave voice to both their fears. "This could be my last night here."

"Hope not," Tobin croaked, his throat tight.

It seemed like a long time before Ki fell asleep. Tobin lay still until he was certain, then slid out of bed and carried a candle into the dressing room.

Their traveling bundles were piled on the floor. Opening his he reached down to the bottom and pulled out the doll. He knew he didn't need to touch it to cast the summons, but he distrusted Brother more than ever now and wasn't taking any chances here.

Alone in the dark, he realized he was again afraid of the ghost, more than he had been since Lhel gave him the doll. But even that didn't stop him from whispering the words; Brother sometimes knew the future, and Tobin couldn't sleep until he'd at least asked.

When Brother appeared, bright as a flame in the dim little chamber, he still had that too-real look.

"Will Orun send Ki away tomorrow?" asked Tobin.

Brother just looked at him, still and silent as a painting.

"Tell me! You've told me other things." *Mean, hurtful things, and lies.* "Tell me!"

"I can only tell what I can see," Brother whispered at last. "I don't see him."

"See who? Orun or Ki?"

"They're nothing to me."

"Then you're no good me!" Tobin shot back bitterly. "Go away."

Brother obeyed and Tobin hurled the doll back into its old hiding place atop the dusty cupboard.

Returning to the bed, he climbed in and snuggled close to Ki. Rain was pattering on the roof and he listened to it, waiting in vain for sleep to take him.

Chapter 6

It was raining even harder the next morning. All around the Companions' wing servants were setting out pails and basins to catch the water leaking through the ancient ceiling.

The weather had never made any difference to Master Porion. Tobin woke Ki as soon as he heard servants moving past in the corridor, and they made certain they were the first ones waiting for the swordmaster at the palace doors. Despite what Mago had said, the stocky old warrior seemed genuinely glad to have them back.

"All well, are you?" he asked, looking them over. "You don't look much the worse for wear."

"We're fine, Master Porion," Tobin assured him. "And we practiced while we were gone, too."

That earned them a skeptical look. "We'll see about that, won't we?"

They had both mended. Even Ki, who'd been the sickest, kept up with the others as they set off on their morning run. Splashing though puddles and squelching through mud with their short cloaks flapping wetly against their thighs, the Companions ran the long circuit around the park, past the tomb and the drysian grove, around the reflecting pool and past the New Palace, and ending as they always did at the Temple of the Four at the center of the park.

The boys' morning offerings were usually cursory affairs, but today Tobin spent several minutes at Sakor's altar, whispering fervently over the little wax horse before casting it into the flames. Then, when he thought no one was looking, he sidled over to the white marble altar of Illior and cast one of Iya's owl feathers onto the incense-laden coals.

Lord Orun's summons came just as they were finishing their bread and milk in the messroom. Tharin must have been keeping watch, because he came in with the messenger. Dressed in a fine blue tunic, with every buckle and brooch polished, he cut an impressive figure. Korin gave Tobin an encouraging wink as he and Ki went out.

When they were out of earshot, Tharin dismissed the messenger and turned to Ki. "Wait for us at Tobin's house, why don't you? We'll meet you there on our way back."

Tobin and Ki exchanged grim, knowing looks; if the worst did come to pass, they wouldn't risk shaming themselves in front of the other Companions.

Ki punched Tobin on the shoulder. "Stand your ground with him, Tob. Good luck." With that he strode away.

"You'd better change out of those wet things," said Tharin.

"I don't give a damn what Orun thinks!" Tobin snapped. "I just want this over with."

Tharin folded his arms and gave Tobin a stern look. "So you're going to go before him dressed like a common soldier, muddy to the knees? Remember whose son you are."

Those words again, and this time they stung. Tobin hurried back to his chamber, where Molay had a steaming basin and his best suit of clothes ready for him. Washed and changed, Tobin stood in front of the polished mirror and let the valet comb his black hair smooth. A grim, plain boy in velvet and linen scowled back at him, ready for battle. Tobin looked into his own reflected eyes, feeling for a moment as if he were sharing a secret with the stranger hidden behind his face.

*   *   *

Orun's grand house stood in the maze of walled villas clustered on the New Palace grounds. Bisir met them at the door and ushered them into the reception hall.

"Good morning!" Tobin greeted him, glad to find one friendly face here. But Bisir hardly spoke and wouldn't meet his eye. It was as if a single night back in his master's house had undone all the good his time at the keep had accomplished. He looked as pale as ever, and Tobin saw new bruises on his wrists and neck.

Tharin had seen, too, and an angry flush came over his face. "He has no right—"

Bisir shook his head quickly, stealing a quick glance toward the stairs. "Don't trouble yourself on my account, my lord," he whispered, then, aloud, "My master is in his chamber. You may wait in the reception chamber, Sir Tharin. The Chancellor will speak with the prince alone." He paused, clasping his hands nervously, and added, "Upstairs."

For a moment Tobin thought Tharin was going to storm up with them. The man's dislike of Orun was no secret, but Tobin had never seen him so angry.

Bisir stepped nearer to Tharin, and Tobin heard him whisper, "I'll be close by."

"See that you are," Tharin muttered. "Don't worry, Tobin. I'll be right here."

Tobin nodded, trying to feel brave; but as he followed Bisir upstairs, he drew out the ring and seal and kissed them for luck.

He'd never been upstairs before. As they continued down a long corridor toward the back of the house, Tobin was amazed at the opulence of the house. The carvings and tapestries were of the best quality and the furnishings rivaled anything in the New Palace. Young servant boys scattered out of their way as they passed. Bisir ignored them as if they didn't exist.

He stopped at the last door and let Tobin into the

enormous chamber beyond. "Remember, I'll be right out here," he whispered.

Trapped, Tobin looked around in surprise. He'd expected a private sitting room or salon, but this was a bedchamber. An enormous carved bedstead dominated the center of the room. Its hangings—thick yellow velvet edged with tiny golden bells—were still closed. So were the draperies at the windows. The paneled walls were hung with tapestries of green woodland scenes, but the room was as hot as a smithy and heavy with the aroma of cedar logs blazing and snapping on the enormous stone hearth.

Even Prince Korin's room was not so lavish, Tobin thought, then started as bells on the bed hangings tinkled softly. A plump white hand emerged and drew back one of the heavy curtains.

"Ah, here is our little wanderer, returned at last," Orun purred, waving Tobin closer. "Come, my dear, and let me see how you weathered your illness."

Propped up against a mass of pillows, Lord Orun was wrapped in a yellow silk dressing gown; a large velvet bed cap of the same color covered his bald head. A crystal lamp hung from a chain, casting shadows that made his face seem more sallow than ever, his heavy flesh slacker on his bones. The counterpane was strewn with documents and the remains of a large breakfast lay on a tray beside him.

"Come closer," Orun urged.

The edge of the mattress was nearly level with Tobin's chest. Forced to look up at the man, Tobin could see the grey hairs in his guardian's large nose.

"Do have a seat, my prince. There's a stool just behind you."

Tobin ignored it, letting his scorn show as he set his feet and clasped his hands behind his back so this man wouldn't see them trembling. "You sent for me, Lord Orun, and I am here. What do you want?"

Orun favored him with an unpleasant smile. "I see your time away hasn't improved your manners. You know why you're here, Tobin. You've been a naughty boy and your uncle has heard all about your little escapade. I wrote him a long letter as soon as we discovered where you'd gone. Of course, I did my best to shield you from his displeasure. I put the blame where it belonged, on that ignorant peasant squire you're lumbered with. Though perhaps we shouldn't blame poor Kirothius too much. I daresay he suits you well enough out there in the wilds, but how could he be expected to keep proper watch over a princess' son at court?"

"He serves me well here! Even Korin says so."

"Oh, you're all very fond of the boy, I know. And I'm sure we can find some suitable situation for him. In fact, in my letter I even offered to take him into my household. I can assure you, he'll be properly educated here."

Tobin clenched his fists, recalling the bruises on Bisir's wrists.

"As to why you're here, well, surely you wish to pay your respects to me after such long absence?" Orun paused. "No? Well, no matter. I'm expecting the king's reply with this morning's dispatches and thought it would be pleasant to read the good news together."

This was far worse than anything Tobin had imagined. Orun was much too pleased with himself. He probably had spies among the king's entourage and already knew the answer. Tobin's heart sank even lower; Ki wouldn't last two days in this household without getting into serious trouble.

Clucking his tongue in feigned concern, Orun lifted a delicate painted plate from the tray and held it out to him. "You're looking very pale, dear boy. Have a bit of cake."

Tobin fixed his gaze on the counterpane's embroidered edge, resisting the urge to knock the plate across the room. Bed ropes creaked as Orun settled back, and Tobin heard his guardian's satisfied chuckle. He wished now he'd accepted the stool but was too proud to move. How long until the dispatches arrived? Orun hadn't said, and the heat was making Tobin dizzy. Sweat prickled across his upper lip and ran down between his shoulder blades. He could hear cold rain spattering against the shutters and wished he were outside again, running with his friends.

Orun said nothing, but Tobin knew he was being closely watched. "I won't put Ki aside!" he gritted out, looking up defiantly.

Orun's eyes had gone like black flints, though he was still smiling. "I sent the king a list of prospective replacements, young men of suitable background and breeding. But perhaps you've someone to add? I don't wish to be unreasonable."

No doubt Orun's list had been a very short one, made up of favorites who would carry tales. Tobin knew who was at the head of it, judging by the Toad's smug demeanor last night.

"Very well, then," he said at last, glaring up at Orun. "I'll have Lady Una."

Orun laughed and clapped his soft hands, as if Tobin had made a particularly brilliant joke. "Most amusing, my prince! I must remember to tell your uncle that one. But seriously, young Moriel is more than willing, and the king did already approve him once—"

"Not him."

"As your guardian—"

"No!" Tobin nearly stamped his foot. "Moriel will *never* serve me. Not if I have to go naked and alone into battle!"

Orun settled back against his cushions again and picked up a cup from the tray. "We'll see about that."

Despair crept over Tobin. For all his brave words to Ki and Tharin, he knew he was no match for the man.

Orun sipped softly at his tea for a moment. "I understand you wish to visit Atyion."

So Moriel was already at work. Or perhaps it had been Alben. He'd heard Orun favored the dark, arrogant boy.

"The estate is mine now. Why shouldn't I go? Korin said I might."

Orun smirked. "Assuming our dear prince recalls anything he said last night. But you're not planning to go today, surely? Just listen to that rain. It's certain to last for days this time of the year. I wouldn't be surprised if it begins to freeze soon."

"It's only a day's ride—"

"So soon after your illness, my dear?" Orun shook his head. "Most unwise. Besides, I should think you've had enough adventures for a while. When you're stronger, perhaps. It's a lovely place in the spring, Atyion."

"The spring? It's my father's house. *My* house! I have a right to go there."

Orun's smile broadened. "Ah, but you see, dear boy, you have no rights at all just yet. You're only a child, and in my charge. You must trust me to decide what is best for you. As your esteemed uncle would be sure to tell you, I have only your best interests at heart. You *are* the second heir, after all." He returned to his breakfast. "For now."

Tobin felt a chill in spite of the heat. Behind that smiling mask, Orun was still furious with him. This was the beginning of his punishment.

Too frightened and angry to speak, Tobin strode to the door, intending to leave no matter what Orun said. Just as he reached it, however, it swung open and he collided headlong with Bisir.

"Forgive me, my prince!" Tobin saw pity in the man's eyes and steeled himself. The king's messenger must have arrived.

Instead, it was Niryn who swept in.

Caught off guard, Tobin blinked up at the tall wizard, then quickly filled his mind with his anger at Orun, imagining it swirling through his head like smoke in a closed room.

Raindrops glistened in the wizard's forked red beard as he bowed to Tobin. "Good morning, my prince! I'd hoped to find you here. How nice that you've returned in time for the Festival of Sakor. And I understand you've brought a wizard back with you, too?"

His words gave Tobin a nasty turn. Had Niryn looked into his head after all, or did he have spies of his own? "Mistress Iya was a friend of my father's," he replied.

"Yes, I remember," Niryn murmured as if it didn't interest him much. Arching an eyebrow, he turned to Orun. "Still abed at this hour, my lord? Are you ill?"

Heaving himself out of bed, Orun pulled his gown around him with imperious dignity. "I was not expecting official visitors, Lord Niryn. The prince has come to visit me after his absence."

"Ah, yes, the mysterious illness. I trust you're quite recovered, Your Highness?"

Tobin could have sworn the man winked at him. "I'm very well, thank you." Tobin expected any moment to feel the wizard's creeping touch in his mind but Niryn seemed far more interested in baiting Orun.

Eyeing his unexpected visitor suspiciously, Orun waved him and Tobin to seats by the fire. Both men waited until Tobin was seated before taking their own chairs.

The old hypocrite, Tobin thought. So long as there was anyone else around to see, Orun treated him with the proper courtesy.

"The prince and I are expecting a messenger from the king," said Orun.

"And as it happens, it is in that capacity that I come to you today." Niryn took a rolled parchment from one deep sleeve and smoothed it over his knee. The heavy royal seals dangled from silk ribbons at the bottom of it. "I received this early this morning. His Majesty asked that I deliver it to you personally." Niryn glanced down at the document, but Tobin could tell he already knew the contents. "His Majesty begins by thanking you for your care of his royal nephew." He looked up at Orun and smiled. "And he hereby relieves you of all further responsibility in that regard."

"What?" Orun's velvet cap slid askew as he lurched forward in his chair. "What—what does this mean? What are you saying?"

"It's perfectly clear, Orun. You're no longer Prince Tobin's guardian."

Orun gaped at him, then held out a shaking hand for the letter. Niryn relinquished it and watched with obvious satisfaction as the other man read it. By the time Orun had finished, the wax seals were clattering together on their ribbons. "He says nothing of why! Have I not discharged my duties faithfully?"

"I'm certain there's no need for concern. He thanks you most graciously for your service." Niryn leaned forward and pointed out a section. "Just there, you see?"

Niryn made no effort to hide how pleased he was with Orun's reaction. "The duke's death was so unexpected, and you were right there, offering your aid," he went on smoothly. "But King Erius wishes to impose on you no longer, for fear you'll be too distracted from your duties at the Treasury. He will appoint a new guardian when he returns."

"But—but my understanding was that the position was permanent!"

Niryn rose and gave him a pitying look. "Surely you, of all people, are no stranger to the king's whims."

Tobin had sat transfixed through all this, but found his voice at last. "My—the king, he's coming home?"

Niryn paused in the doorway. "Yes, my prince."

"When?"

"I cannot say, my prince. Depending on the current negotiations with Plenimar, perhaps sometimes in the spring."

"What does this mean?" Orun mumbled, still clutching the letter. "Niryn, you must know the king's mind in this?"

"It is dangerous for anyone to presume to know King Erius' mind these days. But if I may, my old friend, I would suggest that your reach has finally exceeded your grasp. I believe you know what I speak of. The blessings of the Four be with you both. Good day to you, my prince."

He swept out and, for a moment, the only sounds were the crackle of the fire and the incessant patter of the rain. Orun's lips moved silently as he stared into the flames.

The air felt charged, the way it did just before a storm. Tobin looked longingly at the closed door, anxious to get away. When Orun didn't move, he rose slowly. "May—may I go?"

Orun looked up slowly and Tobin's knees nearly gave way. Naked hatred twisted the man's features. Lurching to his feet, he loomed over Tobin. "May you *go*? This is your doing, you ungrateful brat!"

Tobin took a step back but Orun followed. "With your smirking and your insults. Old Slack Guts, isn't that what you and that country bastard call me behind my back? Laughing! At me, who has served two rulers? Oh, you think there's anything that goes unheard, do you?" he snarled, though Tobin had said nothing. Grabbing him by the arm, Orun shook the king's letter in his face. "This is your doing!"

"No, I swear!"

Orun tossed the letter aside and jerked Tobin closer. Spittle flew from the man's lips as he snarled, "Writing to the king behind my back!"

"No!" Tobin was truly frightened now. Orun's fingers dug into his arms like claws. "I wrote nothing, I swear—"

"Lies. Writing lies!" Orun clutched the neck of Tobin's tunic and shook him. His fingers tangled in the chain and it dug painfully into Tobin's neck.

"Turning him against me, his most faithful servant!" Orun's eyes narrowed in their folds of fat. "Or was it that lackey of yours downstairs? Good Sir Tharin!" Sarcasm curdled the words. "So humble. So faithful. Always fawning on your father like some pathetic stray dog. And always turning up where he's not wanted—" Tobin saw something new and dangerous come into Orun's face. "What did *he* tell the king? What did he *say*?" he hissed, shaking Tobin so hard he had to grasp at Orun's arms to stay on his feet.

Orun's grip tightened, making it harder to breathe. "Nothing!" Tobin wheezed.

Orun was still ranting at him, still squeezing, but Tobin could hardly make out the words over the buzzing in his ears. Black spots swam before his eyes and Orun's face looked as big as the moon. The room was spinning, going dim. His legs wouldn't hold him.

"What did you say?" Orun screamed. "Tell me!"

Then Tobin was falling and something deathly cold passed over him. As his vision cleared he saw Orun backing away from him, hands thrown up in terror. But it wasn't him Orun was looking at, Tobin realized, but a writhing mass of darkness taking shape between them.

Still sprawled where he'd fallen, Tobin watched numbly as the shape coalesced into a familiar, menacing form. He couldn't see Brother's face, but Orun's expression was mirror enough.

"What sorcery is this?" the man whispered in horror. He looked uncomprehendingly from Tobin to the ghost as Brother glided closer. Orun tried to back away but fetched up against the wine table. It toppled over, blocking his escape.

Too dizzy to stand, Tobin watched in confusion as Brother raised one spectral hand. The ghost usually descended like a whirlwind, flinging furniture and striking out wildly. This slow, deliberate advance was worse. Tobin felt the rage and menace emanating from his twin; it sapped what little strength he had left. He tried to cry out, but his tongue wouldn't work.

"No," Orun whimpered. "How—how can this be?"

And still Brother did not attack. Instead, he simply reached out and touched the terrified man's chest. Orun let out an agonized shriek and toppled backward over the fallen table as if he'd been thrown. Sparks flew up when one outstretched hand landed in the fire.

The last things Tobin remembered were Orun's slippered feet twitching in the firelight and the smell of scorched flesh.

Chapter 7

Word had traveled quickly through the Old Palace. Mago and his cronies made faces at Ki during the morning run. At the temple Alben bumped into him, and whispered, "Farewell, grass knight!" too softly for anyone but Ki to hear.

As soon as Tobin and Tharin left, he'd taken Tharin's advice. Slipping out through a servant's passage, he hurried away to Tobin's house. The steward answered his knock, looking as if he'd been expecting him. He took Ki's wet cloak and set a chair for him by the hearth.

"The men are at practice in the back court and Mistress Iya is in the guest chamber. Should I inform them of your arrival, sir?"

"No, I'll just sit here." The steward bowed and left him.

Despite the fire on the hearth, the hall was cold and shadowy. Soft grey mist pressed at the windows and rain drummed on the roof above. Too miserable to sit still, Ki paced the room and fretted. How long would Tobin be? What if Orun found some reason to keep him there? Would Tharin come back to give him the news, or would he be stuck here forever with his belly in knots?

Looking up, he found himself at the bottom of the carved staircase. He'd only gone up there once, and that had been enough. Tobin's father had abandoned that part of the house years ago; the rooms had been stripped of their furnishings and left to the mice. Ki was sure he'd felt ghosts there, leering at him from dark corners.

The duke had used the ground floor when he was in the city. Since his death, Tharin and the guard had been the only regular occupants. Tharin had a room just down the passage, and the men were quartered at the back of the house, but they kept the hall in use. It always had a home-like smell of house altar incense and embers on the hearth.

Leaving the hall, Ki wandered down the main passage. Iya's door lay on the right, and it was closed. The duke's old bedchamber, now Tobin's and therefore Ki's by default, lay to the left. He paused at the door, then went instead to the one beside it.

Tharin's chamber was as spare and orderly as the man who lived there. His room at the keep barracks was just the same. Ki felt more at home here than anywhere else in Ero. He kindled a fire and sat down to await his fate.

But even here he couldn't sit still, and soon he was pacing a furrow in Tharin's carpet. The rain drummed against the windows and his thoughts raced: *What will I do when Orun sends me away? Go back to Oakmount and herd pigs?*

The idea of returning to his father in disgrace was unthinkable. No, he'd join Ahra's regiment and patrol the coast, or go to the battlefields in Mycena and offer his sword as a common soldier.

Such thoughts gave no comfort. The only place he wanted to be was where he was, with Tobin.

He buried his face in his hands. *This is my fault. I should never have left Tobin alone that day, knowing he was sick. A few weeks at court and I forgot everything Tharin taught me!*

On the heels of that came the question he'd been trying not to ask himself ever since the night he'd followed Brother back to Alestun. What had made Tobin run all the way back there in the first place? It wasn't that he didn't believe Tobin's explanation . . . He sighed. Well, he *wanted* to believe it, but something just didn't ring true. And whatever had ailed Tobin that night, something was different between them now.

Or maybe, he thought guiltily, *he felt something different from me.*

The filthy accusations Mago and Arius had thrown at
Ki that day in the stable, implying that he and Tobin did
more than just sleep together, had cut deep. After that Ki
had caught himself pulling away from Tobin sometimes.
The hurt look on his friend's face when he'd kept to his
side of the bed at night came back to haunt him. Was that
why Tobin had left him behind the day he ran off? *I was a
fool, listening to anything those lackwits had to say.* In
truth, with all the uproar of the past month, he'd all but forgotten it all until now. But had Tobin?

Guilt and uncertainty made his belly churn. "Well,
whatever it is, he'll tell me when he's ready," he muttered.

The air went cold behind him, and mean, whispery
laugh raised gooseflesh on his arms. Ki spun around,
reaching instinctively for the horse charm around his neck.
Brother stood beside Tharin's bed, watching him with
hate-filled black eyes.

Ki's heart knocked painfully against his ribs; the ghost
looked more solid than he remembered, a starved, hollow-
eyed parody of his friend. Ki thought he'd gotten used to
Brother that night they'd traveled together, but all his fears
came rushing back.

"Ask Arkoniel," whispered Brother.

"Ask him what?"

Brother disappeared but his hissing laugh seemed to
hang in the air where he'd been. Shaken, Ki pulled a chair
closer to the fire and huddled there, feeling lonelier than
ever.

Lost in his unhappy reverie, he was nearly dozing
when the sound of shouting roused him. Flinging open the
door, he nearly collided with Iya. They dashed to the hall
and found Tharin there, holding Tobin's limp body in his
arms.

"What happened?" Iya demanded.

"His chamber, Ki," Tharin ordered, ignoring her. "Open the door."

"I have a fire lit in yours." Ki ran ahead and turned down Tharin's bed. Tharin laid Tobin down gently and began chafing his wrists. Tobin was breathing, but his face was drawn and beaded with sweat.

"What did Orun do to him?" Ki growled. "I'll kill him. I don't care if they burn me alive for it!"

"Mind your tongue, Ki." Tharin turned to the servants and soldiers crowding in the doorway. "Koni, ride to the grove for a drysian. Don't stand there staring, man, go! Laris, you set a guard on all doors. No one enters except members of the royal household. And fetch Bisir. I want him here now!"

The old sergeant saluted, fist to chest. "Right away, Captain."

"Ulies, fetch a basin of water," Iya said calmly. "The rest of you make yourselves useful or get out of the way."

The others scattered and Tharin sank into a chair by the bed, cradling his head in his hands.

"Close the door, Ki." Iya bent over Tharin and gripped his shoulder. "Tell us what happened."

Tharin shook his head slowly. "I don't know. Bisir took him upstairs, to Orun's chamber. A while later Lord Niryn arrived with a message from the king. He soon came down again and I thought Tobin would follow. But he didn't. Then I heard Bisir cry out. When I got upstairs, Orun was dead and Tobin was lying senseless on the floor. I couldn't wake him, so I carried him back here."

Iya undid the lacings of Tobin's tunic and her face darkened ominously. "Look. These marks are fresh."

She opened the linen shirt beneath, showing Tharin and Ki long red marks already darkening to bruises on Tobin's throat. A thin abrasion on the left side of his neck was beaded with droplets of drying blood. "Did you notice any marks on Orun?"

"I didn't stop to look."

"We'll find who did this," Ki growled. "We'll find him and we'll kill him."

Tharin gave him an unreadable look and Ki shut his mouth. If it hadn't been for his foolishness, Tobin wouldn't have been with Orun today at all.

Ulies returned with the basin, and Tharin took it from him. "Send someone for Chancellor Hylus and Lord Niryn."

"No need for that." The wizard stepped in and approached the bed with every appearance of concern. "A servant came after me with the news. How is the prince? He was perfectly well when I left them. They both were."

Without thinking, Ki blocked his way before he could reach Tobin. Niryn's eyes locked with his. Ki felt a nasty chill but he stood his ground.

"If you please, my lord, I'd rather we waited for the drysians before we disturb him," Iya said, standing by Ki. She spoke respectfully, but Ki sensed it was not a request.

"Of course. Most wise." Niryn took the chair by the hearth. Ki stationed himself at the foot of the bed, keeping a surreptitious eye on the wizard. Tobin had always been scared of Niryn, which was reason enough for Ki to distrust him. And now he was, by his own admission, the last person to see Orun and Tobin before they were struck down. Or so he claimed.

Niryn caught him looking and smiled. Another nasty, slithery feeling went through Ki and he hastily averted his eyes.

A moment later Tobin lurched up with a gasp. Ki clambered awkwardly onto the bed and grasped his hand. "Tob, you're safe. I'm here, and Tharin and Iya."

Tobin gripped his hand so hard it hurt. "How—how did I get here?" he asked in a hoarse whisper.

"I brought you." Tharin sat down on the edge of the bed and put an arm around him. "Seems I'm always carrying you somewhere these days. It's all right now. Can you tell us who hurt you?"

Tobin's hand flew to his throat. "Orun. He was so angry—He grabbed me and—" He caught sight of Niryn and froze. "It was Orun."

The wizard rose and came closer. "He offered you violence?"

Tobin nodded. "The king's message," he whispered. "He grabbed me and—I must have fainted."

"I shouldn't wonder," said Iya. "It appears he tried to throttle you."

Tobin nodded.

A brown-robed drysian arrived and ordered everyone but Iya and Niryn out of the room. Ki hovered in the doorway, watching anxiously as the woman examined Tobin. He crept back to the foot of the bed as she mixed a poultice for the bruises and she let him stay.

When she'd finished, she went out and spoke with Iya and Tharin for what seemed like a long time. Tharin came back in looking more concerned than ever.

"Lord Niryn, they've got Bisir in the hall and Chancellor Hylus just arrived."

Tobin struggled up again. "Bisir didn't do anything!"

"We just want to talk to him," Tharin assured him. "You rest. Ki will keep you company."

"Lord Niryn?" croaked Tobin.

The wizard paused in the doorway. "Yes, my prince?"

"That message you had from the king—I didn't read it. Is Ki still my squire?"

"The king made no mention of the matter. For the time being, it seems your squire's position is secure. See that you remain worthy of it, Sir Kirothius."

"Yes, my lord." Ki waited until the wizards and Tharin were gone, then shut the door and made a luck sign. "He looks like a snake when he smiles. But at least he brought some good news." He sat down on the bed and tried to look into Tobin's eyes, but his friend kept turning away. "How are you? Really?"

"I'm fine." Tobin rubbed at the wet bandage around his neck. "This is helping."

He was still hoarse, but Ki could hear the fear that Tobin was struggling to hide.

"So Orun finally laid hands on you?" Ki shook his head in wonder.

Tobin let out a shuddering sigh and his chin began to tremble.

Ki leaned closer and took his hand again. "There's more to it than you let on, isn't there?"

Tobin cast a frightened look at the door, then brought his lips to Ki's ear. "It was Brother."

Ki's eyes widened. "But he was here. He came to me while you were gone."

Tobin let out a startled gasp. "What did he do?"

"Nothing! I was in here waiting for you, and suddenly there he was."

"Did he say anything?"

"Just that I should ask Arkoniel about—" Ki broke off.

"About what?"

Ki hesitated; he'd felt disloyal before, doubting Tobin, and it was worse now. "He wouldn't say. Is he like that with you, too?"

"Sometimes."

"But you say he came to Orun's? Did you call him?"

Tobin shook his head vehemently. "No! No, I swear it by the Four, I didn't!"

Alarmed, Ki searched his friend's face. "I believe you, Tob. What's the matter?"

Tobin gulped hard, then leaned in again. "Brother killed Orun."

"But—how?"

"I don't know. Orun was shaking me. Maybe he was going to kill me. I don't know. Brother got between us and just—just touched him and Orun fell—" Tobin was shaking. Tears spilled down his cheeks. "I didn't stop him, Ki! What if—What if somehow I *did* make him do it?"

Ki hugged him close. "You'd never do that. I know you wouldn't."

"I don't remember doing it." Tobin sobbed. "But I was so scared, and I hated Orun and he said bad things about you and—"

"Did you call for Brother?"

"Nuh—no!"

"Did you tell him to kill Orun?"

"No!"

"Of course you didn't. So it's not your fault. Brother was just protecting you."

Tobin raised his tear-stained face and stared at him. "Do you think so?"

"Yes. He's spiteful and all, but he *is* your brother and Orun was hurting you." He paused, touching a thin, faded scar on his neck. "Remember when the catamount came after you that day? You said Brother got between you and it before I showed up, like he was going to protect you."

"But it was Lhel who killed it."

"Yes, but he came. And he came when Orun was hurting you. No one's ever done that to you before, have they?"

Tobin wiped his face on his sleeve. "No one, except—"

"Who?" Ki demanded, wondering which of the Companions he'd have to deal with.

"My mother," Tobin whispered. "She tried to kill me. Brother was there, then, too."

Ki's outrage drained away, leaving him speechless.

"You can't tell anyone about this," Tobin said, wiping his nose. "About Orun, I mean. No one can know about Brother."

"Niryn himself couldn't get it out of me. You know that."

Tobin let out another shuddering sigh and rested his head on Ki's shoulder. "If that letter said you had to go, I'd run away again."

"Leaving me to catch up with you like last time?" Ki tried to make light of it, but his throat was suddenly tight. "Don't even try it. I'm putting you on a tether rein."

"I told you I won't. We'd run away together."

"That's all right, then. You should rest now."

Instead, Tobin threw off the blankets and wiggled past him off the bed. "I want to see Bisir. He didn't have anything to do with this."

*T*obin was almost to the hall when a new thought momentarily blotted out all other concerns. What had Bisir seen? He cursed his own weakness, fainting like some lady in a ballad. Had Brother stayed with him after he killed Orun? If Orun could see the ghost, then surely anyone else could have. Steeling himself, he strode into the hall.

Bisir stood wringing his hands by the hearth, surrounded by Tharin and the others. Chancellor Hylus was the only person seated and he must have come straight from court, for he still wore his robe of state and the flat black velvet hat signifying his office.

"Here is the prince, and looking rather better than I expected, thank the Four!" he exclaimed. "Come sit by me, dear boy. This young man was just telling us of the abominable treatment you've suffered."

"Go on, Bisir. Tell Prince Tobin what you told us," said Iya.

Bisir gave Tobin an imploring look. "As I was saying to them, my prince, I saw nothing except the two of you lying on the floor when I came in."

"But you were eavesdropping," Niryn said sternly.

"No, my lord! That is, there is a chair for me by the door. I always stay there, in case Lord Orun calls for me."

Hylus raised a frail, age-mottled hand. "Calm yourself, young man. You are not accused of any crime." He motioned to Ulies to bring the frightened valet a mazer of wine.

"Thank you, my lord." Bisir took a sip and some color returned to his thin cheeks.

"Surely you must have heard something?" the old man prompted.

"Yes, Lord Chancellor. I heard my master speaking angrily to the prince. It was wrong of him, speaking to Prince Tobin like that." He paused and gulped nervously. "Forgive me, my lords. I know I shouldn't speak ill of my master, but—"

"It's of no consequence," Iya said impatiently. "So you heard Orun shouting. Then what?"

"Then came that terrible cry! I ran in at once and found them senseless on the carpet. At least I thought—When I saw my master's face—" His gaze flickered to Tobin again, and this time there was no mistaking the fact that Bisir was scared. "Lord Orun's eyes were open, but—By the Four, I'll never forget the way he looked, with his eyes bulging and his face gone all black—"

"It's as he says," Tharin concurred. "I hardly recognized him. It looked like an apoplexy to me."

"Then Sir Tharin burst in and carried the prince away before I could tell if he—I feared he was dead, too!" He gave Tobin a bobbing bow. "Thank the Four you are well."

"If I may, my lord?" said Niryn.

Hylus nodded and the wizard approached the quaking man. "Give me your hand, Bisir."

Niryn seemed to grow larger and the air darkened around him. It made every hair on the back of Tobin's neck stand up. Ki stepped closer and his hand brushed Tobin's.

Bisir let out a hiss of pain and sank to his knees, his hand locked in Niryn's. When Niryn released him at last, Bisir cowered where he was, cradling his hand against his chest as if it had been burned.

Niryn shrugged and sat down on the hearth bench. "He speaks the truth as he knows it. It would seem the only person who knows what really happened in that room is Prince Tobin."

For one awful moment, Tobin thought the wizard meant to put him to the same test, but Niryn simply stared at him with hard red-brown eyes. Tobin felt no strange sensations this time, but summoned the mind trick Arkoniel had taught him just in case.

"He grabbed me roughly, accused me of trying to turn the king against him—"

"And did you?" Niryn asked.

"What? No! I never wrote anything to my uncle."

Niryn gave him a sly smile. "Never tried to exercise any influence with him at all? It was no secret that you despised Orun. Not that I blame you in that, of course."

"I—I don't have any influence with the king," Tobin whispered. Was Niryn growing larger again? Was the air growing dark and thick around him?

"It would never have occurred to the prince," Tharin interjected, and Tobin saw that once again he was holding his anger in check. "He's only a child. He knows nothing of court ways."

"Forgive me, I was only thinking how far a noble heart will go for love for a worthy friend." Niryn glanced at Ki as he bowed to Tobin. "Please accept my most humble apology, my prince, if I in any way gave offense." His hard gaze slewed back to Tharin. "Perhaps others took it upon themselves to plead the prince's case?"

Tharin shrugged. "For what reason? Rhius chose Ki as his son's squire. The king understands that bond."

Niryn turned to Ki again. "And what about you, Squire Kirothius? Where were you while Prince Tobin was with his guardian?"

"Here, my lord. The steward can vouch for me."

"No need for that. I was only curious. Well, it seems there's nothing more to be learned here."

Lord Hylus nodded gravely. "No doubt your guess is right, Tharin. Strong emotion is a dangerous thing in an old man. I believe it is safe to assume that Lord Orun was the author of his own destruction and brought on a fit of apoplexy."

"Unless it was some dark magic."

Everyone stared at Niryn.

"There are spells that could bring on such a death. The man certainly had enemies and there are wizards who can be bought. Don't you agree, Mistress Iya?"

Iya held out her hand. "If you are accusing me, my lord, by all means put me to the test. I have nothing to fear from you."

"I assure you, Mistress, if it had been you, I would already know it."

Tharin cleared his throat. "With all respect, my lords, Prince Tobin has had a difficult day. If there is no more to be learned, perhaps we should give him some peace?"

Hylus rose and patted Tobin on the back. "You are a brave boy, my dear prince; but I think your friend is right. Rest now, and put this unpleasantness behind you. I shall act as your guardian until your uncle declares another, if you have no objection."

"I'd like that very much!"

"What's to become of Lord Orun's household, Lord Hylus?" Bisir asked softly, still crouched on the rushes.

"On your feet, lad. Go home and tell the steward that the house and staff are to be maintained until the estate is settled. Hurry along now, before everyone bolts with the silver!"

"Come along, Prince Tobin. Let's get you settled," Iya said, just as if she were Nari.

"Couldn't Bisir come live here?" he whispered, letting her and Ki lead him away to his own room.

But Iya shook her head. "Forget him. Light a fire, Ki."

Tobin bridled. "How can you say that? You saw how he was at the keep all those weeks. And he did try to help me today. Ask Tharin—"

"I know. But appearances are very important here and it wouldn't do." When Tobin stood his ground she relented a little. "I'll keep an eye on him for you, then."

Tobin gave a grudging nod, his old distrust for her resurfacing. He wouldn't have had to argue with Arkoniel this way.

Chapter 8

Returning to the Companions the following morning, Tobin and Ki found themselves the center of much unwanted attention. Korin and the others would have had the tale told three times over during the morning run if Master Porion hadn't finally threatened to make them muck out the stables if they didn't leave Tobin alone.

As the day went on, however, even his threats weren't enough to stop the whispers and wide-eyed questions. As they stood blowing on their fingers in the archery lists, everyone wanted to know what Orun looked like when he died. What sort of sounds did he make? Was there any blood? Tobin told them what he could and was glad when Ki finally threatened to knock down the next person who pestered him.

Word traveled quickly around the Palatine. For the next few days courtiers and servants alike stared at Tobin, whispering to each other behind raised hands as he passed. He and Ki kept to their rooms as much as possible or retreated to Tobin's house.

As with most gossip, however, the story was soon sucked dry and within the week the curious had moved on to other scandals. When Caliel challenged him to a game of bakshi at dinner one night, Tobin left Ki to his duties with the other ushers and went to fetch the gaming stones from his room.

He was almost to his door when Lady Una stepped out from the shadows of an empty room across the corridor. Surprise gave way to outright shock when the normally shy girl took him by the hand and pulled him into his chamber. Molay and Baldus were off having their dinner in the kitchen. Tobin was alone with her.

Pushing the door closed, she gazed at him for a moment in silence, brown eyes shining.

"What is it?" he asked, utterly perplexed.

"Is it true?" she demanded.

"Is—is what true?"

"There's a rumor going around that before he died, Lord Orun tried to make you choose another squire, and that—well—" She blushed furiously, but looked him squarely in the eye. "People are saying that you named me!"

Tobin blinked. He'd only said it to anger Orun, then forgotten all about it. Bisir must have overheard and carried the tale.

He wanted to sink through the floor as she clasped his hand again, pressing his knuckles to her bodice. "Is it true, Prince Tobin? Did you put me forward for the Companions?"

When he managed a nod she clutched his hand even tighter, looking hard into his face. "Did you mean it?"

"Well . . ." Tobin hesitated, not liking to lie to her. "I think you'd make a fine squire," he managed, settling for a half-truth. He wished she'd let go of his hand. "If girls could be squires, you'd be a good one."

"It's so unfair!" she cried, eyes flashing with a passion he'd never seen before. "Women have always been warriors in Skala! Ki told me all about his sister. Ahra really is a proper warrior like he says, isn't she?"

"Oh yes!" Tobin had only met Ahra once, but she'd shown him a thing or two about grappling in a fight. He'd back her against most men in a duel.

"It's just so unfair!" Releasing his hand, she folded her arms and frowned. "If I wasn't a noble, I could join the ranks like she did. My grandmother was a general, you know. She died gallantly in battle, defending the queen. And I'll tell you a secret," she confided, leaning alarmingly close again. "She comes to me in my dreams sometimes, on a great white charger. I have her sword, too. Mother gave it to me. Father won't let me train with a proper arms master, though. Not even at light fencing. But one day, if only I could learn . . ." She broke off, giving him an embarrassed little smile. "I'm sorry. I'm being silly, aren't I?"

"No! I've seen you shooting in the lists. You're as good as any of us with the bow. And you ride like a soldier. Even Master Porion said so."

"He did?" Una positively glowed. "But it's no good unless you can use a sword. I have to make do with treatises and what I can pick up watching you boys train. I get so jealous sometimes. I should have been born a boy instead!"

The words struck Tobin in a way he didn't fully understand, and without thinking he blurted out, "I could teach you."

"Really? You're not just being charming, or teasing me like the other boys do?"

Tobin wanted to take the words back as soon as he'd said them, but he couldn't, not with her looking at him like that. "No, I'll teach you. Ki, too. Just so long as no one finds out."

Without warning Una leaned forward and kissed him square on the mouth. It was an awkward kiss, bruising Tobin's lip against his teeth. She fled before he could recover, leaving him agape and blushing beside the open door.

"Bilairy's balls!" Tobin muttered, tasting blood on his lip. "What did I do that for?"

As bad luck would have it, Alben and Quirion happened to be passing just then. *That figures*, thought Tobin; Quirion stuck to the older boy like dog shit on a shoe.

"What's the matter? Did she bite you?" Alben drawled.

Tobin shouldered angrily past them, bakshi stones forgotten.

"What's the matter?" Quirion called after him. "Don't you like being kissed by *girls?*"

Whirling to make some retort, Tobin tripped over his

own feet and fell against one of the ancient tapestries that lined the corridor. The hanging pole snapped and the whole dusty mess came down on him like a collapsed tent. The other boys howled with laughter.

"Blood, my blood. Flesh, my—" Tobin whispered, then clamped a hand over his mouth. Their laughter faded away down the corridor, but Tobin stayed where he was, horrified at what he'd almost done. Hugging himself in the musty darkness, he searched his memory again, wondering if he'd somehow summoned Brother against Orun, after all.

He confided the encounter with Una to Ki and Tharin the next day as they sat by the fire in Tharin's room, but leaving out the unpleasant aftermath with Alben. He was none too pleased when his friends burst into laughter.

"Tob, you bump brain!" Ki exclaimed. "Una's had her cap set for you since we got to Ero."

"Me?"

"Yes, you. You mean to say you haven't noticed how she's always watching you?"

"I've thought so, myself," Tharin said, still chuckling.

"But she's a—just a girl!"

"Well, you do fancy girls, don't you?" Ki laughed, unwittingly echoing Quirion's taunt.

Tobin scowled down at his boots. "I don't fancy anyone."

"Let him be, Ki," said Tharin. "Tobin's young yet, and not used to court. I was the same myself, at his age. As for this sword-training business, though." His expression turned serious. "She said it herself; her father doesn't hold to the old ways, and Duke Sarvoi's not a man to cross. She'll do better to stick with her shooting and riding."

Tobin nodded, though a disapproving father scared him a great deal less than the girl's regard. His lip still hurt where she'd kissed him.

"All the same, you may feel differently in a year or

two," said Tharin. "She's a fine girl from a powerful family. A pretty little thing, too."

"I'll say!" Ki put in warmly. "If I thought she'd look twice at a lowly squire, I'd be happy to stand in your shoes."

The sudden warmth in Ki's voice and his wistful smile made Tobin's belly tighten, as if he'd eaten something bitter.

Why should I care if Ki fancies her? But he did. "Well, I only told her that to be kind, anyway," he grumbled. "She's probably forgotten all about it."

"Not that one," said Ki. "I've seen the way she watches us."

Tharin nodded. "What she told you about her grand-mother is true. General Elthia was the equal of any man in the field, and a cagey strategist, too. Your father thought very highly of her. Yes, I can see a bit of the old warrior in young Una. That's the trouble with these new ways. There are too many girls with the blood of heroes in their veins and the stories still green in their hearts, kept in skirts by the fire."

"No wonder she's jealous of a common soldier like Ahra," said Ki.

"I don't imagine Erius will let that go on much longer, either. And then where will they all go?"

"You mean there are lots of them? Women warriors?" asked Tobin.

"Yes. Just think of old Cook—or Sergeant Catilan, as she was known before—working away in your father's kitchen all these years. Erius forced out a lot of the older ones. She was too loyal to argue, but it hurts her pride still. There are hundreds more like her, scattered about the land. Maybe more."

Tobin stared into the fire, imagining a whole army of dispossessed women warriors, riding like ghosts into an unknown distance. The thought sent a shiver up his spine.

Chapter 9

Arkoniel stretched the stiffness from his shoulders and went to the workroom window. Unfolding the letters Koni had brought that morning, he slowly reread them.

Outside, the afternoon was quickly waning. The tower shadow stretched like a crooked finger across the new snow blanketing the meadow. Except for the churned-up trail left by Koni's horse, it was smooth and white as a new bed sheet: no snow forts beyond the barracks house, no foot trails snaking away to the river or woods.

And no echoing laughter outside his door, Arkoniel thought glumly. He'd never been lonelier. Only Nari and Cook remained now; the three of them rattled about the place like dice in a cup.

He sighed and turned back to the letters. His presence here remained a secret, so they were ostensibly addressed to Nari. Arkoniel smoothed the first parchment against the windowsill, rubbing his thumb idly over the broken seal. Both boys had written to him of Orun's death. Iya had sent word earlier, but he was most interested in their versions.

Tobin's was brief: Orun had had some sort of fit, brought on by bad news. Ki's was the more useful, though he'd not been with Tobin when it happened. Arkoniel smiled as he unfolded the double sheet. Despite Ki's initial resistance to writing, and a less-than-beautiful hand, words seemed to flow as easily from the boy's pen as they did from his lips. His letters were always the more detailed. He told of the bruises on Tobin's neck and the fact that he'd been carried home unconscious. Strangest of all, he'd closed with the line: *Tobin still feels awful bad about it*. Iya had made no mention of any regrets in her letter, but Arkoniel guessed that this was no idle platitude. Ki knew Tobin better than anyone, and had shared his friend's loathing for their guardian. Why would Tobin feel badly about the man's passing?

Arkoniel folded Tobin's letter into his sleeve to return to Nari, but added Ki's to the neat stack on his writing table.

I nearly killed him, but I did not, he reminded himself, as he did each time he placed a new letter on that pile. He wasn't sure why he kept them, perhaps as proof against the nightmares that still haunted him, dreams in which he did not hesitate and Ki did not wake up ever again.

Arkoniel pushed the memory away and glanced at the window to check the sun's progress. Yesterday he'd stayed too late.

When he'd first come here, the keep had been a tomb haunted by both the living and the dead. He and Iya had cajoled the duke into restoring it to a proper home for his child, and for a time it had been. It had become Arkoniel's home, too, the first he'd known since leaving his father's house.

The place was falling back to rot and ruin now. The new tapestries and painted plaster already looked faded. The plate in the hall was tarnished with disuse, and spiders had reclaimed their kingdom in the rafters of the great hall. Without regular fires in most of the rooms, the whole place was once more damp and cold and dim. It was as if the boys had taken the very life from the place with them.

He turned back to the desk with a sigh to complete the day's notes. When the journal was safely locked away, he cleared up the wreckage of his latest failed efforts.

He was nearly finished when something brushed softly past the door, no louder than a mouse's whisker. Arkoniel caught his breath. The glass rod he'd been cleaning slipped from his fingers and shattered at his feet.

Just a rat. It's too early. Golden light still lingered in the eastern sky. *She never comes down this early.*

Gooseflesh prickled his arms as he lit a candle and walked slowly to the door. His hand trembled and a rivulet of hot wax ran down over his fingers.

Nothing there. Nothing there, he repeated, like a child in the dark.

As long as Tobin and the others had been downstairs, he'd managed to hold his fear at bay, even when Bisir's unexpected stay had trapped him up here for days on end. With others in the house, he didn't mind so much the half-heard whispers in the corridor.

Now that the second floor lay empty, however, his rooms were suddenly much too far from Cook's warm kitchen and much too close to the tower door. That door had been locked since Ariani's death, but that didn't stop her restless spirit from wandering out.

Arkoniel had climbed the tower stairs only twice since his first encounter with her angry ghost. Driven by curiosity and guilt, he'd gone up the day after Tobin left for Ero that first time, but felt nothing. Relieved but unsatisfied, he'd worked up the courage to return at midnight—the same hour Tobin had taken him there—and this time he'd heard Ariani weeping as clearly as if she were just behind him. Torn between fear and anguish, he fled and slept in the kitchen with the tower key clutched in his hand like a talisman. The next morning he threw it in the river and moved his bedchamber to the toy room downstairs. He would have shifted his workroom, too, but the furnishings were too heavy and it would have taken him the rest of the winter to carry down all the books and instruments he'd amassed. Instead, he resigned himself to keeping daylight hours.

But today he'd lingered in the workroom too long. Taking a deep breath, Arkoniel gripped the latch and opened the door.

Ariani stood at the end of the corridor, tears streaming down her bloody face, her lips moving. Frozen in the doorway, Arkoniel strained to hear, but she made no sound.

She'd attacked him the first time they met after her death, but still he waited, wanting desperately to hear her words, to give some answer. But then she took a step toward him, face shifting to an angry mask, and his courage failed.

The candle cast antic shadows around him as he bolted, then it went out. Squinting in the sudden darkness, he went down the stairs two at a time and missed his footing before his eyes could adjust. He trod air for an instant, then fell heavily, tumbling down the last few steps into the welcome lamplight of the second floor corridor. Resisting the impulse to look back, he limped quickly toward the stairs to the hall.

One of these days he was going to make a ghost of himself.

Chapter 10

Lord Orun had left no heir. That being the case, his property went to the Crown, absorbed into the very Treasury he'd so ably administered. It had been, in Niryn's estimation, the only good work the man had ever done. Orun's exacting honesty when it came to his official duties had always amazed the wizard.

The house and its furnishings were soon disposed of, and the new Treasury Chancellor installed. That left only Orun's household servants to be dealt with, and few on the Palatine would have taken the gift of them.

The more notorious spies were quietly put out of the way by those they'd helped compromise. Orun had had a passion for blackmail. Not for money—he had wealth enough of that sort—but for the sadistic love of control over others. Given that, together with his other unpleasant pastimes, none but a select few mourned his passing.

And so his spies were poisoned or garroted in alleys, the prettier catamites whisked quietly away into certain other households, and the rest sent from the city with good references and gold enough to keep them away.

Niryn followed these proceedings closely and had made a point of attending Orun's burning. It was there that a young man standing among the few mourners caught his eye.

His face was familiar and after a moment Niryn recognized him as a minor noble named Moriel, whom Orun had tried to force on the prince as a squire. Orun had left the fellow a small bequest in his will, no doubt for services rendered. He looked to be fourteen or fifteen, with a pale, bitter face and sharp, intelligent eyes. Curious, Niryn brushed the boy's mind as they stood by the pyre and was pleasantly unsurprised at what he found there.

The following day he sent the promising young fellow an invitation to dine with him, if his grief allowed. The messenger soon returned with the expected reply, written in the same purple ink his late protector had favored: Young Moriel would be delighted to dine with the king's wizard.

Chapter 11

Iya was not sorry to see Orun out of the way, and had shared Tobin's obvious relief when Chancellor Hylus appointed himself temporary guardian. She hoped Erius would leave the good old fellow in charge. Hylus was a decent man, a relic of the old times before Erius and his mad mother had tarnished the crown. As long as Erius still valued his counsel, perhaps Niryn's sort would not triumph.

She clung to that hope as she fastened the hated Harrier brooch to her cloak each day in Ero.

She had to pass the Harriers' headquarters when she left the Palatine. White-robed wizards and their grey-uniformed guard were always about in the yards around the old stone inn. It reminded her of a hornet's nest and she treated it as such, passing on the far side of the street. She'd been inside only once, when they numbered her in their black ledger. She'd seen enough during that visit to know that a second visit would probably prove fatal.

So she kept her distance and was circumspect in seeking out others like herself, ordinary wizards forced to wear the shameful numbered badge. There were far fewer in Ero these days and most of them were too frightened or suspicious to speak to her. Of all the taverns once patronized by their kind, only the Golden Chain was still open and it was full of Harriers. Wizards she'd known for a lifetime greeted her with suspicion and few offered her hospitality. It was a frightening change in the city that had once most honored the free wizards.

*　*　*

She was wandering disconsolately through the half-deserted market in Dolphin Court one evening when she was suddenly engulfed by a searing blast of pain. Struck blind, she couldn't hear or cry out.

They have me! she thought in mute agony. *What will become of Tobin?*

Then, as in a vision, she saw a face framed in white fire, but it wasn't Tobin's. Stretched with agony surpassing her own, the man seemed to stare straight into her eyes as the flesh shrank and sizzled on his skull. She knew that face. It was a wizard from the south named Skorus. She'd given him one of her tokens years ago and not thought of him since.

The tortured face disappeared and she found herself sprawled facedown on the dirty cobbles, gasping for air.

He must have had the talisman with him when they burned him, she thought, too overcome to move. But what did this mean? The little pebbles were minor charms, containing the tiniest spark of magic to find and draw the loyal ones when the time came. She'd never imagined they could also act as a conduit back to her. But this one had, and through it she'd experienced a fraction of the agony he'd felt as he died. Dozens of wizards had been burned, perhaps scores, but he must be the first of her chosen to be caught. She was amazed at how quickly the pain passed. She'd expected to find her own skin blistered, but fortunately the charm had channeled only the dying wizard's last feelings, not the magic that killed him.

"Old mother, are you ill?" someone asked.

"Drunk, more like it," another passerby laughed. "Get up, you old hag!"

Gentle hands helped her to her knees. "Kiriar!" she gasped, recognizing the young man. "Are you still with Dylias?"

"Yes, Mistress." He'd been an apprentice the last time they'd met. He had a proper beard now and a few lines on his face, but his clothes were as ragged as a beggar's. Only the Harrier badge at his throat marked him for what he was. His number was ninety-three.

He was looking at hers, as well. "Two hundred and twenty-two? It took them longer to find you, I see." He gave her a rueful look. "It's something we notice nowadays, sad to say. Are you feeling better? What happened?"

Iya shook her head as he helped her to her feet. Kiriar and his master Dylias had always struck her as good sorts, but she was still too badly shaken to judge or trust. "It's a hard business, getting old," she said, making light of it. "I could do with a drink, and a bite to eat."

"I know a good house, Mistress. Let me stand you a hot dinner for old times' sake. It's not far and the company's good."

Still wary, but intrigued, Iya leaned on his arm and let him lead her out of Dolphin Court.

She felt a moment's alarm when Kiriar turned his steps back toward the Palatine. Was he a clever betrayer after all, luring her to the Harrier stronghold?

A few streets later, however, he turned aside into one of the goldsmith's markets. Hard times had struck here as well, she noted; many of the shops were deserted. She'd passed half a dozen before it struck her that most of them had belonged to Aurënfaie artisans.

"Gone home, a lot of them," Kiriar explained. "The 'faie don't hold with the new ways, as you can well imagine, and it's growing clear that the Harriers don't trust them. Now, if you'll just stop a moment."

He disappeared into a darkened stable. A moment later he returned and led her through a lane behind it. This in turn led to a narrow alley, overhung by sagging balconies and the strange, spicy aromas of 'faie cookery.

Narrow side ways branched off among the buildings here and there. Reaching one such juncture, her guide stopped again.. "Before we go any farther, Mistress, I must ask you this. What do you swear by?"

"By my hands and heart and eyes," she answered, catching sight of a crescent moon scrawled on the wall just above his shoulder. The telltale shimmer of a blast aura flickered around it as she spoke. "And by the Lightbearer's true name," she added for good measure.

"She may pass," someone whispered from the shadows to their right, as if that wasn't already evidenced by the fact that the blast aura had not struck her down. Iya looked at her ragged companion with new interest. He hadn't left that powerful spell there, or his master; she could count on one hand the wizards she knew who could have.

Kiriar gave her an apologetic shrug. "We have to ask. Come, it's just down here."

He led her into the dirtiest side street she'd yet seen. The smell of piss and decay was strong. Skinny, notch-eared cats slunk past in shadows, or hunched watching for rats in the garbage piled along the wall. The buildings on either side nearly touched overhead, shutting out the waning winter light.

Three cloaked figures emerged from the murk just ahead. Another appeared from a doorway behind them as they passed. They looked like footpads, but all four bowed to her, touching their hearts and brows.

"This way." Kiriar pointed her down a set of steep, crumbling cellar stairs. The door at the bottom looked ordinary enough, but magic of some sort tingled pleasantly through her fingertips as she lifted the rusty latch.

To an ordinary person, the blackness beyond would have been impenetrable, but Iya easily made out the long blades protruding from the walls at various heights along the subterranean passage. Anyone blundering blindly here would soon come to harm.

At the far end she opened another magically warded door and found herself blinking in the cheerful firelight of a tavern. A dozen or so wizards turned to see the new-comer and she was delighted to find familiar faces among them. Here was Kiriar's master, stooped old Dylias, and be-side him a pretty sorceress from Almak named Elisera, who'd turned Arkoniel's head one summer. She didn't know the others, but one of them was Aurënfaie, and wore the red-and-black sen'gai and facial tattoos of the Khatme clan. *The blast aura was probably her work,* thought Iya.

"Welcome to the Wormhole, my friend!" Dylias cried, coming to greet her. "Not the most elegant establishment in Ero, but surely the safest. I hope Kiriar and his friends didn't give you too much of a turn."

"Not at all!" Iya looked around in delight. The paneled oak walls gave back a cozy golden glow from the brazier flickering at the center of the room. She recognized bits and pieces from many of their old haunts—statues, hang-ings, even the golden brandywine distillers and water pipes that had been the pride of the now deserted Mer-maid Inn. There was no menu board, but she smelled meat roasting. Someone put a silver mazer of excellent wine in her hand.

She sipped it gratefully, then raised an eyebrow at her guide. "I'm beginning to suspect you didn't just happen upon me today."

"No, we've watched you since—" Kiriar began.

Dylias silenced him with a sharp look under his beetling white brows, then turned to Iya and laid a finger to the side of his nose. "Less known, the better kept, eh? Suffice it to say the Harriers aren't the only ones who keep an eye out for wizards in Ero. It's been years! How are you, my dear?"

"Not well when I found her," Kiriar told him. "What happened, Iya? I thought your heart had failed."

"A momentary weakness," Iya replied, not yet daring to say more. "I'm fine now, and better for being here with all of you! Still, isn't it risky, gathering like this?"

"Those are 'faie-built houses over our heads," the

Aurënfaie woman told Iya. "It would take an army of those paltry Harriers to even find all the magics here, and another army to break through them."

"Bravely stated, Saruel, and we all pray your trust is well-founded," said Dylias. "All the same, we are cautious. We have a number of guests who depend upon it. Come, Iya. We'll show you."

Dylias and Saruel led Iya through a series of cramped cellar rooms beyond the tavern where more wizards were living.

"For some of us, this stronghold is a prison, as well," Dylias said sadly, pointing out a hollow-eyed old man asleep on a pallet. "It would be worth Master Lyman's life to show his face in the city. Once you're on the Harriers' hunting roster, there's little chance of escape."

"Twenty-eight have been burned on Traitor's Hill since the madness started," Saruel said bitterly. "And that's not counting the priests murdered with them. It's hideous, how they kill the Lightbearer's servants."

"Yes, I have seen it." Iya now knew better than most what a death that was.

"But is it any worse than being buried alive here?" Dylias murmured, closing the sleeping man's door.

Returning to the tavern, Iya sat with the others and listened to their stories. Most were still at large in the city, carefully pretending loyalty and earning their living in the small ways the king's ordinances still allowed. They could make useful items and cast helpful household spells for pay. The greater magics were reserved for the Harriers. The mere charming of a horse was a capital offense now.

"They've made tinkers of us!" an elderly wizard named Orgeus sputtered.

"Has anyone tried to resist?" Iya asked.

"You haven't heard about the Maker's Day riots?" a man named Zagur asked. "Nine young hotheads barricaded themselves in the temple on Flatfish Street, trying to protect two others who were marked for execution. Have you been by the place?"

"No."

"Well, it isn't there anymore. Thirty Harriers appeared out of nowhere, and two hundred grey-backs with them. They didn't last an hour."

"Did they use any magic against the Harriers?"

"A few tried, but they were mostly charm makers and weather tellers," Dylias replied. "What chance did they have against those monsters? How many in this room could strike back? That's not what the Orëska teaches."

"Perhaps not your half-blooded Second Orëska," Saruel said disdainfully. "In Aurënen there are wizards who can level a house if they choose, or summon a hurricane down on their enemies."

"No wizard has that kind of power!" a Skalan woman scoffed.

"Do you think the Harriers would let one of us live if they thought so?" someone else said.

The Aurënfaie retorted angrily in her own language and more joined in.

Dismayed, Iya thought again of Skorus, dying alone in agony.

It is time, she thought. She held up a hand for silence.

"There are Skalans who know such magics," Iya said. "And it can be taught to others who have the talent for it." Rising, she downed the last of her wine and placed the silver cup on the stone floor. She could feel the others watching her as she spread her hands above it. Chanting softly, she drew the power down and focused it on the cup.

The rush came more quickly than it normally did. It was always so in company, though it took no power away from the others.

The air around the cup shimmered for a moment, then the rim began to melt, slumping in on itself like a waxwork on a hot summer's day. She broke the spell before the cup collapsed completely and cooled it with a breath. Prying it loose from the flagstones, she handed it to Dylias.

"It can be taught," she said again, watching the faces of the others as they passed it from hand to hand.

Before she left the Wormhole that night, every wizard in the room—even proud Saruel—had accepted one of her little stones.

Chapter 12

Tobin had only just gotten used to having Iya at the house when she announced that she was leaving. He and Ki watched glumly as she packed her few belongings.

"But the Festival of Sakor is only a few days away!" exclaimed Ki. "You want to stay for that, don't you?"

"No, I don't," Iya muttered, stuffing a shawl into her bag.

Tobin knew something was troubling her. She'd spent a great deal of time down in the city and didn't appear to approve of what she found there. Tobin knew it had something to do with the Harriers, but she wouldn't even let him speak the word aloud anymore.

"Stay away from them," she warned, reading his thoughts or his face. "Don't think of them. Don't speak of them. That goes for you, too, Kirothius. Even the magpie chatter of little boys doesn't go unnoticed these days."

"Little boys?" Ki sputtered.

Iya paused in her packing and gave him a fond look. "Perhaps you have grown just a bit since I found you. All the same, the pair of you added together are nothing but a blink of a wizard's eye."

"Are you going back to the keep?" asked Tobin.

"No."

"Where, then?"

Her faded lips quirked into a strange little smile as she laid a finger to the side of her nose. "Less known, the better kept."

She wouldn't say more than that. They rode with her to the south gate and the last they saw of her was that thin braid bouncing against her back as she cantered into the crowd on Beggar's Bridge.

The Festival of Sakor was celebrated with great fanfare, though everyone said that the king's absence and the rumors of ill luck brought back by returning veterans put a damper on the usual glory of the three-day celebration. But to Tobin, who knew only the rude country observances in Alestun, it was impossibly grand and magical.

On Mourning Night the Companions and principal nobles of Ero stood with Korin in the city's largest Sakor Temple, just down the hill from the Palatine gate. The square outside was jammed with people. Everyone cheered as Korin, standing in his father's place, killed the Sakor bull with a single stroke. The priests frowned over the entrails and said little, but the people cheered again when the young prince raised his sword and pledged his family to the defense of Skala. The priests presented him with the sacred firepot, the temple horns sounded, and the city began to go dark, as if by magic. Beyond the walls, in the harbor and distant steadings, it was the same. On this longest night of the year, every flame in Skala was extinguished to symbolize the yearly death of Old Sakor.

The Companions stood the vigil with Korin all through that long, cold night and at dawn they helped carry the year's new fire back to the city.

The next two days were a blur of balls and rides and midnight parties. Korin was the most sought-after guest in the city; Chancellor Hylus and his scribes had prepared a list of homes, temples, and guildhouses he and the Companions must appear at, many only long enough to pour the new year's libation.

True winter soon set in after that. Rain turned to sleet, and the sleet to wet, heavy snow. Clouds sealed the sky from the sea to the mountains and soon Tobin felt like he'd never see the sun again.

Master Porion kept up with their mounted battle practice and the morning temple run, regardless of the weather, but sword fighting and archery were moved indoors. Their feasting hall was cleared and the bare floor chalked with archery lists and fighting circles. The clash of steel was deafening at times, and everyone had to be careful not to walk between archers and their targets, but otherwise it was not unpleasant. The other young bloods and girls of the court hung about as always, watching the Companions and sparring among themselves.

Una was there most days and Tobin noted with a guilty pang how she followed him with her eyes. His duties had kept him too busy to make good on his promise, or so he told himself. Every time he looked at her, he seemed to feel her lips on his again.

Ki twitted him about it and asked more than once if he was going to keep his word.

"I will," Tobin always retorted. "I just haven't found the time yet."

Winter brought other changes in their daily routine. During the cold months all the noble boys had lessons with General Marnaryl, an elderly warrior who'd served King Erius and the two queens before him. His hoarse, croaking voice—the result of a blow to the throat in battle—had earned him the nickname "the Raven," but it was said with great respect.

He taught by recounting famous battles, many of which he'd fought in himself. Despite his age, the Raven was a lively teacher and salted his stories with amusing asides about the habits and peculiarities of the people he'd fought with and against.

He also illustrated his lectures in a manner Tobin admired. When describing a battle, he would get down on the floor and sketch out the battleground with chalk, then use painted pebbles and bits of wood to represent the different forces, pushing them about with the ivory tip of his walking stick.

Some of the boys squirmed and yawned through these lessons, but Tobin enjoyed them. They reminded him of the hours he and his father had spent with the model of Ero. He also took secret delight whenever Raven talked of famous women generals and warriors. The old man made no distinction and had only cutting looks for those who snickered.

Tobin's friend Arengil was among the noble youths who joined the Companions for lessons and his friendship with Tobin and Ki soon deepened. Quick-witted and humorous, the Aurënfaie had a great talent for acting and could mimic anyone at court. Gathered with the younger Companions in Tobin's room at night, he'd reduce them all to helpless laughter with his haughty, mincing impression of Alben, then seem to transform into another body as he became hulking, sullen Zusthra or stooped old Raven.

Korin and Caliel sometimes joined them, but more often now the older boys slipped out on their own to the lower city. The morning after such excursions they'd turn up for the temple run with bloodshot eyes and superior smirks, and regaled the younger boys with their exploits when they thought Porion wasn't listening.

The others listened with a mix of admiration and envy, but Ki soon grew concerned for Lynx. Everyone knew he was hopelessly smitten with Orneus, but his lord now thought of nothing but keeping up with the prince in drinking and carousing, something Orneus was remarkably ill suited for.

"I don't know what poor Lynx sees in that wastrel anyway," Ki would grumble, watching the sad-eyed squire clean up his friend's sour vomit, or carrying Orneus back to their room when he was too drunk to walk.

"He wasn't like that when they first came here," Ruan confided as they sat toasting lumps of hard cheese over the hearth at Tobin's house one night. Snow was falling and everyone was feeling cozy and grown-up without the older boys around.

"You're right about that," Lutha agreed around a mouthful of cheese. "My father's estate is near his and we saw each other often at festivals and parties before we came to the Companions. He and Lynx were like brothers, but then—" He shrugged, blushing. "Well, you know how it goes with some. Anyway, Orneus is a good enough fellow, but I think the only reason he got chosen as a Companion was on account of his father's influence at court. Duke Orneus the Elder has a holding almost as big as yours at Atyion."

"If I'm ever allowed to go there, I'll see what you mean," Tobin grumbled. Even with Orun out of the way, bad weather had put an end to their travel plans for now and Korin seemed to have forgotten his promise.

"That's how it goes," Nikides said. "It's not like I'd be sitting here if I wasn't the Lord Chancellor's only grandson."

"But what you lack in fight, you make up for in brains," Lutha replied, always quick to bolster his friend. "When the rest of us are getting bravely hacked to pieces on some battlefield, you'll be here with your grandfather's velvet ashcake on your head, running the country for Korin."

"And poor Lynx will probably still be tying Orneus into the stirrups because he's too drunk to ride," Ki added with a laugh.

"It's Lynx who should be the lord," Barieus piped up hotly. "Orneus isn't worthy to do up his boots." When everyone turned to stare at him, he hastily busied himself with a toasting fork. The swarthy little squire usually said very little about anyone, and never against a Companion.

Ki shook his head. "For hell's sake, doesn't anyone like girls but me?"

*T*obin kept quiet during Raven's lessons for some weeks. He didn't always understand what the old man was talking about, but listened intently and questioned the other boys afterward. He always made certain to ask Korin, but quickly discovered that Caliel and Nikides were more knowledgeable. Caliel, the son of a general, had a good mind for strategy. Nikides had the best head for history and had read more books than the rest of them put together. When Tobin and Ki both showed a genuine interest in the old stories, it was Nikides who introduced them to the royal library, located in the same wing as the abandoned throne room.

In fact, it took up nearly that entire wing, room upon room overlooking the eastern gardens. At first Tobin and Ki felt lost among the endless towering racks of scrolls and tomes, but Nik and the black-robed librarians showed them how to read the faded labels on each rack, and soon they were delving into treatises on arms and battle, as well as colorful books of poetry and stories.

Tobin soon learned his way around and discovered a whole room devoted to the history of his family. He asked the librarian about Queen Tamír, but there were only a few dusty scrolls, dry records of the few laws and taxes she'd passed. There was no history of her brief life or reign and the librarian knew of no other sources.

Tobin recalled Niryn's strange reaction, that day at the Royal Tomb, when Tobin had mentioned what he'd been taught of her murder. The wizard had vehemently denied it, though both his father and Arkoniel had told him the same story. Her brother had killed her, and ruled briefly in her place before coming to a bad end himself.

Disappointed, Tobin slipped away from his friends and walked down to the sealed doors of the old throne room. Pressing his palms to the carved panels, he waited, hoping to feel the murdered queen's spirit through the wood the way he'd sometimes felt his mother's ghost at the tower door. The Old Palace was supposed to be haunted by all sorts of spirits. Everyone said so. According to Korin, their own grandmother's bloody specter still wandered these halls on a regular basis; that was why his father had built the New Palace.

It seemed every chambermaid and door warder had some ghost story to tell, yet except for one glimpse of Tamír inside the throne room, Tobin had never seen anything. He supposed he shouldn't complain—he'd had enough of ghosts already—but sometimes he wished Tamír would come back and make herself clearer. Given what he now knew about himself, he was certain she'd been trying to tell him something important when she'd offered him her sword. But Korin and the others had distracted him, and before he could speak to her, she'd vanished.

Was she trapped inside, unable to come out? he wondered.

Returning to the library, he found an unoccupied chamber not far from the throne room. Unlatching one of the windows, he pushed it open and climbed out onto the wide stone ledge that ran along the walls just below. Snow filled his shoes as he inched along to the broken window they'd entered by the night Korin and the others had played at being ghosts.

It had been too dark to see much then. Tobin squeezed through and found himself standing at one side of a huge, shadowy hall. Pale winter light filtered dimly through cracks in the tall, shuttered windows.

The worn marble floor still showed the marks where benches and fountains had been. Tobin got his bearings and hurried toward the center of the room, where the massive marble throne still stood on its raised dais.

He'd been too scared to examine it closely last time, but saw now that it was beautiful. The arms were carved like cresting waves, and symbols of the Four were inlaid in bands of red, black, and gold across the high back. There must have been cushions, but they were gone and mice had built a nest in one corner of the broad seat.

The chamber had a sad, neglected air about it. Sitting

down on the throne, Tobin rested his hands on the carved armrests and looked around, imagining his ancestors hearing petitions and greeting dignitaries from far-off lands. He could feel the weight of years. The edges of the dais steps were worn smooth in places, where hundreds of people had knelt before the queens.

Just then he heard a sigh, so close to his ear it made him jump up and look around.

"Hello?" He should have been afraid, but he wasn't. "Queen Tamír?"

He thought he felt the cool brush of fingertips against his cheek, though it could have been nothing more than an errant stir of breeze through one of the broken windows. He heard another sigh, clearer this time, and just off to his right.

Following the sound with his eyes, he noticed a long, rectangular stain on the floor beside the dais. It was about three feet long, and no wider than his palm. The rusted stumps of iron bolts and a few bits of broken stonework still marked where something had stood.

Something. Tobin's heart leaped.

Restore . . .

The voice was faint but he could feel her now.

Feel them, he amended, for other voices joined in. Women's voices. *"Restore . . . Restore . . ."* Sad and faint as the rustle of wind through distant leaves.

Even now Tobin wasn't frightened. This felt nothing like Brother or his mother. He felt welcome here.

Kneeling, he touched the place where the golden tablet of the Oracle had stood.

So long as a daughter of Thelátimos—

From Ghërilain's time, through all those years and queens, the tablet's carved words had proclaimed to all who approached this throne that the woman who sat upon it did so by Illior's will.

Restore.

"I don't know how," he whispered. "I know I'm supposed to, but I don't know what to do. Help me!"

The ghostly hand caressed his cheek again, tender and unmistakable. "I'll try, I promise. Somehow. I swear it by the Sword."

Tobin said nothing of the experience to anyone, but spent more time that winter reading in the library. The history Arkoniel and his father had labored to teach him came to life as he read firsthand accounts of events written by the queens and warriors who'd lived them. Ki caught his enthusiasm and they sat up late into the night, taking turns reading aloud by candlelight.

Raven's chalk drawing battlefields took on new meaning as well. Watching the old general push his pebble cavalry and wood chip archers about, Tobin began to see the logic of the formations. At times he could imagine the scenes as clearly as if he were reading Queen Ghërilain's account, or the histories of General Mylia.

"Come on now, someone must have an opinion!" the old man snapped one day, tapping his stick impatiently on the diagram in question. It showed a large open field flanked on either side by curving belts of trees.

Without thinking, Tobin stood up to answer. Before he could change his mind everyone was looking at him.

"You have a strategy, Your Highness?" Raven asked, raising a bushy eyebrow doubtfully.

"I—I think I'd hide my horsemen in the grove of trees on the east flank under cover of night—"

"Yes? What else?" His wrinkled face gave nothing away.

Tobin pressed on. "And half or more of my archers over here in woods on the other side." He paused, thinking of a battle he'd read about a few days earlier. "I'd have the rest set stakes here, with the men-at-arms in ranks behind them." Warming to his subject, he squatted and pointed to the narrow strip of open ground between the copses, at the

Skalan-held end of the field. "It would look like a thin front from the enemy's side. I'd have my horsemen keep their mounts quiet, so the enemy would think it was only foot soldiers they were facing. They'd probably make the first charge at dawn. As soon as their horsemen were committed, I'd send mine out to cut them off and have the hidden archers shoot at the enemy's foot soldiers to panic them."

The general tugged thoughtfully at his beard, then rasped, "Divide their forces, eh? That's your plan?"

Someone snickered, but Tobin nodded. "Yes, General Marnaryl, that's what I'd do."

"Well, as it happens, that's very much like what your great-grandmother did at the Second Battle of Isil and it worked rather well."

"Well done, Tobin!" Caliel cried.

"He's my blood, isn't he?" said Korin proudly. "I'll be glad to have him as my general when I'm king, I can tell you."

Tobin's pleasure dissolved to panic at the words and he took his seat quickly, hardly able to breathe. For the rest of the day, his cousin's praise haunted him.

When I'm king.

Skala could have only one ruler, and even Tobin couldn't imagine his cousin simply stepping aside. When Ki was asleep that night, he rose and burned an owl feather in the night lamp flame, but he didn't know what prayer to send with it. As he struggled for some words to say, all he could think of was his cousin's smiling face.

Chapter 13

A cold draft across his bare shoulders woke Arkoniel. Shivering, he fumbled in the darkness and pulled Lhel's bearskin robe up to his chin. She'd let him spend the night with her more often since midwinter and he was grateful, both for the companionship and the chance to escape the haunted corridors of the keep.

The bracken-stuffed pallet crackled as he burrowed deeper under the covers. The bed smelled good: sex and balsam and smoky hides. But he was still cold. He groped for Lhel, but found only a patch of fading warmth where she'd been.

"Armra dukath?" he called softly. He was learning her language quickly and always spoke it here though she teased him, claiming his accent was thicker than cold mutton stew. He'd learned the true name of her people, as well. They called themselves the *Retha'noi*, "people of wisdom."

There was no answer, only the clacking of the bare oak branches overhead. Assuming she'd gone out to relieve herself, he settled back, longing for her naked heat against his back. But he couldn't get back to sleep, and Lhel didn't return.

More curious than worried, he wrapped himself in the fur robe and felt his way to the small, leather-curtained doorway. Pushing it aside, he looked out. In the two weeks since Sakor-tide it had snowed less than it usually did here; the drifts surrounding the oak were only shin deep in most places.

The sky was clear, though. The full moon hung like a

new coin against the stars, so bright on the sparkling snow that he could make out the fine whorls on his fingertips by its light. Lhel said a full moon stole the heat of the day to be so bright, and Arkoniel could well believe it. Each breath showed silver white for an instant, then fell away in tiny crystals.

Small footprints led in the direction of the spring. Shivering, Arkoniel found his boots and followed.

Lhel was squatting at the water's edge, staring intently at the little circle of roiling open water at its center. Wrapped to the chin in the new cloak Arkoniel had given her, she held her left hand over the water. Her fingers were crooked to summon the scrying spell and Arkoniel stopped a few yards away, not wanting to disturb her. The spell could take some time, depending on how far she was trying to see. He saw only undulating silver ripples across the spring's black surface, but Lhel's eyes glinted like a cat's as she watched whatever it was that she'd summoned. Shadow filled the lines around her eyes and mouth, showing her years in a way the sun never did. Lhel claimed not to know her age. She said her people reckoned a woman's age not by years, but by the seasons of her womb: child, child bearer, elder. She still bled with the waning moon, but she was not young.

Presently she lifted her head and glanced at him with no apparent surprise.

"What are you doing?" he asked.

"I had a dream," she replied, kneading the stiffness from her back as she stretched. "Someone is coming, but I couldn't see who, so I came out here."

"Did you see in water?"

She nodded and took his hand, leading him back to the tree. "Wizards."

"Harriers?"

"No, Iya and another I couldn't see. There's a cloud around that one. But they're coming to see you."

"Should I go back to the keep?"

Smiling, she stroked his cheek. "No, there's time, and I'm too cold to sleep alone." The years fled her face again as she reached under his robe and stroked a chilly hand down his belly. "You stay and warm me."

Arkoniel returned to the keep the next morning, expecting to find lathered horses in the courtyard. But Iya did not come that day, or the next. Puzzled, he rode up the mountain track in search of Lhel, but the witch did not show herself.

Most of a week passed before her vision proved true. He was at work on a transmutation spell when he heard the sound of sleigh bells on the river road. Recognizing the high-pitched tinkling, he went on with his work. It was only the miller's girl, making the monthly delivery to the kitchen.

He was still engrossed in the complexities of transforming a chestnut into a letter knife when the rattle of the door latch startled him. No one disturbed him here this time of the day.

"You'd better come down, Arkoniel," said Nari. Her normally placid face was troubled and her hands were balled in her apron. "Mistress Iya is here."

"What's wrong?" he asked, hurrying to follow her downstairs. "Is she hurt?"

"Oh, no, she's well enough. I'm not so sure about the woman she brought with her, though."

Iya was sitting on the hearth bench in the hall, supporting a hunched, bundled figure. The stranger was closely wrapped but he could see the edge of a dark veil visible just below the deep hood.

"Who's this?" he asked.

"I think you remember our guest," Iya said quietly.

The other woman lifted her veil with a gloved hand and Nari let out a faint gasp.

"Mistress Ranai?" It was an effort not to recoil. "You're—you're a long way from home."

He'd met the elderly wizard only once before, but hers was a face not easily forgotten. The ruined half was turned toward him, the scarred flesh standing out in waxy ridges. She shifted to see him with her remaining eye and smiled. The undamaged side of her face was soft and kind as a grandmother's.

"I am glad to meet you again, though I regret the circumstance that brings me to you," she replied in a hoarse, whispery voice. Her gnarled hands trembled as she laid her veil aside.

Centuries ago, during the Great War, this woman had fought beside Iya's master, Agazhar. A necromancer's demon had raked her face into this lopsided mask and crippled her left leg. She was much frailer than he recalled, and he could see the reddened weal of a recent burn on her right cheek.

The first time they'd met, he'd felt her power like a cloud of lightning so strong it raised the hair on the back of his arms. Now he could scarcely feel it.

"What's happened to you, Mistress?" Remembering his manners he took her hand and silently offered her his own strength. He felt a slight flutter in his stomach as she accepted the gift.

"They burned me out," she wheezed. "My own neighbors!"

"They got wind of a Harrier patrol on the way to Ylani and went mad," Iya explained. "Word's been put round that any town that shelters a dissenting wizard will be put to the torch."

"Two centuries I lived among them!" Ranai gripped Arkoniel's hand harder. "I healed their children, sweetened their wells, brought them rain. If Iya hadn't been with me that night—" A coughing fit choked off her words.

Iya gently patted her back. "I'd just reached Ylani and saw the Harrier banner in the harbor. I guessed what that meant in time, but even so, I was nearly too late. The cottage was burning down around her and she was caught under a beam."

"Harrier wizards stood outside and held the doors shut!" Ranai croaked. "I must be old indeed if a pack of young scoundrels like that can best me! But oh, how their spells hurt. It felt like they were driving spikes into my eyes. I was blind—" She trailed off querulously and seemed to shrink even smaller as Arkoniel watched.

"Thank the Light she was strong enough to hold off the worst of the flames, but as you can see, the ordeal took its toll. We've been nearly two weeks getting here. We rode the last bit in a miller's sledge."

He brushed at a streak of flour on Iya's skirt. "So I see."

Nari had disappeared at some point, but she and Cook returned with hot tea and food for the travelers.

Ranai accepted a mug with a murmur of thanks, but was too weak to lift it. Iya helped the old woman raise it to her lips. Ranai managed a slurping sip before another rattling cough took her. Iya held her as the spasm shook her wizened frame.

"Fetch a firepot," Nari said to Cook. "I'll make up the duke's room for her."

Iya helped the old woman take another sip. "She's not the only one driven out. You remember Virishan?"

"That hedge wizard who takes in wizard-born orphans?"

"Yes. Do you recall the young mind clouder she had with her?"

"Eyoli?"

"Yes. I met him on the road a few months back and he told me she and her brood had fled into the mountains north of Ilear."

"It's that monster's doing," Ranai whispered vehemently. "That viper in white!"

"Lord Niryn."

"Lord?" The old woman mustered the strength to spit into the fire. The flames flared a livid blue. "The son of a tanner, he was, and a middling mage at best, last I knew. But the whelp knows how to drip poison in the royal ear. He's turned the whole country on us, his own kind!"

"Is it so bad already?" asked Arkoniel.

"It's still just in pockets in the outlying towns, but the madness is spreading," said Iya.

"The visions—" Ranai began.

"Not here," Iya whispered. "Arkoniel, help Nari get her to bed."

Ranai was too weak to climb the stairs, so Arkoniel carried her. She was as light and brittle in his arms as a bundle of dry sticks. Nari and Cook had made the musty, long-empty room as comfortable as they could. Two firepots stood beside the bed and someone had laid life's breath leaves on the coals to ease Ranai's cough. The pungent smell filled the room.

As the women undressed Ranai to her ragged shift and tucked her into bed, Arkoniel caught a glimpse of the old scars and new burns that covered her withered arms and shoulders. Bad as they were, he found them less worrisome than the strange ebb in her power.

When Ranai was settled, Iya sent the others out and pulled a chair close to the bed. "Are you comfortable now?" Ranai whispered something Arkoniel could not catch. Iya frowned, then nodded. "Very well. Arkoniel, fetch the bag, please."

"It's there beside you." Iya's traveling pack lay in plain sight by his mistress's chair.

"No, the bag I left with you."

Arkoniel blinked, realizing which one she meant.

"Fetch it, Arkoniel. Ranai told me something quite surprising the other day." She looked down at the dozing wizard, then snapped, "Quickly now!" as if he were still a clumsy young apprentice.

Arkoniel took the stairs two at a time and pulled the dusty bag from under the workroom table. Inside, shrouded in spells and mystery lay the clay bowl she had charged him never to show to anyone except his own successor. It had been Iya's burden for as long as he'd known her, a trust passed with the darkest oaths from wizard to wizard since the days of the Great War.

The war! he thought, seeing the first inkling of a connection.

Iya saw Ranai's eyes widen when Arkoniel returned with the battered old leather bag.

"Shroud the room, Iya," she murmured.

Iya cast a spell, sealing the room from prying eyes and ears, then took the bag from Arkoniel. Undoing the knotted thongs, she eased out the mass of silk wrappings and slowly undid them. Wards and incantations winked and crackled in the lamplight.

As the last of the silk fell away Iya caught her breath. No matter how often she held this plain, crude thing, the malevolent emanations always rocked her. To one not wizard-born, this was nothing but a crude beggar's bowl, unglazed and poorly fired. But her master Agazhar had felt nausea when he touched it. Arkoniel suffered a searing headache and feverish pain through his body in its presence. Iya experienced it as a miasma like fumes from a rotting, ruptured corpse.

She glanced at Ranai with concern, fearing the effect it would have on her in her weakened state.

But instead the old woman seemed to find new strength. Lifting her hand, she sketched a spell of protection on the air, then reached out hesitantly, as if to take the bowl.

"Yes, there's no mistaking it," she rasped, withdrawing her hand.

"How do you know of it?" Arkoniel asked.

"I was a Guardian myself, one of the original six . . . I've seen enough, Iya. Put it away." She lay back and sighed deeply, not speaking until the cursed thing was safely wrapped again.

"You understood the Oracle's meaning all too well, even without the knowledge lost when your master died," she told Iya.

"I don't understand," said Arkoniel. "I never heard of other Guardians. Who are the six?"

Ranai closed her eyes. "They're all dead, except for me. I'd never have revealed myself to your mistress, but when I saw that she no longer had the bag with her, I feared the worst. You must forgive an old woman's weakness. Perhaps if I'd spoken when you came to Ylani a few years back—"

Iya took the clawed left hand in hers. "Never mind that. I know the oaths you swore. But we're here now and you've seen it. What is it you have to tell us?"

Ranai looked up then. "There can be only one Guardian for each secret, Iya. You've passed the burden to this boy. What I have to say, only he can hear."

"No, she only left it with me for safekeeping. Iya's the true Guardian," Arkoniel told her.

"No. She passed it down."

"Then I give it back!"

"You can't. The Lightbearer guided her hand, whether she knew it or not. You are Guardian now, Arkoniel, and what I have to say can only be said to you."

Iya recalled the Afran Oracle's cryptic words: *This is a seed that must be watered with blood. But you see too far.* And she thought of the vision she'd had that day, of a grand white palace filled with wizards, but seen from a distance, with Arkoniel looking out at her from a tower window.

"She's right, Arkoniel. You stay." Unable to look at either of them, she hurried out.

Sealed out by her own magic, she sagged against the wall and covered her face, letting the bitter tears come.

Only then did the demon child's cryptic words come back to haunt her.

You shall not enter.

Arkoniel stared after Iya in disbelief, then turned back to the ruined creature in the bed. The revulsion he'd felt the first time he'd seen her rushed back now.

"Sit, please," Ranai whispered. "What I tell you now is what was lost with Agazhar's death. Iya has acted in ignorance. No fault of hers, but it must be made right. Swear to me, Arkoniel, as all Guardians before you have sworn, by hands, heart, and eyes, by the Light of Illior, and by the blood of Aura that runs in your veins, that you will take on the full mantle of guardianship, and that as Guardian, you will lock all I tell you away in your heart until you pass the burden to your successor. Protect these secrets with your life and allow no one who discovers them to live. No one, you understand me? Not friend or foe, wizard or plain-born, man, woman, or child. Give me your hands and swear. I'll know if you lie."

"Secrecy and death. Is that all the Lightbearer will ever ask of me?"

"Many things will be asked of you, Arkoniel, but none more sacred than this. Iya will understand your silence."

He'd seen the grief in Iya's face and knew Ranai spoke the truth. "Very well." He grasped Ranai's hands and bowed his head. "I do swear, by hands, heart, and eyes, by the Light of Illior and by the blood of Aura in my veins, to carry out whatever duty is required of me as Guardian, and to reveal the secrets you give me to no one but my successor."

A blast of raw energy shot through him from their clasped hands, engulfing him. It was like being struck by lightning. It seemed impossible that Ranai's wasted body could still contain such power, but when it passed, it left them both gasping.

Ranai regarded him solemnly. "You are truly the

Guardian now, more so than your mistress was, or even her master. You are the last of the six to carry that which must be hidden. All the rest have failed or laid their burden down."

"And you?"

She raised a hand to her scarred cheek and grimaced. "This was the price I paid for my failure. But let me speak, for my strength is going.

"The greatest wizard of the Second Orëska was Master Reynes of Wyvernus. It was he who rallied the wizards of Skala to fight under Queen Ghërilain's banner, and he who led those who finally defeated the Vatharna. You understand the word?"

Arkoniel nodded. "It's Plenimaran for 'the chosen one.' "

"The chosen one." The old woman's eyes were closed now, and Arkoniel had to lean closer to hear her. "The Vatharna was a great general, chosen by the necromancers to take on the form of Seriamaius."

She still held his right hand, but he made a warding sign with his left. Even priests hesitated to speak the name of the necromancer's god aloud. "How could such a thing be done?"

"They forged a helm and the one who wore it, the Vatharna, became an earthly vessel for the god. It did not happen at once, thank the Four, but gradually, though even the initial guise was terrible enough.

"The helm was completed and their general put it on. Reynes found him only just in time. Hundreds of wizards and warriors were killed in that battle, but the helm was captured. Reynes and the most powerful wizards still alive dismantled it somehow. But before they could do more, the Plenimarans attacked again. Only Reynes escaped, and with only six of the pieces. He never revealed how many there were in all. He put a glamour on those he had, wrapped them as yours is wrapped, and placed them in a darkened tent. Then he chose six of us—wizards who'd taken no part in the other ceremonies—and sent us in one at a time. We were to take the first bundle our hand found in the darkness, then depart alone, unseen. No matter what the cost, the pieces were to be scattered and hidden. Not even Reynes would know where they were."

She coughed weakly and Arkoniel held a cup of water to her lips. "So they couldn't put it back together?"

"Yes. Reynes was very careful, not trusting even himself to know the full truth. None of us had witnessed the ritual of dissolution, or the true form of what we carried. None of us knew what the others had, or where they went."

"So Agazhar was one of the original Guardians?"

"No. He wasn't powerful enough to be considered. Hyradin was the first of your line. He and Agazhar came to be friends later on, but Agazhar knew nothing of the burden he carried. It was only by chance that he was with Hyradin when the Plenimarans found him. Mortally wounded, Hyradin gave Agazhar the bundle and held off the enemy long enough for him to escape. Years later when he and I met again, I saw what he carried and knew Hyradin must be dead."

"And all the other pieces were lost?"

"Mine was, and two others that I know of. Hyradin's you carry. But one of us returned, saying she'd accomplished her purpose. The sixth was never heard of again. As far as I know, I'm the only one who failed and lived. It was years before I healed, and longer before I learned of Hyradin's fate. By rights Agazhar should have killed me and I told him so, but he wouldn't, saying I was a Guardian still. As far as I know, yours is the only fragment yet in Skala. I told Agazhar it should be hidden somewhere secure, but he thought he could better protect it by keeping it with him." She fixed Arkoniel with her good eye. "He was wrong. It *must* be hidden somewhere it cannot be lost or stolen. Tell Iya that much, at least. I've had visions of fire and death since we last met, and of the girl who is hidden."

She smiled, seeing his startled look. "I don't know who she is, or where, only that she has been born. And I'm not the only one, as Iya knows. The Harriers who came for me had heard of her from others. If you know, and they ever capture you, kill yourself before they can wring it from you."

"But what does this thing have to do with her?" Arkoniel asked, perplexed.

"I don't know. I don't think Iya knows, but it is what the Afran Oracle showed her. This evil you carry is bound up with the fate of the future queen. You must not fail."

Ranai accepted another sip of water. Her voice was fading and there was no color left in her face. "There's something else, something only I know. Hyradin had a dream while he was Guardian, a vision that came to him again and again. He told it to Agazhar before he died and, not knowing what it meant, Agazhar told me before I knew enough to stop him. Perhaps that was Illior's will, for it would have been lost otherwise. Take my hand again. The words I speak to you will never leave your memory. They must be passed on through all your successors, for yours is the last line. I pass them to you now as Agazhar should have, and a gift of my own with them."

She clutched his hand and the room went black around Arkoniel. Her voice came to him out of the darkness, strong and clear as a young woman's. "Hear the Dream of Hyradin. 'And so came the Beautiful One, the Eater of Death, to strip the bones of the world. First clothed in Man's flesh it came, crowned with a dread helm of darkness and none could stand against this One but Four.'"

Her voice changed, deepening to a man's. The darkness parted and Arkoniel found himself in a forest clearing, facing a fair-haired man in ragged clothes. The stranger held the cursed bowl in his hands, offering it to him. "First shall be the Guardian, a vessel of light in the darkness," he said to Arkoniel. "Then the Shaft and the Vanguard, who shall fail and yet not fail if the Guide, the Unseen One, goes forth. And at the last shall again be the Guardian, whose portion is bitter, bitter as gall when they meet under the Pillar of the Sky."

The voice and vision faded away and Arkoniel blinked around at the familiar chamber. The words were etched in his mind, as Ranai had promised. He had only to think of them and the wizard's voice seemed to speak in his ear. But what did they mean?

Ranai's eye was closed, her face peaceful. It was a moment before he realized that she was dead. If she knew the meaning of the dream, she'd taken that knowledge with her to Bilairy's gate.

He whispered the prayer of passing for her, then rose to find Iya. As he stood up his clothing fell away in ashes. Even his shoes had been reduced to cinders by the rush of the old woman's power, yet his body was unmarked.

Wrapping himself in a blanket, he went to the door and let Iya in. She took the situation in at a glance. Cupping Arkoniel's face between her hands, she gazed into his eyes, then nodded. "She passed her life force to you."

"She made herself die?"

"Yes. She had no successor. By channeling her soul through yours as she died, she was trying to impart some of her power to you."

"A gift," Arkoniel murmured, sitting down by her. "I thought she meant the—" He caught himself. He'd spoken freely to Iya all his life; he felt like a traitor now, keeping secrets.

She sat on the end of the bed and gazed sadly at the dead woman. "It's all right. No one understands better than I how things stand. Do what you must."

"I won't kill you, if that's what you mean!"

Iya chuckled. "No, the Lightbearer has work for me yet. This is the proof of it. There are others, many others, who've had a glimpse of what Tobin will become. Illior is choosing those who will help her. For so long I thought I was the only one, but it seems I'm only the messenger. Others must be gathered and protected before the Harriers take them all."

"But how?"

Iya reached into a pouch at her belt and tossed Arkoniel a small pebble; he'd lost track of how many of these little tokens she'd left with other wizards. "You've been safe enough here, all these years. I'll send the others here for now. How do you feel?"

"No different." Arkoniel rolled the pebble between his fingers. "Well, maybe a bit more scared."

Iya rose and hugged him. "So am I."

Chapter 14

Tobin returned to the throne room several times, but had no more ghostly visitations. He was still a child, and in the way of children, it was easy to put his fears aside once the moment passed. The ghosts or gods or Iya would tell him when it was time to step forward. For now, he was simply Tobin, beloved cousin of a young prince, nephew of a king he'd never met. The Companions were cheered wherever they went, and Korin was everyone's darling.

Hard as Porion and Raven worked the boys, winter was a time of special pleasures. The theaters of Ero staged their most lavish productions in the dark months; true marvels featuring live animals, mechanical devices, and fireworks. The Golden Tree surpassed all the other houses with a lengthy play cast entirely with real centaurs from the Ashek Mountains, the first of their kind Tobin and Ki had seen.

The markets were fragrant with the scent of roasting chestnuts and mulled cider, and bright with fine woolen goods from the northlands beyond Mycena. Street vendors sold sweets made of honey and fresh snow that glistened like amber in the sunlight.

Chancellor Hylus was a kindly guardian and saw to it that Tobin had ample pocket money, far more than Orun had seen fit to give him. Still unused to having gold or anywhere to spend it, Tobin would have let the coins gather dust in his room if Korin hadn't insisted on visits to his favorite tailors, swordsmiths, and other merchants. Encouraged, Tobin got rid of the faded black velvet hangings in his bedchamber, replacing them with his own, blue and white and silver.

He also visited the artisans in Goldsmith Street and began making sculptures and bits of jewelry again. One day he shyly took a brooch he was rather proud of to show to an Aurënfaie jeweler whose work he especially admired. It was a filigree piece cast in bronze and fashioned to look like bare, intertwined branches. He had even included a few tiny leaves and set it with a scattering of tiny white crystals. He'd been thinking of the night sky over Lhel's clearing and the way the stars winked through the oak branches on winter nights.

Master Tyral was a thin, silver-haired man with pale grey eyes and a bright blue sen'gai. Tobin was fascinated by these exotic folk and could already recognize half a dozen different clans by their distinctive headcloths and manner in which they wrapped the long strips of wool or silk around their heads. Tyral and his workmen all wore theirs in a sort of squat turban wrapped low on their heads, the long ends hanging over their left shoulders.

Tyral greeted him warmly as always, and invited Tobin to lay out his work on a square of black velvet. Tobin unwrapped the bronze brooch and put it down.

"You made this?" Tyral murmured in his soft, lilting accent. "And this, as well, yes?" he asked, pointing to the gold horse charm Tobin wore around his neck. "May I see it?"

Tobin handed it to him, then fidgeted nervously as the man examined both pieces closely. Looking around at the beautiful necklaces and rings on display around the fine shop, he began to regret his audacity. He'd come to enjoy the praise of his friends for his work, but they weren't artists. What would this master craftsman care for his clumsy attempts?

"Tell me about this brooch. How did you achieve such fine lines?" Tyral asked, looking up with an expression Tobin couldn't immediately interpret.

Tobin haltingly explained how he'd sculpted each tiny branch in wax, then woven the warmed filaments together and packed them in wet sand to receive the molten metal. Before he'd finished, the 'faie chuckled and held up a hand.

"Indeed, you are the artist. Forgive my doubt, but I seldom see such skill in a Tírfaie of your age."

"You think they're good?"

The 'faie picked up the horse charm. "This is very nice. You wisely kept the lines simple, suggesting detail rather than cluttering the little body up with it. One can feel the beast's vitality in the stretch of the neck and the way you've positioned the legs, as if it is running. Lesser artisans would leave the legs straight, like a cow's. Yes, it is a fine little piece. But this one!" He picked up the brooch and cradled it in the hollow of his palm. "This shows more than skill. You were sad when you made this. Homesick, perhaps?"

Tobin nodded, speechless.

Tyral took Tobin's right hand and examined the fingers and palm the same way he'd looked at the brooch. "You train to be a warrior, but you were born to be an artist, a maker of things. Do they train you for that as well, up there on the hill?"

"No, it's just something I do. My mother made things, too."

"She gave you a great gift, then, Prince Tobin. One perhaps you have not been taught to value as you should. The Lightbearer has put skill in these rough young hands of yours." He sat back and sighed. "Your family is renowned for their prowess in battle, but I will tell you a true thing. With such hands as these, you will always be happier creating than you ever will be destroying. I am not flattering you or currying favor when I say that if you were a common boy rather than a prince, I would invite you to work here with me. I've never said that to any Tírfaie, either."

Tobin looked around at the workbenches, with their

rouge stones, crucibles, and racks of scarred mallets, tiny hammers, dies, and files.

Tyral smiled sadly, reading the longing in his eyes. "We do not choose our births, do we? It would not be seemly for a prince of Skala to become a common craftsman. But you will find ways, I think. Come see me whenever you like and I will give you what help I can."

The jeweler's words stayed with Tobin for a long time afterward. It was true that he couldn't sell his work like a common craftsman, but he could keep on as he had, making gifts. He made charms and cloak pins decorated with animal heads and gems for his friends. Nikides commissioned an emerald ring for his grandfather's birthday and Hylus was so pleased with it he was never seen without it again. Word spread and soon commissions were coming in from other nobles, who brought him gold and gems to work with. Apparently, as Ki observed, Tobin could work for his own kind.

When Porion allowed them the occasional day off, Korin took the younger boys around to his new favorite haunts: taverns where pretty girls in low-cut bodices were quick to sit on the older boys' laps and to pet and coo over the younger ones. Actress and actors welcomed them backstage at the finest theaters, and merchants in the richer districts always seemed to have some special items held back just for them.

Now and then—usually when Korin had been drinking, as Ki was quick to note—he even brought the younger ones along on his nocturnal rambles. This required giving Master Porion the slip, but that was part of the fun. On frosty moonlit nights they played catch-me through the crooked streets, then headed down to some of the meanest waterfront neighborhoods. Even in the dead of winter these streets stank of shit and dead dogs, and the wine in the filthy taverns was vile. Yet Korin seemed happier here than anywhere else, bawling drunkenly along with raw-throated minstrels or elbowing in beside sailors, dock-hands, and less savory fellows to watch a street fight or a bear baiting.

The older boys were already well-known in such places, and Korin was greeted as "young Lord No-Name" with knowing winks and nods. More than once the older boys left the others waiting on some cold unlit street corner while they had their whores against alley walls. Of all the older boys, only Lynx refused to join in these unsavory revels. Waiting in the cold with Tobin and the others, listening to the yelps and grunts that echoed out, he often looked downright ill. Barieus hovered near him, anxious to offer comfort, but Lynx took no notice.

"I don't understand it!" Ki exclaimed in disgust as they rode home on their own one night. "Those lowborn sailors and whores would knife their own mothers for one night in a decent house, but these spoiled young blades roll downhill like horse turds into places even my brothers wouldn't even set a toe in. They wallow in it like pigs and Korin is the worst of 'em. I'm sorry, Tobin, but it's true and you know it. He's our leader and he sets the tone. I wish Caliel would talk sense into him." They both knew that wasn't likely to happen.

It wasn't all gutter crawling, though. Invitations arrived daily to parties, bonfires, and hunts. Creamy scrolls written in colored inks piled up like fallen leaves in the Companions' mess. The Companions had always been much sought-after guests in the king's absence, and were all the more so now that Korin was nearing marriageable age.

The prince was not one to turn down invitations. Fifteen, and already man-grown with a fine new beard on his chin, Korin drew admiring stares wherever he went. His hair hung in a mane of black ringlets around his shoulders, framing a square, handsome face and flashing dark eyes. He knew how to make women of any age melt with a smile or a kiss on the hand; girls gathered around him like cats to cream while their mothers hovered anxiously, hoping for some sign of favor.

Those with younger daughters began to cast their eyes in Tobin's direction, as well, much to his friends' envious amusement and Tobin's secret dismay. He was rich, after all, and of the best family in Skala. Twelve was not too young to consider a contracted union. The shy glances of the girls and their mothers' naked appraisal made Tobin cringe. Even if he had been who they imagined him to be, he doubted he'd have welcomed such predatory looks. After the obligatory greetings with their hosts of the evening, he quickly sought out a corner in which to hide.

Ki, on the other hand, took to the life like a duck to water. His good looks and easy, laughing manner attracted attentions he was more than happy to return. He even took to dancing.

The other Companions teased Tobin about his shyness, but it was Arengil who at last found a way to put him more at ease.

In mid-Dostin Caliel's mother, the Duchess Althia, hosted a ball in honor of her son's sixteenth birthday at her villa near the Old Palace. It was a grand affair. The hall was lit with hundreds of wax tapers, tables groaned with food of the best sort, and two bands of minstrels played by turns for the bejeweled gathering.

Caliel's younger sister Mina cajoled Tobin into a dance, and he embarrassed himself as usual, tripping over his feet and hers. As soon as the song ended he excused himself and took cover in a corner. Ki came over to keep him company, but Tobin could tell from the way he followed the dancers with his eyes, tapping his feet and drumming his hands on his knees in time to the music that he'd rather be out dancing.

"Go on, I don't mind," Tobin grumbled, as several pretty girls wandered past, making eyes at them.

Ki gave him a guilty grin. "No, that's all right."

Chancellor Hylus was speaking with Nikides nearby. Spying Tobin there, they came over.

"I've just been having the most interesting conversation with my grandson," Hylus told Tobin. "It seems you've been badly overlooked."

Tobin looked up in surprise. Hylus was smiling and Nikides looked very pleased with himself. "How do you mean, my lord?"

"Nothing's been done about your heraldry, my prince! I should have noticed myself, but it was Nikides." He pointed to the main entrance of the hall, where the banners of all the noble guests were displayed. Korin's red occupied the highest pole, with Tobin's blue just below it.

"You've every right to display your father's banner, of course," Nikides told him, as if Tobin would know what he was talking about. "But as a prince of the blood, you should incorporate your mother's, as well. In a case such as yours, they could be combined."

"With your permission, my prince, I will send word to the college of heralds to begin on your new arms at once," the old man offered.

Tobin shrugged. "Very well."

Clearly delighted, the pair moved on, already discussing escutcheons and bars.

Ki shook his head. "Nik could do with a bit more dancing himself."

The song ended and Arengil emerged from the press, looking very handsome and exotic. In addition to his green-and-yellow sen'gai, he wore a long white tunic of Aurënen make, and a thick golden torque and bracelets set with smooth round sapphires and crystals. Tobin had seen similar work in the shops of the Aurënfaie jewelers, but nothing so fine as these pieces.

"You've retreated earlier than usual," Arengil noted, smiling as Tobin took his wrist to examine a bracelet more closely.

"This is beautiful!" Tobin exclaimed, wishing he had

something to sketch out the intricate raised pattern work. "It's old, isn't it?"

"Never mind that now!" Arengil laughed, pulling his hand free. "Come on. Every girl in the room is waiting for you to ask her for a dance!"

Tobin folded his arms. "No they're not. I'm like the bull with three legs. Did you see Quirion laughing at me? Bilairy's balls, I wish Korin would just let me stay home!"

Una glided over, looking very pretty in blue satin with strands of pearls and lapis braided into her dark hair. She never flirted the way other girls did, but Tobin could tell she was enjoying the looks she drew tonight. Fluttering a jeweled fan under her chin in a very grown-up way, she bowed low to Tobin. "Hiding again, my prince?"

"I was just telling him that it's his duty to ornament these gatherings," Arengil remarked.

"An ornament. That's just what I feel like," Tobin muttered. "It's so boring, all this talking and standing around!"

"You seemed to enjoy conversing with that elderly duke earlier," Una observed.

Tobin shrugged. "He's an artist. He admired a pendant I made for his granddaughter and invited me to see his work."

"Watch that one," Arengil warned, lowering his voice. "He invited someone we both know to see his 'work,' then tried to kiss him in the carriage."

Una made a face. "But he's *old*!"

Arengil snorted and tossed the long, fringed ends of his sen'gai back over his shoulder. "The old ones are the worst." He looked around quickly, then confided, "I've heard a thing or two about Lord Orun. You must have been glad to be rid of him."

Ki screwed his face up in disgust. "Old Slack Guts? I'd have put a knife in him! By the Four, Tobin, tell me he never—"

"No!" Tobin replied, shuddering at the thought. "He was bad enough without that."

"And he's gone, so forget him. Come on, Prince Tobin. Dance with me!" Una urged gaily, holding out a hand to him. "I don't care if you step on my toes."

Tobin shrank back. "No, thanks. I've had enough of being laughed at for tonight." He hadn't meant it to come out so gruffly, and he felt bad, seeing the laughter die in her eyes.

"It's true," said Ki, not noticing. "He's like an ox on ice."

"Really?" Arengil made a show of looking Tobin over. "You should be a natural, the way you fight and sit a horse." Tobin shook his head but the older boy wouldn't be put off. "You've got the balance and rhythm and that's all you really need to dance. Come on, I want to try something."

Ignoring Tobin's protests, he led them to an unoccupied chamber down the corridor. The walls were decorated with battle trophies. Arengil took down two swords and tossed one to Tobin.

"Come on, my prince, partner me." Arengil struck a defensive stance, as if they were going to practice.

"Here? There's too much furniture in the way."

The 'faie raised a challenging eyebrow. "Frightened, are we?"

Scowling, Tobin took his place facing him. "Are you saying I should attack my dancing partner with a sword? Because I might be able to manage that."

"No, but it is similar. If I do this—" Arengil took a quick step forward, and Tobin fell back, braced to parry. "Right, you do that. And if you want to make me retreat?"

Tobin pushed the Aurënfaie's blade with his own and made a quick feint. Arengil fell back a step. "Keep pressing. What next?"

Tobin made a quick succession of mock attacks, driving Arengil back across the room.

"Now let me drive you." Slowly and deliberately, Arengil moved him backward. Reaching the place where they'd started, he lowered his weapon and bowed. "Thank you for the dance, my prince."

Tobin rolled his eyes. "What are you talking about?"

"That's brilliant!" Una exclaimed. "That's all dancing is, Tobin. The lady responds to the step her partner takes. It's just like sword fighting."

Arengil tossed the sword to Ki and struck a dancing pose. Right hand raised, left at the small of his back, he shot Tobin another challenging look.

Feeling very silly, Tobin hesitantly took his place facing in the opposite direction and placed his right palm against Arengil's.

"Good. Now, if I do this—" Arengil took a small step forward and pressed his hand against Tobin's. "What must you do?"

Tobin took a step forward, then another and they circled one another. Arengil turned sharply on his heel and changed hands. Tobin followed awkwardly.

"You, too!" Una took Ki's hand. A far more willing pupil, he wrapped an arm around her waist and spun her around, laughing.

Distracted, Tobin tripped over Arengil's foot. The older boy caught him around the waist to steady him, and whispered, "Don't worry. She won't let Ki steal her away." Giving Tobin a wink, he propelled him backward for a few steps. "I'm on the offensive now, pushing you. Unless you mean to fight me or fall over, you must allow yourself to be driven. Now let's try this."

He faced Tobin and raised both hands. Reluctantly, he did the same and stepped back on his left foot as Arengil stepped forward on his right.

And on it went, as they transformed one dance step after another into a battle drill. It was grim work, but Tobin did begin to see the patterns.

Ki and Una were making better progress. He whirled her around the room, whistling a country jig.

"But this isn't really dancing. It's too simple," Tobin

complained. He jerked a thumb at the others spinning past. "You have to add in all those jumps and twists and things."

"Those are just the flourishes," Arengil assured him. "As long as you remember the order of the steps and keep to the beat, it's all just fancy advance and retreat."

"That reminds me," Una called, escaping Ki's embrace to fan herself. "Can you teach me to fight by pretending we're dancing?" She paused, and Tobin saw her smile falter again. "You haven't forgotten your promise, have you?"

Glad of any excuse to escape the dancing lesson, Tobin grabbed up the discarded swords and handed one to her. Una's skirts swirled around her as she took her stance and saluted him. When Tobin answered, she turned slightly and fell into a reasonably good defensive stance.

Arengil raised an eyebrow. "*You* want to learn sword-play?"

"I've warrior blood in my veins, the same as you!" she retorted.

Several revelers passed the doorway just then. "What's this, a duel?" a man asked, grinning at the sight of Una with a sword.

"Just playing, Lord Evin," she said, waving the blade clumsily about.

"Mind you don't hurt her, boys," the man warned, and disappeared after his companions. Una raised the blade again, steady this time.

"Do you think this is wise?" Arengil whispered. "It's bad enough if word gets back to your father that you were alone in here with three boys. If he thought—"

"Evin won't say anything."

"But someone else might. It's hard to keep a secret anywhere on the Palatine. The servants carry on like a flock of crows."

"Then we'll have to go somewhere they won't see," she said. "Meet me on Tobin's balcony tomorrow after-noon after your lessons."

"The balcony?" Ki scoffed. "There's only about a thousand windows facing over it around the gardens."

"You'll see," Una teased, and was gone with a last challenging look over her shoulder.

"Girls with swords?" Arengil shook his head. "She's going to get us all in trouble. In Aurënen, women keep to womanly things."

"In Skala warfare is a womanly thing," Tobin shot back, then hastily amended, "Or it used to be."

All the same, he found this new boldness in Una rather disconcerting.

The following day Tobin and the others were on the balcony outside his room at the appointed hour, but there was no sign of her.

"Maybe she isn't so bold in daylight," Arengil said, shading his eyes to scan the snowy gardens.

"Here!" a voice called from overhead.

Una stood grinning down at them from the eaves above the balcony. She was dressed in a plain tunic and leggings and her dark hair was bound in a tight braid. The cold winter air had put roses in her cheeks, as Nari used to say, and her dark eyes were bright with a mischief Tobin had never seen before.

"How'd you get up there?" Ki demanded.

"Climbed, of course. I think you can use that old trellis over there." She pointed to a shadowy recess several feet from the left-hand railing.

"That was you, wasn't it, that first morning after we came to Ero?" Tobin exclaimed, remembering the mysterious figure who'd taunted them and disappeared.

Una shrugged. "Maybe. I'm not the only one who comes up here. Come on, unless you're too scared to try it?"

"Not likely!" Ki shot back.

Going to the railing, they found a rickety wooden framework festooned with prickly brown rose canes.

"We'll have to jump," said Tobin, gauging the distance.

"And hope the damn thing holds." Ki looked down, frowning. The ground fell away sharply below the balcony. Missing the trellis meant a fall of twenty feet or more.

Una rested her chin in one gloved hand. "Should I go look for a ladder?"

This was a side of Una Tobin had never seen. She was clearly enjoying herself, taunting them from her high perch. Pulling on his gloves, Tobin climbed onto the railing and jumped. The trellis creaked and groaned and the rose thorns pierced his gloves, but the framework held. Swearing under his breath, he clambered up to join her.

Una caught his wrist as he reached the eaves and helped him up. Ki and Arengil scrambled up beside them and looked around in surprise.

The palace was a huge, rambling structure and the snow-covered roofs stretched out before them like a gently rolling countryside: acres of sloping slates and low gables. Chimney pots jutted up like blasted trees, bleeding soot around their bases. Dragon statues, many with broken wings or missing heads, dotted ridgelines and cornices, their peeling gilt faded to cheap brass in the afternoon light. Behind Una, a line of footprints made a dotted path.

"I saw this once, but from higher," said Tobin. When the others looked at him strangely, he explained, "A wizard showed me the city in a vision once. We flew over it, like eagles."

"Oh, I love magic!" cried Una.

"Now what?" Ki demanded, impatient to get started.

"Follow me, and walk where I do. There are lots of rotten spots."

Picking her way among the peaks and chimneys, she led them to a broad, level stretch sheltered between two high ridgelines. It was about fifty feet square and guarded by three undamaged roof dragons. They were far from the edge, and well away from prying eyes.

Several wooden crates stood under a slight overhang to their right. Una opened one and took out four wooden swords. "Welcome to my practice ground, my lords." Grinning, she made them a deep bow. "Will this do?"

"You say you're not the only one who comes up here?" Tobin asked.

"No, but most people only come up at night in the summer, to—you know."

Ki nudged him with his elbow. "We'll have to remember that!"

Una blushed, but pretended not to hear. "If you go over that way, you can see the practice grounds," she said, pointing west through a valley of roof pitches. "And if you go that way, to the north, you'll eventually come to my family's villa at the far end of the palace—if you don't get lost or fall through someone's ceiling."

Arengil picked up one of the wooden blades and made a few practice feints. "I still don't know what you want with sword lessons. Even if you do learn, the king will never let you fight."

"Maybe it won't always be this way," Una shot back. "Maybe the old ways will come back."

"She can learn if she wants to," Tobin said, liking her more than he ever had before. He paused, then added wryly, "Maybe we could continue with my dancing lessons here, too."

𝒯hat winter was not a mild one, even by coastal reckoning, but there was more rain than snow. For Tobin and the others, this meant frequent chances of clear footing for their stolen rooftop lessons, though they were often soaked. They met on the roof whenever the weather and their other lessons allowed, and though Una had sworn them all to secrecy, she was the first to break it.

One sunny afternoon Tobin and Ki arrived to find another dark-haired girl waiting for them with Una and Arengil. She looked familiar.

"You remember my friend Kalis?" Una asked, shooting a mischievous look in Ki's direction. "She wants to learn, too."

Ki colored a bit as he bowed and Tobin recognized her as one of the girls Ki had danced with at Caliel's birthday ball.

"You don't mind, do you?" Una asked.

Tobin shrugged and turned away, the lie burning in his cheeks.

*T*wo more girls joined them after that, and Tobin brought in Nikides, who needed more practice than any of them. Of course, Lutha couldn't be left out for long, or their squires. Ki dubbed the group "Prince Tobin's Sword Fighting Academy."

Tobin rather enjoyed having his own secret cabal, and was grateful to Una for another reason, as well. The roof was a safe place to call Brother. He stole up alone at least once a week and spoke the words.

He did it unwillingly at first. The scar on Ki's forehead served as a reminder of one transgression, and Orun's death still haunted Tobin's dreams. The first few times he called Brother here he brought the doll and wouldn't let Ki come with him, not yet trusting the ghost to behave.

But Brother was very quiet these days, and showed no interest in Tobin or their surroundings. Tobin wondered if he'd fade again, the way he had before their father's death. But as the weeks passed Brother retained his strangely solid appearance. Was it the new binding, Tobin wondered, that had given him the strength to kill?

When he brought Ki up at last, they discovered that he couldn't see Brother unless Tobin told Brother to show himself.

"Just as well. I don't much want to see him," said Ki.

Tobin didn't, either. Ki's scar might be fading, but not the memory of how it got there.

*A*s the winter went on it became clear to Tobin that some of the girls in his "Academy" were more interested in meeting with boys than in the lessons, and that the boys had no objection to this situation. Kalis and Ki occasionally wandered off among the chimney pots, and returned sharing secret smiles. Barieus stopped pining for the unattainable Lynx; he lost his heart to red-haired Lady Mora after she broke his finger during a bout and was much more cheerful after that.

Una didn't try to kiss Tobin again, but he sometimes sensed she wanted to. Grappling during practice fights, he couldn't help noticing the emerging curves of her body. Girls ripened sooner, Ki said, and got ideas sooner, too. That was all well and good for him, Tobin thought miserably.

Even if he'd wanted girls to like him, he couldn't imagine what Una saw in him. Sparring on the roof, or dancing at a ball, he could feel her waiting for some sign that her feelings were returned. It made him feel guilty, though he was certain he'd done nothing to mislead her. It was all very confusing, and he only made things worse when he made her a gold pendant in the shape of a sword. Mistaking the gesture, she wore it openly like a love token.

During lessons, at least, he could offer her something honest. They were well matched in size and often paired off against each other. She learned quickly, surprising them all with her progress.

Tobin found a more formidable opponent in Arengil. Though the 'faie appeared no older than Urmanis, he had years more training than any of them. He didn't lord it over anyone, though, but taught them the Aurënfaie style of dueling, which relied more on skillful dodging than grappling. Before long Tobin and the other boys were putting Arengil's techniques to good use during practices with the other Companions. The others began to remark on it, especially after Ki managed to split Mago's lip with his elbow. Ki grinned about that for two days and gifted Arengil his best dagger the next time they met.

Chapter 15

As the last storms of Klesin blew themselves out across the sea, the Companions waited anxiously for news of renewed fighting; surely the king couldn't keep Korin hidden away like a daughter, now that he was grown? Reports came of a few skirmishes along the frontier, but neither King Erius nor the Plenimaran Overlord seemed in any hurry to rejoin the battle.

As always, Nikides was the first to hear news. "Grandfather says there's talk of a truce," he informed the others glumly over breakfast one morning.

Everyone groaned. Peace meant no chance to prove themselves in battle. Korin said nothing, but Tobin knew his cousin suffered more than the rest of them, knowing that he was the reason they'd all been held back for so long.

Wine flowed ever more freely in the mess after that, and the boys grumbled and snapped at each other at practice.

No more news came, but within the week Tobin had a nightmare he hadn't had in months.

In it, he huddled in a corner, watching his mother pace the tiny room at the top of the watchtower. Ariani rushed from window to window, clutching the rag doll to her breast like an infant. Brother crouched in the shadows, staring at Tobin with knowing black eyes.

"He's found us again!" Ariani cried, then she was grasping Tobin by the arm, pulling him across the room, toward the west window, the one that overlooked the river.

"He's coming," Brother agreed from his corner.

Tobin woke to find Brother watching him from the foot of the curtained bed.

He's coming. The ghost's thin lips did not move as he echoed his dream self.

Ki stirred beside him, mumbling blearily into the pillow.

"It's nothing. Go back to sleep." His head throbbed from all the wine he'd drunk at mess that night, but it wasn't that making his stomach so queasy.

"The king is really coming back?" he whispered to Brother.

The ghost nodded and faded away.

Too upset to sleep, Tobin slipped out of bed and wrapped himself in the woolen robe Molay always left ready for him on a nearby chair. The draperies were still pulled across the balcony windows, but early light was creeping in around the edges. Outside, crows were arguing somewhere in the garden.

"Do you need me, my prince?" Baldus called sleepily from his pallet.

"No, go back to sleep."

Tobin went out onto the balcony. Three crows sat in a budding oak just below the rail, fluffing their breasts against the cold. All over the city, smoke from breakfast hearths rose straight up in the still air, threads of blue against the pink-and-gold sky. Beyond the harbor mouth the sea sparkled with whitecaps. Tobin gazed out at the horizon, imagining the king out there somewhere, maybe even now sailing for home.

But we'd have heard! The king wouldn't just sneak into Ero like some raider in the night. He'd been gone for years; there would be fanfare and festivals.

Tobin sat down on the stone balustrade, waiting for the oppressive feel of the dream to pass. Instead, it grew stronger, making his heart beat so fast that dark spots began to dance in front of his eyes.

He tried Arkoniel's mind-clearing trick, concentrating

on the crows' shining feathers. Gradually the panic receded, leaving him with the more immediate problem of Brother's warning.

Chilled through, he went inside and curled up in an armchair by the banked hearth. Someone walked quickly past his room, but otherwise the Companions' wing was still quiet. The daily bustle of palace life hadn't yet begun.

What if he comes today? Tobin wondered, hugging his knees. Then a happy inspiration came to him. Tharin knew the king! He'd know what to do.

"What could he do?" Brother hissed at him from the shadows behind his chair.

Before Tobin could think of an answer a loud slam and a string of laughing curses came from the direction of the dressing room. Someone had come through the secret passage that connected Tobin's room to Korin's. He ordered Brother away just as Korin and Tanil burst in, still dressed in their nightshirts. Baldus leaped up with a startled squeak and Ki let out a muffled complaint from the bed.

"Father's coming home!" Korin shouted, pulling Tobin from his chair and dancing him around the room. "A messenger just arrived. His ship put in at Cirna three days ago."

He's found us again!

"The king? Today?" Ki stuck his head out through the bed curtains, shaking tangled brown hair out of his eyes.

"Not today." Releasing Tobin, Korin flung back the bed curtains and vaulted in beside Ki. "The seas are still rough, so he's coming the rest of the way overland. We're to meet him in Atyion, Tob. Looks like you're going to get your birthday wish at last!"

"Atyion?" The good news barely registered.

Tanil flopped down on Ki's other side and used him for an armrest. "Finally, a reason to get out of the city! And we all get to be part of the king's procession back to the city!" Tanil looked as pleased as Korin.

"Why Atyion?" Tobin asked.

"To honor you, I imagine," Korin replied. "After all, Father hasn't seen you since you were born."

No, but I've seen him, thought Tobin, remembering the glint of sunlight on a golden helm.

Korin jumped up and began pacing like a general planning a campaign. "The messenger came to me first, but it won't be long before everyone knows. The whole city will be in an uproar within the hour, and half the damn court will want to come with us." He tousled Ki's hair and yanked the coverlet off him. "Up now, squire, and to your duty. You and Tobin help wake the others. Tell everyone light packs only; no servants or baggage. We can be gone before anyone's the wiser."

"Now? Right now?" Tobin stammered, wondering if he'd have time to speak with Tharin before they left.

"Why not? Let's see. My guard and yours should satisfy Lord Hylus—" Korin headed back toward the dressing room. "With an early start, we can be there by supper tomorrow." He paused, beaming at Tobin. "I can't wait for him to meet you!"

*T*he expected uproar was already beginning as Tobin and Ki went to wake the others. Lutha and Nikides were up, but it took some pounding to rouse Orneus.

Ki grinned at the string of muffled curses that greeted them from inside. A moment later the door inched open and Lynx peered out at them. Even wine sick, he was his usual agreeable self. "What's going on?" he asked, yawning. "Orneus is still, uh—asleep."

"Asleep?" Ki wrinkled his nose as a whiff of sour vomit floated into the corridor.

Lynx gave a rueful shrug, but brightened when he heard their news. "Don't worry, I'll have him ready!"

Master Porion praised Korin's plan. "Meet the king like warriors, boys, not a pack of soft courtiers!" he said, slapping the prince on the back.

Molay and Ki insisted on overseeing everything.

Baldus was dispatched to Tharin with orders to ready the men and horses. While everyone else was busy, Tobin slipped into the dressing room.

If leaving the doll behind meant being free of Brother for a few days, it would have been an easy choice, but the ghost's new habit of showing up where and when he pleased was getting out of hand. Tobin took the doll down from its hiding place and shoved it to the bottom of his pack. As he yanked the straps tight, it occurred to him that Atyion should have been Brother's home, too.

Despite their haste, it was almost noon before Korin had his column properly formed up in the front courtyard. The Companions wore the colors and arms of their own houses, as was the custom when riding out from the city, and lord and squire alike wore the scarlet baldric bearing the Prince Royal's white dragon crest. Their helms and shields shone bravely in the midday light.

Korin's guard was resplendent in scarlet and white, and Tobin's wore blue. Tharin, as always on such occasions, wore noble dress and a baldric of Tobin's colors.

A crowd of courtiers had gathered to see them off, cheering and waving scarves and hats.

"Look Tobin, there's your lady," Korin called. Una stood with Arengil and several girls from the secret sword school. The other Companions heard and laughed. Blushing, Tobin followed Ki over to say good-bye.

Arengil made them an exaggerated bow. "Behold the glorious warriors of Skala!" He stroked Gosi's nose, admiring the golden rosettes that adorned the gelding's new harness. "So much for the peasant prince, eh? You look like you just stepped out of a tapestry."

"Yes," said Una. "I suppose we'll have to let our dancing lessons go for now. How long will you be gone?"

"I don't know," Tobin told her.

"Come on!" Korin shouted, wheeling his horse about

and brandishing his sword. "Let's not keep my father waiting. To Atyion!"

"To Atyion!" the others cried, leaping into the saddle.

As Tobin turned to go, Una kissed him on the cheek, then disappeared into the crowd.

Swept up in the excitement of the preparations, Tobin had been able to forget his fears for a little while, but the inevitable boredom of a long ride gave them space to creep in again.

He was going to meet the king. Because of this man, his mother had never been queen. Perhaps if she'd worn the crown, she wouldn't have gone mad. And perhaps Brother wouldn't have died and they could have grown up together at court, or in Atyion, instead of hidden away in the mountains.

If not for him, Tobin thought with startling bitterness, *I'd have grown up knowing my true face.*

Chapter 16

Word of the king's return had reached Niryn by secret messenger a week earlier. It seemed his business in Ilear would have to wait; the king's brief letter ordered the wizard to meet him quietly at Cirna.

Nothing could have suited Niryn better. Under cover of darkness, he left the city with a small contingent of Harrier Guard, riding north.

Situated at the narrowest point of the isthmus, the fortress at Cirna belonged to Prince Tobin, at least in name. After Orun's timely death, the king had seen fit in his wisdom (and with some subtle manipulation) to make Niryn Lord Protector here. Built on a rocky, windswept scrap of ground inhabited by a few goatherds and fishermen, bounded on either side by precipitous cliffs, the Cirna fortress was, in its own way, as important as Atyion. Its power lay not in resources, but in location. The master of Cirna guarded the only land route into Skala.

The massive walled fortress stood at the center of the isthmus, straddling the only road. On either side stone walls twice the height of a man and thick as a house ran from its outer walls to the cliffs on either side, and had withstood the attacks of Plenimaran armies, Zengati raiders, even the witches of the hill folk. The tolls collected at its gates were not inconsiderable, and Niryn's share had already enlarged his own coffers.

But gold was not what made his heart swell as the grim fortress loomed out of the salt-laden mist ahead of him. Cirna represented the consolidation of his power over the king.

It had not been easy to turn the king against Rhius. But turning him against the odious Orun had been another matter entirely. In the latter case, there had been more than enough evidence against the man's character. But Duke Rhius's life had been above reproach, and the bonds forged between the men as Companions seemed to hold for life. Perhaps Erius had pressed Rhius to marry his only sister, thus safely binding the powerful holdings at Cirna and Atyion to the throne, but his affection for the man had been genuine. That had presented a significant obstacle in the early days of Niryn's rising influence. But at last Rhius had been so unwise as to speak openly against the killing of female Kin, and the king's patience had worn thin. When Rhius was finally killed in battle, only Niryn guessed at the relief behind the king's extravagant show of grief.

That had removed one obstacle from Niryn's path. Today he would deal with an even greater threat.

The isthmus road took Niryn and his riders along the top of the eastern cliffs and from here, through a lowering curtain of drizzle, he saw the royal flagship and her escorts riding at anchor in the little harbor below.

Crossing the Inner Sea so early in the spring was a risky undertaking and the vessels all showed signs of damage. Aboard the king's ship sailors were swarming busily at their repairs in the sheets.

Riding down the muddy switchback road to the village, Niryn found several men of the King's Guard waiting for him on the shingle. They rowed him out in a longboat and Lord General Rheynaris was there to greet him as he hoisted himself over the ship's rail.

"Welcome aboard, Lord Niryn. The king's waiting for you below."

Niryn glanced around as he followed Rheynaris. Across the deck a cluster of younger nobles was watching him with apparent curiosity. One of them made a warding sign when he thought Niryn wasn't looking.

"Tell me, Rheynaris, who is that young fellow there?"

"With the yellow hair? That's Solari's oldest son, Nevus. He's one of the king's new equerries."

Niryn frowned; he'd heard nothing of this. Lord Solari had been one of Rhius' liegemen.

"How is the king?" Niryn inquired when they were out of earshot of the others.

"Glad to be home, I'd say." Rheynaris paused as they neared the cabin. "He has been more—changeable since we left Mycena. It's always worse when he's away from battle."

Niryn nodded his thanks for the warning and the general tapped lightly at the door.

"Enter!" a gruff voice called.

Erius reclined on the cabin's narrow bunk, writing on a lap desk propped across his knees. The wizard waited at respectful attention, listening to the busy scratch of the goose quill. The cabin was unheated; Niryn could see his breath, but Erius had his tunic unbuttoned like a common soldier. His hair and beard were greyer, the wizard noted, and framed a face more careworn.

Finishing with a flourish of the quill, Erius set the desk aside and swung his legs over the edge of the bunk. "Hello, Niryn. You've wasted no time. I didn't expect to see you before tomorrow."

The wizard bowed. "Welcome home, Majesty."

Erius pushed a stool his way with one foot. "Sit, and give me news from home."

Niryn quickly touched on general news, downplaying a recent wave of plague that had decimated several northern towns. "The high priest of the Achis temple is being held for treason," he went on, moving on to more important business. "He was heard on at least three occasions speaking of that mythical queen they keep seeing in their fever dreams."

Erius frowned. "You told me that was all done with."

"They're only dreams, my king, born of fear and wishful thinking. But, as you know all too well, my liege, a dream can be dangerous if allowed to take root in ignorant minds."

"That's what I have you for, isn't it?" Erius lifted a sheaf of parchments from the desk. "Chancellor Hylus reports more dead of plague, and winter crops failing as far inland as Elio and Gormad. No wonder the people think themselves cursed and dream of queens. I'm beginning to wonder how much of a kingdom I'll have left to pass on." The corner of his left eye twitched. "I destroyed the tablet, pulled down the steles, but the words of the Oracle have not faded."

Niryn's fingers hardly moved as he cast a soothing spell. "Everyone is speculating on whether the truce will hold. What do you think, Majesty?"

Erius sighed and rubbed a hand over his beard. "It's a farmers' truce, at best. As soon as the Plenimarans get a harvest in and replenish their granaries, I expect we'll find ourselves marching back across Mycena. In the meantime, we'd better do the same. These damn droughts are as much our enemy as the Overlord's armies. All the same, I'm not sorry for a bit of a rest. I'll be glad of music and decent food again, and sleeping without an ear cocked for alarms." He gave the wizard a rueful smile. "I never thought I'd grow weary of war, my friend, but truth is I'm glad for this truce. I don't suppose my son will be, though. How is Korin?"

"Well, Majesty, very well. But restless, as you say."

Erius chuckled darkly. "Restless, eh? That's a nice way of putting it, much nicer than the reports I get from Porion—drinking, whoring, carrying on. Not that I was any better at his age, of course, but I was blooded by then. Who can blame him for itching to fight? You should read the letters he sends me, begging to join me in Mycena. By the Flame, he doesn't know how it's galled me keeping him wrapped in silk for so long."

"And yet what choice did you have, Majesty, with no other heir but a sickly nephew?" This was an old dance between them.

"Ah, yes, Tobin. But not so sickly, after all, it seems. Orun's reams of complaints aside, Korin and Porion both give him nothing but praise. What do you make of the boy, now that you've seen him for yourself?"

"He's an odd little fellow, in most respects. Rather sullen from what I've seen, but something of an artist. In fact he's already made a name for himself at court with bits of jewelry and carvings."

Erius nodded fondly. "He gets that from his mother. But there's more to him than that, I hear. Korin claims the boy is almost as good with a sword as he is."

"He does seem skilled, as is that peasant squire of his."

The instant the words left his lips Niryn knew he'd taken a misstep; the sudden wild glare was in the king's eyes, presaging a fit.

"Peasant?"

Niryn skittered back off his stool as Erius lurched up, knocking the lap desk to the floor. The lid flew open, scattering wax, parchments, and writing implements in all directions. The sand shaker and a pot of ink burst, spreading a gritty black puddle across the worn boards. "Is that how you refer to a Companion of the royal house?" he roared.

"Forgive me, Majesty!" These passions came on so suddenly, so unpredictably, that even Niryn could not forestall them. As far as he knew, Erius cared nothing for the boy.

"Answer my question, damn you!" Erius shouted as the rage built in him. "Is that how you speak of a Companion, you scullion's spunk? You limp pizzle of—"

Spittle flew from his lips. Niryn fell to his knees, fighting the urge to wipe his face. "No, Majesty."

Erius stood over him, still screaming abuse. It began with insults, but soon devolved to incoherent raving, then to a choked, wheezing snarl. Niryn kept his gaze downcast as one did when faced with a vicious dog, but he watched from the corner of his eye in case the king reached for a weapon. It had happened before.

The outburst ceased abruptly, as they always did, and Niryn slowly raised his head. The king swayed slightly, chest heaving, fists clenched at his sides. His eyes were as blank as a doll's.

Rheynaris looked in at the door.

"It's over," Niryn whispered, waving him off. Rising, he took the king gently by the arm. "Please, Your Majesty, sit down. You're weary."

Docile as an exhausted child, Erius let himself be guided back into the bunk. Leaning back against the wall, he closed his eyes. Niryn quickly gathered up the desk and its scattered contents, then dragged a small rug over the spilled ink.

By the time he'd finished the king's eyes were open again, but he was still lost in that strange fog that always followed these fits. Niryn sat down again.

"What—what was I saying?" the king croaked.

"Your nephew's squire, my king. We were speaking of how some at court have been unkind about the boy's upbringing. They call him a 'grass knight,' I believe. Prince Korin has always been very passionate in his defense."

"What? Passionate, you say?" The king blinked at him, struggling to regain his composure. Poor man, he still believed that the fits were momentary, that no one noticed. "Yes, passionate, like his dear mother. Poor Ariani, they tell me she's killed herself . . ."

No wonder General Rheynaris had sounded so relieved when he'd reported the king's departure from the field. Over the past year his secret missives had been full of these episodes. The report of Orun's death had sent the king into a rage so fierce it had required a drysian's draught to calm him. Strange, since his regard for the man had cooled markedly over the past few years. Niryn had worked carefully at that, finally convincing Erius to relieve him of his guardianship. Orun's influence over the boy had been easily construed as treason. Why would the man's death upset him?

Erius rubbed at his eyes. When he looked up, they were clear and shrewd again. "I've sent word to the boys to meet us at Atyion." He chuckled. "My son wrote me quite a letter a while back, chastising me for not letting his cousin see his estates."

"That was Orun's doing, of course," Niryn told him. "He replaced the steward with his own man and had already begun to line his pockets."

"The greedy fool saved me the trouble of executing him." He sat up and clapped Niryn on the shoulder. "Seems you were right about him. He finally overreached. I should have listened to you sooner, I know, but he was a good friend during my mother's dark times."

"Your loyalty is legend, Majesty. His death has left certain complications, however. Atyion cannot be left without a Protector."

"Of course not. I've given the post to Solari."

"Lord Solari, my king?" Niryn's heart sank as he recalled the young man he'd seen on deck.

"Duke Solari, now. I've made him Protector of Atyion."

Niryn clenched his fists in the folds of his robe, struggling to hide his disappointment. He'd expected Erius to consult him on the decision of a successor. Now the greatest plum in the kingdom had fallen beyond his reach.

"Yes, he's a much better choice than Orun. He was one of Rhius' generals, you know; loyal enough, but ambitious, too." Erius' mouth tightened into a humorless smile. "The garrison at Atyion trusts him. So does Tobin. I've sent Solari ahead to settle in."

"I see the wisdom in your choice, but I wonder what Tharin will have to say? Perhaps he had hopes in that direction, as well."

Erius shook his head. "Tharin's a good man, but he never did have any ambition. If it weren't for Rhius, he'd still be a landless third son, breeding horses at Atyion. I don't think we need concern ourselves with what he thinks."

"He is very protective of the prince, however. He won't be parted from him."

"Poor fellow. All he ever cared for was Rhius. I suppose he'll end his days hovering around the boy, nursing old memories."

"And is Solari as loyal to the prince?"

The hard smile returned. "He's loyal to me. He'll protect the prince as long as it preserves my favor. Should that favor change for some reason, I daresay we'll find him a man ready to serve his king. Now, what's all this about Korin knocking up some chambermaid? Do you know anything of it?"

"Why—yes, Majesty, it's true, but I hadn't thought to trouble you with it until you returned." For once, Niryn was caught completely off guard. He'd only learned of it a few weeks before, thanks to one of his more observant spies among the Old Palace servants. Korin didn't know; the girl had been too wise to brag of the child's paternity. "She's of low birth, as you say. Kalar, I think the name is."

Erius was still watching him closely, no doubt wondering why his chief wizard had sent no word.

"May I speak candidly, Majesty?" Niryn's mind raced, already turning the situation to his advantage.

"You know I depend on your counsel."

"I'm neither a father nor a warrior, so forgive me if I misspeak out of ignorance, but I'm increasingly concerned for Prince Korin. You've been gone for so long, you hardly know the young man he's become. These girls he beds, and the drinking—"

He paused, watching for warning signs, but Erius merely nodded for him to continue.

"For he is a man now, strong and well trained. I've heard Master Porion say more than once that young warriors are like fine coursing hounds; if you keep them from the field, they either grow fat and lose their spirit, or turn vicious. Let him be the warrior you've made him to be, and all the rest will fall by the wayside. He lives to please you.

"But more than that, my king, the people must see him as a worthy successor. His excesses are already common gossip around the city and without the strength of deeds to balance them?" He paused meaningfully. "And now he's throwing bastards. Surely you see where this could lead? With no legitimate heir, even a by-blow might gather supporters. Especially if the child should be a girl."

Erius' knuckles went white, but Niryn knew how to play this tune. "The thought of your ancient line tainted with such common blood—"

"You're quite right, of course. Kill the bitch before she whelps."

"I will see to it personally." He would have in any event; his Nalia needed no competitors, even a servant's brat with royal blood in her veins.

"Ah, Korin, Korin, what am I to do with you?" Erius shook his head. "He's all I have, Niryn. I've lived in fear of losing him since his poor mother and the other children died. I haven't been able to get another child on any woman since. Every one has been stillborn, or a monstrous thing that couldn't live. This bastard, now—"

Niryn did not have to touch the king's mind to know his heart, and the words he could not bring himself to say. *What if my son's children are monsters, too?* That would be the final proof of Illior's curse on his line.

"He'll soon be old enough to marry, Majesty. Pair him with a healthy wife of good family and he'll give you fine, strong grandchildren."

"You're right, as always." The king let out a long sigh. "What would I do without you, eh? I thank the Four that wizards live so long. You're a young man now, Niryn. The knowledge that you'll still be standing by the throne of Skala generations from now is a great comfort to me."

Niryn bowed deeply. "I live for nothing else, Majesty."

Chapter 17

The country north of Ero was a rolling mix of forest and open farmland that stretched from the sea's edge to the mountains just visible in the west. The trees were just beginning to bud, Ki noted, but crocus and blue cockscomb brightened the muddy fields and ditches. In the villages they passed, the temples and roadside shrines were decorated with garlands of them for the Dalna feasts.

The ride to Atyion was a long one and the Companions and their guard entertained each other with songs and stories to pass the time. It was all new country to Tobin, but Ki had traveled this road with his father and later with Iya when she brought him south to the keep.

Early on the second day a great island chain came into view ahead of them, rising like huge breaching whales to the horizon. When they slowed to rest the horses, Porion, Tharin, and Korin's captain, a dark, weathered lord named Melnoth, helped pass the time trading stories of fighting pirates and Plenimarans in those waters, and of the sacred island of Kouros where the first hierophant and his people had made landfall and established their court.

"You can feel the magic in the very stones, there, boys," Porion told them. "And it's no magic known to the Four."

"That's because the Old Ones scratched their spells all over the rocks and painted them in the caves above the surf," said Melnoth. "The hierophant brought the worship of the Four across the water with him, but couldn't displace the old powers that still lurk there. They say that's why his son moved the court to Benshâl."

"I always had strange dreams there," Tharin mused.

"But aren't there the same sort of marks on the rocks all along the coast?" asked Korin. "The Old Ones lived all around the Inner Sea."

"Old Ones?" asked Tobin.

"The hill tribes they're called now," Porion explained. "Little dark folk who practice the old ways of necromancy."

"They're great thieves, as well," one of Korin's guardsmen added. "Proper folk used to hunt them like vermin."

"Yes we did," old Laris muttered, but he looked sad as he said it.

"So long as what's left of them keep to the mountains, they're safe enough," Korin said, cocksure as if he'd driven them there himself.

Others added tales of their own. The hill folk sacrificed young men and children to their evil goddess. They rutted like animals in the fields under certain moons and always ate their meat raw. Their witches could change into beasts and demons at will, kill by blowing through a hollow branch, and summon the dead.

Tobin knew that these were Lhel's people they spoke of. He had to press his lips together to keep from arguing when some of the older soldiers spoke of bewitchments and withering curses, and could tell that Ki was no happier hearing such stories. He loved the witch who'd twice saved his life. Lhel was just a healer, an herb witch, and she'd been a wise friend to them both.

All the same, Tobin couldn't deny that she'd used blood and bits of Brother's bones in her magic. That did seem like necromancy, now that he thought of it. A fleeting image flashed to mind: a needle flashing in firelight, and Brother's bloody tears falling through the air. The binding scar began to itch and Tobin had to rub at it to make it stop.

"There are plenty of good Skalan families who'd find a bit of that blood in their own veins, if they thought to ask their grandmothers," Tharin was saying. "As for their magic, I guess I'd have used whatever I had at hand, too, if a pack of strangers decided to take my lands from me. And so would the rest of you."

This got only a few grudging nods, but Tobin was grateful. Lhel always spoke well of Tharin. Tobin wondered what he'd make of her.

The road gradually turned inland, taking them through dense woodland far from the sound of the sea. At midafternoon Tharin called a halt and pointed to a pair of granite pillars flanking the road. They were weathered and mossy, but Tobin could still make out the faint outline of a spreading oak carved on them.

"Do you know what those are?" Tharin asked.

Tobin pulled out his father's oak tree signet; the design was the same. "This is the boundary, isn't it?"

"Ride forward and enter your lands, coz," said Korin, grinning at him. "All hail Tobin, son of Rhius, Prince of Ero, and rightful scion of Atyion!"

The rest of the company cheered and beat their shields as Tobin nudged Gosi forward. He felt silly with all the fuss; it was the same thick forest on both sides of the markers.

A few miles farther on, however, the woods ended and the road wound on through an open plain toward the distant sea. Topping a crest in the road, Korin reined in and pointed. "There it is, the finest holding outside Ero."

Tobin gaped. "That's all—mine?"

"It is! Or will be, anyway, when you come of age."

In the distance, a large town lay in the bend of a meandering river that snaked its way to the sea. The farmlands were dotted with tidy steadings and laced with low stone walls. Sheep and large herds of horses grazed in some, while others enclosed fields and budding vineyards.

But Tobin had eyes only for the town and massive castle that dominated the plain by the river. High stone curtain walls studded with round bastions and corbels and overhung by extensive hoardings of stone and wood enclosed the landward sides of both. The castle itself was square, and dominated by two large towers of reddish brown stone. Almost as large as the New Palace and more heavily fortified, it dwarfed the town below.

"That's Atyion?" Tobin whispered in disbelief. He'd heard of its great wealth and grandeur, but with nothing to compare it to, he'd imagined it simply a larger sort of keep.

"I told you it was big," said Ki.

Tharin shaded his eyes and squinted at the long banners flying from the towers and the peaked roofs of the corbels. "Those aren't your colors."

"I don't see Father's, either," said Korin. "Looks like we're in time to give him welcome, after all. Tobin, you take the lead and let the lazy fools know you're coming!"

The standard-bearers galloped ahead down the muddy, rutted road to announce them. The Companions followed at a fast trot. The farmers and drovers they met cheered their approach. By the time they reached the gates a crowd had gathered to greet them. Tobin's standard was mounted on the tall pole over the gate, but just below it hung another, one he and Tharin recognized—Solari's golden sun on a green field. It wasn't quite the same, though. The device at the top of the standard pole was not the bronze ring of a lord, but the silver crescent of a duke.

"Looks like Father has chosen Atyion's new Lord Protector already," said Korin.

"And promoted him, too," Tharin noted.

"He was your father's liegeman, wasn't he?" asked Korin.

Tobin nodded.

"Well, that's an improvement over the last choice!" Tharin said. "Your father would be pleased."

Tobin wasn't so certain. He'd last seen Solari when he came with the others to bring home his father's ashes. Solari and Lord Nyanis had been his father's most trusted liegemen. The day Solari had come to take leave of Tobin, however, Brother had appeared, whispering of treachery.

He told his captain he would be lord of Atyion himself in a year—

"He's lord of Atyion now?" he asked.

"No, that passed to you by right," Tharin assured him. "But Atyion must have a Protector until you come of age."

Alerted by the standard-bearer's arrival, a larger crowd had gathered in the market square beyond the gate. Hundreds of people pressed forward to catch a glimpse of him, laughing and waving kerchiefs and scraps of blue cloth in the air. Korin and the others fell back, letting Tobin take the lead. The roar took on a rhythm; the crowd was chanting his name.

"To-bin! To-bin! To-bin!"

He gazed around in wonder, then raised his hand in a tentative wave. The cheering doubled. These people had never laid eyes on him before, yet they seemed to know him on sight, and to love him.

His heart swelled with a pride he'd never felt before. Drawing his sword, he saluted the crowd. They parted before him as Tharin led the way down a winding, cobbled street to the castle.

Children and dogs ran excitedly beside their horses and women leaned out of windows, waving scarves at the men below. Looking back over his shoulder, Tobin saw that Ki looked as happy as if he owned the place himself.

Catching Tobin's eye, he hollered, "I told you, didn't I?"

"Home at last!" Tharin cried, overhearing.

Tobin had always thought of the keep as home, but Tharin had been born here, and his own father, too. They'd ridden these streets together, played along the walls and riverbank, and in the castle looming ahead.

Tobin pulled out the signet and ring and clasped them, imagining his father bringing his bride here to the same sort of welcome. But his new sense of homecoming was already mingled with something darker; this should have been his home, too.

The town was clean and prosperous. The market

squares they passed were lined with shops and stalls, and the stone-and-timber buildings well built and in good repair. Corrals filled with fine horses seemed to be everywhere, too.

They were nearly to the castle walls before it occurred to Tobin that he'd seen no beggars in the streets and no signs of plague.

A wide moat separated the town from the castle walls. The drawbridge was down and they crossed it and galloped through the gate into an enormous bailey.

Inside the safety of the curtain wall stood a small village of barracks and stables, cottages, and rows of workmen's stalls and forges.

"By the Light," Lutha exclaimed. "You could fit most of the Palatine in here!"

There were more horse corrals, and herds of sheep, goats, and pigs watched over by children who waved excitedly to him as he passed.

Ranks of soldiers lined the way; some wearing his colors, others in Solari's. They shouted his name and Korin's, called out to Tharin, and beat their shields with their sword hilts and bows as the entourage passed. Tobin tried to count them, but couldn't. There were hundreds. He was glad to recognize a few faces here and there; men who'd served with his father.

"About time you brought the prince home!" an old veteran called out to Tharin, restraining a huge boarhound on a chain. The dog barked and struggled; it seemed to Tobin the creature was looking at him.

"I told you I would one day!" Tharin shouted back. This drew even more cheering.

Solari and a blond noblewoman stood waiting for them at the head of the castle's broad entrance stair.

Solari's herald raised a trumpet and sounded a shrill salute, then cried out in a loud, formal voice: "Greetings to Korin, son of Erius, Prince Royal of Skala, and to Prince Tobin, son of Rhius and Ariani, Scion of Atyion. Duke

Solari, lord of Evermere and Fair Haven and Lord Protector of Atyion and his good lady, Duchess Savia, bid you most welcome."

Tobin swung down from the saddle and let his Protector come to him. Solari's curly black hair and beard showed a thicker sprinkling of grey now, but his ruddy face was still youthful as he dropped to one knee and presented his sword hilt to Tobin.

"My liege, it is my very great honor to welcome you to your father's house, now yours. His Majesty, King Erius, has appointed me Lord Protector of Atyion until you come of age. I humbly seek your blessing."

Tobin clasped the hilt and looked hard into the man's eyes. Despite Brother's warning, he saw only welcome there and respect. Could Brother have been wrong, after all, or lying to make trouble, as he had with Ki?

As Solari smiled up at him, Tobin wanted Brother to be wrong. "You have my blessing, Duke Solari. It's good to see you again."

Solari rose and presented his lady. "My wife, Your Highness."

Savia curtsied deeply and kissed him on both cheeks. "Welcome home, my prince. I've wanted to meet you for so long!"

"I suppose it wouldn't be dignified for me to swing you up on my shoulders as I used to?" Solari said, dark eyes twinkling.

"I guess not!" Tobin laughed. "Allow me to present my royal cousin. And you remember Sir Kirothius, my squire."

Solari clasped hands with Ki. "You've both grown up so, I hardly recognize you. And here's Tharin, too! How are you, old friend? It's been too long."

"Indeed it has."

"I've felt like an intruder, wandering these halls without you and Rhius. But with his son here at last, things begin to feel right with the world again."

"How long have you been here?" asked Tharin. "We had no word you'd been appointed."

"The king invested me before we sailed from Mycena and sent me ahead to make the house ready for Prince Tobin and his own arrival."

"Is Lord Nyanis well?" Tobin asked. Nyanis had been Tobin's favorite among his father's generals. That sad day at the keep had been the last time he'd seen him, too.

"As far as I know, my prince. I've had no word otherwise." Solari ushered them up the stairs. "I've been with the king at the royal camp this past year. Nyanis is still entrenched with General Rynar above Nanta until we see if the truce holds."

As they passed beneath the arched portal the carved panel over the doors caught Tobin's eye; it showed a gauntleted hand holding Sakor's garlanded sword. He touched his heart and hilt as he passed under it and Korin did the same. But Tharin was frowning, first at the carving, and then at a swarthy, wide-set man wearing the silver chain and long tunic of a steward, who bowed low to them as they entered.

"Where's Hakone?" he asked Solari.

"He's finally grown too frail to carry out his duties, poor old fellow," Solari told him. "Orun replaced him with some squint-eyed fellow of his own, but I got rid of him quick enough and took the liberty of installing Eponis here, a trusted man of my own household."

"And of flying your own colors from the battlements," Tharin noted pointedly. "For a moment Prince Tobin thought he'd come to the wrong house."

"Highness, the fault is mine," Eponis rumbled, bowing to Tobin again. "I will see it is remedied at once."

"Thank you," said Tobin.

Solari and his lady led them on through a receiving chamber where heady incense burned before a household shrine as large as a shop. A black cat sat at the foot of it, tail curled around its feet, and watched them pass with eyes like gold coins. A grey-muzzled old bitch lay companion-ably beside it, but at Tobin's approach she lurched up stiffly and slunk away. The cat blinked placidly at him, then went on washing its face.

Beyond this, through a pillared gallery, lay the great hall. Entering for the first time, Tobin caught his breath in amazement.

Light streamed in through tall windows set high over-head, but even with the bright midday light flooding in, the peaks of the ceiling vaults were lost in shadow. Rows of stone columns supported the roof and cordoned off side chambers. The floor was made of colored bricks set in zigzag patterns, and the walls were hung with enormous tapestries. Gold and silver seemed to glint at him from all directions—plates on high shelves, shields and other war trophies hanging on the pillars, statues, and gracefully shaped vessels on the shelves of a dozen or more long sideboards. A company of servants in blue livery stood waiting at the center of the room.

A white cat lay beneath a nearby table, nursing a lit-ter of yellow and white kittens. Across the hall two more cats—one black and white, the other striped yellow—were leaping and rolling in play. A huge black tom with a white blaze on its chest sat washing its hind leg among the silver vessels on a nearby sideboard. Tobin had never seen so many cats indoors. Atyion must be plagued with mice, to need so many.

Tharin chuckled softly beside him, and Tobin realized he'd been gaping like a yokel. And he wasn't the only one.

"By the Flame!" Lutha gasped, and got no further than that. Even Alben and his friends were impressed.

"I've assigned servants to each of the Companions, since none of you are familiar with the house," Eponis in-formed them. "It's very easy to get lost if you don't know your way around."

"I can believe that!" Lutha exclaimed, and everyone laughed.

"Sir Tharin can guide me," Tobin said, anxious to keep his friend close by.

"As you wish, my prince."

"Any word of my father?" asked Korin.

"He's expected tomorrow, my prince," Solari replied. "All has been made ready." He turned to Tobin and smiled. "The servants can take you to your chambers if you'd like to rest. Or perhaps you'd like to see some of your castle, first."

Your castle. Tobin couldn't help grinning. "Yes, I would!"

They spent the afternoon exploring, with Solari and Tharin as their guides. The main living quarters lay in this tower and a wing flanking the gardens between it and the second. The other one served as fortress, granary, armory, and treasury. Tobin was amazed to learn that an army of several thousand men could be quartered there in time of siege.

A second wing parallel to the other closed the rectangle of ground and housed the servants' quarters, kitchens, laundries, brewing rooms, and other household offices. One large chamber was filled with weavers working at great clacking looms; in the next scores of women and girls sat singing together as they spun flax and wool into thread for the weavers.

Inside the rectangle formed by the towers and wings lay an expanse of gardens and groves, with an elegant little temple dedicated to Illior and Sakor. Pillared galleries on the upper floors of the main tower overlooked the grounds.

Tobin and the others were footsore and dazzled by the time Solari left them at their chambers to prepare for the evening feast.

The Companions had rooms high in the royal wing, along a gallery overlooking the gardens. Tobin and Korin

were given private chambers. The rest were divided between two large guest rooms.

Alone with Ki and Tharin, Tobin looked around his
room, heart beating faster. It had belonged to some young
man of his family, he could tell. The bed hangings were
worked with running horses, and there were weapons and
shields on the walls. A few toys lay carefully arranged on a
chest: a miniature ship, a wheeled horse, and a wooden
sword.

"These are just like the ones Father gave me!" Then his
heart skipped a beat. "These were his, weren't they? This
was my father's room."

"Yes. We slept here until—" Tharin paused and cleared
his throat roughly. "It would have been yours. It should
have been."

Just then a woman appeared in the doorway. She was
dressed like a courtier and her faded golden hair was
arranged in braids around her head. A heavy bunch of
keys hung on a golden chain at her girdle. She was accompanied by a battle-scarred yellow tom, who stalked over to
sniff at Tobin's boots.

The woman's face was lined with age, but she stood
straight as a warrior and her pale eyes were bright with joy
as she dropped gracefully to one knee before Tobin and
kissed his hand. "Welcome home, Prince Tobin." The cat
rose on his hind legs and butted his scabby head against
their hands.

"Thank you, my lady," Tobin replied, wondering who
she was. Her face seemed familiar somehow, though he
was certain he'd never met her before. Then, as Tharin
stepped to her side, Tobin realized that they had the same
pale eyes and hair, the same straight, strong nose.

"Allow me to present my aunt Lytia," Tharin said, obvi-
ously trying hard not to laugh at the look on Tobin's face.
"I still have a few cousins about the place, too, I think."

Lytia nodded. "Grannia oversees the pantries, and Oril
is Master of Horses now. I was a lady-in-waiting to your

grandmother, my prince, and to your mother, too, while she lived here. Afterward, your father made me keeper of the keys. I hope you'll accept my service?"

"Of course," Tobin replied, still looking from one to the other.

"Thank you, my prince." She looked down at the cat, who was winding himself around Tobin's ankles and purring loudly. "And this rude fellow is Master Ringtail, Atyion's chief rat slayer. He recognizes the master of the house, I see. He doesn't go to many except for me and Hakone, but he's certainly taken a liking to you."

Tobin knelt and gingerly stroked the cat's striped back, expecting it to turn on him the way dogs did. Instead, Ringtail thrust his whiskered muzzle under Tobin's chin and kneaded long sharp claws into his sleeve, demanding to be picked up. He was a strong, heavy animal, and had extra toes on each foot.

"Look at that! Seven toes. I pity the rat that comes in reach of them," Tobin exclaimed, delighted. The cats he'd seen in barns and stables were wild, hissing things. "And look, he must be a great warrior. All his wounds are in the front. I accept your service, too, Master Ringtail."

"There's another room he should see, Tharin," Lytia murmured. "I asked Lord Solari to leave it to us to show him."

"What room is that?" asked Tobin.

"Your parents' chamber, my prince. It's been kept just as they left it. I thought you might like to see it."

Tobin's heart knocked painfully against his ribs. "Yes, please. You, too, Ki," he said when his friend hung back.

Still cradling the heavy cat against his chest, Tobin followed Lytia and Tharin down the corridor to a large door carved with fruit trees and birds with long, flowing tails. Lytia took a key from her belt and unlocked the door.

It swung open on a handsomely appointed room bathed in late afternoon light. The bed hangings were dark blue worked with pairs of white swans in flight; the tapestries covering the walls echoed the theme. The balcony

doors stood wide, overlooking the gardens below. Someone had burned incense and beeswax within recently.
Tobin caught the underlying staleness of a room where no
one had lived for a long time, but it had none of the musty
rot smell he'd known at home. It was nothing like the sad,
half-empty rooms at the Ero house, either. This room had
been well tended, as if its occupants would soon return.

There were a number of fancy boxes and caskets
arranged on a dressing table, and the usual implements on
the writing desk that stood in front of one of the tall, mul-
lioned windows. Brightly enameled mazers lined a wine
board across the room, and carved ivory figures stood
ready on a gleaming game board by the hearth.

He let Ringtail down and the cat trailed after him as he
walked around the room, touching the bed hanging, picking up a game piece, running a fingertip over the inlaid lid
of a jewel box. He ached to find some echo of his father
here, but he was too aware of the others watching him.

"Thank you for showing me," he said at last.

Lytia gave him an understanding smile as she placed
the key in his hand and folded his fingers around it. "All
this is yours now. Come here whenever you like. It will always be kept ready."

She gave his hand a gentle squeeze and Tobin guessed
that she knew what he'd been seeking, and that he hadn't
found it.

Chapter 18

They feasted in the great hall that night at three long tables arranged in a half circle. Solari and his family sat
with Tobin and Korin. His eldest son by a previous wife
was off serving with the king. Savia's children, two young
boys and a pretty little daughter named Rose, sat with
them. The little girl spent most of the meal on Korin's
knee. The rest of the company was made up of the Companions, Solari's friends and generals, and a number of rich
merchants from the town. It was a raucous, clattering affair
made louder by a steady procession of minstrels and
bards.

Tobin had the seat of honor at the canopied head
table, but it was clear that Solari was the host. His men
served at table, and he ordered the courses, wines, and the
minstrels and entertainers. He fussed over Tobin and Korin
throughout the evening, choosing the choicest bits from
each platter and extolling the quality of each wine, the fruit
of Atyion's fine vineyards.

Course followed course, each a banquet in itself. Lady
Lytia stood by the servers' entrance and inspected each
dish closely before it was carried to the head table. The
first course alone was made up of beef with mustard, roast
woodcock, partridge, plover, and snipe. A fish course followed: eels in jelly, gurnard with syrup, fried minnows,
smoked pike in pastry, and boiled mussels stuffed with
bread and cheese. The desserts included cakes of three
kinds, pies both sweet and savory, with brightly decorated
pastry crusts.

Dozens of the castle cats kept them company, leaping

onto the tables in search of scraps and getting under the servers' feet. Tobin looked for his new friend, but Ringtail was nowhere to be seen.

"The cooks here put the royal kitchens to shame, my lady!" Korin exclaimed to Savia, licking his fingers happily.

"The credit belongs to Lady Lytia," the duchess replied. "She oversees the menus and the cooks, even the buying of the food. I don't know what we'd do without her."

"Ah, and here she comes now with tonight's centerpiece!" cried Solari.

Lytia led in two servers bearing a huge pastry on a litter. At her command, they placed it before Tobin. The golden crust was decorated in fine detail with Atyion's oak flanked by two swans, all fashioned of pastry and colored glazes.

"For your amusement on your first night with us, Prince Tobin," she said, offering him a long knife decorated with blue ribbon.

"It's a shame to spoil it," Tobin exclaimed. "You have my compliments, lady!"

"Cut it, cut it!" little Rose cried, bouncing on Korin's lap and clapping her hands.

Wondering what the filling could be, Tobin thrust the knife into the center of the crust. The whole elaborate creation fell to pieces, releasing a flock of tiny blue-and-green birds that fluttered up to circle the table. The cats sprang onto the table after them, much to the amusement of the guests.

"Your esteemed aunt is a true artist!" Solari called down the table to Tharin, who acknowledged the praise with a nod.

Lytia waved in a second litter and presented them with an identical pastry filled with plums and brandy custard.

"All from your estate and cellars, my prince," she told him proudly, serving Tobin the first helping.

A half-grown black-and-white kitten leaped into his lap and sniffed at his plate.

Tobin stroked its soft fur. "I've never seen so many cats!"

"There have always been cats at Atyion." Lytia gave the kitten a bit of custard on the end of her finger. "They're favored by Illior because they love the moon."

"My old nurse told me that's why they sleep all day and can see to hunt in the darkness," Korin said, coaxing the kitten into Rose's lap. "It's too bad Father can't bear the sight of them."

The kitten jumped back into Tobin's lap but just then Ringtail appeared from under the table with a growl. Leaping onto the arm of Tobin's chair, he cuffed the kitten out of the way and took its place.

"You must be well favored with the Lightbearer, if that one comes to you," Solari observed, eyeing Ringtail with distaste. "I can't get near the brute." He reached to scratch his head but the big cat laid his ears back and hissed at him. Solari hastily withdrew his hand. "You see?" He shook his head as the tom licked Tobin's chin, purring loudly. "Yes, well favored indeed!"

Tobin stroked the cat's back, thinking once again of Brother's warning.

Nuts and cheese followed the pastry, but Tobin was too full to manage more than a few sugared almonds. A new set of minstrels was introduced with the sweets and some of the guests began to play dice among the wine cups. No one showed any sign of going to bed.

Exhausted and dizzy from too many wines, Tobin excused himself as soon as he could politely do so, pleading weariness.

"Good night, sweet coz!" Korin cried, rising to clasp him in an unsteady embrace. Not surprisingly, he was far drunker than Tobin.

Everyone rose to bid him good night. Tobin guessed that the feast would continue well into the night, but they'd have to do so without him. Tharin and Ki escorted him out, with Ringtail trotting ahead as vanguard, his striped tail straight as a standard pole.

Tobin was more grateful than usual for Tharin's company as he guided them through the warren of corridors and staircases. Reaching an unfamiliar junction, Tharin paused. "If you're not too tired, Tobin, there is someone else I'd like you to meet."

"Another relative?"

"Practically. Hakone has served your family since your great-grandfather's time. He's longed to meet you ever since word came of your birth. It would mean a great deal to him to see you."

"Very well."

Turning aside, they left the main tower, descended a staircase, and made their way through the gardens to an entrance leading to the kitchens. The aroma of baking bread filled the passageway. Passing an open door, Tobin saw an army of cooks at work over pastry boards. He caught sight of a tall, grey-haired woman across the room, discussing something with another as she stirred something in a large cauldron.

"My cousin, Grannia, and the head cook," Tharin told him. "There's no purpose in stopping; they're like a couple of generals, planning tomorrow's feast for the king."

Moving on past other kitchens, they climbed a flight of narrow stairs. The servants they met along the way greeted Tharin warmly and Tobin with awe.

"It's almost as if they know you already, isn't it?" said Ki.

Halfway down a plain, rush-strewn corridor, Tharin stopped and opened a door without knocking. Inside, the oldest man Tobin had ever seen lay dozing in an armchair by a brazier. A few wisps of white hair still fringed his shiny pate, and a thin, yellowed beard hung halfway to his belt. An equally ancient yellow cat lay on his lap. Ringtail jumped up and touched noses with it, then curled up beside it to have his ears washed.

The old man woke and squinted down with rheumy eyes, feeling Ringtail's head with crabbed, red-knuckled fingers. "Oh, it's you, is it?" His voice was as creaky as a rusty hinge. "Come to visit your old mother, but brought her no gift, you heedless fellow? What do you say to that, Ariani?"

Startled, it was a moment before Tobin realized that the man was addressing his cat. This Ariani was holding Ringtail down now with one seven-toed foot, washing his face. The big tom submitted contentedly.

"He didn't come alone, Hakone," Tharin said, raising his voice. Crossing the room, he took the old man's hand in his, then motioned for Tobin and Ki to join him.

"Theodus, home at last!" Hakone exclaimed. Catching sight of Tobin and Ki, he broke into a fond, toothless grin. "Ah, and here are my dear boys. Tell me now, Rhius, how many grouse have you brought me? Or is it rabbits today? And you, Tharin, did you have any luck?"

Tharin bent closer. "Hakone, I'm Tharin, remember?"

The old man squinted at him, then shook his head. "Of course, my boy. Forgive me. You caught me dreaming. But then, this must be . . ." He gasped and fumbled for the walking stick lying by his chair. "My prince!" he exclaimed, dislodging the cats as he struggled to rise.

"Please, don't get up," Tobin told him.

Tears spilled down Hakone's sunken cheeks as he fell back in the chair. "Forgive an old man's weakness, my prince, but I'm so very happy! I was beginning to fear I wouldn't live long enough to see you!" He reached out and cupped Tobin's face in his trembling hands. "Ah, and if only I could see you better! Welcome home, lad. Welcome home!"

A lump rose in Tobin's throat as he thought of how the old man had mistaken him for his father. He took Hakone's hands in his. "Thank you, old father. And thank you for your long service to my family. I—I hope you're comfortable here?"

"Very kind of you to ask, my prince. There's a stool just there. Tharin, fetch the prince a chair! And move the lamp closer."

When Tobin was seated by him, Hakone peered more closely into his face. "Yes, that's better. Just look at you! Your dear mother's eyes in the duke's face. Don't you think so, Tharin? It's like seeing our Rhius reborn."

"So it is," Tharin said, giving Tobin a wink. They both knew he little favored either of his parents, but Tobin liked the old man already and was pleased to make him happy.

"And this must be the squire you told me of," Hakone said. "Kirothius, isn't it? Come boy, let me see you."

Ki knelt by his chair and Hakone felt at his shoulders, hands, and arms. "A good strong lad, yes!" he said approvingly. "Hands hard as iron. You've warriors' hands, both of you. Tharin tells me nothing but good things, but I suppose you get into all sorts of mischief, just as Rhius and this rascal did."

Tobin exchanged a smirk with Ki. "Tharin was a rascal?"

"The both of them!" Hakone cackled. "Brawling with the village children, raiding the orchards. Tharin, do you recall the time Rhius shot your mother's best milk ewe? By the Light, it seems like I was after you two with the switch every other day."

Tharin mumbled something, and Tobin saw with delight that the man was blushing.

Hakone let out another rusty chuckle and patted Tobin's hand. "Filled the salt cellars with sugar just before a banquet for the queen herself, one time, if you can imagine such a thing! Of course young Erius was in the middle of that one, but Tharin took the blame, and the whipping." The memory loosened another spate of laughter, but it quickly changed to a coughing fit.

"Calm yourself, Hakone," Tharin urged, fetching him a cup of wine from the sideboard and holding it to the old man's lips.

Hakone managed a slurping sip and wine dribbled

down into his beard. He sat wheezing for a moment, then let out a long sigh. "But that's all done and gone now, isn't it? You're grown and Rhius is dead. So many dead . . ." He trailed off and closed his eyes. Tobin thought he'd gone to sleep. An instant later, however, he sat up again and said sharply, "Tharin, the duke has no wine! Get down to the cellars—" He broke off and looked around at them. "No, I'm wandering again, aren't I? That's your duty now, Kirothius. Serve your prince, boy."

Ki jumped up to obey but Tobin stopped him. "That's all right, old father. We've just come from the hall and had more wine than we can hold."

Hakone lay back again and the old cat returned and settled in his lap. Ringtail curled up at Tobin's feet.

"I was sorry to find a stranger wearing your chain," said Tharin, taking Hakone's hand again. "I thought Lytia would be the one to take your place."

Hakone snorted. "That was Lord Orun's doing. The king had already sent us half a dozen new servants after the princess died—may Astellus carry her softly." He kissed his fingertips reverently and pressed them to his heart. "And then as soon as Rhius passed, Orun sent his own man. It was time for a change, of course—I'm blind as Bilairy's goat and my legs are failing me—but this was a shifty-eyed, pasty-faced bastard and no one was sad when Solari replaced him. But it should have been your auntie, then, as you say. She's been steward in all but name these past few years."

"I'll tell Solari to make her steward," said Tobin.

"I'm afraid you can't do that yet," said Tharin. "Until you're of age, the Lord Protector decides those things."

"Then I'm not lord of Atyion, am I? Not really."

Hakone found Tobin's hand and clasped it. "You are, my boy, and no other. I heard them cheering you in today. That's the heart of your people you saw out there. They've longed for you as much as I have. Solari is a good man, and keeps your father's memory alive among the men. Let him keep you safe for now, while you serve the prince."

Just then they heard a soft shuffling in the passage. Ki opened the door and found a cluster of cooks and kitchen maids crowding in the corridor.

"Please, sir, we just wanted to see the prince," an old woman said, speaking for all of them. Behind her, the others nodded hopefully and craned their necks for a glimpse of Tobin.

"Be off with you! It's too late to be troubling His Highness," Hakone rasped.

"No, please, I don't mind," said Tobin.

Ki stepped aside and the women came in, curtsying and touching their hearts. Several of the older ones were weeping. The woman who'd spoken knelt and clasped Tobin's hands.

"Prince Tobin. Welcome home at last!"

Overwhelmed anew, Tobin bent and kissed her on the cheek. "Thank you, old mother. I'm very glad to be here."

She raised a hand to her cheek and looked back at the others. "There, you see that? I told you blood would tell! None of the rest of it matters."

"Mind your tongue, Mora!" Hakone snapped.

"It's all right," Tobin told him. "I know what they say about me, and my mother. Some of it's even true, about the demon and all. But I promise you I'll try to be worthy of my father's memory, and a good lord to Atyion."

"You've nothing to worry about in him," Hakone told the women gruffly. "This is Rhius reborn. You pass that on belowstairs. Go on now, back to your duties."

The women took their leave, all but the one Tharin had pointed out as his cousin.

"What is it?" Tobin asked her.

"Well, my prince, I—" She stopped, twisting her chapped hands in her apron front. "Should I speak, Hakone?"

The old man looked to Tharin. "What harm can there be in asking?"

"Go on, Grannia."

"Well, my prince," she said. "It's just that—well, a good many of us Atyion women served in the ranks once. Catilan, your cook up at Alestun keep? She was my sergeant. We were among your grandfather's archers."

"Yes, she told me about that."

"Well, the thing is, Prince Tobin, that your father gave permission for us to keep in training, quiet-like, and to teach those of the young girls as wanted to learn. Is it your pleasure that we keep on with that?"

And there it was, that same mix of hope and frustration he'd seen so often in Una. "I would never change what my father willed," he replied.

"Bless you, my prince! If you should ever need us, you've only to send word."

"I won't forget," Tobin promised.

Grannia gave him a last awkward curtsy and hurried out, her apron pressed to her face.

Well done, Tobin," Tharin said as they made their way back to Tobin's chamber. "Your reputation will spread through the house by dawn. You did your father proud tonight in every way."

Koni and Sefus were standing guard at the end of the corridor near his room.

"Will you stay here with us?" Tobin asked, as they reached the door. "This was your room, after all."

"Thank you, Tobin, but it's yours now, and Ki's. My place is with the guard. Good night."

A steaming tub stood ready in their room and Tobin sank happily into it as Ki and a page lit the night lamps.

Tobin submerged to his chin and watched the ripples lap at the smooth wooden sides. He thought again of Una, and all the women who'd been denied their honor as warriors. Grannia's face rose in his mind's eye, so hopeful and sad all at once.

He shivered, sending more ripples across the water's surface. If Lhel and Iya were right, if he *did* have to become a woman someday, would the generals still follow a woman? Those soldiers had cheered Duke Rhius' son today. Would he lose everything by showing what the wizards claimed was his true face?

Tobin looked down at himself: the strong, tight-muscled arms and legs, his flat chest and hard belly, and the pale, hairless worm between his thighs. He'd seen enough naked women on his harbor rambles with Korin to know women didn't have those. If he changed . . . He shuddered, cupping his hands over his genitals, and felt the reassuring stir of his penis under his hand.

Maybe they're wrong! Maybe—

Maybe he'd never need to change. He was a prince, Ariani's son and Rhius'. That was good enough for the soldiers he'd met here. Maybe it would be good enough for Illior, too?

He ducked under the water and scrubbed his fingers through his hair. He wouldn't think of such things tonight, of all nights. All his life he'd been called a prince, never until today had he truly felt like one. In Ero he'd always felt the gulf that lay between him and those who'd spent their lives at court. He was plain and unknown and awkward, someone none of the fine courtiers would have looked at twice if not for his title. In his mind, he was as much a grass knight as Ki, and happy with it, too.

But what he'd seen today had changed all that. Today he'd watched the wonder in the other Companions' faces when they saw this castle. His castle! Let Alben and the others try and look down their long noses at him now!

And he'd basked in the adulation of the people. His father's warriors had beaten their shields for him and chanted his name. Someday, no matter what else happened, he would lead them. In his mind he conjured battlefields and the clash of arms. He'd lead the charge, with Tharin and Ki at his side.

"Prince of Skala, Scion of Atyion!" he murmured aloud.

Ki's laughter brought him back to earth. "Is his august Highness going to stay in that tub until the water's cold for his humble squire, or do I get a turn?"

Tobin grinned at him. "I'm a prince, Ki. A real prince!"

Ki snorted as he cleaned the day's mud from one of Tobin's boots with a rag. "Who said you weren't?"

"I don't think *I* believed it. Not until today."

"Well, you've never been anything else in my eyes, Tob. Or anyone else's, either, except maybe Orun and look what that got him? Now, then—" He made Tobin an exaggerated bow. "Shall I duck your royal head under the water, or scrub your noble back? We lesser sorts like to get to sleep before dawn."

Laughing, Tobin made quick work with the sponge and gave up the tub before the water had cooled.

Ki managed little more than a mumbled good night before he dozed off. But tired as he was, Tobin couldn't sleep. Staring up at the horses of Atyion chasing each other across the green pastures of tapestry, he tried to imagine some ancestor of his, his father's grandmother perhaps, working the pattern on her fine loom. His own father had looked up at these same horses, with Tharin asleep beside him—

Before he moved down the hall to the swan bed with his bride, thought Tobin. His parents had lain there together, made love there.

"And his parents before him, and theirs, and—" Tobin whispered aloud. Suddenly he wanted to know the faces of his ancestors and find his own plain face among them, an assurance that he really was of the same blood. There must be portraits somewhere in the house. He'd ask Tharin and Lytia tomorrow. They'd know.

Sleep still eluded him and his thoughts returned to that

room just down the hall. Suddenly he wanted to open those boxes he'd seen, and the wardrobes, looking for— what?

He left the bed and went to the clothes rack. Reaching into his purse, he took out the key Lytia had given him and stared down at it. It felt heavy against his palm.

Why not?

Stealing past the sleeping page, he inched the door open and peeked out. He could hear the low, comforting rumble of Tharin's voice from around the corner, but there was no one else in sight. Taking one of the night lamps with him, he crept out into the corridor.

I don't need to skulk around like a thief in my own house! he thought. All the same, he hurried on tiptoe to his parents' door and held his breath until it was locked again behind him.

Casting about with his lamp, he found another and lit it, then walked slowly around the chamber, touching things that his parents had touched: a bedpost, a chest, a cup, the handles of a wardrobe. Alone here at last, it didn't feel like just another room anymore; it was *their* room. Tobin tried to imagine what it would have been like if they'd all lived here happily together. If everything hadn't gone so terribly wrong.

At the dressing table he opened a box and found a woman's hairbrush. Some dark strands were still twined among the bristles. He plucked a few free and wound them around his finger, pretending for a moment that his parents were down in the hall, laughing and drinking with their guests. They'd come upstairs soon and find him waiting to bid them good night . . .

But it was no good; he couldn't imagine what that would be like. Reaching into his tunic, he unfastened the chain and slipped his mother's ring on his finger, searching the two profiles carved in the beautiful purple stone—the stone his father had traveled all the way to Aurënen to choose because he loved his bride so much.

Try as he might to think otherwise, the proud, serene pair on the ring were strangers to him. They'd shared this room, shared that bed and a life Tobin had never known, never been a part of.

But his curiosity grew, fed by the loneliness that never quite went away. Still wearing the ring, he opened another box and found a few jewels his mother had left behind: a necklace of carved amber beads, a golden chain with links shaped like dragons, and a pair of enamelwork earrings set with smooth stones the color of a summer sky. Tobin marveled at the craftsmanship; why would she leave these things behind? He replaced them, then opened a large ivory casket. Inside were a set of heavy silver cloak pins and a horn-handled penknife. A man's things. His father's.

He went to the wardrobes next. The first held nothing but a few old-fashioned tunics on pegs. Taking one down, Tobin pressed it to his face, seeking his father's scent. He held the garment up, thinking of the armor his father had given with him, with the promise that he would be old enough to go to battle when it fit him. He hadn't tried it on for a long time.

He pulled the tunic on over his nightshirt. For all his growth this past year, the hem still fell well past his knees and the sleeves hung below his fingertips.

"I'm still too small," he muttered, replacing it and moving to the next wardrobe. He swung the doors wide, then stifled a cry of dismay as his mother's perfume wafted over him. It wasn't her spirit, though; the scent came from bunches of faded flowers hung on hooks to freshen the folded gowns.

Tobin knelt to look at them, marveling at the colors. She'd always favored rich tones and here they were—wine dark reds, deep blues, saffron gold, greens like the colors of a summer forest in brocades, silks, velvets, and lawn. He touched the fabrics, hesitantly at first, then hungrily as his fingers found the raised work of embroidery, trimmings of fur, and colored beads.

A guilty yearning seized him and he stood up and lifted out a green gown trimmed with winter fox. He paused, listening for steps in the passage, then carried it to the long mirror near the bed.

He held the dress up in front of him and saw that he must be as tall as she had been, for the hem just brushed his toes. He shook out the wrinkles and held it up under his chin again; the full skirt spread out around him in graceful folds.

What would it feel like—?

Embarrassed by this unexpected longing, Tobin quickly thrust the dress back into the wardrobe. In doing so, he knocked a long cape of cream brocade from the peg it had been hanging on. It had a high collar of ermine and was stitched over the shoulders with rays of blue and silver.

Tobin had only meant to replace it, but somehow he found himself at the mirror again, draping it over his shoulders. The heavy fabric settled around him like an embrace, the dark satin lining cool as water against his skin. He fastened the golden clasp of the collar and dropped his arms to his sides.

The soft white fur caressed his throat as he slowly raised his eyes to his reflection. It was an effort to meet his own gaze there.

My hair is like hers, Tobin thought, shaking it out over his shoulders. *And I have her eyes, just as everyone always says. I'm not beautiful like she was, but I have her eyes.*

The cloak whispered around his ankles as he went to the dressing table and took out one of the earrings. Feeling sillier by the minute, yet unable to stop himself, he carried it back to the mirror and held the jewel to his ear. Perhaps it was the earring, or the tilt of his head, but Tobin thought he caught a glimpse of the girl Lhel had shown him. The blue stone complemented his eyes, just as the embroidery on the cape did, making them seem bluer.

In the forgiving light of the small lamp, she looked almost pretty.

Tobin touched the face in the glass with trembling fingers. He could see the girl, that stranger who had looked back at him from the surface of the spring. There hadn't been time then, but now Tobin gazed in growing wonder and curiosity. Would a boy look at her the way his friends looked at the girls they fancied? The thought of Ki looking at him like that sent a hot, shivery feeling down through Tobin. The sensation seemed to pool between his hipbones like the moontide pains, but this didn't hurt. Instead, he felt himself starting to go hard under his nightshirt. That made him blush, but he couldn't look away. Suddenly lonely and unsure again, he called the only witness he could.

Brother made no reflection in the mirror, so Tobin had him stand beside it instead so that he could compare their faces.

"Sister," the ghost murmured, as if he understood the nameless ache growing in Tobin's heart.

But the fragile illusion was already broken. Standing side by side with his twin, Tobin saw only a boy in a woman's cloak there in the mirror.

"Sister," Brother said again.

"Is that what you see when you look at me?" Tobin whispered.

Before Brother could answer, Tobin heard voices outside the locked door. He froze like a frightened hare, listening as Koni and Laris exchanged greetings. It was only a change of guard, he knew, but he still felt like a thief about to be caught. What if someone noticed that he was gone from his room and came looking?

What if Ki found him here like this?

"Go away, Brother!" he hissed, then hastily put away the cloak and earring. Extinguishing all the lamps, he felt his way to the door and listened until the voices had faded away down the corridor.

He made it back to his own chamber without meeting anyone and Ki didn't stir as he climbed back into bed. Pulling the covers over his head, Tobin closed his eyes and tried hard not to think of the swirl of heavy silk around his bare legs, or how, for a disjointed moment, his eyes had looked back at him in the glass from a different face.

I'm a boy, he told himself silently, squeezing his eyes shut. *I'm a prince.*

Chapter 19

Korin had everyone up at dawn the next morning to be ready for the king. The sun was out and mist was rising in long streamers from the river and off the wet fields.

The Companions dressed in their mail and corselets, and wore their finest cloaks. Going downstairs, they found the house in an uproar.

Armies of servants were at work everywhere Tobin looked. The great hall was already hung with the king's colors and all the gold plate lay ready. Outside, smoke billowed from the kitchen chimneys, and from several pits in the kitchen garden, where whole stags and boars were being roasted Mycenian style on buried beds of coals. Entertainers of all sorts milled in spare rooms and courtyards.

Solari was once again master of the situation. Breaking his fast with Tobin and the others, he outlined the evening's entertainments and courses, with the steward and Lytia hovering at his elbow. Every few minutes he would pause, and ask, "Does this meet with your approval, my prince?"

Tobin, who knew nothing of such things, nodded silent agreement to everything presented.

When he'd finished, Lytia summoned two servers bearing cloth-draped boxes. "Something special for the highest-ranking guests. A specialty of this house since your great-grandparents' day, Prince Tobin." Whisking aside one of the covers, she lifted out a glass vase filled with delicate glass roses. Tobin gasped; worked glass of this sort was worth a dozen fine horses. His eyes widened further when Lytia casually broke off one ruby petal and popped it into her mouth, then offered him one.

Tobin hesitantly touched it to his tongue, then laughed. "Sugar!"

Solari chuckled as he helped himself to a flower. "Lady Lytia is a true artist."

"Your great-grandmother sent my grandmother to Ero to train with a famous confectioner," said Lytia. "She passed the craft down to my mother, and she to me. I'm glad my little flowers please you, but what do you think of this?" Reaching into the second box, she lifted out a translucent sugar dragon. The hollow body was red like the rose petals, with delicate gilded wings, feet, and drooping facial spines. "Which would you prefer for tonight?"

"They're both astonishing! But perhaps the dragon is proper, for the king?"

"Good, then you won't be needing this!" Korin exclaimed, and tapped the sugar vase with his knife. It shattered with a delicate tinkle and the boys scrambled for the large pieces.

"It's a shame to break them," Tobin said, watching them.

Lytia smiled as she watched the Companions elbowing each other to snatch up the last morsels. "But that's why I make them."

As soon as Solari released Tobin, Korin insisted on riding down to the town gates to stand watch. Porion insisted on coming with them, and Tharin came along, too, but Korin wanted no other guard.

Tobin recognized that mix of longing and excitement in his cousin's eyes. He remembered loitering around the barracks yard, waiting for his father to ride out from the trees at the bottom of the meadow. He wished he could share Korin's excitement instead of feeling sick to his stomach the way he did. He'd kept a worried eye out for Brother all morning, but there'd been no sign of him.

A crowd gathered around them as they sat their horses just outside the gate, admiring the Companions' arms and horses. Everyone seemed to know Tharin.

Soldiers loitering around the square found reasons to come over, too, and Tobin found them easy to talk to. He'd been around fighting men all his life. He asked them about their scars and admired their swords or bows. With a little encouragement, they shared stories of his father and grandfather, and some of his aunts who'd fought under the queen's banner in years gone by. Many started their tales with, "You'll have heard this one . . ." But Tobin hadn't, mostly, and wondered why his father had told him so little of his own history.

Noon came and went. Food vendors brought them meat and wine and they ate in the saddle like picket riders. At last, bored with waiting and tired of being stared at, Tobin rallied his friends and they passed the time giving children rides up and down the road. Korin and the older boys stayed by the gate, flirting with the local girls. They'd put on their best dresses for the occasion and reminded Tobin of a flock of bright, chattering birds as they giggled and preened for the boys.

The sun was halfway down the sky when an outrider arrived at last, announcing the king's arrival.

Korin and the others would have ridden out in a mob if Porion hadn't caught them up with a sharp shout.

"Form up properly, now!" he ordered, keeping his voice down in deference to the princes. "I've taught you better than this. You don't want the king thinking bandits are attacking him, do you?"

Chastened, they formed up in a proper column, each noble with his squire beside him, and Korin and Tobin in the lead. Solari and Savia rode down just in time to join them, dressed in festival splendor.

"They look like a king and queen themselves, don't they?" Ki whispered.

Tobin nodded. Both glittered with jewels and their horses' tack was fancier than Gosi's.

They took the north road at a gallop, the princes' banners and Solari's bright against the afternoon sky before them. A mile or so on they caught sight of answering colors, and a long column of soldiers coming their way. A score of armed warriors and the king's standard-bearer led the way. Behind them Erius rode with his principal lords. Tobin couldn't see his face yet, but knew him by his golden helm. They were dressed for battle, but carried hawks and falcons rather than shields. Dozens of noble standards snapped in the crisp late afternoon breeze.

A long column of foot soldiers marched behind them, like a red-and-black serpent with glinting scales of iron.

Porion held the boys to a formation canter, but they called out excitedly to each other as they spied the banners of their fathers or kinsmen.

They quickly closed the distance between the two companies, and Korin reined in and dismounted.

"Down, Tob," he murmured. "We greet Father on foot."

Everyone else had already dismounted. Swallowing his fear, Tobin steeled himself to hate this stranger who shared his blood. He handed Gosi's reins to Ki and followed his cousin.

He'd glimpsed his uncle only once before, but there was no mistaking the man now. Even without the golden helm and a gold-chased breastplate, Tobin would have known Erius by the sword that hung at his left side: the fabled Sword of Ghërilain. Tobin had learned to recognize it from the little painted kings and queens his father had given him, then seen it carved with differing skill on the stone effigies at the Royal Tomb. If he'd had any doubt that this was the sword he'd been offered by the ghost of Queen Tamír that long-ago night, they were laid to rest now. This was the one.

He'd never seen the king's face, though, and when he

looked up at the man at last he let out small gasp of surprise; Erius looked just like Korin. He had the same square, handsome face and dark, merry eyes. There were thick streaks of white in his hair, but he sat his tall black horse with the same soldierly dash that Tobin's father had, riding up the river road to the keep.

Korin dropped to one knee and saluted his father. Tobin and the other Companions did the same.

"Korin, my boy!" Erius exclaimed, as he swung down from the saddle to meet them. His voice was deep and filled with love.

Instead of fear or hate, Tobin felt a sudden stab of longing.

Abandoning any pretense of dignity, Korin threw himself into his father's arms. A roar of acclaim went up from the ranks as the pair hugged and pounded each other on the back. The Companions cheered the king, beating their sword hilts against their shields.

After a moment Korin noticed Tobin still kneeling and dragged him to his feet. "This is Tobin, Father. Cousin, come and greet your uncle."

"By the Flame, look how you've sprouted up!" laughed Erius.

"Your Majesty." Tobin started to bow, but the king caught him in a strong embrace. For a dizzying instant Tobin was back in his father's arms, enveloped in the comforting smells of oiled steel, sweat, and leather.

Erius stepped back and gazed down at him with such fondness that Tobin's knees went weak.

"The last time I saw you, you were a babe asleep in your father's arms." Erius cupped Tobin's chin in one hard, callused hand and a wistful look came over his face. "Everyone said you have my sister's eyes. I can almost see her looking out at me," he murmured, unknowingly sending a superstitious chill up his nephew's spine. "Tobin Erius Akandor, have you no kiss for your uncle?"

"Forgive me, Your Majesty," Tobin managed. All his

hate and fear had melted away at that first warm smile. Now he didn't know how to feel. Leaning forward, he brushed his lips against the king's rough cheek. As he did so, he found himself looking at Lord Niryn, who stood just behind the king. Where'd he come from? Why was he here? Tobin stepped back quickly, trying to cover his surprise.

"How old are you now, boy?" Erius asked, still clasping him by the shoulders.

"Twelve and a half, almost, Your Majesty."

The king chuckled. "That old, eh? And already a dangerous swordsman, by all reports! But you mustn't be so formal. From this day forth, I'm 'Uncle' to you, and nothing else. Come now, let me hear it. I've waited a long time."

"As you wish—Uncle." Looking up, Tobin saw his own shy, traitorous smile mirrored in the king's dark eyes.

It was a relief when Erius turned away. "Duke Solari, I've brought your own son back to you, too, safe and sound. Nevus, go and greet your parents."

He's your enemy! Tobin told himself, watching the king laugh with Solari and the young noble. But his heart wasn't listening.

Korin and Tobin flanked the king as they rode on to the castle. Solari and his family rode ahead with the standard-bearers.

"What do you think of your new guardian?" Erius asked.

"I like him a great deal better than Lord Orun," Tobin answered truthfully. Knowing now that Brother sometimes lied, he was prepared to believe better of the man. Solari had treated him no differently than he ever had, always kind.

Erius chuckled at his bluntness and gave Tobin a wry wink. "So do I. Now, where's this squire of yours?"

This is it, Tobin thought, tensing again. He'd been given no warning of a new guardian. Did the king have a new squire for him hidden among the ranks, as well? Putting on a brave face, he waved Ki up. "May I present my squire, Uncle? Sir Kirothius, son of Sir Larenth of Oakmount steading."

Ki managed a dignified bow from the saddle, but the hand he pressed to his heart was shaking. "Your Majesty, please accept my humble service to you and all your line."

"So this is the troublesome Sir Kirothius? Sit up and let me look at you, lad."

Ki did as he was told, gripping the reins with white-knuckled hands. Tobin watched them both closely as the king sized up his friend. Fitted out in fine new clothes, Ki looked the equal of any of the Companions; Tobin had seen to that.

"Oakmount?" the king said at last. "That would make your father Lord Jorvai's man."

"Yes, my king."

"Odd place for Rhius to seek a squire for his son. Wouldn't you agree, Solari?"

"I thought so myself at the time," Solari replied over his shoulder.

Would Erius nullify the bond right here in front of everyone? Ki's expression didn't change, but Tobin saw his friend's hands clench harder on the reins.

But Solari wasn't done. "As I recall, Rhius met Larenth and some of his sons in Mycena and was impressed with their fighting ability. Strong country stock, he said, not spoiled with court manners and intrigues."

Tobin stared down at Gosi's neck hoping his surprise didn't show. Of course his father had had to lie, but it had never occurred to him to wonder what he might have said to explain Ki's presence.

"A wise choice, judging by this fine young fellow," said Erius. "Perhaps more of my lords should take Rhius' advice. Do you have any brothers, Kirothius?"

Ki broke into a buck-toothed grin. "A whole pack of

them, Your Majesty, if you don't mind 'em rough and plain-spoken."

This won a hearty, full-throated laugh from the king. "We could do with more country honesty at court. Tell me, Kirothius, and be honest now, how does this son of mine strike you?"

No one but Tobin noticed Ki's slight hesitation. "It's a great honor to serve Prince Korin, Majesty. He's the best swordsman of us all."

"Just as he should be!" Erius clapped Ki on the shoulder, then gave Tobin a wink. "Your father chose well, my boy, just as I thought. I won't break the bond he blessed, so perhaps now the pair of you can stop looking like dogs in need of green grass."

"Thank you, my king!" Tobin managed, his rush of relief so strong he could hardly get his breath. "Lord Orun was so set against him—"

The king's mouth quirked into an odd little smile. "You see where that got him. And call me uncle, remember?"

Tobin raised his fist to his heart. "Thank you, Uncle!"

The king turned back to Korin, and Tobin gripped the saddlebow, dizzy with relief. Ki's place was safe, after all. For that, at least, he could love his uncle a little.

All of Atyion turned out to greet the king, but it seemed to Tobin that the cheering wasn't quite as loud as it had been the day before. And this time it was Solari's troops in the forefront at the castle yard, rather than his own.

That night's feast more than made up for any disparity in the welcome. Lytia had been busy.

The tables were draped with red and strewn with fragrant herbs. Flat wax candles floated in silver basins, and hundreds of torches burned in sconces on the pillars that lined the room, so that even the painted ceiling vaults were illuminated.

Under the direction of Lytia and the steward, a steady

procession of dishes was carried in, more exotic and varied than anything Tobin had ever seen. Huge pike quivered in glistening aspic skins. Humble grouse were encased in new pastry bodies, shaped and painted to look like mythical birds, complete with brilliant plumed tails of real feathers. Companies of spiced crabs stood at attention, holding tiny silk banners in their claws. A roast stag was carried in on a shield, its belly filled with mock entrails made of dried fruit and nuts threaded on strings and glazed with honey and nutmeg. The sweet courses included pears filled with sweet brown cream whipped to peaks, pastry apples filled with dried fruit and chopped veal, and another bird pie, this one filled with tiny red warblers. As they burst free and swirled up toward the rafters, the king's men released their hawks and roared with laughter as the soft red feathers floated down around them.

Lytia's sugar dragons were presented on a silver platter the size of a war shield. Each was made in a slightly different pose, some rearing, some crouched as if to pounce, and arranged as if doing battle with each other. The spectacle was borne around to all the tables before the dragons met their ultimate fate.

The squires served the head table. Tobin and the noble Companions sat to the king and Korin's right. Niryn, Solari and his wife, and other nobles had the king's left. Tobin was pleased to see Tharin seated among the king's friends.

"Were some of these men in your Companions, too, Uncle?" he inquired, as the panters worked, cutting the first round of bread trenchers and laying the upper crusts before the king and his kin.

"Your swordmaster was a squire, before his lord was killed in battle. General Rheynaris was one of my boys, and that duke beside him was his squire. Tharin was our butler. Your squire puts me in mind of him at that age. Look at them, Tharin," Erius called down the table, pointing to the Companions. "Were we as fine a company in our day?"

"I daresay we were," Tharin called back. "But we'd have found them a fair match on the sword ground."

"Especially your son, my king, and those wild young ruffians," Porion called, pointing to Tobin and Ki. "Those lads will match any swordsman in the court when they get their growth."

"It's true, Father," Korin said, slopping wine from his mazer as he saluted Tobin. "Tobin and Ki have dusted the jackets of most of us."

"They had good teachers." The king raised his mazer to Tharin and Porion, then clapped Korin on the shoulder. "I've brought some gifts for you and your friends."

These proved to be Plenimaran longswords for Korin and Tobin, and handsome belt knives for the rest. The steel had a dark blue tinge not seen in Skala and it took a cruel, sharp edge. The workmanship was exceptional and the boys excitedly compared their gifts. Tobin's sword had a curved guard of bronze and silver, and the metal had been worked to look like intricately intertwined briars or vines. He turned it admiringly in his hands, then looked at Korin's, which had guards made in the shape of wings.

"Beautiful work, isn't it?" said Erius. "The eastern craftsmen stick closer to the old styles. There are weapons in the treasury vaults dating from the Hierophantic Era just like them. I captured these myself; they belonged to generals."

He sat back and exchanged a wink with Korin. "I've one more gift to bestow, though I won't take credit for thinking of it. Boys?"

Korin, Caliel, and Nikides left the hall and returned with a bulky cloth-wrapped bundle and Tobin's standard pole. The banner was furled and muffled in white cloth.

Korin gave the bundle to his father's page and grinned at Tobin. "Lord Hylus sends his regards, coz."

Erius rose and addressed the hall. "I've been gone a long time, and have a great deal of business to attend to now that I'm home. The first duty I'm pleased to discharge tonight regards my nephew here. Rise, Prince Tobin, and receive from my hand your new coat of arms: the might of Atyion married to the glory of Skala."

Nikides unfurled the banner and the king opened the bundle and shook out a dagged silk surcoat, both worked with Tobin's arms.

The arms shield was divided by a vertical impalement of red, which, together with the silver dragon crest at the top, proclaimed his royal blood. The left side showed the oak of Atyion in white on a black ground edged with silver silk. The right side of the shield bore the red dragon of Illior beneath the golden flame of Sakor on azure edged in white, his mother's colors.

"They're wonderful!" Tobin exclaimed. He'd almost forgotten the conversation he'd had with Hylus and Nikides. He shot Nikides a grateful look, suspecting he'd had something to do with this.

"It's a brave device," Erius told Tobin. "You must have your battle shield repainted and new tunics for your guard."

Tobin dropped to one knee, holding the surcoat across his chest. "Thank you, Uncle. I am honored."

The king ruffled his hair. "And now it's time to pay the piper."

"Uncle?"

"I've heard great things about this squire and you—I'd like to see for myself. Pair off with some of the others. Helms and hauberks, that will do. Squire Kirothius, fetch your master's armor. Clear the floor, you minstrels, and we'll have proper warrior's entertainment."

"You take on Garol, Ki," Korin ordered. "Who'll face Tobin?"

"I will, my prince," Alben called out before anyone else could answer.

"Bastard!" Ki muttered. Any of the other boys might have gone easy on Tobin, let him make a good first showing for the king. But not jealous, proud Alben.

"Yes, let my son test your nephew!" called one of the nobles down the table *This must be the famous Baron Alcenar*, thought Tobin. The man was dark and handsome like his son, and looked just as arrogant.

Ki and Garol fought first. Taking their places, they saluted the king, then began to circle each other. The nobles pounded the tables and traded wagers.

The betting was all on Garol at first. He was older than Ki and more heavily muscled. The odds seemed justified at first, as he drove Ki back with a series of powerful opening swings. The two had sparred often enough to know each other's tricks; Ki would have to win with speed and skill.

Working grimly, he blocked Garol's blows and slowly began turning him, so as not to get trapped against the tables. It put Tobin in mind of the dancing lessons they'd had with Arengil and Una. Ki might be the one backing up, but he was the leader, making Garol open his guard as he was forced to follow his retreating foe. Tobin grinned, guessing what Ki was up to. Garol's greatest weakness was impatience.

Sure enough, the older boy quickly tired of the chase and sprung at Ki, nearly knocking him over. Quick as a snake, Ki spun on his heel, ducked under Garol's arm, and smacked him across the back of the neck with the flat of his blade, knocking him on his face. Everyone heard the hiss of his blade across the mail coif; it would have been a killing blow. Arengil had taught them that move.

The audience bellowed and hooted as gold changed hands. Ki helped Garol up and threw an arm around his shoulders, steadying him. Garol rubbed ruefully at his neck, looking a little dazed.

Then it was Tobin's turn. He was already nervous, and didn't like the smirk Alben exchanged with Urmanis as he took his place. As much as he disliked Alben, Tobin knew better than to underestimate him; he was a strong, cunning fighter and could be counted on to do anything to win.

Rolling his shoulders and flexing his arms to settle the heavy mail shirt more comfortably, Tobin took his place.

When they'd saluted the king, Alben struck a defensive stance and waited, forcing Tobin to make the first move or appear a fool. It was a calculated strategy, and Tobin narrowly missed getting a belly stroke when Alben side-stepped his first feint. It unbalanced him and Alben pressed the advantage with a quick series of punishing swings. Tobin danced and ducked, but still caught a ringing blow across the top of his helm that nearly knocked him to his knees. He recovered just in time to turn a swing, and the tip of his blade caught Alben in the face, sliding across the coif to nick him on the cheek.

Alben swore and redoubled his assault, but Tobin's blood was up now, too. He would not be shamed in front of the king, or in his own hall.

"For Atyion!" he cried, and heard the challenge echoed in a deafening chorus at the lower tables. Chained at the far end of the hall, the castle hounds bayed and howled. The cacophony lifted Tobin on wings of fire. His sword felt as light as a dry stick in his hands.

After that, all he knew was the clash of steel and his opponent's ragged breathing as they battered each other around the floor, toiling like harvest threshers with the sweat burning their eyes and soaking the tunics under their hauberks.

Hoping to lure Alben into a fatal overreach, Tobin stepped back, but caught his heel on something and fell on his back. Alben was on him in an instant. Tobin still had his sword but Alben trapped his wrist under his foot and raised his blade for the killing stroke. Pinned, Tobin saw that Alben's blade wasn't turned; if he struck, it would take him edge on, breaking bones or worse.

Just then two hissing, yowling streaks shot from beneath the nearest table and ran between Alben's legs. Startled, he rocked off-balance just enough for Tobin to wrench his arm free and bring his blade up, leveling it at his opponent's face, the tip just inches from Alben's left eye. Alben flailed with his arms, trying not to pitch forward, and Tobin hooked his legs out from under him with one foot. The other boy toppled back and Tobin scrambled up to straddle him. Yanking back Alben's coif, he pressed the edge of his blade to his throat.

Alben glared up at him, eyes burning with pure malice.

Why do you hate me? Tobin wondered. Then Ki and the other Companions were pulling him to his feet and thumping him on the back. Urmanis and Mago tried to help Alben up, but he shook them off. Making Tobin a mocking salute, he stalked back to the table.

Looking around, Tobin found Ringtail innocently washing his face under the head table.

"Well done!" the king cried. "By the Flame, you're both as good as Porion claims!" Unfastening the golden brooch from the throat of his tunic, he tossed it to Ki. The startled boy caught it, then pressed it to his heart and fell to one knee. Erius presented Tobin with his gold-hilted dagger.

"Now then, let's see the rest of you at it. Korin and Caliel, you first, and show me that you haven't forgotten what I taught you!"

Korin won his match, of course. Tobin was certain he saw Caliel drop his defense at least once, letting Korin score a hit. The rest of the boys fought hard and Lutha earned special praise for winning his bout after Quirion broke his little finger in the first assault. Tobin paired with Nikides, and made certain his friend got in a few good hits before Tobin dispatched him.

Erius saluted them with his wine cup when they'd finished. "Well done, every one of you! The Plenimarans are giving us a rest just now, but there are still raiders and pirates." He gave his son a wink.

Korin jumped up and kissed his father's hand. "We're yours to command!"

"Now, now, I'm not making any promises. We shall see."

The final course of soft cheeses and gilded nutmeats

was brought out on painted porcelain plates and the minstrels played old ballads as they ate.

"Here's a new conceit from the Ylani potters," Solari told them when the dainties had been eaten. Turning his plate over, he showed the king a verse painted on the underside. "Each one has a riddle or song, which the owner of the plate must deliver to the company, standing on his chair. If I may demonstrate."

Amid much laughter and table pounding, Solari mounted his chair and declaimed a very silly parody with maudlin dignity.

Delighted, Erius was the next one up, declaiming a blisteringly obscene verse in the tender tones of a pale court poet.

The game was a great success and went on for over an hour. Most of the pieces were equally bawdy, and a few were worse. Tobin blushed hotly when Tharin climbed onto the table and, with a perfectly straight face recited a poem about a young wife satisfying her lover in a pear tree while her ancient, nearsighted husband stood below, urging his wife to pluck the plumpest fruit she could find.

To Tobin's relief, his plate just had a riddle. "What fortress can withstand fire, lightning, and siege, yet can be defeated by a soft word?"

"A lover's heart!" Korin cried, and received a round of good-natured catcalls as his reward.

"Show Tobin the great sword, Father," Korin urged when the plate game was over.

The king's baldric bearer came forward and presented it to the king on bended knee. Drawing the long blade free of the studded sheath, Erius held it up for Tobin to admire. Yellow torchlight slid along the polished steel, glinting warmly on the worn gold dragons set in raised relief on the sides of the curved quillons.

Erius offered the hilt to Tobin and he had to stiffen his arm to hold it; it was much longer and heavier than his own blade. Even so, the hilt of yellowed ivory wrapped with braided gold wire felt good in his hand. Lowering the point, he examined the large ruby carved with the Royal Seal of Skala set in the fluted gold pommel. This was a pattern he'd seen often in reverse, pressed into the wax at the bottom of his uncle's letters: Illior's dragon bearing Sakor's Flame in a crescent moon on its back.

"The very sword King Thelátimos gave to Ghërilain," Korin said, taking it and turning the blade to catch the light. "All these years later, it's come back to a king's hand."

"And one day to yours, my son," Erius said proudly.

Tobin stared at the sword, trying to imagine his fragile, unpredictable mother wielding this blade as a warrior. He couldn't.

Suddenly, for the second time that day, he was aware of Niryn watching him. Pride replaced fear. Thinking only of the feel of the sword in his hand, he returned the wizard's stare. This time he was not the first to look away.

Chapter 20

It was well after midnight when Solari and the Companions accompanied Erius and his party from the feasting hall. Tobin kept close to Tharin and as far as he could from Niryn as they wended their noisy way upstairs.

He couldn't help stealing glances at the king, trying to square this jovial, laughing man with the stories he'd grown up with. But it was like trying to measure his body to its long evening shadow; the two simply didn't match. Confused, he gave up trying. His fickle heart yearned for a new father, but his mother's memory still haunted him too strongly to abandon all caution.

Of one thing he was certain, however, from all Iya and Lhel had told him, and what he'd seen here; for good or ill, the king held the threads of his life in those square warrior's hands. Erius had put Orun over him, and now he'd given charge of Atyion to Solari. Despite the seeming freedom he enjoyed among the Companions, his life in Ero was as ruled by others as it had been at the keep, and this time by people he did not dare trust. For now, it was safer to pretend to love the man he must call Uncle. And for now, the feeling seemed to be honestly reciprocated.

The king's room lay next to the one that had belonged to Tobin's parents. Pausing outside his door, Erius clasped hands with Tharin, then took Tobin's chin in his hand again, gazing into his eyes. "By the Light, it is almost like seeing your mother again. So blue! Blue as the evening sky in summer." He sighed. "Ask me a boon, child. For my sister's sake."

"A boon, Uncle? I—I don't know. You've already been too generous."

"Nonsense, there must be something."

Everyone was staring at him. Tharin shook his head slightly as if in warning. Standing with the other squires, Ki grinned and gave Tobin a tipsy little shrug.

Perhaps it was the wine that made Tobin bold, or seeing Mago smirk just then. "I don't need anything for myself, Uncle, but there is something I'd like." He didn't dare look at Ki as he plunged on. "Could you please ennoble my squire's father?"

"It's a fair boon," Korin chimed in drunkenly. "Ki's as good as any of us. It's not his fault he's only a grass knight."

Erius raised an eyebrow and chuckled. "Is that all?"

"Yes," said Tobin, encouraged. "I'm not yet of age to grant it, so I humbly ask Your Majesty to do so in my name. I wish to make Sir Larenth Duke of—" He searched his memory for all the lands he owned but had never seen. One seemed as good as another. "Of Cirna."

As soon as the words were out he knew he'd taken a serious misstep of some sort. Tharin went pale, and Lord Niryn made a faint, strangled noise. Several of the others gasped.

The king's smile disappeared. "Cirna?" He released Tobin and stepped back. "That's an odd parcel to make a gift of. Did your squire ask this of you?"

The black look he shot Ki send a thrill of dread through Tobin. "No, Uncle! It was just the first place that came into my head. It—it could be any holding, so long as it comes with a title."

But Erius was still staring from Tobin to Ki, and something unpleasant had crept into his eyes. Tobin knew he'd made a grave error but couldn't imagine what it had been.

To Tobin's surprise, it was Niryn who came to his rescue. "The prince has his mother's noble soul, my king, generous to a fault. He does not know his lands yet, and so could not know what he offered." Something in the way he looked at the king just then unsettled Tobin even more, though the wizard was apparently trying to help him.

"Perhaps not," Erius said slowly.

"I believe Prince Tobin owns a very suitable tract north of Colath," Niryn offered. "There's a fortress there, at Rilmar."

Erius brightened noticeably. "Rilmar? Yes, a very good choice. Sir Larenth shall be Marshal of Roads. What do you think, Squire Kirothius? Will your father accept?"

It was a rare thing for Ki to be speechless, but all he managed was a jerky nod as he sank to one knee. Erius drew his sword and rested it across Ki's right shoulder. "On behalf of your father and all his descendents, do you swear fealty to the throne of Skala, and to Prince Tobin as your liege lord?"

"I do, my king," Ki whispered.

Erius held the point before Ki's face and he kissed the tip of it.

"Then rise, Kirothius, son of Larenth, Marshal of Rilmar. Give the kiss of fealty to your benefactor before these witnesses."

Everyone clapped, but Tobin could feel Ki's fingers shaking as he took his hand and kissed it. Tobin's were, as well.

When they'd bidden the king good night, Tharin followed Tobin and Ki to their room. He sent their page off for hot water, then dropped into a chair and held his head in his hands, saying nothing. Ki kicked off his boots and sat cross-legged on the bed. Tobin settled on the hearthrug and poked at the embers, waiting.

"Well, that was unexpected!" Tharin said, recovering himself at last. "And when you tried to give away Cirna—By the Light, did you have any idea what you were doing?"

"No. Like I said, it was the first place I thought of. It's only a small holding, isn't it?"

Tharin shook his head. "In acreage, perhaps, but the man who holds Cirna holds the bulwark of Skala, not to mention the Protector's share of revenues collected in your name. And at the moment, Lord Niryn is that man."

"Niryn?" Ki exclaimed. "What's Fox Beard doing with a commission like that? He's no warrior."

"Never mock him, Ki, not even in private. And whatever the reason, it's between him and the king." He stopped and rubbed at his beard, thinking. "I suppose it's between you and Niryn, too, Tobin. Cirna is yours, after all."

"Does that make Niryn my liegeman?" Tobin shivered at the thought.

"No, and neither is Solari. They're the king's men. But don't worry. You'll hardly see either of them, and you're under the king's protection. He has say over you before anyone else."

"That's good," said Ki. "Korin thinks the sun rises and sets on Tobin, and now the king likes him, too, doesn't he?"

Tharin stood and ruffled Tobin's hair. "I'd say so."

"But I did do something wrong, didn't I? I saw it in the king's face."

"If you'd been a few years older—?" Tharin shook his head, casting off some dark thought. "No, he saw you spoke from an innocent heart. It's nothing to worry about. You two get to bed, now. It's been a long day."

"You could sleep here tonight," Tobin offered again. There was more to the king's reaction than Tharin was letting on and it still scared him.

"I promised Lytia I'd visit with her tonight," Tharin said. "But I'll check on you on my way back. Sleep well."

With the door safely closed behind him, Tharin sagged against the wall, hoping the sentries down the corridor would put his sudden weakness down to too much wine. He'd recognized the look in Erius' eyes—suspicion. If Tobin had been sixteen, instead of twelve, his request might have marked him and Ki both for death. But he was only a child, and an unworldly one at that. Erius still had enough good left in him to see that.

All the same, Tharin spent a long time in aimless conversation with the sentries, keeping an eye on the king's door, and Niryn's.

You didn't have to do that, you know. Waste a king's boon on me," Ki said when Tharin was gone. Tobin was still sitting on the rug, hugging his knees the way he did when he was feeling troubled. "Come get into the bed. The fire's out."

But Tobin stayed where he was. "Will your father be angry?"

"Not hardly! But what made you think of it, Tob? My old dad's a lot of things, but noble isn't one of them. I can see it now, him and my brothers using the king's warrant to steal horses."

Tobin looked around at him. "You always said he wasn't a horse thief!"

Ki shrugged. "Guess I've lived around decent folk long enough to know what my people are."

"They can't be so bad, Ki. You're as good as any of us. Anyway, now no one can call you grass knight."

But they still will, some of them, thought Ki.

"I made you a promise the day we left the keep," Tobin said earnestly.

"I don't remember any promise."

"I didn't say it out loud. Remember how hateful Orun was being to you and Tharin? I promised Sakor that day that I'd make you and Tharin great nobles so Orun would have to bow to you and be polite." He clapped a hand to his forehead. "Tharin! I should have asked something for him, too, but I was so surprised I couldn't think. Do you think I hurt his feelings?"

"I think he was probably glad you didn't."

"Glad? Why?"

"Think about it, Tob. You gave my dad Rilmar fortress,

and off he goes; nothing changes for me in that. But if you made Tharin lord of some important holding, like he deserves, he'd have to go and administer it. That means leaving us—you, I mean, and he wouldn't like that much."

"Us," Tobin corrected, coming to join him on the bed. "I never thought of that. I'd miss him, too. Still—" He pulled his boots off and settled back against the bolsters. His mouth had that stubborn set to it that Ki knew so well. "Bilairy's balls, Ki! Tharin deserves better than to be just a captain of my guard! Why didn't Father ever promote him?"

"Maybe Tharin asked him not to," Ki said, then wished he'd kept his mouth shut.

"Why would he do that?"

Now I've done it, thought Ki, but it was too late to take it back.

"Why would Tharin do that?" Tobin demanded again, reading his face like a book.

You couldn't hide much from Tobin, that was certain. So it was either tell or lie, and he'd never lie to Tobin. *It's not like Tharin cares who knows. He said so himself.*

Ki pushed himself up against the footboard, squirming inwardly as he tried to make a start on it. "Well, it's just that—Well, when they were young, in the Companions, they—your father and Tharin, that is—uh—loved each other and—"

"Well, of course they did. You and I—"

"No!" Ki held up a hand. "No, Tobin, not like us. That is, not *just* like us."

Tobin's eyes widened as he caught Ki's drift. "Like Orneus and Lynx, you mean?"

"Tharin told me so himself. It was only when they were young. Then your father married your mother and all. But Tharin? Well, I don't think his feelings ever changed."

Tobin was staring at him now, and Ki wondered if they'd fight over it, they way Ki used to fight people who accused his father of horse thieving.

But Tobin only looked pensive. "That must have been sad for Tharin."

Ki recalled Tharin's expression when he'd spoken of it that rainy night. "You're right about that, but they stayed friends all the same. I don't think he could've stood being parted from your dad any more than I could've if Orun had sent me away." Tobin was watching him again, looking a little odd. "Not that I—Well, you know. Not like that," Ki hastily amended.

Tobin looked away quickly. "No! Of course not."

The silence drew out so long between them that Ki was grateful when the page banged back in with the water pitcher.

By the time the boy had built up the fire and gone out again, Ki could look Tobin in the face. "So, what was it like, meeting your uncle?"

"Strange. What do you think of him?"

"He's not how I expected, exactly. I mean Korin always speaks well of him, but he's his father, right?" Ki paused, lowering his voice just to be safe. "My dad never had much good to say about the king, on account of him keeping women out of the ranks. And there's all that with the female heirs and the Harriers and such. You notice we weren't the first to greet him, either? There's Old Fox— Niryn, I mean—riding close as his shadow. How'd he get to the king before we did?"

"He's a wizard." Tobin had that distant, guarded look again, the one that came over him whenever Fox Beard was around.

Seeing it, Ki crawled up beside him. Not touching, but close enough to let him know he wasn't alone, being scared of the man. "I think if I met the king at some tavern and didn't know who he was, I'd take him for a good fellow," he offered, going back to the subject at hand.

"So would I, after today. All the same . . ." He trailed off and Ki realized he was trembling. When he spoke again, it was barely a whisper. "My mother was so afraid of him!"

Tobin almost never spoke of his mother.

"Brother hates him, too," he whispered. "But still, after today? I hardly know how to feel except—Maybe the stories aren't true? I mean, Mother was mad, and Brother lies . . . I just don't know!"

"He likes you, Tob. I could tell. And why wouldn't he?" Ki settled closer, shoulder to shoulder. "About the stories, though, I don't know . . . I'm just glad you weren't born a girl."

Tobin's sudden stricken look dropped the bottom out of Ki's belly. "Oh hell, I'm sorry, Tob. I let my tongue run away from me again." He took his friend's hand. In spite of the fire, it was ice-cold. "Maybe they are just stories."

"It's all right. I know what you meant."

They sat a moment like that, and the quiet between them felt good. The room was warming and the bed was soft. Relaxing back against the bolsters, Ki closed his eyes and chuckled. "I know someone who *is* going to have trouble with the king, and soon. Did you see the looks Erius was giving the butler toward the end, when Korin was so drunk?"

Tobin let out a rueful laugh. "He was well down into it, wasn't he? I'm afraid I was, too. Who knew Atyion made so many kinds of wine, eh?"

Ki yawned. "Mark my words. Now that the king's back, Master Porion is going to get his way and there'll be no more drink in the mess for any of us." He yawned again. "And that's fine with me, if it means not having to watch Korin and the others drink themselves stupid every other night."

Tobin grunted sleepy agreement.

Ki felt himself drifting. "Room's spinning, Tobin."

"Mmmm. Guess Korin wasn't the only one who had too much. Don't sleep on your back, Ki."

They both chuckled.

"You say Brother hates the king, too?" Ki mumbled, thoughts wandering toward sleep. "Good thing he didn't show up at the feast, eh?"

Ki's sleepy mutterings drove the sleep from Tobin's mind. Perhaps Brother could see into the king's heart, know if he was kind or evil? Deeper than that, however, lay the ever-present, lonely knowledge that liar and demon that he was, Brother was the only other one Tobin could completely confide in.

When Ki was snoring, Tobin blew out the night lamps and took the doll from his pack. Feeling his way to the hearth, he knelt, heart pounding in his ears. Did he dare call him at all? The day the king had come to the keep Brother had gone wild, thrashing around like a whirlwind. What would he do now, with Erius just down the corridor?

Tobin clutched the doll tightly, as if that would restrain Brother. "Blood, my blood. Flesh, my flesh. Bone, my bone," he whispered, then braced for violence. But Brother simply appeared, kneeling in front of him like a reflection. The only sign of his anger was the terrible, bone-aching chill he brought with him.

"The king is here," Tobin whispered, ready to order him away if Brother moved.

Yes.

"You aren't angry with him?"

The chill grew unbearable as Brother leaned forward. Their noses almost touched; if he'd been alive, Tobin would have tasted his breath as he hissed, "Kill him."

Pain shot through Tobin's chest, as if Brother had torn the hidden stitching open.

He fell forward on his hands, willing himself not to faint. The pain slowly faded. When he opened his eyes again, Brother was gone. He listened fearfully, expecting some outcry nearby, but all was silent. He whispered the spell again to make certain Brother was actually gone, then hurried back to the bed.

"Did he come?" Ki asked softly, awake after all.

Tobin was glad he'd blown out the lamps. "You didn't hear?"

"No, nothing. I thought maybe you'd changed your mind."

"He came," Tobin said, relieved Ki hadn't overheard the dangerous words. He shifted, bumping Ki's bare foot with his.

"Damn, Tobin, you're chilled through! Get under the covers."

They shucked off their clothes and pulled the blankets and counterpanes over them, but Tobin couldn't seem to get warm. His teeth chattered so loudly that Ki heard and moved over to warm him.

"Bilairy's balls, you're cold!" He chafed Tobin's arms, then felt his brow. "Are you sick?"

"No." It was hard to talk with his teeth chattering like that.

A pause, then, "What did Brother say?"

"He—He still doesn't like the king."

"No surprises there." Ki rubbed Tobin's arms again, then settled close against him, yawning again. "Well, like I said—it's a lucky thing you're not a girl."

Tobin squeezed his eyes shut, glad again of the sheltering darkness.

That night the woman pains returned. He sometimes felt a dull ache under his hipbones when the moon was full, but this was the same stabbing ache he'd felt before he'd run away. He'd forgotten the sack of leaves Lhel had given him. Scared and miserable, he curled himself tighter, grateful for Ki's warmth against his back.

Niryn was about to let his valet undress him when he felt it again, that strange little shiver of energy. As usual, it was gone before he could tell what it was, but this was the first time he'd encountered it outside Ero. Waving the man away, he fastened his robe again and went in search of the troubling magic.

He thought he caught a whiff of it again outside Prince Tobin's door, but when he cast a sighting inside, he found the boys fast asleep, curled up together like puppies.

Or lovers.

Niryn's lip curled into a sour smile as he stored away this nugget of information. One never knew when such knowledge might prove useful. Prince Tobin was too young to be a threat, but the king was already showing signs of favor. And there was that embarrassing moment when the stupid brat had tried to take Cirna from him. Niryn would not forget that. No indeed.

Chapter 21

The king was in no hurry to return to Ero. The following day he announced that the royal retinue would honor his nephew by spending the next fortnight in Atyion. Within the week Chancellor Hylus and the other chief ministers arrived and the castle hall became the Palatine in miniature, with the king conducting business between hunting parties and feasts. Only the most pressing matters were allowed and Hylus carefully evaluated each petition and suit, sending away those that could wait. Even so, the hall was filled from dawn to dusk.

With the truce in force, most of the business centered on strife within Skala's own borders. Loitering with the other boys, Tobin heard reports of new outbreaks of plague, bandit raids, tax disputes, and failed crops.

He was also keenly aware of his dependent status among the nobles. His banner might hang highest beneath the king's and Korin's, but the adults paid him little mind except at banquets.

This left Tobin and the other boys free to explore the town and the seashore beyond the castle and they found themselves welcome wherever they went.

The town was a thriving one, and had none of Ero's filth or disease. Instead of a shrine, there were temples to each of the Four set around a square, fine buildings of carved and painted wood. The Temple of Illior was the largest, and Tobin was awed by the painted ceilings and the black stone altar. Priests in silver masks bowed to him as he burned his owl feathers there.

The people of Atyion were well fed and friendly, and every merchant vied eagerly for the honor of serving Atyion's scion and his friends. They were cheered, toasted, and blessed everywhere they went, and gifted royally.

The taverns were the equals of any in Ero. Bards from as far away as Mycena and northern Aurënen plied their craft there, and knew how to please the Companions with tales of their ancestors' prowess.

Tobin was accustomed to living in Korin's benevolent shadow, but here he was the shining light. Korin received great praise and honor, of course, but it was clear that in Atyion Tobin was the people's darling. Though Korin made light of it, Tobin sensed he was jealous. It came out most clearly when Korin had been drinking. For the first time since Tobin had known him, he found himself the butt of the more cutting jokes usually reserved for Orneus or Quirion. Korin began to find fault with the taverns, the theater, the whores, and even Lytia's excellent feasts. He and the older cohort soon went back to their old ways, going off on their own at night and leaving Tobin behind.

Ki was furious, but Tobin let it go. It did hurt, but Tobin understood what it felt like to be second-best. Trusting that things would return to normal back in Ero, he kept his own friends around him and made the most of his time at Atyion.

They were sitting in the sunny window of the Drover's Inn by the market one day, listening to a balladeer sing of one of Tobin's ancestors, when Tobin caught sight of a familiar face across the room.

"Isn't that Bisir?" he said, elbowing Ki to make him look.

"Bisir? What would he be doing here?"

"Don't know. Come on!"

Leaving Nik and Lutha behind, they hurried out in time to see a slim, dark-haired man in the rough tunic and wooden clogs of a farmer disappearing around a corner across the street. They hadn't seen the young valet since Lord Orun's death, but despite the incongruous clothing, Tobin was certain it was he.

Giving chase, Tobin caught up with the man and saw that he was right.

"It is you!" he exclaimed, catching him by the sleeve. "Why did you run away?"

"Hello, Prince Tobin." Bisir was still pretty and soft-spoken, and had that same startled hare look about him, but he was thinner, too, and ruddy as a peasant. "Forgive me. I saw you go in there and couldn't help wanting a better look at you. It's been a long time. I didn't think you'd remember me, really."

"After that winter at the keep? Of course we do!" Ki laughed. "Koni still asks about you now and then."

Bisir blushed and rubbed his hands together nervously, the way he used to. They were brown and callused, with dirt under the nails. Looking at them, Tobin realized that the former valet was ashamed to be seen like this.

"What are you doing here?" he asked.

"Mistress Iya brought me here after—after the troubles in Ero. She said you told her to look after me, but that I wasn't to trouble you. That it would reflect badly on you to be associated with anyone from that household." He gave Tobin a self-deprecating shrug. "She was right, of course. She found me a place in a dairyman's household, just outside the town. And I'm much happier here."

"No, you're not. You're miserable," said Tobin, sizing him up at a glance. Iya must have dumped him at the first likely-looking place.

"Well, it is quite a change," Bisir admitted, staring down at his muddy clogs.

"Come back to the castle with me. I'll speak to Lytia for you."

But Bisir shook his head. "No, Mistress Iya said I mustn't

go there. She was very strict and made me swear, my prince."

Tobin let out an exasperated sigh. "All right then, what would you rather do?"

Bisir hesitated, then looked up shyly. "I'd like to train as a warrior."

"You?" Ki exclaimed.

"I don't know—" Tobin couldn't think of anyone less suited to arms than Bisir. "You're a bit old to be starting," he added, to spare the man's feelings.

"Perhaps I can be of some help, my prince," an old woman in a long grey cloak said.

Tobin glanced at her in surprise; he hadn't noticed her standing there. She looked a bit like Iya somehow, and he thought she must be a wizard until she showed them the intricate dragon circles on her palms. She was a high priestess of Illior. He'd never met one not wearing the silver mask before.

She smiled as if she knew his thoughts. Pressing her hands to her heart, she bowed to Tobin. "I am Kaliya, daughter of Lusiyan, chief priestess of the temple here in Atyion. You don't recognize me, of course, but I've seen you many times, there and around the town. If you'll forgive an old woman's meddling, I think I might be able to suggest a more suitable situation for your young friend here." She took Bisir's hand and closed her eyes. "Ah, yes," she said at once. "You paint."

Bisir blushed again. "Oh, no—Well, a little, when I was a child, but I'm not very good."

Kaliya opened her eyes and regarded him sadly. "You must forget all your former master told you, my friend. He was a selfish man, and had his own uses for you. You do have the gift, and it's far more likely to come out with training than swordplay. A friend of mine is a maker of fine manuscripts. Her shop is in Temple Square and I believe she's seeking an apprentice. I'm sure your age would be of no consequence to her."

Bisir stared down at his dirty hands for a moment, as if he didn't quite recognize them. "You really saw that in me? But Mistress Iya?" Hope and doubt warred in Bisir's eyes as he looked imploringly at Tobin.

He shrugged. "I'm sure she won't mind, as long as you stay out of the castle."

But Bisir still hesitated. "This is so sudden. So unexpected. I don't know what Master Vorten will say. There's the winter forage to bring in and the muck to spread. I'm to help build the new stalls, too—" His chin was trembling now.

"Oh, don't take on like that!" Ki said, trying to cheer him. "Your master can't very well say no to Tobin, can he?"

"I suppose not."

"He won't say no to me, either," the priestess said, taking Bisir's arm. "There's no need to trouble the prince with this. We'll go speak with Vorten and my friend, Mistress Haria, right now. She'll make you work, but I believe I can promise you no more muck spreading."

"Thank you, my lady. And thank you, my prince!" Bisir exclaimed, kissing their hands. "Who would have imagined, when I followed you in there—?"

"Run along home, now," Kaliya told him. "I'll be along shortly."

Bisir clattered away in his clogs. Kaliya laughed as she watched him go, then turned to Tobin and Ki. "Who would have imagined?" she said, echoing Bisir. "Who, indeed, would have imagined that a prince of Skala would cross the street to help a dairyman's laborer?"

"I knew him in Ero," Tobin explained. "He was kind to me, and tried to help me."

"Ah, I see." Her smile was as enigmatic as a silver mask; Tobin couldn't read this face at all. "Well, if the Scion of Atyion should ever be in need of help, I hope you will remember me. May the Lightbearer's blessings be on you both." With that she bowed and went on her way.

Ki shook his head as she disappeared into the market day crowd. "Well, that was damned strange!"

"A bit of good luck, I'd call it," Tobin said. "I'm glad we found Bisir again. A dairyman? Can you imagine?"

Ki laughed. "Or a warrior? It's a good thing for him that woman happened along when she did."

Despite Tobin's status among the townspeople, Duke Solari continued to play host in the hall at night, and managed all the estate business.

"Hosting a court is an expensive undertaking," he told Tobin one night. "But don't worry. We'll recoup the loss by taxing the inns and taverns."

There were taxes for using the roads and the seaport at the mouth of the river, as well, and each noble was charged for housing their own retinue and guards inside the castle.

Still torn between loyalty and distrust of his father's former liegemen, Tobin consulted Tharin, who in turn steered him to Lytia and Hakone.

"Oh yes, it's always done this way," Hakone assured him as they sat around the old steward's hearth one night. "The lord of the estate—that being you in this case—gains honor by hosting the king, but he foots the bill, too, and passes it down to the town. You needn't worry, though. If the duke didn't collect a copper from the tolls and taxes, the treasuries of Atyion could withstand a good many royal visits." He paused and looked up at Lytia. "Why, he's never seen it, has he?"

"Is there a lot of gold?" asked Tobin.

"Mountains of it, I always heard!" Ki exclaimed.

"Very nearly." Lytia chuckled. "I'd show you, but that's one key I don't have." She rattled the heavy chain at her girdle. "You'll have to ask your uncle or the duke about that. Tharin, see that he does ask. It's not just coin, Prince Tobin. There are the spoils of battles all the way back to the Great War and beyond, and gifts from a dozen queens."

"Get him to show you, Tob," Ki urged. "And make sure I get to come along!"

*T*he next day Tharin spoke to Solari, and Tobin invited all the Companions to tour the treasury.

It was located deep under the west tower, and dozens of armed men and three sets of ironbound doors guarded it.

"We've kept it all safe for you, my prince," the captain of the watch told Tobin proudly. "We've just been waiting for you to come home and claim it."

"When he's of age," Solari murmured, as they started down the steep stairs. He smiled as he said it, but Tobin noted the remark.

Just then Ringtail appeared out of nowhere and darted between Solari's feet. He staggered, then kicked at the cat. Ringtail hissed and clawed at his foot, then ran back the way he'd come.

"Damn that creature!" Solari exclaimed. "That's the third time he's done that today. I nearly broke my neck coming down to the hall this morning. And he pisses in my bedchamber, too, though how he gets in I don't know. The steward should have him drowned before he kills someone."

"No, my lord," said Tobin. "Lady Lytia says the cats are sacred. I won't have any of them harmed."

"As you wish, my prince, but I must say, there are more than enough of the creatures about."

Lytia's description had done nothing to prepare Tobin for the sight that greeted them as the final door swung open. It was not one huge room but a whole maze of them. Gold there was in plenty, and silver too, in leather bags stacked like sacks of oats. But this was not what made Tobin's eyes pop. Room after room was filled with armor, swords, tattered banners, jeweled harnesses and saddles. One held nothing but golden cups and platters, shelves of them shining in the torchlight. In the middle of it a huge double-handled vessel stood on a velvet-draped trestle. It was large enough to bathe a small child in and decorated under the rim with writing that Tobin did not recognize.

"It's the old tongue, the language spoken in the courts of the first hierophants!" Nikides exclaimed, pushing in between Tanil and Zusthra for a better look.

"I suppose you can read it," sneered Alben.

Nikides ignored him. "It's what they called an endless inscription, I think. One that creates magical powers or blessings when a priest reads it." He had to walk around the vessel to see all the words. "I think it starts here—'The tears of Astellus on the bosom of Dalna sprout the oak of Sakor that stretches its arms to Illior's moon that brings down the tears of Astellus on the—' Well, you see what I mean. It was probably used in a temple of the Four to catch rainwater for ceremonies."

Tobin grinned, happy to see his friend shine. Nikides might not be the greatest swordsman, but no one could best him at learning. Even Solari took a second look at the vessel. For a moment Tobin saw his Protector's face mirrored in the curved golden surface, distorted into a yellow, greedy mask. He glanced at the man, feeling the same uneasy chill that he had the day Brother whispered his accusations. But Solari looked no different and seemed genuinely pleased to show Tobin his inheritance.

Despite the king's duties, Erius still made time to hunt and hawk and visit the horse breeders with the boys, and had them at his table every night. Tobin continued to wrestle with his own heart. The more he saw of his uncle, the less of a monster he seemed. He joked and sang with them, and was free with gifts and rewards after the hunts.

They feasted every night, and Tobin couldn't imagine where so much food and drink could come from. Lines of wagons rumbled up the roads every day and Solari had to send out crews to keep the roads mended. He took the boys out to see the progress. The roadways were still soft from the spring rains, so the soldiers laid logs down crossways to the road, drove stakes to keep them tightly in place, then sent carts loaded with stones to pack them down.

Every day seemed to bring some new diversion, and Tobin slowly grew used to the idea that this great castle, its riches and lands all belonged to him. Or would someday, at least. The court business was interesting, but Tobin still felt most at home in Hakone's room or wandering among the soldiers in the castle's enormous barracks yards. He always found a warm welcome there.

Iris and hag sorrel were tall in the ditches, and foals and spring lambs gamboled in the fields as the king's column set off for Ero at the fortnight's end.

Korin and the Companions rode with the king for a while, discussing hawking and the best hunts they'd had. But Erius' mind was already in the city and he was soon conducting business on horseback, listening to petitions read out by mounted scribes. Bored, the boys fell back and left him to it.

Someone back in the ranks started a ballad and soon the whole column joined in. It was an old one, from the time of the Great War, and told of a general who'd died defeating the Plenimaran necromancers. The song ended, and talk turned to dark magic. None of the boys had any real knowledge of such matters, but they'd all heard lurid tales and eagerly shared them.

"My father told me a story passed down through all my grandfathers," Alben said. "One of our ancestors led a force against a necromancer's castle on an island near Kouros. It was fenced all around with the bodies of Skalan warriors, nailed up like scarecrows. Inside the castle, all the books were bound with human skin. The servants' shoes and belts were made of it, and all the cups were made of skulls. We have one in the house treasury. Father says we should have exterminated every necromancer when we had the chance."

They hadn't seen Niryn all morning, but suddenly there he was, riding beside Korin. "Your father speaks wisely, Lord Alben. Necromancy has deep roots in Plenimar, and it's growing stronger again. Their dark god demands innocent blood and flesh in his temples. The priests make a feast of it and their wizards use the bodies like the carcasses of cattle, just as you say. Their filthy practices have even come to our shores, and some wearing the robes of the Four secretly practice the red arts. Traitors, every one of them. You boys must be vigilant; their influence is a canker in the heart of Skala, and death is the only cure. They must be hunted down and destroyed."

"As you and your Harriers do, my lord," Alben said.

"Bootlicker," Lutha muttered, then busied himself with his reins when the wizard's hard brown gaze flickered momentarily in his direction.

"The Harriers serve the king, just as you boys do," the wizard replied, touching his brow and heart. "The wizards of Skala must defend the throne from these foul traitors."

He rode forward again, and Zusthra and Alben excitedly launched into the stories they'd heard of such executions. "They burn them alive," said Zusthra.

"They only hang the priests," Alben corrected. "They have a special magic for the wizards."

"How can they do that?" Urmanis demanded. "They must catch only the weak ones. The strong ones could just use their own magic to escape."

"The Harriers have their ways," Korin told him smugly. "Father says that Niryn was gifted with binding magic in a vision from Illior and told to purify his kind for Skala's sake."

Word of the king's progress went before them and every village was decked out to greet him. Bonfires blazed on hilltops and people lined the road, cheering and wav-

ing as they passed. It was no different when they reached
Ero just before dusk of the second day. The whole city was
ablaze with light and the north road was lined for half a
mile out with well-wishers.

Erius happily acknowledged the welcome, waving and
throwing fistfuls of gold sesters to the crowd. At the gate
he saluted the carved emblems of the gods, then drew his
sword and held it up for all to see. "In the name of
Ghërilain and Thelátimos, my ancestors, and in the name
of Sakor and Illior, our protectors, I enter my capital."

This set off an ever-louder roar of acclaim. It rolled like
a wave into the city. As the echoes died, Tobin could hear
the distant cheering on the Palatine.

Inside the walls the streets were decked with banners,
flags, and torches, and people had strewn the street with
hay and sweet herbs to make the king's way soft. Clouds of
incense billowed up from every corner shrine and temple.
People poured out of the shops and houses, gathered in
the markets, hung from windows, calling out to the king
and waving whatever they could find—hats, kerchiefs,
rags, cloaks.

"Is the war over?" they cried. "Are you home for good?"

It was the same on the Palatine. Nobles decked in their
finest clothes massed along the royal way, throwing flowers and waving red silk banners.

Reaching the New Palace, Erius dismounted in the garden and made his way through the happy throng, clasping
hands and kissing cheeks. The Companions and officers
followed in his wake and were cheered just as loudly.

At last they gained the palace steps, and the crowd beyond parted before them as the king strode to the audience
chamber.

Tobin had been here once before, soon after he first
came to Ero. Still a bumpkin then, he'd been awed by the
huge pillared hall, with its grand fountains, colored windows, and huge shrines. Today, he could scarcely see any
of it beyond the masses of people who filled the corridors.

Phalanxes of the King's Guard formed a cordon between the dragon pillars, opening an arrow-straight concourse to the dais. The Harrier wizards flanked the stairs, a line of white against the red backdrop of the Guard. Lord Chancellor Hylus stood waiting at the bottom of the steps, dressed in full regalia. He bowed low as Erius approached and bade him welcome, as if he hadn't seen him only a few days earlier in Atyion.

Niryn, the Companions, and the rest of the entourage took their places in the front rank before the dais, but Korin and Tobin followed the king.

"Just do as I do, but on the other side," Korin had instructed him earlier.

Following his cousin's lead, Tobin took his place behind the throne and stood at attention, left hand on his sword hilt, right fist over his heart.

The ceremonial cloak was still draped over the throne, as it had been throughout the king's absence, and the tall, gem-studded crown rested on the seat. This crown was not a round circlet, but square, like a house with a fancy spire at each corner. When Erius reached the throne, noble equerries reverently lifted the square crown and bore it away on a large velvet cushion. Others draped the cloak over the king's shoulders, fastening it at his shoulders with jeweled brooches. Tobin saw with an unpleasant start that one of the equerries was none other than Moriel the Toad. Solemn in his red tabard, Moriel finished with the brooch and took his place at the bottom of the dais stair. The other Companions had formed up just beyond and Ki shot Tobin a bemused look. The Toad gave no sign that he'd seen either of them.

Erius faced the throng and raised his sword again. "By the blood of my ancestors and the Sword of Ghërilain, I claim my throne!"

Everyone except Korin and Tobin sank to their knees, fists to hearts. From where Tobin stood it looked like a field of oats suddenly flattened by a strong wind. His heart gave a painful little hitch; no matter what Arkoniel or Lhel said, Erius was a true king, a warrior.

Erius took the throne and laid the sword across his knees.

"The Sword of Ghërilain has returned to the city. Our Protector has returned," Hylus announced in a surprisingly loud voice for such a frail old man.

The cheer was so loud this time that it reverberated in Tobin's chest. He felt the same exhilaration he'd experienced entering Atyion. *This is what it is to be king,* he thought.

Or queen.

Chapter 22

The king's return put an end to the Companions' easy, insular life in the city. Erius wanted Korin with him at court nearly every day, and the Companions went with him.

Or half of them. Split already by age, they now found themselves further divided by blood and title. Tobin had slowly come to understand the subtle distinction between squire and noble, although the squires were the sons of noble families themselves. But now those distinctions were thrown into still sharper contrast. When Korin and the others went to court, the squires remained behind at their lessons at the Old Palace.

Tobin didn't care much for this new arrangement, for it meant being separated from Ki.

He was walking through the Companions' wing in search of him one afternoon not long after their return when he heard a woman sobbing somewhere nearby. Rounding a corner, Tobin saw a maid hurrying away down the corridor with her apron over her face.

Puzzled, he went on, only to hear more weeping as he approached his own door. Inside, his page Baldus was huddled sobbing in one of the armchairs. Ki stood over him, awkwardly patting his shoulder.

"What's wrong?" Tobin exclaimed, hurrying over. "Is he hurt?"

"I just got here myself. All I've gotten out of him so far is that somebody's dead."

Kneeling, Tobin pulled the boy's hands away from his face. "Who is it? Someone in your family?"

Baldus shook his head. "Kalar!"

The name meant nothing to Tobin. "Here, take my handkerchief and wipe your nose. Who was she?"

Baldus drew a hitching breath. "She brought the laundry around and changed the hallway rushes . . ." He dissolved into tears again.

"Oh, yes," said Ki. "The pretty blond with the blue eyes who was always singing."

Tobin knew who he meant. He'd liked her songs and she'd smiled at him. He'd never thought to ask her name.

They could get nothing more out of Baldus. Ki gave him some wine, then tucked him into the disused squire's alcove to cry himself to sleep. Molay came in and set about his duties, but he was uncharacteristically silent and grim.

"Did you know this Kalar, too?" asked Tobin.

Molay sighed as he hung a discarded tunic in the wardrobe. "Yes, my prince. Everyone knew her."

"What happened?"

The man pulled a few socks from under Tobin's workbench and shook off the bits of wax and metal shavings. "She died, my lord."

"We know that!" said Ki. "What happened to her? It wasn't plague, was it?"

"No, thank the Light. It seems she was pregnant and miscarried last night. Word came a little while ago that she did not survive." The man's careful reserve gave way for a moment and he wiped at his eyes. "She was hardly more than a girl!" he exclaimed in a low, angry voice.

"That's nothing unusual, losing a child early on like that, especially the first one," Ki mused when Molay was gone. "Most don't die of it, though."

It was several days before the servants' gossip made its way into the Companions' mess. The child was rumored to have been Korin's.

Korin took the news philosophically; after all, it had only been a bastard, and a servant's child at that. Red-haired Lady Aliya, who'd been the focus of his attention for some time now, was the only one who seemed pleased with the news.

The girl was soon forgotten as the boys came to grips with another unpleasant development, and one that struck closer to home. Not only had Moriel somehow gotten appointed to the king's retinue, but he was already a favorite.

Korin was no more pleased than Tobin was with this unexpected addition to his father's household. Promotion had not improved the Toad's manners, as far as they could see, but the king doted on him. A tall, pale, arrogant boy of fifteen now, Moriel stuck close to the king, always at hand, always obsequious.

His new duties frequently brought him into the Old Palace, as well, though equerries had seldom been seen there before. There was always some message to deliver or some object the king needed from one of the old wings. It seemed to Tobin that every time he turned around the Toad was disappearing around a corner, or hanging about with Mago and his friends among the squires. In that, he'd gotten his wish, after all, if only peripherally.

Korin detested him even more than anyone. "He's in Father's chambers more than I am!" he grumbled. "Every time I go there, there *he* is, smirking and fawning. And the other day, when Father was out of earshot, he called me by my first name!"

Things came to a head between the two boys a few weeks later. Tobin and Korin had gone to the king's chamber to invite Erius to hunt and found their way blocked by Moriel. Instead of bowing them in, he stepped out and closed the door behind him.

"Go tell my father I wish to see him," Korin ordered, already bristling.

"The king does not wish to be disturbed, Highness," Moriel replied, his tone just short of rude.

Tobin watched his cousin size the other boy up. He'd never seen Korin really angry, but he was now.

"You will announce me at once," he said in a tone that anyone would have been foolish to ignore.

To Tobin's amazement, Moriel shook his head. "I have my orders."

Korin waited the space of a heartbeat, then back-handed Moriel so hard that he went sprawling and slid several feet along the polished marble floor. Blood trickled down from his nose and a split lip.

Korin bent over him, shaking with fury now. "If you *ever* dare speak to me in such a tone again—if you fail to obey my command or forget to address me properly, I will have you impaled on Traitor's Hill."

With that he wrenched his father's door open and strode inside, leaving Moriel cowering. Tobin might have pitied the boy, but the poisonous glare Moriel shot after Korin killed the sentiment.

From the antechamber, he could hear Korin raging to his father, and the murmur of the king's amused reply. Entering the room, he found Niryn with them, standing just behind the king's chair. He said nothing, but Tobin was certain he caught a hint of Moriel's smirk in the wizard's eyes.

Aside from these disruptions, the summer flowed on smoothly enough for a while. It was the hottest in memory and the countryside suffered. Petitioners at court brought tales of drought and wildfires, murrains and dry wells.

Standing by the throne each day, Tobin listened with interest and sympathy, but felt little touched by it, busy as he was with his new duties.

The noble Companions often served at the king's table now, just as the squires served them. By right of birth, Tobin acted as their panter, cutting the different breads for each course. Korin was an expert carver, flashing the six kinds of knives skillfully about as he served up the meats. The other boys fell out by age and family, with hulking Zusthra as butler and Orneus making a clumsy job of

mazer, despite all Lynx's attempts to train him. The second
time he slopped wine on the king's sleeve he was sum-
marily demoted to almoner and Nikides took charge of the
king's cup.

Afternoon arms practice and their lessons with old
Raven continued in spite of the heat, but the mornings
were spent at the audience chamber. Korin and Tobin sat
next to the king. Hylus and the others stood just behind
them, often for hours at a time. Erius began consulting
Korin on the smaller matters, letting him decide the fate of
a miller found to be short measuring, or an alewife selling
sour brew for good. The king even allowed him to try
some of the lesser criminals and Tobin was surprised at
how quick his cousin was to mete out floggings and
brandings.

With the exception of Nikides, the other boys found attending court tedious duty. Even with its high, pillared roof
and tinkling fountains, the throne room was like an oven
by noon. But Tobin found it fascinating. He'd always had a
knack for reading faces and now he had an endless assort-
ment to study. Soon he could almost see the thoughts form-
ing as the petitioners cajoled, complained, or tried to curry
favor. The tone of voice, the way a person stood, or where
their gaze went as they spoke—all of it stood out like letters on a page. Liars fidgeted. Honest men spoke calmly.
Scoundrels wept and carried on louder than the honest.

His favorite studies were not the Skalans, however, but
the foreign envoys. Tobin marveled at the intricacies of
diplomacy, as well as the visitors' exotic clothing and ac-
cents. Mycenians were the most common, an earnest,
hardheaded lot concerned with harvests, tariffs, and the
defense of their borders. The Aurënfaie were the most di-
verse; there were dozens of different clans, each with their
own distinctive headclothes and dealings.

One day the king received a half dozen men with
swarthy skin and curly black hair. They wore long blue-and-
black-striped robes of a type Tobin had never seen before,

and heavy silver ornaments dangled from their ears. These, he was surprised to learn, were Zengati tribesmen.

Arengil and Tobin's friends among the Aurënfaie craftsmen always spoke of Zengat with hatred or disdain. But, as Hylus later explained, the Zengati were as clannish as the 'faie, and some clans were more trustworthy than others.

The heat brought more than drought again that summer. From their secret rooftop practice ground, Tobin, Una, and the others could see great brown swaths marring the distant fields, where blight had destroyed the crops.

The summer sky was marred, as well. The Red and Black Death had broken out along the harbor outside the walls. Whole neighborhoods were burned flat and great columns of smoke hung over the water. To the west, a smaller column rose with darker urgency from the funeral grounds. Even people who'd died with no taint of plague on them were quickly disposed of.

Reports came from the inland towns of dead horses and oxen, and more disease. Erius ordered livestock and grain to be disbursed by the wealthy lords in each stricken district. Niryn's Harriers hanged any who spoke of a curse on the land, but that did not stop the murmurs from growing. At the temples of Illior, the amulet makers had more business than they could keep up with.

Safe atop the Palatine, the Companions thought themselves untouched by such events until Porion forbade them to go farther into the city than Birdcatcher Street. Korin complained bitterly for days, cut off from his haunts in the harbor stews.

One thing they still had plenty of was wine, in spite of disapproving rumblings from the king. It flowed more freely than ever and even normally sensible Caliel began to show up for sword practice with red eyes and a sour demeanor.

*   *   *

$\mathcal{T}$obin's set followed lead and drank their wine well watered. Thanks to this, they were generally the first up in the morning, and the first to learn that Korin's squire was finding other places to sleep.

"What are you doing here?" Ruan demanded the first time they found Tanil curled in a blanket by the messroom hearth. He gave the older squire a playful nudge with his boot. Tanil usually answered such liberties by throwing the offender down and tickling him, signaling the others to pile on for an all-out wrestle. Instead, he stalked out without a word.

"Who pissed in his soup?" Ki muttered.

The others snickered, except for the crestfallen Ruan, who idolized Tanil.

"I wouldn't be too chipper either, if I spent the night on the floor," said Lutha. "Maybe he's tired of Korin's snoring."

"Korin hasn't been doing much snoring lately," Ki confided. Living next door to the prince, he and Tobin had heard enough late night thumping and whispering to guess that Korin didn't often go to bed alone.

"Well, I guess we know it's not Tanil," said Ruan.

"It never was!" Lutha scoffed. "No, Korin's after another chambermaid."

"I don't think so," Nikides mused later, trudging along beside them as they set off on the morning run. He'd gotten a bit more growth over the summer and lost most of his boyish fat, but he was still the slowest.

"What do you mean?" asked Ki, always eager for gossip.

Nikides looked ahead to make sure none of the older boys were in earshot. "I shouldn't say anything—"

"You already have, blabbermouth. Tell!" Lutha urged.

"Well, when I was dining at Grandfather's the other night, I overheard him saying something to my cousin the Exchequer about the prince and—" He looked ahead again, making certain Korin was still well ahead of them. "That he was—dallying with Lady Aliya."

Even Ki was shocked. Servant girls were one thing, or other boys, even, but the noble girls were strictly kept.

Worse yet, none of them liked Aliya. She was pretty enough, but she had a mean, teasing way with everyone except Korin. Even Caliel avoided her when he could.

"Haven't you noticed?" said Nikides. "She's always with him, and from the way the maids have been sulking and moping, I'd say she'd pushed the rest of them out of his bed."

"And Tanil," Ruan reminded them.

Lutha let out a whistle. "Do you suppose he's in love with her?"

Barieus laughed. "Korin in love? With his horses and hawks, maybe, but *her*? Bilairy's balls, I hope not. Picture her as queen!"

Nikides shrugged. "You don't have to love 'em to bed 'em."

Lutha pretended to be shocked. "Is that any way for the Lord Chancellor's grandson to talk? For shame!" He gave his friend a playful cuff on the ear.

The other boy yelped and swung at Lutha, who easily veered out of reach without breaking stride.

"You six, double time!" Porion shouted, falling out of the line to glare at them. "Or would you rather do a second round to build up your strength?"

"No, Master Porion!" Tobin called, and lengthened his stride, leaving Nikides to fend for himself.

"Nik's right, you know. Just look at him," said Ki. Korin was loping at the head of the pack, dark eyes sparkling as he shared some joke with Zusthra and Caliel. "He's too wild to give his heart away. All the same, though, if Aliya is his favorite now, she'll be worse than ever!"

Chapter 23

By late summer the city was unbearable. Many Palatine nobles fled to their country estates, and those who stayed built bathing pools. In the lower parts of the city, the weak and the elderly died by the dozens.

The king and Porion relented a bit with the boys. Released from court duties, the Companions rode in the wooded hills and bathed in the sea. The men of the princes' guard were as grateful for this light duty as the Companions. At the pools and sea coves, everyone stripped off and swam. Soon they were all as brown as farmers, and Ki was the brownest of them all. He was starting to fill out like the older boys, too, Tobin couldn't help but notice. He, on the other hand, was not.

Riding back through the city after an excursion in mid-Lenthin, Tobin was suddenly struck by the near silence. The streets were always quiet on these blistering days; most people stayed indoors to escape the heat and the stench. Even so, those who were about always cheered the prince's banner as the Companions rode past. This morning had been no different, but now many looked away, or stared darkly after them. One man even spat on the ground as Korin passed.

"Has something happened?" Korin called out to a harness maker fanning himself on a crate in front of his shop. The man shook his head and went inside.

"What rudeness," Zusthra exclaimed indignantly. "I'll thrash the fellow!"

To Tobin's relief, Korin shook his head and kicked his horse into a gallop.

They were within sight of the Palatine gate when someone threw a cabbage from the upper window of a house. It missed Korin's head by inches and struck Tanil on the shoulder, knocking the squire from his horse.

Korin reined in furiously as the Companions closed ranks around him. "Search that house. Bring me the man who dares attack the king's son!"

His captain, Melnoth, kicked the door down and stormed in with a dozen men. The rest formed a circle around the Companions, weapons drawn. Screams and the sound of breaking crockery soon came from inside.

A crowd gathered as Korin helped Tanil back into the saddle.

"I'm all right," Tanil insisted, rubbing his elbow.

"You're lucky it isn't broken," said Ki. "Why the hell is someone shying cabbages at us all of a sudden?"

The soldiers dragged three people from the house: an old man and woman, and a young fellow in the blue-and-white robes of an Illioran temple initiate.

"Which of you attacked me?" Korin demanded.

"I threw the cabbage!" the priest shot back, staring arrogantly up at Korin.

The prince was visibly taken aback by the man's brazen vehemence. For a moment he looked more like a hurt child than an angry noble. "But why?"

The man spat on the ground. "Ask your father."

"What's this to do with him?"

Instead of answering, the young priest spat again, and began yelling, "Abomination! Abomination! Murders! You are killing the land—"

Captain Melnoth struck him on the head with his sword hilt and the man fell senseless to the ground.

"Is this your kin?" Korin demanded of the cowering elderly couple.

The toothless old man could only whimper. His wife

wrapped her arms around him and looked imploringly up at Korin. "Our nephew, my prince, just in from the country to serve at the Dog Street temple. I had no idea he'd do such a thing! Forgive him, I beg you. He's young . . ."

"Forgive?" Korin let out a startled laugh. "No, old mother, I don't forgive such an act. Captain, take him to the Harriers and see that he's questioned."

The old woman's wailing followed them as they rode on.

Erius made light of the incident that night as the boys feasted with him in his private courtyard. The squires served at table, assisted by a few of the king's young men. Moriel was among them, and Tobin was amused to see how he was careful to stay out of Korin's reach.

Niryn, Hylus, and a handful of other nobles dined with them. Everyone had heard of the incident with the young Illioran, of course, but had to have it again from Korin.

When he was done, Erius sat back and nodded. "Well, Korin, perhaps it's time you see that it's not all cheers and roses, ruling a great kingdom. There are traitors everywhere."

"He called me an abomination, Father," said Korin. The accusation had been eating at him all day.

"What else would you expect from an Illioran?" Niryn sneered. "I wonder sometimes that you let their temples remain open in the city, Majesty. Priests are the worst traitors of all, corrupting the simpleminded populace with their wives' tales."

"But what did he mean, telling me to ask you about it?" Korin persisted.

"If I may, my king?" asked Lord Hylus, looking grave. "The man's remarks were most certainly in reference to the executions announced today."

"Executions?" Korin turned expectantly to his father.

"Yes, that's why I invited you here tonight, before this other unpleasantness occurred," his father replied. "I've something special planned, my boys. Tomorrow night there's to be a burning!"

Tobin felt cold despite the lingering heat of the day.

"A wizard burning?" Korin exclaimed, delighted. "We've been wanting to see one of those!"

Lynx leaned over Tobin's shoulder to fill his cup. "Some of us have," he muttered without much enthusiasm.

"Your father understands that you are no longer a child, my prince," Niryn said with an obsequious smile. "It's time you and your Companions witness the full power of Skalan justice. Thanks to your quick thinking this afternoon, we'll have one more rope on the gibbet pole."

"And you won't have far to go to see it done," the king said, comfortable over his wine and nuts. "The East Market is being cleared as we speak."

"Then you mean to go forward with this, my king?" Hylus asked softly. "You will not reconsider?"

The chamber went silent.

Erius turned slowly to his chancellor, and Tobin recognized the sudden change in his uncle's jovial countenance. It was the same look he'd given Tobin when he'd foolishly asked that Cirna be given to Ki's father. This time Niryn did not intervene.

"I believe I made myself clear on the matter this morning. Do you have something more to say?" the king replied, his voice dangerously low.

Hylus looked slowly around the table, but no one would meet his eye. "Only to reiterate that such matters have always been dealt with outside the city walls. In light of today's incident, perhaps Your Majesty should—"

Erius lurched to his feet, clutching his mazer in one upraised hand, ready to hurl it at the old man. His face had gone dark red and sweat beaded his brow. Caught behind the Lord Chancellor's chair, Ruan clutched the empty alms basin to his chest. Hylus lowered his head and pressed a hand to his heart, but did not flinch.

Time seemed to stop for one awful moment. Then Niryn rose and whispered something in the king's ear.

Erius slowly lowered the cup and slumped back in his chair. Glaring around at the table, he demanded, "Does anyone else object to the execution of traitors?"

No one spoke.

"Very well, then," Erius said thickly. "The executions will proceed as I order. *Where* I order. Now if you will all excuse me, I have other matters to attend to."

Korin rose to follow his father, but Niryn shook his head and accompanied the king himself. Moriel followed. Korin stared after them in silent outrage, cheeks flaming.

It was Hylus who broke this silence. "Ah, my prince, these are trying times. I should not have questioned your good father. I pray you will convey my apologies to him."

"Of course, my lord." Korin was still shaken, too.

Everyone rose to leave, but Tobin sat a moment longer, heart pounding in his ears. He'd grown complacent again, basking in his uncle's favor. Tonight he knew he'd had a true glimpse of the man his mother had feared, the man who could in cold blood order the death of children.

Chapter 24

"Traitors or not, I don't like the feel of this," Ki muttered as they finished dressing the following evening. "It's bad business, killing priests. My dad used to say that's what brought on all the famines and sickness there've been since the king—" Ki bit his tongue and looked quickly at Tobin to see if he'd offended him; the king was his uncle, after all. He kept forgetting that.

But Tobin was staring off with that distracted look he still sometimes got since his illness. Ki wasn't sure if he'd even heard him.

Tobin tugged on his new surcoat and let out a troubled sigh. "I don't know what to think, Ki. We're pledged to fight all traitors against Skala, and I will! But the way the king looked at Hylus?" He shook his head. "I grew up with my mother's madness. I know the look of it, and I swear that's what I saw in the king's eyes when he was shouting at that poor old man. And no one else said anything! They all acted like it was nothing. Even Korin."

"If he is mad, who'd dare say anything? He's still king," Ki reminded him. "And what about Niryn? He looked pretty damn pleased, I thought."

A soft knock came at the door and Nikides and Ruan slipped in. Ki noted with alarm that Nikides was close to tears.

"What's wrong?" Tobin asked, guiding him to a chair.

Nikides was too overcome to answer.

"Haven't you heard the rumors?" asked Ruan.

"No," Ki replied. "What is it?"

Nikides found his voice then. "Grandfather is under arrest. For treason! For asking a question!" Nikides choked out, shaking with anger. "All Grandfather did was ask a question. You heard him. The king knows as well as anyone that there's never been an execution inside the city walls, except—Well, you know."

"Except during Queen Agnalain's reign," Ruan finished for him. "Begging your pardon, Prince Tobin, but your grandmother did some dark things."

"You needn't apologize to me. She was mad, just like my mother."

"Don't say that, Tob," Ki begged. Her memory seemed to be on Tobin's mind too much these days. "She never did anything like Mad Agnalain." *Or the king,* he added silently.

"It can't be true," he said to Nikides. "Chancellor Hylus is the wisest, most loyal man in Skala and everyone knows it. You know how rumors are."

"But what if it *is* true?" Nikides fought back tears. "What if he's executed with the others tonight? And—" He looked imploringly up at Tobin. "How could I just sit there and watch?"

"Come on. Korin will know, I bet," said Tobin.

Tanil answered their knock. "Time to go already?" He had on his showiest armor but his boots were still unlaced.

"No, we need to speak with Korin," Tobin replied.

Korin was standing before his long looking glass with his cuirass half-buckled. The Sakor horse charm Tobin had made for him swung against the gilded leather as Tanil wrestled with the stubborn buckles. Two valets, meanwhile, were laying out ceremonial cloaks and polishing the prince's gold-chased helm.

Ki felt a pang of guilt, seeing all this. Tobin still dressed himself, and only let Ki help with the straps he couldn't reach. As much as he admired Tobin's simplicity, he sometimes wondered if he shouldn't try to live a bit more like a royal.

Tobin explained Nikides' concerns, but Korin only

shrugged. "I've heard nothing of it, Nik. You mustn't mind Father. You know how changeable he can be, especially when he's weary. It's this damn heat!" He turned back to the mirror to watch as Tanil draped his maroon-and-gold cloak over his shoulders. "But Hylus should know better than to question Father!"

Any son would stand up for his father, Ki knew; he'd done it often enough himself. All the same, there was an imperious note in Korin's voice he'd been hearing more often lately and it left him uneasy. So did poor Nikides' stricken look.

"I thought it was the Lord Chancellor's role to advise the king," Tobin said quietly.

Korin turned and ruffled his cousin's hair. "An advisor must still show the proper respect, coz."

Tobin started to say something, but Ki caught his eye and shook his head slightly. Nikides' nervous glance told him he'd done the right thing, as well as just how much life at court had changed since the king's return.

*T*he Companions assembled in the mess for Master Porion's inspection before going on to the New Palace. Tobin stayed close to Nikides as the others milled about.

Ki stood with them, but his eye was on Korin. The prince was in high spirits, chattering on with the older boys like it was some festival they were going off to. Some of them had seen hangings, but tonight wizards would be burned!

"I hear they turn black and shrivel up like a spider in the fire," said Alben, clearly relishing the idea.

"I heard they explode into colored smoke," Orneus countered.

"We'll show 'em how traitors are served in Ero!" Zusthra declared, brandishing his sword. "Bad enough to have enemies over the water without worrying about vipers here at home."

This was greeted with a hearty cheer.

"Wizards are the most dangerous sort of traitor, with their magic and free ways," Orneus declared, and Ki guessed he was quoting something he'd heard his father say.

"Rogue priests are the next worst, like that bastard who attacked Korin," Urmanis chimed in. "And these damn Illiorans who still claim that only a woman can rule Skala? It's like shitting on all the victories King Erius has given them."

"My father says all Illiorans still secretly believe that," said Alben. "Bunch of ingrates! King Erius saved this land."

Lynx was quiet, Ki noted. That was nothing unusual, but Ki had heard him mention having an uncle who was a wizard and guessed he was more troubled than he let on. Maybe, like Nikides, he was scared of seeing a familiar face tonight.

"Wizards, priests—they're all moonstruck," Zusthra declared. "It's Sakor who puts the strength in our arms."

Porion strode in just then, looking like a thundercloud. Leaping up on a table, he shouted for their attention.

This was the first time Ki had seen the arms master in full armor. His cuirass was oiled and polished, but showed the scars of many battles, as did the great scabbard swinging at his side and the steel helmet he carried beneath his arm.

"Line up!" he barked, glowering around at them. "Listen to me now, boys, and listen well. It's no pleasure jaunt we're going on tonight, so I don't want any more of that kind of talk. The servants can hear you at the other end of the corridor."

He set his helmet down and folded his arms. "Traitors or not, the men and women who die tonight are Skalans, and some of them will have supporters in the crowd—friends, family, and the like. As you know, this is the first time in a long time that an execution has been held inside the city walls instead of at Traitor's Hill. It's not for me to say whether that's wise or right, but I can tell you it's not popular among some factions here in Ero. So keep your mouths shut, your eyes open, and your swords at the ready. You Companions are coming into your own tonight. What's your purpose?"

"To guard Prince Korin!" Caliel replied.

"That's right. You've all trained for this and tonight you could be called on to live up to your oath. We're to ride before the king to the market and back, with king's men flanking us. At the first sign of trouble, we close ranks around Korin and get him back here any way we can. The king's men may help us, but the honor and duty are ours."

"What about Father?" Korin demanded. "I'm not going to be carried off like baggage if he's in danger!"

"The king will be well protected. Your task, my prince, is to stay alive to rule after him. So no heroics tonight, do you understand?" He held Korin's eye until the boy nodded, then gave the rest of them a dark look. "And no more carrying on like a bunch of little girls on a picnic, either! This is solemn business." He paused and rubbed at his grizzled beard. "And a risky one, too, if you ask me. Blood will be spilled in the capital tonight; the blood of priests. Whatever their crimes, it's an unlucky thing, so stay sharp and be ready for trouble every inch of the way until we're safe back here again."

He jumped down from the table and began to sketch out a battle plan on the floor with a bit of chalk. "I'm the most concerned about the market square; that's where the crowd will be thickest, and most contained. We'll be here, before the platform at the center. Korin, you and the nobles will flank the king to his right. Squires, you'll each sit your horse behind your lord and I want you to keep an eye on the crowd while the others are watching the executions. If the worst happens, you stay with Korin and we'll fight our way back to the gate. Do you all understand?"

"Yes, Master Porion!" they answered with one voice.

He paused again, looking around at them. "Good. And it's rule of war tonight. Anyone who panics and deserts the prince, I'll kill myself."

"Yes, Master Porion!" Ki shouted with the others, knowing it was no idle threat.

As they filed out he gave Tobin's wrist a quick, furtive squeeze. "Ready?"

Tobin glanced at him, perfectly calm. "Of course. You?"

Ki nodded, grinning. He wasn't scared either, but swore secretly that if trouble did come, his first concern would not be for Korin.

A yellow full moon hung over the city, painting a rippling golden path across the face of the harbor below. The air was dead still, as if the whole city was holding its breath. No sea breeze cut the fetid summer smell of the streets. Ki's torch hardly flickered as they rode slowly along. The tall stone buildings that lined the high street gave back the clatter of hooves and the mournful throbbing of the drums.

Tobin rode beside Korin and Porion, of course, which put Ki just behind them with Caliel, Mylirin, and Tanil. All the squires carried torches. The King's Guard flanked them and brought up the rear. Ki was glad of the line of red tunics to either side. Tonight he felt the full weight of the responsibility that underlay all their training and banquets and mock battles.

Looking back, he could just see the king over the heads of the other Companions. The torchlight turned Erius' crown to a wreath of fire around his brow, and glanced from his upraised sword.

"He looks like Sakor himself, doesn't he?" Mylirin whispered admiringly, following Ki's gaze.

Ki nodded, distracted by a flash of silver and white beside the king. Lord Niryn rode at the king's side like a general.

The crowds outside the Palatine had been smaller than they'd expected, and quiet. Passing through a neighborhood populated mostly by Aurënfaie nobles and rich merchants, however, Ki looked around nervously. It was not late, but hardly a light showed.

A herald rode ahead of the main column, calling out, "The king's justice will be served. Long live King Erius!"

A few bystanders returned the call, but others faded back into shadowed doorways, watching their progress in silence. Looking up, Ki saw people watching them from their windows. He braced for more cabbages, or worse.

"Priest killer!" a lone voice shouted from the darkness. Ki saw several of the guards look around for the dissident, and a sense of unreality swept over him. These streets he'd ridden so freely suddenly felt like enemy territory.

Tobin and Korin rode at saddle attention, stiff as a pair of pokers, but Tobin was glancing around, alert to any threat. Ki wished he could see his friend's face, read in those blue eyes what Tobin thought of all this, for suddenly he was more aware than he ever had been of the gulf that separated them—not of wealth, but of blood and history and position.

The crowds were thicker near the East Market. Many held up torches to light the king's way and Ki scanned their faces: some looked sad, others smiled and waved. Here and there he saw people weeping.

Ki tensed, sweeping the crowd now for the glint of a blade or curve of a bow. He shivered with a mix of relief and dread as the gate finally come into sight ahead of them. He could already hear the sounds of a huge crowd.

This was the largest square in the city. Located halfway between the Palatine and the harbor, it was surrounded on three sides by tall buildings, including a theater the Companions had often patronized. The paved square sloped to the east and was bounded on that side by a low stone parapet overlooking a small wooded park and the harbor below.

Ki hardly recognized the place tonight. All the stalls had been cleared away and people stood shoulder to shoulder except for a processional way kept clear by

Niryn's grey-backs. Even the shrine of the Four was gone. That, even more than the sight of all those Harrier guards, gave him a strange sinking feeling in the pit of his stomach.

At the center of the square a broad, banner-draped platform rose like an island above the sea of faces. It was guarded on all sides by ranks of grey-backs armed with hand axes and swords. Eight white-robed wizards stood waiting there. Torches set at the four corners illuminated their silver-stitched robes, and the two large wooden frames looming just behind them.

They look like upended bedsteads, or doorways with no walls around them, thought Ki, already guessing their purpose from the stories he'd heard. Just behind them loomed a more familiar device: the stark frame of a gibbet. Ladders were propped ready against the crossbeam and Ki counted fifteen halters hanging ready.

A crowd of ministers and nobles sat their horses in the cleared space in front of the platform and Ki was glad to see Lord Hylus among them. No doubt Nikides was breathing a sigh of relief, too, though the old man looked to have aged ten years since the night before.

The crowd fell silent at the king's approach. The only sounds were the drums and the sound of hooves on the cobblestones.

Korin and the Companions lined on the king's right, as ordered. Taking his place just behind Tobin, Ki steadied Dragon and rested his hand on his sword hilt.

Niryn dismounted and followed the herald onto the platform. The drummers ceased their playing and for a moment Ki could hear the sea. The Harrier wizards bowed low to the king, then formed up in a semicircle behind their master.

"Witness, all you who have gathered here, the sacred justice of the king!" cried the herald. "By order of King Erius, Heir of Ghërilain, Holder of the Sword, and Protector of Skala, these enemies of Skala will be put to death before this gathering and the Four. Know that they are traitors against the throne and all lawful people."

Some cheered this proclamation, but most only murmured among themselves in low voices. In the distance someone shouted angrily, but he was quickly drowned out by other voices.

The herald unrolled a scroll heavy with seals and read out the names of the condemned and the charges against them. The fourth was the young priest who'd thrown the cabbage. His name was Thelanor and he was charged with treason, sedition, and assault against the person of the Prince Royal. He'd already been branded across the mouth with the traitor's T, the mark of a heretic priest. Guards on the far side of the platform hoisted the bound prisoners into the waiting arms of the hangmen.

The condemned wore long sleeveless tunics of coarse, unbleached muslin. There were a few women among them, but most were men and boys. Most bore the traitor's brand on their foreheads and all were gagged. Only two others, an old man and woman with grey hair and thin, wrinkled faces, were branded on the mouth like Thelanor. They held their heads high as the guards pushed them to the ladders.

Ki had gone with his family to see thieves and brigands hanged in Colath. The crowds had roared for blood and pelted them with whatever came to hand. Ki and his brothers and sisters had thought it great fun, scavenging stones and rotten apples to throw. His father had given them a copper groat for each hit to spend later at the sweet seller's booth.

Ki looked around with growing unease. Only a few people threw things and he didn't see many children at all, except for those standing under the gibbet. One of the boys looked so much like his brother Amin that Ki almost called out to him in alarm before he heard the stranger's name read.

The drummers beat out a quick tattoo. Soldiers braced

the ladders against the gibbet beam and, one by one, the prisoners were forced up to the halters. A cheer went up from the other Companions as the first man was pushed off to jerk at the rope's end.

Korin brandished his sword, shouting "Death to Skala's enemies! Long live the king!"

The others were quick to do the same and none quicker than eager Orneus. Ki was sure he saw the boy look to see if Korin was watching him and despised him for it.

Tobin had drawn his sword with the rest, but didn't wave it about or cheer. Ki couldn't muster much enthusiasm, either.

The second man struggled and cried and had to be pried free of the ladder. This panicked some of the other prisoners and for a moment it looked as if the soldiers might have to force them all.

The crowd was warming up now, and a flurry of rotten vegetables rained down on the condemned and their guards.

A woman was the next hanged, and then it was young Thelanor's turn. He tried to shout something through his gag, but no one could have heard him over the noise anyway. In the end he went to his death like a man, leaping off the ladder before the guards could push him.

A few of the remaining prisoners had to be forced up, but most of them must have been braver, or shamed by the priest's example. One man made the warriors' salute as best he could with his bound hands and flung himself off. The jeering of the crowd failed for an instant, then redoubled as the next man clung to the rungs, struggling and pissing himself as the guards beat him about the head. The young boys and women went more quietly.

The old priests' turns came last. They didn't hesitate, except to raise their bound hands to their hearts and brows before they climbed the ladders. This impressed even the lowest sort in the crowd and no one threw anything at them. Both tumbled off the ladders without struggle or protest.

The crowd was almost silent now. Ki thought he heard weeping. The old people had died quickly, their frail necks snapping like dry sticks. But the women and children were light and the warriors had necks like bulls; most struggled hard and long before Bilairy claimed them. Ki had to force himself to watch, not wanting to shame Tobin by turning away. Usually hangmen gave the strugglers a good yank on the legs to put them out of their misery, but no one helped them tonight.

When it was finally over the drumming resumed with a sharper, faster rhythm. A large, high-sided cart rumbled into the square, pulled by a pair of black oxen and surrounded by ranks of grey-backs with shields and upright swords. Six Harrier wizards stood in the back of the cart, facing inward with their arms linked.

No one dared throw anything at them, but an ugly muttering swelled to screams of anger and outrage. Ki shivered, feeling the sudden fury like a wave of nausea. But whether it was the Harrier wizards or their unseen prisoners who were jeered, he could not tell.

*T*obin had never seen an execution before and it had taken all his willpower tonight not to kick Gosi into a gallop and flee. What little dinner he'd managed roiled and burned at the base of his throat and he swallowed convulsively, praying Korin and Porion would not see his weakness. None of the others seemed to be bothered by the spectacle; Korin was acting like this was the finest entertainment he'd ever seen, and shared whispered bets with some of the others on which of the hanged prisoners would last the longest.

As the cart reached the platform a sudden, irrational fear overwhelmed Tobin. What if it was Arkoniel they pulled out, or Iya? Gripping the reins so tight his fingers ached, he watched as two naked prisoners were dragged from the cart.

It's not them! he thought, dizzy with relief. Both were men and neither was hairy like Arkoniel. There was no reason to think that it would have been him, he realized, but for an instant the possibility had seemed all too real.

Both men had elaborate patterns painted in red on their chests, and iron masks strapped over their faces. These were featureless except for slanting slits where the eyes and nose would be and gave the prisoners an evil, inhuman appearance. Metal shackles bound their wrists.

The guards forced them to their knees and Niryn stepped behind them, raising his hands above their heads. He'd always struck Tobin as rather bookish, but now he seemed to swell and grow taller, looming over the condemned.

"Behold the enemies of Skala!" he cried in a voice that carried to the farthest corners of the square. He waited until the renewed roar died away, then went on, "Behold these so-called wizards, who would overthrow the rightful ruler of Skala. Witches! Blighters of crops and flocks, preachers of sedition, these storm bringers call down lightning and fire on the innocent people of their villages. They defile the sacred name of Illior with perverse magics and threaten the very safety of our land!"

Tobin shuddered; these were charges of the most serious nature. Yet as he looked at the condemned wizards, it struck him how helpless and ordinary they looked. It was hard to imagine them hurting anyone.

Niryn pressed both hands to his brow and heart, then bowed low to the king. "King Erius, what is your will?"

Erius dismounted and climbed up to join him. Facing the crowd, he drew Ghërilain's sword and planted the tip between his feet, hands folded over the hilt. "Cleanse the land, loyal wizards of Skala," he cried. "Protect my people!"

No soldier stepped forward. Instead, Harrier wizards dragged the condemned to the upright frames. Three stood a little apart, chanting steadily as the prisoners were loosed from their shackles and quickly bound spread-eagle to the frames with silver ropes.

One of them seemed drugged or ill. His legs would not support him and he had to be held upright as he was lashed into place. The other one was not so passive. Just as the wizards reached to tie his hands, he suddenly twisted loose and staggered forward. Raising his hands to his face, he let out a muffled scream and the iron mask shattered in a cloud of smoke and sparks. Blood spattered the robes of the closest wizards. Tobin watched in horrified fascination, unable to look away. The man's bloody face was horribly torn, and twisted with agony. Shattered teeth showed in a defiant snarl as he raised his fists at the crowd, screaming, "Fools! Blind cattle!"

The wizards grappled with him, but the man fought wildly, throwing them off. "Your reckoning will come!" he shouted, pointing at the king. "The True Queen is at hand. She is among us already—"

He jerked away as another wizard seized him and suddenly he was staring straight down at Tobin.

Tobin thought he saw a spark of sudden recognition in those crazed eyes. A strange tingling sensation spread over him as they stared at each other, locked eye to eye, for what felt like a long time.

He sees me! He sees my real face! Tobin thought numbly as something like joy came into the man's eyes. Then the others were on him again, dragging him back.

Freed from that gaze, Tobin looked around in panic, wondering if the crowd would let him flee if Niryn denounced him. From the corner of his eye he saw the wizard and king standing apart from the scuffle, but didn't dare look directly at them. Were they staring at him? Had they understood? When he finally chanced a look, however, both were watching the execution proceed.

The Harrier wizards hauled the struggling man back

by his arms and hair, yanking his head down so that another could gag him.

"Lightbearer will not be mocked!" he managed as they forced a loop of the silver rope between his teeth. Even then he kept fighting. Transfixed, Tobin didn't notice the king move until he'd plunged the Sword of Ghërilain into the man's belly.

"No!" Tobin whispered, horrified to see that honorable blade stained with a prisoner's blood. The captive thrashed once, then crumpled forward as Erius withdrew the blade.

The wizards held the man upright and Niryn pressed his hand to the man's brow. Still alive, the prisoner spat at him, leaving another red stain on his white robes. Niryn ignored this insult and began to chant softly.

The prisoner's eyes rolled up in their sockets and his legs gave way. After that it was a simple matter to bind him into place on the frame.

"Proceed," Erius ordered, calmly wiping his blade clean.

With order restored, the wizards formed a circle around the frames and began a new chant. It grew louder and louder until white flames, brighter than anything Tobin had ever seen blossomed over the condemned men's bodies. There was no smoke, and none of the stench that sometimes wafted into the city from the burning grounds outside the walls. The doomed wizards struggled for a few seconds, then were consumed as quickly and completely as a moth's wing in a candle flame. Within a few seconds nothing remained of them but their charred hands and feet, still hanging in the silver bonds at the corners of the scorched wooden frame.

The searing brightness left dark spots before Tobin's eyes. He tried in vain to blink them away as he stared at the frame on the left, remembering that look of recognition he'd glimpsed in the man's pain-wracked face. Then the world was tilting crazily around him. The square, the jeering crowd, the pathetic, shriveled scraps on the frames, it all disappeared and Tobin was staring instead at a gleaming golden city set on a high cliff above the sea.

Only Ki was close enough to hear Tobin's faint cry as he slumped slowly over Gosi's neck, and he didn't understood the single word Tobin gasped out, nor would Tobin remember it for a long time.

"Rhíminee!"

No one, not even Niryn, noticed a tiny charred pebble lying among the ashes of the wizards.

Twenty miles away, under that same yellow moon, Iya rested her head on a tavern tabletop, gasping as white fire filled her vision as it had that day in Ero. In it she made out another doomed face, twisted in agony. It was Kiriar. Kiriar of Meadford. She'd given him a talisman that night in the Wormhole.

The pain passed quickly, but left her badly shaken. "O Illior, not him!" she moaned. Had they tortured him, learned of the little band of wizards hidden away under their feet?

Slowly she became aware of the tavern noise around her.

"You've hurt yourself." It was a drysian. Iya had noticed her earlier, healing village children outside the shrine. "Let me tend to you, old mother."

Iya looked down. The clay wine cup she'd been drinking from had shattered in her hand. The shards had cut her palm, crosshatching the faded scar Brother had given her the night she'd brought Ki to the keep. A sliver still jutted from the swell of flesh just below her thumb. Too weak to reply, she let the drysian wash and dress her wounds.

When she'd finished, the woman laid her hand on Iya's head, sending a cool soothing energy through her. Iya smelled fresh green shoots and new leaves. The sweet tang of springwater filled her dry mouth.

"You're welcome to sleep under my roof tonight, Mistress."

"Thank you, Mistress." Better to sleep on Dalna's hearth tonight, than here where too many curious idlers were still watching the crazy old woman to see what foolishness she'd do next. Better, too, to be with a healer if the awful pain returned. Who knew how many wizards Niryn might burn tonight?

The drysian helped her down the muddy street to a small cottage at the edge of the village and settled her on a soft bed by the fire. Names were neither asked for nor given.

Lying there, Iya was glad of the thick bands of protective symbols carved in the beams and the hanging bags of charms. Sakor might be at war with the Lightbearer in Skala, but the Maker still watched over all equally.

Despite that, Iya found little comfort that night. Every time sleep claimed her she dreamed of the sybil in Afra. The girl looked up at her with shining white eyes and spoke with the Lightbearer's voice.

This must stop.

In the vision, Iya fell on her face before her, weeping.

Chapter 25

Arkoniel had watched the Alestun road hopefully in the months since Iya's visit. Spring had passed with no visitors. Summer burned the meadow brown, and still no one but tradesmen and Tobin's messengers raised any dust above the trees.

It had been another blisteringly hot summer; even the valley around Alestun, spared the worst of the ongoing droughts for years, was struck. Crops withered in the fields and new calves and lambs died in the meadows. The river shrank to a gurgling stream between cracked, stinking expanses of mud and dead water plants. Arkoniel stripped to a linen kilt again and the women went about in their shifts.

He was working in the kitchen garden late one afternoon in Lenthin, helping Cook dig the last of the yellowed leeks, when Nari shouted down to them from a second floor window. A man and a boy were coming up the road.

Arkoniel stood and brushed the dirt from his hands. "Do you know them?"

"No, it's strangers. I'll go."

Watching from the gate, however, Arkoniel recognized the broad-set, grey-bearded man walking beside Nari, but not the little boy perched among the baggage on the swayback horse the man led.

"Kaulin of Getni!" Arkoniel called, crossing the bridge to meet them. It had been ten years or more since he'd watched Iya give the man one of her pebble tokens. Kaulin had been solitary then. His little companion looked no older than eight or nine.

"Iya said I'd find you here," Kaulin said, clasping hands with him. He gave the younger wizard's stained kilt and sunburned chest a wry look. "Turned farmer, have you?"

"Now and then," Arkoniel laughed. "You look like you've had some hard traveling."

Kaulin had always been ragged, but it was the boy who concerned Arkoniel. He seemed healthy enough, and was brown as a trout, but he kept his gaze on the horse's dusty withers as Arkoniel approached and he read more fear than shyness in those wide grey-green eyes.

"And who's this, then?" asked Nari, smiling up at the child.

The boy didn't look up or reply.

"Did a crow steal your tongue?" she teased. "I've got some nice cold cider in the kitchen. Would you like some?"

"Don't be rude, Wythnir," his master chided, when the child turned his face away. Grasping the back of the boy's ragged tunic, Kaulin hoisted him down like a sack of apples. Wythnir promptly retreated behind the man's legs and stuck a finger in his mouth.

Kaulin scowled down at him. "It's all right, boy. You go with the woman." When Wythnir didn't move, he grabbed him by the shoulder and steered him none too gently to Nari. "Do as you're told!"

"There's no need for that," Nari said tartly, taking the child's hand. Then, more gently to the boy, "You come along with me, Wythnir. Cook has some lovely cakes baking and you shall have the largest one, with cream and berries. It's been a long while since we've had a little boy to spoil."

"Where did you meet with Iya?" Arkoniel asked, following with Kaulin. "I've had no word from her in months."

"She found us up north a few weeks back." Kaulin pulled a pouch from the neck of his tunic and shook out a small speckled stone. "Claimed she found me by this and told me to come here to you." He looked around the tidy kitchen yard and his expression softened a little. "Said we'd be safe here."

"We'll do our best," Arkoniel replied, wondering what Iya expected him to do if Niryn and his Harriers were the next ones up the road.

Like all those Iya would eventually send him, Kaulin had seen glimpses of chaos and a rising queen in his dreams. He'd also watched fellow wizards consigned to the Harrier's fire.

"Your mistress won't say what her purpose for us is, but if she stands against those white-robed bastards, then I'll stand with her," Kaulin declared, as he and Arkoniel sat in the shadowy hall after the evening meal. It was too hot still for even a candle, and so they made do with a light orb Arkoniel cast in the hearth.

Cook had made up a bed for Wythnir upstairs, but the boy silently refused to be parted from his master. Arkoniel hadn't heard him speak all afternoon.

Kaulin looked down sadly at the child curled asleep on the reeds. "Poor lad. He's had reason enough not to trust strangers, these past few months."

"What happened?"

"We were up in Dimmerton, back at the end of Nythin. Stopped at an inn there, hoping to earn our supper. One young fellow in particular was taken with my tricks, and stood me a jug of good wine." He clenched a fist angrily against his knee. "It was strong, and perhaps fortified with something else, for next thing I know I'm running off at the mouth about the Afran Oracle and how I thought the king had brought the plagues on by ignoring it. He was agreeable to my opinions and we parted friends, but that night a maidservant woke me, saying a mob was coming for us and we'd better run for it.

"I wasn't so fuddled I couldn't fend off a pack of drunken wizard baiters, but who should be leading them but my drinking companion? Only now he wore the Harrier's robe. There was only one, thank the Light, but he managed to give me this mark before we got free of him." He pushed back his sleeve, showing Arkoniel a livid, puckered scar that ran the length of his forearm.

Arkoniel's heart sank. "Did you tell him anything of the visions?"

"No, that's locked safe away in my heart. Only you and Iya have heard me speak of—" Kaulin hesitated and cast a furtive look around. "Of *her*." Kaulin pushed his sleeve down and sighed. "So, what are we to do here? We're not so far from Ero that the Harriers might not find us again."

"I don't know," he admitted. "Wait and keep each other safe, I guess."

Kaulin said nothing to this, but Arkoniel could see by the way he glanced around that he wasn't reassured by this vague battle plan.

Later, Arkoniel sat at his window and watched the moonlight glimmering on the river. Kaulin had been halfway up the hill before anyone had noticed him. The day Orun's men had come thundering up the road to demand Tobin, his only warning had been a cloud of dust above the trees, and that had given them little enough time. Without Tobin here, he'd grown lazy.

Now there was even more reason for vigilance. Sheltering wizards who fled the king's Harriers was a far riskier undertaking than guarding a child whom no one was yet seeking.

Chapter 26

In the weeks following the execution, none of the Companions dared speak openly about the king's frightening outburst or the fact that he'd killed a bound man with his sword. Tobin's fainting fit was another matter, however.

The king had been furious that a member of his own family would mar the event with such a show of weakness. Ki was quick to point out that Tobin hadn't actually fallen all the way off his horse, though he'd come close to it. By the time Ki got to him Tobin had already righted himself, but people had seen and the damage was done. By the following day it was the talk of the Palatine, at least behind upraised hands.

The more charitable gossips had put it down to Tobin's youth and sheltered upbringing; others were not so kind. Though none of the Companions dared tease Tobin to his face, or say anything in front of Korin, more than once Ki caught Alben and his friends pantomiming a girlish swoon behind Tobin's back

The worst of it for Ki was Tobin's silence with him. Clearly, he was too shamed to speak of it, even to his friends, and Ki hadn't the heart to pry. The burning had been an awful business and he'd come close to puking up dinner himself.

Better to say nothing and just forget it for now, he told himself.

A few weeks after the execution, he and Tobin were heading into the messroom when they caught a bit of conversation from inside that put a knot in Ki's gut.

"Between that, and how he reacted to Lord Orun's death?" That was Alben speaking, spiteful as always. And there was no question of whom he was speaking.

Tobin halted just outside the door and shrank back against the wall to listen. Ki wanted to haul him away before he heard any more, but knew better than to attempt it; Tobin had gone pale. From where he stood Ki could just see half the room, and some of the people loitering there. Alben was leaning at ease against the long table, holding forth to Zusthra and Urmanis. Korin and Caliel must not be around, Ki guessed, or Alben wouldn't dare talk that way about Tobin.

"Oh, who cares about that?" Zusthra growled, and Ki's spirits rose; Zusthra could be rough, but he was usually fair. But what he said next dashed any good feelings. "If he can't take the sight of a bunch of traitors getting their due, what use will he be on the battlefield?"

This was too much. Ki strode in, fists clenched in front of him. "You shut your mouth!" he snarled, not caring that they were lords and he was only a squire. He'd take a beating before he'd let Tobin hear any more of this. When he glanced back, however, Tobin was gone.

Zusthra looked abashed, but the others snickered as Ki backed out again.

The incident was gradually eclipsed by other gossip and more pressing concerns.

Despite his hopeful words in Atyion, Erius still refused to send them out to fight. Every day it seemed there was some new report of brigands terrorizing the villages somewhere, or pirates striking out of the islands at the coast. But as the summer quickly faded, Erius would not consent to his son's pleas to get them blooded.

Perhaps because of this, the older boys turned more often to the pleasures of the lower city, led, as always, by Korin.

The king's return had done nothing to stem the

prince's drinking or his taste for low pleasures. According to Nikides, their conduit to court doings, Erius had winked at Porion's reports, and said, "Let him sow his wild oats while he can!"

Judging by how often Tanil ended up sleeping in the mess or in the squire's alcove in Tobin's room, Korin had plenty of oats to sow, and eventually, a few of them sprouted. A few more chambermaids turned up pregnant, but were quickly banished from court. How many bastards Korin might have fathered on the harbor whores was not known, at least to the Companions.

Even in the aftermath of the execution shame, Korin's regard for Tobin never wavered, but all the same, the older boys began to leave the younger ones behind more often when they went out at night.

If Tobin noticed or cared about this increasing division, he gave no sign of it, even to Ki. As the summer waned into a cooler autumn, Tobin and his friends kept up their secret sword practice with Arengil and Una's warrior girls.

Nearly a dozen showed up most days, though Ki was certain most of them just liked dressing in boy's clothes and sneaking about. Una, Kalis, and a girl named Sylani were the only ones who showed any real skill.

They met there a few days after Tobin's thirteenth name day celebration. When Tobin and Ki arrived, they found the girls laughing among themselves. Una colored indignantly when one of them confessed that they'd been debating whether or not Tobin was old enough for marriage under the royal laws.

"Old enough for battle, that's all I care about," Tobin countered, blushing furiously. He hated it when they flirted with him.

"What about you, then?" said Kalis, turning warm eyes on Ki. "You're fifteen. That's old enough to marry in my town."

"If you want a child for a husband," Arengil scoffed,

shouldering Ki aside. "How about me? I'm old enough to be your grandfather."

"You don't look much like my grandfather," she said, running a hand over the Aurënfaie's smooth cheek.

Jealous, Ki tried to lure her fickle attentions back with a fancy two-handed flourish he'd picked up from Korin. "If you ever want to feel the way a beard tickles, he won't be much use to you." Nikides ducked out of the way as Ki's blade flashed past his shoulder.

"Let's see you put that move to practical use, Squire Kirothius," Una challenged, laughing at him. She knew he fancied Kalis.

Tobin had marveled at the progress Una had made. It was less than a year since they'd started training and she was already a match for Nikides. She wouldn't let any of the other boys give quarter when they sparred, either. She'd had a few split knuckles and bruises to explain away, but bore her wounds proudly.

Watching her now with Ki, he thought again of Grannia in Atyion and the girls she trained in secret there, hoping for the day when a queen would call them to arms. How many more were there all over Skala? And how many like Ahra, who were lucky enough to serve openly?

In the midst of these contemplations, he caught sight of Nikides across the circle. He was staring over the roofline at something, looking positively horrified.

Tobin turned just in time to see the king stride into view less than twenty feet way. Porion and Korin were with him, and their old enemy, Moriel, was leading the way. The king's face was an ominous sight. Korin saw him and shook his head. Porion caught Tobin's eye and gave him a withering look.

One by one the others realized what audience they had. Several of the girls let out cries of dismay. Ki dropped his sword and fell one knee. Arengil, Lutha, Nikides, and their squires quickly did the same. Tobin couldn't move.

Erius strode into their midst and looked around, memorizing faces for future punishment. At last, he rounded on Tobin.

"What's going on here, nephew?" he demanded.

Tobin realized that he was the only one still standing, but his legs still refused to obey him. He glanced quickly into the king's eyes, reading the weather signs there. There was anger, to be sure, but also that quicksilver danger, a hint of madness.

"Well?" Porion prompted gruffly.

"We—we're just playing," Tobin managed at last. Even to his own ears it sounded ridiculous.

"Playing?"

"Yes, Majesty," a trembling voice piped up. It was Una. She placed her sword on the ground in front of her, as if offering it to him. "It's just a game we play—pretending to be warriors."

The king rounded on her. "And whose idea was this?"

"Mine, Your Majesty," she answered at once. "I asked To—Prince Tobin if he'd show us how to play at swords."

The king raised an eyebrow at Tobin. "Is this true? You come all the way up here, hiding away, just to play?"

Moriel was gloating openly now. How long had he spied on them, Tobin wondered, hating him even more. And how much had he told the king?

"Una asked me to teach her and I did," he replied. "We come up here because her father wouldn't approve. And so the older boys wouldn't laugh at us, fighting girls."

"You, Nikides?" asked Erius. "You went along with this as well, and never thought to tell your grandfather?"

Nikides hung his head. "No, Majesty. It's my fault. I should have—"

"You damn well should have!" Erius thundered. "And you know better, too, young miss!" he snapped at Una. Then he was back to Tobin again, face twisted with mounting rage. "And you, my own blood, practicing sedition! If news of this reached my enemies—"

Tobin's knees gave way at last and he knelt before the king, certain the man was about to lay hands on him. Just then he caught a hint of motion from the corner of his eye and an even greater fear froze the breath in his throat.

Brother stood on the ridge where the king had been, framed against the sky. Even at this distance Tobin saw murder in his twin's face. Brother started forward, stalking the king as Erius continued to berate Tobin.

Tobin had been too surprised to react at Orun's house. This time he brought his hands in front of his mouth, as if in supplication, and whispered the words as loudly as he dared behind his fingers.

Brother stopped and looked at Tobin, mouth curled in a silent snarl of rage. He was only a few paces from the king, almost within arm's reach. The spirit's hungry fury rolled across the roof slates like a cold fog but Tobin stared him down, lips moving now in a silent command. *Go away. Go away. Go away.*

Before he could tell if Brother had obeyed, Erius stepped closer, blocking his view.

"What are you whimpering about, you whelp?" he demanded furiously.

Terrified, Tobin waited helplessly for the king to drop dead in front of everyone.

"Are you deaf as well as mute?" Erius shouted.

"No, Uncle!" Tobin whispered. Shifting his weight ever so slightly, he could just see past the king.

Brother was gone.

"Forgive me, Uncle," he said, relief making him giddy and bold. "I just didn't see any harm in it."

"No *harm*? When you know that I expressly *forbid*—"

"We weren't really teaching them, Your Majesty," Ki blurted out. "We just figured if we went along with it and got them alone, they'd let us kiss them. It—it's not like any of them were any good."

Tobin cringed inwardly; Una must know this was an

outright lie, said only to spare them the king's wrath, but Tobin couldn't bring himself to look at her.

"He's lying!" Moriel cried. "I watched them. They were really teaching them."

"Like *you'd* know the difference, you pasty-faced lap-dog!" Ki shot back.

"That's enough out of you!" Porion barked.

But somehow, Ki had managed to say exactly the right thing. Erius stared at him for a long moment, then turned back to Tobin with the beginnings of a grin. "Is this true, nephew?"

Tobin hung his head so he wouldn't have to see any of the girls' faces. "Yes, Uncle. It was just a game. To get them alone."

"And kiss them, eh?"

Tobin nodded.

"That's a new one!" Korin said with a too-loud laugh.

His father burst out laughing. "Well, it's hard to fault you for that, nephew. But you girls should have better sense. Shame on you! Get back to your mothers' houses where you belong, and don't think they won't hear of this!"

Una looked back at Tobin as she turned to go. The doubt in her eyes hurt him worse than anything the king could have said or done.

"As for the rest of you—" Erius paused, and Tobin's belly tightened again. "You can spend the night at the altar of Sakor, meditating on your foolishness. Go on! Stay there until the other Companions come in the morning."

That night, Tobin meditated instead on the king and all he'd let himself forget once again. Despite the lapses he'd already witnessed, he'd let himself be taken in by Erius' fatherly manner and generosity.

Brother's appearance today had broken the spell once and for all, and his heart with it. It was proof that for at least a moment, the king had meant to hurt him, just as Orun had.

But it was not that, or the punishment, that started him softly weeping in the darkest hour of the night. As he knelt there, shattered, exhausted, dozing even as he wavered on aching knees, the breeze shifted and the strange-smelling smoke from Illior's altar enveloped him, and he remembered—remembered how his mother had dragged him to that window, trying to pull him out with her as she fell to her death. He remembered how the river had looked, black between the snow-covered banks. There'd been ice along the edges and he'd wondered if it would break when he landed on it. His mother was going to make him fall. He *had* been falling, but someone had yanked him back at the very last moment and dragged him away from the window, away from the sound of his mother's dying scream.

It had been Brother. But why hadn't he saved their mother, too? Had he instead pushed her out?

Sobs rose in his throat. It took every ounce of will to hold them in. Just when he thought he was going to give way and shame himself again, Ki's hand found his and squeezed it. The grief and fear receded slowly, like the waves of the ebb tide. He didn't disgrace himself, and greeted the morning sun dazed but strangely peaceful. Brother had saved him that day, and again with Orun. And would have today, perhaps, if the king had lost control of himself after all.

He needs you, and you need him, Lhel had said. Brother must know it, too.

Returning to the palace with the others later that morning, he learned from Baldus that Una had disappeared in the night without a trace.

PART II

Had we known where this vision would take us when we started, I don't know that we'd have had the courage to follow it. The Oracle was kind, in her way . . .

—Document fragment, discovered in the east tower of the Orëska House

Chapter 27

That first winter with Kaulin and Wythnir passed quietly. Mail arrived regularly from Tobin and Ki, and from Iya, who now divided her time between her travels and more frequent visits to the city. A few oblique remarks made it clear that she had found allies in Ero, wizards who would be of more use staying where they were than joining him.

The boys wrote of court life, and in Tobin's Arkoniel discovered a dark thread of worry and discontent. Korin was carousing more, the king was changeable in his moods, and the older boys were treating Tobin and the other younger ones like children.

In contrast, Ki reported happily on parties and various girls who were showing interest in them. Arkoniel guessed that Tobin was less pleased with the latter; he said nothing about girls at all, except to report that one whom he'd been friends with had disappeared under mysterious circumstances. He was vague on the details, but Arkoniel was left with the unsettling impression that Tobin thought her murdered.

As winter closed in once more, Arkoniel divided his own attentions between his new guests and the workroom. Kaulin was not much interested in Arkoniel's "indoor magic," as he called it, preferring to wander in the forest in all weathers. Once he'd settled in, he'd proven something of a grumbler, and Arkoniel was content to leave the fellow to himself.

Arkoniel was somewhat perplexed by Kaulin's neglect of Wythnir. He wasn't really unkind to the child, but frequently went off without him, leaving him in Nari's care like an ordinary child in need of a nurse.

Arkoniel remarked on this one morning as Nari bustled about his workroom with her dust rag.

"That's all right," she said. "I'm glad to have a child under this roof again. And Maker knows, the poor little thing can do with some coddling. He's hardly out of clouts, wizard-born or not, and hasn't got a soul to care about him."

Arkoniel caught something sharp in her tone. Setting his half-finished journal aside on the writing table, he turned in his chair and laced his fingers around one updrawn knee. "Kaulin does neglect him a bit, I suppose. The child seemed well enough when they arrived here, though."

"He wasn't starved, I'll grant you, but you've seen how Kaulin is with the child. He hardly has a kind word for him, when he can be bothered to speak to him at all. But what can you expect, eh? Kaulin only took the boy on to repay a debt."

"How do you know that?"

"Why, Wythnir told me," Nari said, and Arkoniel caught her smug little smile as she went to work on the windows. "And I got a bit more out of Kaulin the other day. The poor little thing had been treated very badly by his first master, a drunkard or worse, from what I gathered. I suppose even Kaulin was an improvement, but he doesn't seem to care for the child. It's no wonder Wythnir looks like a little ghost all the time." She flicked dust off a candlestand. "I don't mind having him underfoot, of course. He's not a bit of trouble. Still, he is wizard-born, and the way he's taken to you, perhaps you could show a bit more interest in him?"

"Taken to me? He hasn't even spoken to me since he got here!"

She shook her head. "You mean you haven't noticed how he follows you about and lurks outside the workroom?"

"No, I haven't. In fact, I didn't think he liked me."

Arkoniel's early experiences with Tobin had left him rather shy of quiet children. "Anytime I speak to him he sticks a finger in his mouth and stares at his feet."

Nari snapped her dust rag at him and chuckled. "Oh, you just take some getting used to. You've gone a bit crusty and strange since the boys left."

"I haven't!"

"Oh yes, you have. Cook and I don't pay you any mind, but this is a little boy and I guess I know more about them than you do. Give him a smile! Show him a trick or two and I'll bet you a sester coin he warms right up."

To Arkoniel's surprise, Nari won that wager. Though the child remained quiet and shy, he did brighten noticeably when Arkoniel took the time to show him a trick or ask for his help with some little chore. He was still thin, but Cook's good food had put color into his wan cheeks and brought a bit of luster to his ragged brown hair. Conversation remained difficult; Wythnir seldom spoke except to mumble a reply to a direct question.

In the workroom, however, he watched every move Arkoniel made with alert, solemn eyes. One day, for reasons known only to himself, he shyly offered to show Arkoniel how to make a luck charm out of a bunch of dried thyme and horsehair. It was not the sort of thing most eight-year-olds, even wizard-born, knew how to do. His weaving was a little clumsy, but the spell held firm. Arkoniel's honest praise earned him the first smile he'd seen from the boy.

After this small success Wythnir truly began to blossom. It seemed only natural to teach him, and it only took a few lessons to discover that Kaulin had done a better job with the boy than Arkoniel had guessed. Wythnir had been with the man less than a year, but already knew most of the basic cantrips and fire charms, as well as a surprising amount about the properties of plants. Arkoniel began to suspect that it was not boredom or disappointment that made Kaulin neglect the boy, but resentment of the boy's obvious potential.

The discovery of Wythnir's quickness made Arkoniel more cautious in what he let the boy see of his own studies. What he'd learned of Lhel's witchery was still forbidden knowledge among the free wizards. They worked together each morning, but the afternoons were reserved for Arkoniel's solitary labors.

Since Ranai's spirit gifting, Arkoniel had discovered that certain types of spells—summonings and transmutations in particular—came more easily than they had before. He saw spell patterns more clearly in his mind and found he could hold the wizard eye for nearly an hour without fatigue. Perhaps it was thanks to her, as much as to Lhel, that he finally achieved his first success with what he'd come to think of as his "doorway spell."

He'd given up on it a dozen times or more since he'd first conceived of it, but sooner or later he'd find himself with the old salt box in front of him, trying to force a bean or stone to materialize inside it.

Wythnir was sweeping the workroom one rainy morning in late Klesin while Arkoniel was making another attempt, and wandered over to see what he was grumbling about.

"What are you trying to do?" Even now he spoke in the hushed tones of a temple novice. Arkoniel often wondered what a few days with Ki would do to change that.

Arkoniel held up the recalcitrant bean. "I want this to go inside this box, but without opening the lid."

Wythnir pondered this a moment. "Why don't you make a hole in the box?"

"Well, that would defeat the whole purpose, you see. I mean, I might as well just open the—" Arkoniel broke off, staring at the boy, then the box. "Thank you, Wythnir. Would you leave me for a while?"

* * *

Arkoniel spent the rest of the afternoon and the night cross-legged on the floor, deep in meditation. As dawn broke, he opened his eyes again and laughed. The pattern of magic had come to him at last, so simple and clear in its workings that he couldn't imagine how it had eluded him for so long. No wonder it had taken a child to point it out to him.

Going back to the table, he picked up a bean and his crystal wand. Humming the tones of power that had come to him in the night, he wove lines of light on the air with the tip of his wand: *whirlwind, doorway, traveler, rest.* He hardly dared believe it, but the pattern held and the familiar cold prickling of energy ran down from his brow to his hands. The pattern brightened, then collapsed into a small blot of darkness. Shiny and solid-looking as polished jet, it hung in the air in front of him. Reaching out with his mind, he found that it was spinning. He was so surprised that he lost concentration and it disappeared with a sound like a cork coming out of a wine jug.

"By the Light!" Composing himself, he sketched the pattern again. When it was fixed in the air, he tested it more carefully and found it malleable as clay on a potter's wheel. All it took was a thought to make it expand to the size of a keg head, or shrink to a hummingbird's eye.

It was not a stable spell, but he found he could weave it with ease, and experimented with a succession of them. He could change the position with a thought, moving it around the room and tilting the axis from vertical to horizontal.

Finally, tingling with anticipation, he visualized the salt box without actually looking at it and dropped a bean into the little vortex. The bean disappeared like a stone into a tiny pond and did not fall out the other side. The hole collapsed on itself with the usual dull pop.

Arkoniel stared at the empty air where it had been, then threw back his head and let out an elated whoop that carried his joy all the way to Lhel's camp.

Wythnir, who had evidently gone no farther than the floor outside the door, burst in. "Master Arkoniel, what's wrong? Are you hurt?"

Arkoniel swung the startled child up into the air and danced him around the room. "You're a luck bringer, my boy, do you know that? Illior bless you, you put the key in my hand!"

Wythnir's baffled smile made Arkoniel laugh again.

Over the next few weeks Arkoniel armed himself with a handful of beans and put his new magic to various tests. He successfully sent beans into the box from across the workroom, then from the corridor, and finally, thrillingly, through the closed workroom door.

He also inadvertently made a crucial discovery. If he was careless or hurried, if he didn't visualize the destination carefully and concentrate on his purpose, the unlucky bean simply vanished. He tested this repeatedly and was unable to recover any of the lost ones, or discover where they'd gone.

Doubtless trapped in whatever middle space they occupy between the spell pattern and their final destination, he noted in his journal that night. It was nearly midnight but he was too excited to worry about ghosts. Wythnir had long since been packed off to bed, but Arkoniel kept the lamps burning, unwilling to stop when things were progressing so well. He was more tired than he wanted to admit, however.

He decided to try sending something heavier into the box. A lead fishing weight Ki or Tobin had left behind was just the thing. In his excitement, however, he carelessly brushed the black disk with his hand and felt a distinct tug as the hole closed. For a moment he could only stare stupidly at the spurting stump that was all that was left of his little finger. It was gone, cut clean as a sword stroke just below the second knuckle. It began to throb painfully, but still he stood there, watching the blood flow in disbelief.

The pain soon brought him to his senses. Wrapping the finger in a fold of his tunic, he raced to the table and opened the salt box. There was the lead, intact as expected, but the inside of the box was a spattered mess. The flesh of his finger had been torn from the bones and mangled to bloody gobbets. The bones were undamaged, however, and the nail had survived intact; it lay like a delicate seashell beside the weight.

Only then did the enormity of what he'd done hit him. Collapsing on the stool, he rested his forehead on his left hand. He knew he should call for help before he fainted and bled all over the floor, but it was a moment before he could make himself move.

Lhel warned me never to touch the window spells, he thought, as a wave of nausea rolled over him. No wonder she'd been so hesitant to trust him with this sort of magic.

Because the wound was so clean, it took a bit of doing to get the bleeding stopped. Cook stitched up the end of his finger, smeared it with honey, and tied it up in a bit of clean linen.

He cleaned the box out himself and said nothing of the incident to Kaulin or Wythrin, but he was more careful than ever to keep others away as he cast the spell.

Rather than dampen his zeal, however, the accident spurred him on. He spent the next few days experimenting with different objects: a slip of parchment, an apple, a cloak pin, and a dead mouse from the kitchen traps. Only the metal pin survived. The parchment was shredded to bits, but not burned. The apple and the mouse carcass arrived in very much the same state as his severed finger; the flesh and delicate bones were mangled, but the mouse's skull survived intact.

Having determined that only very solid objects could be safely transported, he then experimented with weight and found that a carved stone book end took no more effort to send across the room than the beans had. Satisfied, he went back to beans and began distance trials.

Nari and the others gave him some odd looks as he dashed around the keep. Stationed by the box, it was Wythnir's task to yell down the stairs as soon as the little travelers appeared.

No matter how far Arkoniel got from the box, no matter how many doors or walls lay between, he only had to imagine a hole in the side of the box itself, concentrate carefully, and the bean would find its way home.

He next tried sending beans to other destinations. The first one made its way successfully from the workroom to the offering shelf of the house shrine. From there, he sent it on to Cook's flour barrel—a messy success in that case—then began sending it outside.

Kaulin remained unimpressed. "Don't see much use in it," he sniffed, watching Arkoniel retrieve a bean from the bole of a willow beside the river.

Arkoniel ignored him, already making a mental list of places in other towns he could picture clearly enough to focus the magic on.

"It is a drawback, of course, not being able to send parchment letters," he muttered aloud. "Still, there must be some way around that."

"You could write them on bits of wood," Wythnir offered.

"I suppose I could," mused Arkoniel. "That's a very good idea, Wythnir."

Kaulin gave them a disdainful look and wandered off about his own business.

Chapter 28

Even in the mountains, that spring and early summer were hotter than the last. Tradesmen raised their prices, complaining of dead livestock and fields blasted with drought and blight. On the mountainsides the birch turned yellow in high summer. Even Lhel seemed to feel it, and Arkoniel had never once heard her complain of heat or cold.

"The curse on this land is spreading," she warned, scratching symbols into the dirt around her camp.

"Tobin is still so young—"

"Yes, too young. Skala must suffer a little longer."

The heat finally broke in late Gorathin with a spate of violent thunderstorms.

Arkoniel had taken to sleeping through the hottest part of the day. The first clap of thunder shook the keep like an avalanche, startling him bolt upright on his damp bed. His first thought as he lurched up was that he must have slept the day away, for the room was nearly dark. Outside, clouds the color of a new bruise were scudding low over the trees. Just then another blinding blue-white flash split the sky and another rending crash shook the house. A puff of damp wind stirred against Arkoniel's cheek, then the rain came, falling in thick, silvery curtains that instantly cut off all view. Fat drops spattered across his sill so hard he felt the spray from three feet away. He went to the window, glad of any respite, but even the rain was warm.

Lightning lanced down in angry tridents, each flash leaving a deafening report in its wake. The storm was so loud he didn't notice that Wythnir had come into his room until he felt the child's hand on his arm.

The boy was terrified. "Will it hit the house?" he asked, voice quavering as he tried to make himself heard.

Arkoniel put an arm around him. "Don't worry. This old place has been here a long time."

As if to contradict him, a bolt struck a dead oak at the edge of the meadow, splitting it from crown to root and setting it ablaze.

"Sakor's fire!" Arkoniel exclaimed, running for the workroom. "Where are those firepots you cleaned the other day?"

"On the shelf close by the door. But—you're not going *out*?"

"Just for a bit." There was no time to explain. Arkoniel knew of at least half a dozen elixirs that could only be brewed with this sort of fire, if he could get to it before the rain put it out.

The pots stood ready on the shelf, pierced brass lids gleaming. Wythnir had been diligent, as always. Their round iron bellies were filled with dry cedar bark and greasy wool. He snatched the largest and ran down the stairs. Kaulin called after him as they passed in the hall, but Arkoniel didn't stop.

The rain pelted his hair flat and plastered his kilt to his thighs as he sprinted barefoot over the bridge and plowed on through the coarse, waist-deep sea of dead timothy and thistle, hugging the pot close to his chest to keep the tinder dry.

Reaching the oak, he was glad to see that he was in time. Flames still hissed and crackled in the fissures of the blasted trunk and he was able to knock a few brands into the pot with his knife before the last of them fizzled out. It was enough; the tinder caught and he had his fire. He was just clamping the lid in place when Kaulin and the boy came panting up to join him. Still frightened, Wythnir cowered as lightning struck again down by the river.

"I only brought the one pot," Arkoniel told Kaulin, not anxious to share his prize. Dividing the fire diminished its potency.

"Not looking for that," Kaulin muttered. Rain ran down his broad back in rivulets as he crouched on the blackened grass at the base of the tree and poked about with a silver knife. Wythnir did the same on the far side and soon straightened up with a cry of triumph. "Look, Master Kaulin, here's a big one!" he cried, juggling something back and forth between his hands like a hot ashcake. It was a rough, dirt-caked black nodule about the size of a man's finger. Kaulin soon found some, too.

"A fine one!" Kaulin exclaimed, taking it and holding it up for the rain to cool.

"What is it?" asked Arkoniel. The man was as pleased with this fruit of the storm as he was with his.

"Sky stone," Kaulin told him, tossing it to him. "Got the power of that lightning bolt fused in it."

It was still very hot, but Arkoniel felt something else as well, a subtle vibration that sent a tingle up his arm. "Yes, I feel it. What will you do with it?"

Kaulin held out his hand and Arkoniel reluctantly surrendered it. "Lots of things," he replied, rolling it in his cupped palm to cool it more. "This here's a couple of months' livelihood, if I find the right one to sell it to. This'll put the hot iron back up an old man's worn-out prick."

"Impotence, you mean? I've never heard of that cure before. How does it work?"

Kaulin slipped the stones into a leather pouch. "The man binds one of these to his member with a red silk cord and leaves it until a thunderstorm comes. As soon as he sees three flashes in the sky, his vitality's restored. For a while, at least."

Arkoniel stifled a grunt of disbelief. Such folk "cures" were seldom more than an idea planted in the customer's mind, sympathetic magic that had more to do with the cully's desperation than any inherent power of the so-called remedy. It was the sort of cheat that gave their kind a bad name. All the same, he had felt something in the stone. Satisfied, the others set off with their find. Rain sizzled on the lid of the firepot as he trudged after them.

Wythnir slowed until he was walking with Arkoniel. Without a word, he pressed something into the wizard's hand, then hurried back to Kaulin. Looking down, Arkoniel found himself holding one of the rough hot stones. Grinning, he pocketed it for later study.

The rain had slackened a bit. Halfway across the meadow, Arkoniel caught the distant jingle of harness on the Alestun road. Kaulin had heard it, too.

Arkoniel passed him the firepot. "Take this to my workroom and stay there, both of you. Don't make any sound until I send word."

They ran for the bridge. Kaulin and the boy disappeared through the main gate, while Arkoniel sprinted for the empty barracks. Inside he crossed to a window overlooking the road and peered out through a crack between the shutters. The rain had increased again and he could see no farther than the bridge, but he didn't dare expose himself.

Presently he heard a heavy snort and the creak of harness. A brown-and-white ox appeared out of the storm, pulling a high-sided cart. Two people sat on the driver's bench, wrapped in cloaks against the storm. The one next to the driver threw her hood back just then and Arkoniel's heart leaped; it was Iya, baring her face to make herself known to anyone watching from the keep. The driver did the same, a fair-haired young man with vaguely 'faie features. It was Eyoli of Kes, the young mind clouder from Virishan's orphan brood. Iya had brought at least one of them to safety. The fact that they'd come by cart gave him hope of others.

Though no great wizard herself, Virishan had earned Iya's respect by gathering up neglected wizard-born children from among the poor, saving them from filthy seaports and backward border towns where their sort were too often abused, exploited, and killed by the ignorant. An outcast herself, Iya had been happy to give Virishan what support she could.

"Ah, there you are, and in this weather!" Iya called, as Arkoniel stepped out to greet them. Eyoli reined in the horse and held a hand down to him. Climbing up the muddy wheel spokes, Arkoniel glanced into the cart. There were only five children huddled there among the baggage and their protector was not with them.

"Where's your mistress?" Arkoniel asked, as they rattled off again.

"Dead of a fever this past winter," Eyoli told him. "It carried off twelve of the children, too. I've had the care of the rest since, but it's hard to make a living with no more magic than any of us has. Your mistress found us begging in Kingsport and offered us sanctuary here."

Arkoniel turned to the shivering children. The older three were all girls. The two little boys were no older than Wythnir.

"Welcome, all of you. We'll have you warm and dry soon, and there's lots to eat."

"Thank you, Master Arkoniel. I'm glad to see you again," one of the girls said, pushing her sodden hood back. She was nearly woman-grown, he saw, and very pretty, with wide blue eyes and a flaxen braid. He must have stared, for her smile faltered. "I'm Ethni, remember?"

"The little bird tamer?" She'd been young enough to sit on his knee the last time he'd seen her.

Ethni grinned and lifted a wicker cage to show him two brown doves. "You helped me with that, and now I've a few new tricks to show you," she said proudly.

I'd like to see them! Arkoniel thought, wondering if she'd still sit on his knee. Catching himself, he quashed the thought with a guilty pang. The fact was, though, that this was the first pretty young girl he'd met since he'd broken celibacy with Lhel. That realization, and his body's warm reaction, were rather disquieting.

"And us! Do you remember us?" the younger girls chided, turning up identical faces. Even their voices seemed the same.

"Rala and Ylina!" one reminded him.

"You made luck knots for us, and sang ballads," her sister chimed in.

Arkoniel smiled at them, but was aware of Ethni's gaze still on him. "And who are these fellows?"

"This is Danil," one of the twins told him, hugging the dark-eyed boy.

"And this is Totmus," said her sister, introducing the shy, pale one.

"Who else has arrived?" asked Iya.

"Kaulin and a little boy."

She pulled her wet cloak closer around her, frowning. "That's all, after all this time?"

"How many did you call?"

"Only a dozen or so since I last saw you. It wouldn't do to have a crowd streaming down the Alestun road. But I'd expected more to be here by now." One of the boys whimpered. "Don't worry, Totmus, we're nearly there."

In the kitchen yard Nari and Cook hustled the shivering children to the kitchen hearth and wrapped them in dry blankets.

Later, when the children were all settled on pallets in the hall, Arkoniel and Iya carried their wine cups up to his bedchamber. The thunder had passed, but the storm raged on. As night fell the wind turned cold, pelting the keep with hailstones the size of hazelnuts. The wizards sipped their wine in silence for a while, listening to it clatter against the shutters.

"Our wizards aren't much of a collection yet, are they?" Arkoniel said at last. "One old faker, a half-grown mind clouder, and a handful of children."

"There'll be more," Iya assured him. "And don't underestimate Eyoli. He may be limited, but he's good at what he does. I think he might do to keep an eye on Tobin for us in the city. It's risky, but he'll attract far less attention than we would."

Arkoniel rested his chin on one hand and sighed. "I miss Ero. And I miss traveling with you."

"I know, but what you're doing here is important. And surely Lhel isn't letting you get too lonesome?" she added with a wink.

He blushed, unable to answer.

She chuckled, then pointed at his right hand, noticing the missing finger. "What happened there?"

"A happy accident, actually." He held up his hand proudly; thanks to Cook, it had healed clean over the bone end. The new skin there was still a shiny pink and a bit tender, but he hardly noticed it anymore. "I've got wonderful news, but it's easier to show you than explain it."

Rummaging in his pocket, he found his wand and a coin. He wove the spell and made a black disk the size of his fist, its surface parallel to the floor. Iya sat forward, watching with interest as he flourished the coin like a conjurer and dropped it into the disk. It disappeared and the black aperture snapped out of existence. He grinned. "Look in your pocket."

Iya reached in and pulled out the coin. A look of wonder slowly spread over her face. "By the Light," she whispered. "By the Light! Arkoniel, I've never seen the like! Did Lhel teach you this?"

"No, it's that spell I've been working on, remember? But I did start with one of her spells as a base." He wove the sigil for the window spell on the air, and had Iya peek through at Nari and Cook knitting by the kitchen fire. "That was the start of it, but I added to it, and visualize it differently."

"But your finger?"

Arkoniel went to his desk and took a taper from the candle box. Weaving the spell again, he thrust the taper partway in and showed her the resulting stump. Iya reached into her pocket and found the missing half.

He held up his finger again. "The one and only time I was careless. So far, anyway."

"By the Four, do you realize how dangerous this is? How big can you make these—these—What do you call them?"

"Doorways. I've made some large enough for a dog to walk through, if that's what you're getting at, but it won't work. I've tried it with rats, but they come through mangled on the other end. Small, solid objects go through just fine. Just imagine being able to send something all the way here from Ero in the blink of an eye! I haven't tried anything that ambitious yet, but it should work."

Iya looked down at the candle stub and coin. "You haven't taught this to Kaulin or the boy, have you?"

"No. They've seen it work, but not how it's cast."

"That's good. Can you imagine how dangerous this could be in the wrong hands?"

"I understand that. It's not perfected yet, either."

She took his damaged hand in hers. "Perhaps this was a blessing. You'll have this before you as a reminder for the rest of your life. I am proud of you, though! Most of us go our whole lives simply learning the magic created by others, without ever making anything new."

He sat down again and sipped his wine. "It's thanks to Lhel, really. I'd never have figured it out without the things she's taught me. She's shown me a good deal about blood magic too. Wonderful things, Iya, and nothing like necromancy. Perhaps it's time we stopped thinking that way about the hill folk and began to learn from them before they all die out."

"Perhaps, but would you trust just anyone with the kind of power she has over the dead?"

"It's not all like that."

"I know, but you know as well as I do there were reasons they were driven out. You can't let your affection for one witch blind you to the rest. Lhel's had her reasons not to show you the dark side of her power but it's there, believe me. I've felt it.

"All the same, what you've accomplished here is marvelous." Iya touched his cheek, and a hint of sadness crept into her voice. "And you'll do more. So much more. Now, tell me about this Wythnir. You seem fond of him."

"There's not much to tell. From what Nari and I have been able to gather, his early life was about like that of those children downstairs. But you wouldn't believe how quickly he takes to everything I show him."

She smiled. "So, how do you like having an apprentice of your own?"

"Apprentice? No, he came with Kaulin. He belongs to him."

"No, he's yours. I saw that the minute he looked at you, down in the hall."

"But I didn't choose him, I just—"

She laughed and patted his knee. "Then this is the first time I've heard of an apprentice choosing the master, but he is yours, whether you and Kaulin have worked it out between you or not. Don't let go of him, my dear. He will be great."

Arkoniel nodded slowly. He'd never thought of Wythnir that way, but now that she'd said it, he knew she was right. "I'll speak with Kaulin. If he's agreeable, will you be our witness?"

"Of course, my dear. But you must settle it tomorrow morning."

Arkoniel's heart sank. "You're leaving so soon?"

She nodded. "There's still so much to do."

There was no arguing with that. They finished their wine in silence.

To Arkoniel's relief, Kaulin had no objection to giving over his bond on Wythnir, especially after Arkoniel offered a handsome compensation for his loss. Wythnir said nothing, but beamed happily as Iya tied his hand to Arkoniel's with a silk cord and spoke the blessing.

"Will you swear the wizard's oath to your new master, child?" she asked him.

"I will, if you tell me what it is," Wythnir replied, wide-eyed.

"Don't guess I ever got 'round to that," Kaulin muttered.

Iya shot him a disdainful look, then spoke kindly to the child. "You swear first by Illior Lightbearer. And you swear by your hands and heart and eyes, that you will always obey your master and strive to serve him the best you can."

"I swear," Wythnir replied eagerly, touching his brow and breast the way she showed him. "By—by Illior, and by my hands and heart and—"

"Eyes," Arkoniel prompted softly.

"Eyes," Wythnir finished proudly. "Thank you, Master Arkoniel."

Arkoniel was surprised by a wave of emotion. It was the first time the child had called him by name. "And I so swear, by Illior, and by my hands and heart and eyes, that I will teach you all I know, and protect you until you are grown into your own power." He smiled down at the boy, remembering when Iya had said these same words to him. She'd kept her word and so would he.

Arkoniel was sorry as always when Iya rode out later that day, but the keep seemed a different house now, with so many people under the roof again. Wizard-born they might be, but they were still children and racketed about the hallways and meadow like farmers' brats. Kaulin grumbled about the noise, but Arkoniel and the women were glad of the new sense of life they brought to the old house.

Their presence brought new problems, as well, he soon discovered. For one thing, they were much harder to hide than quiet little Wythnir. On tradesmen's days he packed them all off into the forest with Eyoli and Kaulin to guard them.

The other children joined Wythnir at his lessons, and Arkoniel found he had a school, as well. Fortunately, Wythnir's remaining shyness fell away around the others and Arkoniel watched with delight as he began to play like a normal child.

Pretty Ethni was a welcome addition to the household, too, but a disturbing one. She flirted with Arkoniel whenever they met. He was flattered, but saddened as well. Though twice Wythnir's age, she had none of his promise. Even so, he encouraged her and praised every small advance. It was rather nice, the way she smiled at him when he did.

Lhel saw the true nature of his feelings for the girl before he did and told him the first time he came to her after the other's arrival.

She chuckled as they undressed each other in the oak house. "I see a pair of pretty blue eyes in your heart."

"She's only a girl!" Arkoniel retorted, wondering what form a witch's jealousy might take.

"You know as well as I do that's not true."

"You've been spying again!"

She laughed. "How else can I protect you?"

Their coupling that day was as passionate as ever, but afterward he caught himself comparing Lhel's brown throat to Ethni's smooth white one and tracing the lines around her eyes. When had they gotten so numerous, and so deep? Sad and ashamed of himself, he drew her close and buried his face in her hair, trying not to see how much greyer it was now.

"You are not my husband," Lhel murmured, stroking his back. "I am not your wife. We are both free."

He tried to read her face but she pulled his head back

down on her breast and stroked him to sleep. As he drifted off, it occurred to him that for all the passion they'd shared here in this oak house, neither of them had ever spoken of love. She'd never taught him the word for it in her language.

Chapter 29

Tobin celebrated his fourteenth name day in Atyion, and Duke Solari saw to it that it was a grand affair. Far grander, in fact, than Tobin would have liked; he'd have been happier with a small hunting party at the keep, with just the Companions and a few friends, but Iya had warned against going there now. She wouldn't say why and Tobin's old resentments against the wizard boiled up. But in the end even Tharin had taken her side and Tobin had grudgingly given in.

All the same, he was glad to visit Atyion again. The townspeople turned out to greet him, and Tobin was pleased that he recognized so many faces among the crowd.

Even the castle cats seemed glad to have him back. Packs of them gathered wherever he sat down, winding around his ankles and curling up on his lap. Lytia's orange tom, Ringtail, slept stretched between Tobin and Ki every night, and followed Tobin around the castle. The cat couldn't abide Brother, though. When Tobin called the ghost in secret, Ringtail would dart under the furniture, growling and hissing until Brother was gone.

To Tobin's great relief, the king did not come out for the name day feast. Solari was disappointed, but still managed to fill the great hall with guests. The high tables were packed with lords Tobin hardly knew—Solari's captains and liegemen mostly—but farther out, soldiers wearing the colors of Atyion sang and yelled out toasts to Tobin's health. Looking out over that sea of faces, Tobin was all too aware of who wasn't there. Una had not been heard from since her disappearance, and Arengil was gone, too, sent home to Aurënen a few days after the embarrassment on the roof. Weeks later it came back to Tobin through palace gossip that the young foreign lord had been deemed a bad influence.

There were a great many gifts this year, and one large pile sent by the people of the town. Most of them were from merchants and represented the sender: a fine pair of gloves from the glove maker, kegs of ale from the brewer, and so on. Tobin gave most of it a cursory glance, until Ki pulled a large scroll from the pile and handed it to him with a grin. Unrolling it, Tobin found a beautifully illuminated ballad about his father, banded along the top and margins with intricate colored scenes of battle. A smaller scrap of parchment had fallen out and on it Tobin found a brief but effusive note from Bisir, who was very happy in his new profession.

Tobin and the Companions stayed at the castle for a fortnight. Whenever they could slip away, he and Ki visited with Tharin's aunt Lytia and Hakone. The old steward had declined over the summer and was growing more feebleminded. This time he could not be dissuaded from the notion that Tobin and Ki were the young Rhius and Tharin. It was rather unsettling.

Tobin was also entertained lavishly by the town's principal guild masters. Most of these banquets were a bore. His hosts were invariably gracious and openhanded, but he sensed that much of it was done to curry his favor.

He much preferred visiting the men of the barracks. He'd never seen his father around actual troops, but he'd always been friendly with his guard and it didn't occur to Tobin to act otherwise. Soon he knew most of the officers and sergeants by name and set up mock challenges between his guard and any swordsman the Atyion men wanted to put forward, even going a few rounds himself.

He was disappointed when they let him win, but Tharin assured him later that it was done out of love and respect, rather than fear.

"You're their lord, and you take the time to learn their names," he told Tobin. "You can't imagine how much that means to a man in the ranks."

He also revisited his parents' room several times, trying again to capture the long-lost echo of who they had been then, but he didn't go near his mother's wardrobe. The memory of his reflection in the mirror made him blush.

Instead, he and Ki came there late at night when everyone else was asleep, and sat at the wine table playing at bakshi. He summoned Brother, too, and let him stalk sullenly around in the shadows as they played. The ghost had shown no signs of wanting to hurt Ki again; Tobin could almost forgive him.

When the fortnight was over, Tobin was reluctant to leave; Atyion now felt almost as much like home as the keep. Perhaps it was the way everyone greeted him on the streets, always smiling, always friendly. In Ero he was the king's nephew, Korin's cousin, the odd little second heir. Just a placeholder, really. In Atyion he was someone's son and the future hope of the people.

Ringtail escorted him to the front court when it was time to leave and sat yowling on the stairs as he rode away. Riding out through the cheering, banner-waving throngs that lined the streets, Tobin almost regretted his place in the Companions.

Chapter 30

They'd been back in Ero for only a few days when Korin surprised them all with news that would change the course of their lives.

It was a crisp, smoke-scented autumn morning and Ki was looking forward to the run, and to the dressing-down Korin and the others were likely to get. The older boys were later than usual, and Porion was already fuming. Korin and his set had escaped to the lower city the night before and come home stinking. Their drunken singing had woken Ki, so he wasn't feeling much sympathy for them as they straggled out.

Alben and Quirion and their squires were the first to emerge. They were wine sick but one glance from Porion was enough to sober them up fast. The others soon followed in ones and twos, looking equally raddled except for Lynx, as usual.

"Where the hell is Korin?" Ki asked, as Lynx stepped into line beside him.

The other squire rolled his eyes. "I don't know. Orneus didn't make it past the second tavern. I had to rent a horse to get him home."

Tanil ran out, still wrapping his belt. "The prince is coming, and sends his apologies, Master Porion."

"Oh, does he?" The arms master's voice dropped dangerously and he gave them all a scathing look. "Is this a festival day, boys? Did I forget the date? A good day to sleep in, was it? Just for that, you can—Ah, Your Highness. So pleased you could join us, my prince. And you, too, Lord Caliel. I trust you both had a fine time of it last night?"

"Thank you, Master Porion, we did," Korin replied, grinning.

Ki's gut tightened; not even Korin spoke back to Porion. He braced for the inevitable, but instead Porion merely ordered a doubling of the usual run.

As they set off Ki could see Korin still grinning.

"What's up with him I wonder?" Tobin muttered.

Zusthra jogged past to catch up with the prince. "He has a secret to share," he murmured, looking smug.

Korin waited until they were at breakfast. "I've got good news!" he cried, throwing an arm over Tobin's shoulders. "I want you to be the first to hear it." He paused, savoring the moment, then announced, "Lady Aliya carries my child. I'm to have an heir, boys!"

Ki and Tobin gaped at each other a moment, then joined in the cheering.

"I told you he'd manage it!" Zusthra cackled, pounding Caliel on the back. "We're free! They can't keep us from battle, now he's got an heir!"

Zusthra had good reason to crow, Ki knew. He was the oldest of them, with a thick red beard on his chin. He would have been off to the wars with his father years ago if not for his place in the Companions.

Everyone was shouting war cries and yelling. Porion sat by for a few minutes, then banged on the table with his spoon for their attention.

"Does your father know, Prince Korin?"

"No, and I mean to tell him myself tonight, so not a word."

"As you wish, my prince." He scowled around at the others, who were still cheering and congratulating each other. "I wouldn't go putting on your armor just yet. The truce is still on, you know."

As soon as Porion released them at midday Tobin and Ki ran all the way to the house to tell Tharin. He was in the back courtyard with Koni, examining a horse.

"Slipped away from your duties, have you?" he said, frowning.

"Just for a minute," Tobin promised, then quickly gave him the news.

Tharin let out a low whistle and shook his head. "So Korin finally got his way, did he?"

"The truce can't last forever!" Ki crowed. "They never do. Are Tobin and I old enough yet to go?"

Tharin scratched under his beard. "If Korin goes, then you all will."

"I guess we can put up with Aliya as consort, if that's the case," Ki said, laughing. "In fact, this could be the best thing to happen. I'll bet you once they've been under the same canopy for a few months, he'll be glad enough to go off to war, just to get away from that sharp tongue of hers."

None of them noticed Moriel lurking by the door or saw when he hurried away.

Niryn's rooms were near the king's wing of the New Palace. No one thought it odd that the king's equerry called there so frequently.

Niryn was taking a solitary breakfast in his courtyard when Moriel was ushered in.

"My Lord Niryn, I happened to be near the Companions' mess just now and overheard something that might be of interest to you."

"Did you? Let's have it."

"Prince Korin just announced that Lady Aliya carries his child! No one else is to know until the prince tells his father."

"And when does he plan to do that?"

"Tonight, he said."

"I suppose the prince and his friends are quite pleased?"

Mingled spite and envy twisted up the corner of the boy's mouth. "Oh yes, they're all cheering because they think they can go off to war now."

"It was good of you to inform me, Sir Moriel. You have my continuing—appreciation." Niryn gave the boy a knowing smile as he bowed. Moriel knew better than to expect anything as crass as gold to pass between them now. A gift would arrive later. Some nameless benefactor would clear his bills with the tailors or wine merchants. And, of course, he would remain in the king's good favor. Moriel had understood the arrangement from the beginning and had since outstripped all the wizard's expectations. Jealousy and malice were the ideal alloys in boys like Moriel; they hardened his soft, craven nature to usefulness, like tin in bronze.

"How do you think His Majesty will take the news?" Moriel asked.

"We shall see. Go back and tell the king I have something of great importance to discuss with him. I'll come within the hour. And Moriel? Say nothing of this."

Moriel looked offended. "I wouldn't think of it, my lord!"

Jealousy, malice, and ego, Niryn amended as he went back to his breakfast. And a traitor's heart. How long would this one remain tractable before overreaching himself?

No matter, he thought, sucking the custard from a pastry horn. *There are always plenty more of that ilk to be had.*

In fact, Niryn had learned of the pregnancy a few days earlier, as he'd known about the others. Prince Korin had kept his spies busy the past year or so, throwing bastards around the city like a farmer strewing barley seed. But this time it wasn't just another kitchen maid or harbor slut, girls one could simply exterminate like troublesome vermin. No, this one had nearly gotten past him. His spy among the Dalnan priests—now deceased—had informed him too late of certain divinations performed for the girl, divinations that set the royal hallmark on the child's paternity. Aliya's mother, a woman as ambitious as she was powerful, had already been told and was eagerly anticipating the formal announcement that would graft her line to the throne.

Closeted with Erius in the king's private study, Niryn spoke carefully, never taking his eyes from the king's face. Erius took the news with disarming calm.

"Lady Aliya, you say? Now which one is she?"

"The eldest daughter of Duchess Virysia."

The king's face, usually so easily read, betrayed little. "Ah yes, that auburn-haired beauty who's always on his knee."

"Yes, my king. She's one of several lovers your son has enjoyed in recent months. As you know, he has been ah— laboring mightily, as the poets put it, to produce an heir so that you will let him go off to battle."

Erius laughed outright at this. "By the Flame, he's as stubborn as I am! Are you certain the child is his?"

"I've looked into the matter carefully, Majesty. The child is his, though a bastard. But even if you forbid the match, the endorsements Prince Korin has already given have done their damage. The child could make claim to the throne on the strength of them."

Niryn watched hopefully for a flicker of anger, but instead Erius slapped his knees and laughed. "They'll make handsome babes between them, and the family's highborn. How far along is she?"

"I believe the child will be born in the month of Shemin, my king."

"If—" Erius began, then pressed a finger to his lips to ward off the bad luck. "Well, the girl is strong and fair . . . We'll hope for the best. Shemin, you say?" He counted on his fingers and chuckled. "If they marry at once, we can pretend it was a hasty birth. That's as good as on the right side of the blanket."

"There is one other thing, my king."

"Yes?"

"Well, there's the matter of the girl's mother. She is a known Illioran sympathizer."

Erius brushed the issue aside. "I suspect she'll be praying at a different altar, now that she's to be the grandmother of the future king or queen, eh?"

"No doubt you're right, my king," Niryn replied, forcing a smile, for it was the truth. "There is just one hindrance. Your son, my king, he's not yet blooded. To my knowledge, no ruler of Skala has married before they've proven themselves in battle."

"By the Four, you're right there! Well, the lad's timing is damn poor. I don't mean to attack Benshâl just to suit him."

"I believe some of the ancient queens faced that same dilemma. But there are always bandits or pirates to be dealt with. I'm certain the Companions would not complain of such a foe. With their youth, it's an honorable enough beginning."

"My grandmother did just the same to marry." Erius sighed and ran a hand over his silver-streaked beard. "But the chick isn't hatched yet. If Korin was killed now, and the child . . ." Again he stopped and made a warding sign.

"Like it or not, Majesty, you must let the boy claim his place as a warrior or the armies will not accept him when, Sakor forfend, the time comes for him to claim the crown. You have only to ask, Majesty, and I will do all in my power to protect your son."

To his surprise Erius did not bridle at the suggestion. "This magic of yours? What would it be?"

"There's no dishonor in it, I assure you. How can there be, any more than to wear armor? A simple amulet would suffice, such as Queen Klie wore in the ballads."

"Very well. I'll have General Rheynaris find a suitable covey for my son to hunt." Erius smiled, looking as if a burden had been taken from his shoulders. "Thank you, my friend, for your good counsel. But not a word to anyone. I want to tell Korin myself. Can you imagine the look on his face?" The king looked boyish himself at the thought. He stood and clapped the wizard on the shoulder. "If I could have only one minister at court, I'd have to keep you. You've been invaluable, as ever."

Niryn pressed his hand to his heart. "May I always be so worthy of your trust, my king."

As he walked back to his own rooms, Niryn sent up a silent prayer of thanks to Illior, but it was mere habit. In truth, it had been a very long time since he'd cared what the gods thought.

Chapter 31

Before Korin could break the news to his father a terse summons arrived, ordering the prince and Master Porion to the New Palace. The rest of the Companions were useless once he was gone. Raven tried in vain to engage them with descriptions of the twenty-third battle of Kouros, but the boys swiveled like weathercocks at every noise from the corridor. Giving up in disgust, he dismissed them.

They loitered around the mess for the rest of the afternoon, anxious not to miss any summons. The mood was tense; if the king had been happy about the news, what was all the waiting about?

Ki made a halfhearted attempt at knucklebones with Barieus and Lynx, but no one could concentrate.

"He's done it now," Tanil fretted, pacing the rushes flat by the door. "I *tried* to tell him to be more careful, but he wouldn't listen."

"He didn't want to be careful and neither did she," Caliel grumbled, stretched out on a bench by the hearth and staring morosely up at the ceiling.

"Will the king blame Porion?" asked Lutha.

"Or us?" said Quirion. "Maybe he thinks the Companions should have kept a better eye on him. What do you think, Tobin?"

"How should I know?" Tobin shrugged, whittling a bit of kindling to slivers.

Ki cast a concerned glance at his friend. Ever since the incident at the execution, something had changed in the king's demeanor toward Tobin.

"I say it's good news for us, no matter what happens," Zusthra declared. "Korin will have his heir—"

"That's for his father to say," Nikides cut in. "The child's a bastard, remember?"

"I can think of at least two queens born on the wrong side of the blanket," Caliel countered.

"Yes, but those were the children of queens," Nikides reminded him.

"So what?" snapped Urmanis. "Bilairy's balls, do you always have to be such a know-it-all?"

Nikides colored and shut up.

"No, Nik's right," said Caliel. "Go on, explain it to him, if he's too thick to see it."

"A woman always knows the child is hers, so a queen can't be cuckolded," Nikides told Urmanis. "Even if she doesn't know which lover was the father, as happened with Klie. But Korin has only Aliya's word, and the drysians', that her child is his. Really, it would be safer not to claim it and get Korin married off properly."

"But he could still be cuckolded, even by a rightful consort," Ki pointed out.

Before they could debate that point, the sound of approaching footsteps brought them all to attention.

It wasn't Korin, or Porion, however, but Moriel. They'd seen little of the Toad since the incident with Tobin and the girls. Perhaps he'd gotten wind of how Tobin's friends planned to get even with him for his treachery.

He didn't look very happy to be here now. "The king wants all of you to dine with him at the palace. You're to come back with me now."

"What's going on with Korin?" demanded Caliel.

Moriel made him a slight bow. "I'm only the messenger, my lord."

Ki guessed from the Toad's sour expression that he knew more than he was saying. "Must be good news for us!" he whispered, nudging Tobin as they went out. "If the king was angry at us for letting Korin run wild, Toad wouldn't be looking like he's got a belly cramp."

There were hundreds of corridors and passages threading the New Palace courts together, a labyrinth for any who didn't live there. Most of the Companions had only been as far as the public wing, in its own right a maze of grand audience and ministerial chambers, armories, treasury rooms, and public gardens, temples, and fountain courts.

Moriel knew his way and led them to a small dining chamber in the king's wing. Tall windows edged in patterns of colored glass overlooked a garden with golden fountains and tall, vine-covered walls. Braziers burned by the long dining table, where a cold supper had been laid ready. Bowing, Moriel withdrew.

The boys stood about uncertainly, not daring to touch the food without the king's leave. Erius came in at last, accompanied by Korin, Porion, and Raven. All of them looked very solemn.

"I suppose you've heard the news regarding my son and Lady Aliya?" the king rumbled, looking sharply around at them.

"Yes, Majesty," everyone said, coming to attention.

He let them dangle a moment longer, then broke into a broad smile. "Well, then, pour a libation and raise a toast to Korin and his lady, and my future grandchild!"

Tobin dutifully kissed his uncle on both cheeks and took his seat on his left. The squires hastened to serve, for there were no other servants.

When Lynx had poured the wine, they tipped the first few drops out onto the flagstones, then drank the successions of healths and blessings.

"It's been too long since we had a simple meal together," Erius said, as the first course was passed.

He kept the conversation to ordinary things while they ate—hunting, their progress at training. Porion and Raven were both uncharacteristically effusive in their praise of the boys.

As Ki and Barieus passed the last trays of sweets, Erius stood and smiled around at them. "Well, boys, are you young warriors ready to try your hand at proper fighting?"

Everyone gaped for a moment, afraid to believe what they'd just heard. Then they burst into new cheers and sloshed their cups about, saluting the king. Ki flung his tray up with a whoop and half strangled Tobin with a hug while quince tarts rained around them.

"There is one impediment, however," Erius went on, giving Korin a wink. "It wouldn't be seemly for Korin to wed before he's properly blooded, but his lady isn't giving us time to start the war up again, so we'll have to make do with what Skala can offer at home."

Everyone laughed. Tobin cast a grateful look Porion's way, certain that the old warrior had finally found a way to press their cause.

When the table was cleared Korin unrolled a map. Leaning in beside him, Tobin recognized a section of the northern coastline.

"Here's where we're going," Korin told them, pointing to an inland location in the mountains. "A strong band of brigands has been reported in the foothills north of Colath. Father wants them cleaned out before winter."

"How many?" Lutha asked eagerly.

"Fifty or so, by the reports we've had," Raven croaked. "By all accounts, they're a disorganized rabble. Until now they've kept on the move, attacking at night without warning, preying on small villages. They're making a winter camp in the hills, so they'll be easy enough to find."

"We'll be going to a fortress not too far from there, at Rilmar."

"Rilmar?" Ki exclaimed.

Erius chuckled. "I thought it was time your father thanked his young benefactor properly. And I don't imagine you'll mind seeing your family again? I understand it's been a long time since you've seen them?"

"Yes, Majesty. Thank you." But he didn't sound pleased. Everyone else was too excited to notice, but Tobin glanced at his friend in concern. He used to love to tell stories about his kin. They sounded like a wild, hot-blooded bunch, and Tobin had always wanted to meet them. But Ki didn't talk of them so much anymore, except for Ahra.

"So it will be us against fifty?" Lutha was asking eagerly.

"Well, Tobin and I will take our guard, so there's forty, plus all you lot," Korin explained. "Lord Larenth can provide another score or so, but this will be our battle.

"And don't worry," he added, ruffling Tobin's hair and looking around at the younger boys. "We *all* go."

"We can be ready by daylight!" said Caliel.

Erius chuckled. "It will take a bit longer than that. The ships are being readied, and supplies packed. You boys will help oversee the preparations, as part of your education. Two days is soon enough." Erius clasped Korin by the shoulder and gave him an affectionate shake. "As soon as you come back with blood on your cheeks, we'll announce this wedding of yours."

Chapter 32

The three-day voyage was Tobin's first experience aboard a ship. Their vessels, two deep-bellied carracks with red sails, were large enough to transport their horses.

Tobin felt a flutter of fear as the ship shifted beneath his feet, but by the time they'd passed the harbor mouth he'd found his sea legs. Behind them, the city glistened in the morning sun, reminding him again of the toy city above its painted harbor. Only then, when it was too late, did he realize that in all the excitement of the preparations, he'd completely forgotten about Brother. The old rag doll was still in its hiding place in the dressing room.

"Don't worry," Ki said, when Tobin confided this to him. "No one ever dusts up there anyway. And it's not like he'd be any good to you in battle."

Porion was their sergeant now, and Tharin and Melnoth were their captains. Korin spent hours with the men, asking a hundred questions and listening to tales of past battles. The rest of the boys gathered around for these lessons and by the time they rounded the headlands at Greyhead, they'd already fought the battle a dozen times over in their heads.

"These aren't trained soldiers you're going against," Porion warned repeatedly. "They can't be counted on to follow the rules of engagement."

"Chances are you won't see half of them at any given moment," Tharin added. "They'll be up in trees, or shooting at you from the bushes. Our best bet is to take them unawares if we can, before they have time to scatter."

* * *

*T*he sea shone green under the pale sun each day. The weather held clear, with a good following wind. On the third morning they dropped anchor at a large fishing village and spent the day unloading the horses and their gear. The coastline was rougher than in Ero, and the forest hugged the sea ledges.

The village was a small, lonely place, without a palisade or market square, or an inn. The Companions spent the night on pallets in the thatch-roofed temple of Astellus, which doubled as a wayfarers' hostel. Their men camped on the beach under canvas lean-tos. The next morning they set off at dawn, following a winding road up into the hills.

The mountains were different, too. They were shorter and rounder, like worn-down teeth, and thickly forested almost to their tops. Their rocky summits showed through like a balding man's pate. The wide valleys between were well watered and dotted with steadings and walled villages.

The keep at Rilmar stood at the mouth of one of the larger valleys, guarding an important road. Tobin had expected something like his old home at Alestun, but Rilmar consisted of a single large round stone tower encircled by a raised earthwork and a weathered stockade wall. The tower was topped by a crenellated terrace and conical wooden roof. The banner flying there showed two green serpents intertwined on a red-and-yellow field.

"That must be your father's new arms," Tobin said, pointing it out to Ki.

Ki said nothing, and he wasn't smiling as he scanned the walls. Tobin could make out the heads of half a dozen men watching them from there. His banner and Korin's should have told the guards who was coming, but no one hailed them or came out to meet them.

Ki peered up, shading his eyes.

"See any of your family?" Tobin asked, anxious to meet the people he'd heard so many stories about.

"Nobody I recognize."

Hounds bayed an alarm from inside as they rode up to the gates.

A dirty, one-eyed warder let them in. He saluted Korin and Tobin, then squinted at the rest of them with surly interest, not appearing to know Ki.

Beyond the gate they entered a barren close. Men and women who looked more like bandits themselves than a lord's warriors were at work there, shoeing horses and chopping wood. A smith was busy at a forge by the inner wall. Other men lounged about at their ease. Two brindle hounds as big as calves rushed at the newcomers, barking furiously until some of the idlers sent them yelping with a few well-aimed stones. Tobin caught Tharin and Porion looking around with pursed lips at such slovenliness. He heard someone among the Companions snicker but Korin silenced them with a quick glare.

Two boys a bit older than Ki and dressed in decent leather armor came bounding down from the rickety wall walk.

"That you, Ki?" the taller of the pair demanded. He had Ki's dark eyes and hair, but he was broader and looked more like a farmer than a warrior.

"It's me, Amin!" Ki said, brightening a bit as he slid out of the saddle to meet his brother.

The other boy gave him a none-too-gentle punch on the arm. "You been gone too long, little brother. I'm Dimias. This here's Amin."

The other boy looked even more like Ki. "Lookit you, the little lordling!" he cried, giving Ki a rough hug.

Both of them spoke with the thick country accent Ki had had when Tobin first met him.

The smith, a fair-haired man in a scorched leather apron, limped over from the forge to meet them. His arms and hands were massive, but he had a clubfoot. He gave Korin an awkward, bobbing bow and touched a fist to his heart. "Welcome to Rilmar, Yer Highness." His eyes kept darting to Ki as he spoke, and Tobin read sour envy in his small, narrowed eyes.

"Hullo, Innis," Ki said, looking no more pleased to see him; Innis had never come off well in Ki's stories. "Prince Korin, may I present my half brother?"

Innis wiped his hands on his apron and bobbed again. "Father's inside wi' gouty foot. Said I's to bring you in when you come. You can leave yer horses and soldiers here. Amin, you an' Dimias see to 'em. Come on, then, Yer Highness."

Porion and the captains stayed with the Companions as they crossed to the crumbling stone wall that enclosed the keep yards. Innis fell in next to Ki, and Tobin heard him growl, "Took you long enough to come home again, didn't it? Too good for yer own folk now, I reckon."

Ki's hands clenched, but he held his head up and said nothing.

Passing under the barbican, Tobin caught his breath, trying not to wrinkle his nose at the odors that greeted them.

Inside the gate a few slatternly-looking women were at work over a soap kettle; the stinging fumes wafted around the dank yard, adding an acrid edge to the overwhelming stink of dung, damp stone, and rotting garbage, which lay everywhere. Woodsmoke hung in heavy layers on the moist air. A pile of broken barrels took up one corner near the stables, and pigs were rooting through a midden just beyond.

The ancient keep was badly in need of repair. The walls were crusted with moss and lichen, and wildflowers had found rootholds between the weathered blocks where mortar had crumbled away. On the upper levels of the tower, shutters hung by one hinge or were missing altogether, giving the place an abandoned look.

The yard was paved with flagstones, but they'd been cracked and heaved by the frosts, and in places they were missing altogether, leaving muddy brown puddles where a few bedraggled chickens and ducks drank. Witchgrass and thistles stuck up through the breaks in the stone. Hollyhock and nightshade had gone to seed near the ironbound front door, and a hoary rose vine climbed over the lintel, a few white blossoms giving the yard its only hint of cheer.

It's as bad as the streets around Beggar's Bridge, Tobin thought. Even in the darkest days of Tobin's childhood, the keep yard at Alestun had been kept tidy and the lower levels of the house in decent repair.

On the far side of the yard, a gang of dirty children was playing in the back of a broken-down cart. An unshaven young man dressed in nothing but a long dirty tunic sat watching the riders from the driver's seat. His lank hair hung in greasy tangles around his bare shoulders and as they got closer, Tobin saw that he had the blank, wideset eyes of an idiot.

Tobin heard more snickers behind him. Ki had gone red to the tips of his ears. He'd long since been trained away from his rough ways and speech, and he'd always been clean and particular in his dress. No wonder he hadn't been anxious to see his own people again.

The children in the cart ran to greet the Companions. The rest of the motley assembly soon followed.

The youngest children circled them like a flock of swallows, laughing excitedly. One little girl with a long blond braid down her back stopped to stare at Korin's gold-chased helmet. "Is you a king?" she lisped, blue eyes solemn.

"No, I'm the king's son, Prince Korin." He took her hand and kissed it gallantly, sending her into screams of laughter.

The idiot boy in the cart let out a hooting bellow, bouncing up and down and making a wet sound that might have been Ki's name.

"Hullo, Kick," Ki called, waving back reluctantly.

"Another brother?" Mago asked with poorly concealed glee.

"Bastard one," Innis grunted.

Entering the keep, they walked through a large, round chamber that served both as kitchen and storeroom and up a creaking staircase to the great hall.

This chamber was lit by a few narrow windows and a fire on the long hearth, but from what Tobin could make out as his eyes adjusted to the smoky dimness, it was little better than the room below. The ceiling beams and long tables were black with age, and the blotched plaster had fallen away in places, revealing bare stone underneath. A few cheap, new tapestries hung in odd places and the silver plate lined up on shelves near the hearth was tarnished. A brindle bitch lay nursing a litter in the middle of the room and lanky, notch-eared cats walked the tables with impunity. The household women darted sharp looks at the guests as they sat twirling their distaffs by a smaller cooking hearth, two half-naked babies rolling on the dirty rushes at their feet. The whole place stank of old grease and piss.

"This isn't where I grew up," Ki whispered to Tobin, then sighed. "This is better, actually."

Tobin felt as if he'd betrayed Ki; he'd never imagined a place like this when the king had granted Larenth the title.

A thin, worn-out woman not much older than Innis came forward to greet them. Dressed in a fine new gown stained with tallow spots across the skirt, she made an awkward job of kneeling to kiss Korin's hand. From the look of her and what Ki had told him over the years, Tobin guessed that Larenth got his new wives from among the servants whenever he'd used up the last with child birthing.

"Welcome to our house, Yer Highness," she said. "I'm Lady Sekora. Come in and be welcome. We thank you—" She paused, searching for the words. "We thank you for honoring us with our new rank, too. My man—my lord's back there, waiting on you wi's foot up."

Korin was trying not to laugh as he raised her by the

hand. "Thank you, my lady. Allow me to present my cousin, Prince Tobin of Ero."

Sekora stared into Tobin's face with obvious curiosity. "Yer Ki's master, then, what that wizard spoke of?" Her teeth were bad and her breath stank.

"Ki is my squire and my friend," Tobin said, taking her thin, rough hand in his as she curtsied again.

She looked from him to Ki and shook her head. "Ki, I 'spect yer dad'll be wanting to see you. Come and eat, then I'll take you all through."

She clapped her hands and the women brought cold food and wine from a sideboard and laid it out for the guests. They ranged in age from a stooped old grandmother to a pair of young girls who blushed and made bold eyes at Tobin and the others.

The food was plain but surprisingly good, considering the household—cold mutton with mint relish on trenchers of fresh parsley bread, boiled onions mired in thick cream spiced with cloves and wine, and the best venison pie Tobin had tasted since he left Cook's kitchen. The hospitality was another matter. Lady Sekora stood with the women, twisting her hands nervously in her skirt front as she watched every mouthful Korin took. Innis ate with them, head low over his trencher, shoveling the food in like a peasant.

"Why is it the master of the house doesn't eat with us?" asked Korin, pushing a bold white tom away from his trencher.

"Ailing, ain't he?" Innis grunted around a mouthful of pie. This was the extent of their entertainment during the meal.

When they'd finished Innis went back to his work and Sekora led Korin, Tobin, and Ki to a smaller room behind the hall.

It was much cozier here, lined with pine paneling gone dark gold with age and warmed by a crackling fire that somewhat masked the smell of a neglected chamber pot. It reminded Tobin of Hakone's room.

Lord Larenth lay dozing in an armchair by the fire, his poultice-swathed foot propped on a stool in front of him. Even asleep, he was a formidable-looking old man. He had a hawkish nose, and faded scars marked his unshaven cheeks. Thinning grey hair fell over his shoulders and a drooping moustache framed his thin-lipped mouth. Like Sekora, he wore new clothes of a fine cut, but they looked like they'd been slept in more than once, and used for a napkin, too. Sekora shook him gently by the shoulder, and he woke with a start, reaching for a sword that wasn't there. His left eye was milky white and blind. Tobin could see nothing of Ki in this man except for his one good eye; it was the same warm brown.

All in all, Lord Larenth was what Ki would call a "rough customer" but it seemed he was better versed in court etiquette than his wife, for he pushed himself up from his chair and made Korin and Tobin deep bows. "Please accept my apologies, Yer Highnesses. I don't get much beyond this chair these days, on account of my foot. My eldest boys is away with the king's army, and my eldest girl ain't back yet. Sekora, is Ahra back yet? No? Well, she said she'd come so I reckon she will—" He trailed off. "Innis should have greeted you."

"He did, and your good lady made us most welcome," Korin assured him. "Sit, please, my lord. I can tell your foot hurts you."

"Fetch chairs, woman!" Larenth snapped, and waited until Korin was seated before he sat down again. "Now then, Prince Tobin, my family owes you a great debt for raising us to this. I'll do me best to be worthy of your trust, and the king's."

"I'm sure you will, my lord."

"And I was sad to hear of yer father's passing. He was a rare, fine warrior, that one. Rare fine!"

"Thank you, my lord." Tobin acknowledged this with a

nod, waiting for the old man to turn to his son, whom he hadn't even acknowledged.

Korin pulled a letter from his tunic and presented it to the old man. "The king sends his greetings, my lord, and orders regarding tomorrow's raid."

Larenth stared at the document a moment before cautiously accepting it. He turned it over in his hands, examining the seals, then shrugged. "Have you anyone to read it out, Yer Highness? We don't hold with such here."

"Squire Kirothius, read the king's letter for your honored father," said Korin, and Tobin guessed that he'd noticed, too.

Larenth's shaggy eyebrows shot up and he squinted with his good eye. "Ki, is it? I didn't know you, boy."

"Hullo, Dad."

Tobin expected them to laugh and hug now, the way Tharin and his kin had when they met. But Larenth was looking at his son as he might some unwanted stranger. "You done all right for yerself, then. Ahra said you had."

The letter trembled in Ki's fingers as he unfolded it.

"Read, too, do you?" Larenth muttered. "All right then, go on."

Ki read the brief missive. It began with the usual greetings, then commanded that Korin lead the raid. Ki didn't stumble once, but his cheeks were red again by the time he'd finished.

His father listened in silence, sucking his teeth, then turned back to Korin. "The thieving bastards moved their camp higher up in the hills a few weeks back, after we took a charge at 'em. Innis can take you out, if Ahra don't come. There's a trail that'll let you flank 'em. If you go up in the night, p'raps they'll be too drunk to hear you. You can take 'em at first light." He paused, squinting at Korin. "How many seasoned men have you?"

"Twoscore."

"Well, you keep 'em close, Yer Highness. They're a hard lot, these bandits. They've raided half the villages in the valley this winter, and made off with a fair number of the women. I've been after them since I got here and we've had a hard time of it. Led 'im meself until my foot went rotten." He stared at Korin again, then shook his head. "Well, you just keep 'em close, you hear? I don't want to answer this here letter with your ashes."

"We've had the best training in Skala, my lord," Korin replied stiffly.

"I don't doubt that, Yer Highness," the old man said bleakly. "But there's no training to match what you get at the sharp end of a sword."

Settling in for the night at that cheerless house, Ki wished that Tobin had left well enough alone. If his father hadn't been made a lord, the king would never have thought to send the Companions to him. It seemed like a lifetime since he'd been among his kin; he hadn't realized just how much he'd changed until he saw them again and saw how they looked at him. Even Amin and Dimias had stolen jealous glances at him around the fire downstairs. The younger children, at least those who remembered him, were happy to see him and begged for stories of the city. His little half sisters and brothers and their bastard siblings clung like baby squirrels to anyone else who'd sit still for it, including Korin, who'd been blessedly good-natured about it all. Whatever else Ki might think of the prince, he had a good touch with people when he wanted to. And Ki did have one moment of pleasure when a toddling boy with a shitty bottom had climbed into Alben's lap.

That didn't make up for the rest of it, though. Now the Companions all knew just how much a grass knight he really was. The sight of his father and poor Sekora in their filthy finery had nearly killed him with shame. "You can put a pig in silk slippers, but it don't make him a dancer," his father liked to say of anyone he thought was getting above themselves. Never had Ki understood the proverb so clearly.

Most of the household went to bed with the sun. The youngest children still slept in haphazard piles on the floor with the hounds and cats. Innis and the older boys sat up with them over more of the dreadful wine, making a desultory attempt at hospitality. Innis, the fourth legitimate child after Ahra, was a slow-witted bull of a man, taciturn to the point of rudeness. He'd shown more aptitude for smithing than he ever had fighting. Because of that and his crippled foot, he'd been left home to manage the household when the others went off to war. Amin and Dimias had both gone off as runners during the last conflicts and it was clear that Innis hadn't forgiven them their good fortune, any more than he would Ki.

Korin made the best of things. He drank cup after cup of the bad wine and praised it as if it were Kallian red. He joked with Amin and even charmed a smirking grin out of Innis by challenging him to arm wrestle and losing. Caliel paid their guesting price by leading a few songs, which brightened things up for a while. But Ki was too aware of the looks Alben, Mago, and their friends kept stealing at him, and their smirks as Sekora tried clumsily to play hostess. She'd always been kind to Ki and he nearly jumped on Arius when he answered her rudely. His brothers had noticed, too, and looked ready to do murder.

Lynx gripped his knee under the table and shook his head. Even here in this wretched place, a royal squire shouldn't shame the king's son or his lord by brawling. Ruan and Barieus gave him sympathetic looks across the table, but that only made Ki feel worse.

Tobin knew how he felt; he always did. Ignoring the rude ones, he talked hunting with Amin and did a bit of swordplay with Dimias. He gave Ki the occasional quick smile, and there was no false brightness in it.

It was a relief when they finally headed off to their chamber. Weaving a bit, Korin threw an arm around Innis and proclaimed him a fine fellow. Tobin and Caliel got hold of him and steered him along behind Sekora. Ki hung back, not yet trusting himself near Mago and the others.

His stepmother led them upstairs to a passably clean guest chamber with two large beds. His father no doubt considered this scandalous luxury, but Ki wanted to sink through the floor when Sekora told Korin that the squires were welcome to the stable loft, as if they were mere servants. Korin was very polite about it, and saw to it that pallets were brought up for them.

The rest of this floor, which should have been the private quarters for the family, had fallen into disrepair and there was no evidence that his father thought it needed changing. The other rooms were empty and musty, their bare floors filthy with the droppings of birds and mice. Since the family still lived and slept in the hall as they always had, it made little difference to them.

"Would you mind if I went back down for a bit, Tob?" he asked softly.

Tobin clasped him by the wrist. "It's all right, Ki. Go on."

So you're back to fight, are you?" Amin said, making room for him on the settle. "Is it true none of you been to the wars?"

"That's right," Ki told him.

"Funny thing, coming all the way up here for it, after living so close to the royals so long," Dimias said. "Bilairy's balls, Ki, even *I* been. Why didn't that duke fellow ever take you, eh?"

"Nobles don't go so young." It was true, but he felt small all the same. Amin had a sword cut on his cheek and was careful to sit so Ki could see it.

"Listen to *him*!" his half sister Lyla said from one of the sleeping piles. "Sounds like quality now."

"They learned me to talk like 'em," Ki snapped, falling back into the old way of speaking. "You don't think they want me squalling like you all around them fine lords an' ladies?"

Dimias laughed and locked an arm around his neck. "That's our Ki! And I say good for you. Maybe you can learn us, too, and find us positions in Ero, eh? I'd fancy city life. Leave all this stink behind without a glance, just like you did."

"Father sold me off," Ki reminded him, but the truth was, he hadn't cared much, leaving.

Lowering his voice, Amin muttered, "I seen how some of 'em looked down their noses at you, though, and you let 'em beat you down, too. Don't give 'em the pleasure of it, y'hear? I seen battle and all. Half these highbred boys'll piss their pants tomorrow, mark my words."

"But not you, eh?" Amin clapped Ki on the shoulder. "Ahra said the pair of you was warrior-born after she seen you again. Sakor-touched, so she said. And he's a good 'un, that Tobin, even if he is sorta runty and girlish."

"You'll stand fast, you and yer prince," Dimias said.

" 'Course we will!" Ki scoffed, "And he ain't girlish!"

They tussled a bit over that, but for the first time that day he was glad to be home, and gladder still to have his brothers speak well of Tobin.

Squeezed into bed between Nikides and Urmanis, Tobin listened to the older boys bragging about how many bandits they'd kill the next day. As always, Korin's voice was the loudest. Tobin kept an eye on the door, waiting for Ki to come up. Tiring of the wait, he went looking for him.

The hall was dark except for the hearth's glow. He was about to go back upstairs when someone whispered, "Ki's outside, Yer Highness, if you're lookin' for 'im."

"Thank you." Picking his way carefully around the piles of sleepers, he made his way down through the kitchen into the stinking courtyard. The sky overhead was cloudless, and the stars looked big as larks' eggs. Torches were burning on the parapet, and he could see the guards patrolling the wall walk. He was heading for the yard gate when he caught sight of two people sitting in the back of the abandoned cart.

"Ki?" he whispered.

"Go to bed, Tob. It's cold out."

Tobin climbed up onto the splintery seat beside them. It was Tharin there with him, sitting with his elbows on his knees. Suddenly he felt like an interloper, but he didn't want to go in again. "What's wrong?"

Ki let out a harsh snort. "You saw." He gestured around at the keep, the yard—everything, probably. "This is what I come from. Think they're going to let me forget it?"

"I'm sorry. I never thought it would be like this. I thought—"

"Yeah? Well, you didn't reckon on my kin."

"He's been gone a good while," Tharin said quietly.

"They're not so bad—some of them. I like your brothers, and your father is a tough old warrior; I can tell."

"He got old while I was gone. I've never seen him laid up like that, half-blind. Five years is a long time, Tob. Looking at them, I start to wonder who I am."

"You are what you've made of yourself," Tharin said firmly. "That's what I've just been telling him, Tobin. Some are born noble but don't have the heart to be any kind of man. Others like Ki here come out noble to the core no matter what. You both saw my family. They weren't much different than your people, Ki, but Rhius raised me up and I hold my head high next to any wellborn man. You're cut from the same cloth. There's not a boy on the Palatine I'd rather stand next to tomorrow."

Tharin gave them both a quick squeeze on the shoulder and climbed down. "Bring him in soon, Tobin. You need your rest."

Tobin stayed by Ki, thinking of his own homecoming in Atyion. He'd honestly supposed Ki would find something of the same welcome here. But the keep was awful;

there was no denying it. Had the king known it, when he'd suggested it?

At a loss for words, he found Ki's hand and clasped it. Ki let out a growl and bumped his shoulder against Tobin's. "I know you don't think less of me, Tob. If I thought that, I'd ride out that gate tonight and never look back."

"No, you wouldn't. You'd miss the fight tomorrow. And Ahra will be here, too. What do you think she'd do to you if you ran off?"

"There's that. Guess I's more 'feared of her than any Companion." Standing, he looked around the yard again and chuckled. "Well, it could be worse."

"How?"

Ki's grin flashed in the darkness. "I could be the heir to all this."

Chapter 33

It was still dark when Tharin and Porion woke them, but Tobin felt the flutter of a dawn breeze through the open window. No one was bragging as they dressed. Tobin's eyes met Ki's as his friend helped him into his hauberk, and he saw his own excitement and fear mirrored there. By the time he'd pulled the surcoat on he was sweating.

As they turned to go he saw that Korin was wearing the horse amulet he'd made for him, and a new one Tobin hadn't seen before.

"What's this?" he asked, leaning in for a closer look. It was a pretty piece, a polished lozenge of horn set in gold.

"A luck piece Father gave me," Korin said, kissing it.

For the first time in a long time, Tobin felt a pang of longing and envy. What would his father have said to him, or given him, before his first battle?

There was no sign of breakfast in the hall. Children and animals watched from the shadows as they clattered down to the yard. Ki's three older brothers were waiting for them out in the close, and Ahra and her riders were with them. From the looks of their clothes they'd ridden all night to get here and had only just made it. A girl of twelve or so, barefoot and dressed in a ragged, mud-spattered tunic sat an equally muddy horse beside Ahra. Both dismounted to hug Ki, then Ahra bowed deeply to Korin and Tobin. "Forgive me being late, my princes. Father sent Korli here after me but she was delayed on the road."

" 'Pologies, Yer Highness," the girl mumbled shyly, dropping them an awkward curtsy. "Hullo, Ki!"

Ki gave her a quick kiss.

Tobin studied her with interest, for Korli looked the most like Ki of anyone he'd seen here. She had his dark good looks, and gave Tobin a hint of the same buck-toothed smile when she saw him looking.

"Is she your full sister?" he asked as Ki went to saddle their horses. It seemed odd he'd never mentioned her.

"Korli? No, she's one of the bastards." He paused, giving her a second look. "Huh. She's sure grown."

"She looks like you."

"Think so?" He strode off in the direction of the stable.

Surprised by this casual dismissal, Tobin stole another look at the girl. Korli was slighter than Ki, but she had the same brown eyes and soft, straight hair, and the same smooth, golden skin. Her features were a little rounder, a bit softer . . .

Like my other face looked in the pool.

A chill ran up Tobin's spine and he turned away quickly, feeling like he'd seen a ghost.

Ahra had twenty riders with her, as hard-bitten a lot as any he'd seen, and at least a third of them were women. Most of the men with them were getting old or were very young; the best fighters were off in the regular regiments. As he turned to look for Ki, one of the boys gave him a quick secretive wave. Tobin hesitated, thinking he'd misunderstood, but the boy signaled him again. Intrigued, Tobin wandered over.

He was beardless, no older than Tobin, and the face that showed under the helmet and warrior braids was smudged with dirt. Something about his eyes was familiar, though, and judging by the grin he was giving him now, he thought he knew Tobin.

"Don't you know me, Yer Highness?"

It wasn't a boy at all.

Tobin's heart leaped as he followed her behind a hayrick. "Una, it's you!"

She pulled off the helmet and shook the hair back

from her face. "Yes! I didn't want to chance Korin and the others seeing me, but I knew you'd keep my secret."

Tobin hardly recognized the highborn girl he'd known. She wore the scarred armor of a common soldier, but the sword at her hip was a fine one of old design.

"Your grandmother's?" he guessed.

"Told you I'd carry it one day. I just didn't think it would be so soon. And I bet you never thought I'd see battle before you, either."

"No! What are you doing here?"

"Where'd you think I'd go, after all Ki's stories?"

"I don't know. We—Ki and I—we were afraid that—" He swallowed the words, not wanting to admit aloud what he and Ki had only speculated on in whispers, that the king had murdered her. "Well, damn, I'm just glad you're here! Have you killed your first man yet?"

"Yes. You were a good teacher." She hesitated, looking him in the eye. "You don't hate me, then?"

"Why would I hate you?"

"It was all my idea, training the girls. Father said you were in awful trouble for doing it, and I heard Arengil was sent back to Aurënen because of it."

"Of course I don't hate you. It wasn't your fault."

"Mount up!" Korin called.

Tobin took her hand in the warrior's grip. "Sakor's Flame, Una. I'll tell Ki!"

Una grinned and saluted him. "I'll be at your back, my prince."

They made a brave show, riding out past the torches with their banners. They carried no lights. Innis and Ahra took the lead, guiding them up the valley as the stars slowly faded. Amin and Dimias rode with them, and Tobin couldn't help admiring the easy way they sat their mounts. Tharin and Captain Melnoth brought up the rear.

After a few miles they left the road and took off across country through stubbled fields and wooded copses still wreathed in chill mist. They reached the first hamlet while it was still too dark to make out much more than a few thatched roofs over the top of the log palisade. As they came closer, however, they caught a familiar smell; it was the ash and burned pork reek of the pyre fields near Ero.

"Bandits?" asked Korin.

"No," Ahra replied. "Plague took this one."

A few miles farther on, however, they came to the remains of one that had been burned by bandits. The sky had gone from indigo to grey, light enough for Tobin to see the broken black stump of a stone chimney and a wooden doll floating in a ditch.

"This happened a few weeks back," Innis told them. "The men was killed and left, but there weren't a women or girl to be found among 'em."

"They're setting up good and solid if they took the girls," said Tharin, shaking his head. "How much farther?"

Innis pointed toward the wooded hills ahead, where a few thin columns of smoke could be seen rising above the trees.

Tobin imagined the captured women making breakfast there and shuddered.

"Don't worry, we'll bring the women back safely," Korin was saying.

Innis shrugged. "Not much point now, is there?"

"Ruined goods, are they? You'd just leave 'em, would you?" Ahra growled.

Innis jerked his thumb back at the ruined houses. "Naught to come back to."

Scowling, Ahra took the lead and they turned west, following a game track into the forest.

"Not a word, anyone. Pass it back," she whispered. Then, to Korin and the others just behind her, "Keep your weapons from rattling if you can. It's a few miles yet, but no sense giving them any warning if they have sentries posted."

Everyone checked their scabbards and bows. Tobin

leaned down and tucked the loose end of Gosi's girth strap under the edge of his saddle, holding it in with his thigh. Beside him, Ki did the same on Dragon.

The sun was just coming up over the valley but it was still almost night dark in the trees. Old firs towered around them, and the rocky ground was strewn with fallen trees.

"Not good ground for a mounted charge, is it?" Korin said softly to Ahra.

"No, but good for ambush. Shall I send lookouts?"

"We'll go!" Dimias offered.

But Ahra shook her head and sent off two of her own people.

Tobin sat straighter in the saddle, scanning the shadows for signs of sentries. He wasn't scared, exactly, but it felt like there was an empty space under his heart.

Looking around, he guessed the others were feeling it, too. Korin's face was set in a grim mask under his helm, and Tanil was counting the arrows in his quiver. Glancing back, he saw the others all making last checks, or watching the woods nervously. Ki caught Tobin's eye and grinned. Was Una scared, Tobin wondered, or did your first battle cure you of it? He wished he'd had time to ask her.

They'd gone less than a mile into the forest, steadily climbing, when Ki caught the scent of cooking fires. The air was damp and it carried the smoke low through the trees. Soon they could see wisps of it curling just below the dripping roof of branches. He began scanning the trees more carefully, unable to shake off the image of sharp eyes watching him down the length of an arrow shaft.

But nothing happened. The only sounds were the soft thud of hooves on moss and the waking calls of the birds.

They reached a clearing and dismounted. The officers and Companions gathered around Ahra while the squires took charge of the horses.

"Not much farther," she whispered, gesturing to where

the track continued out the eastern side. "The camp is less than half a mile that way, down in a little dell."

All eyes turned to Korin. He conferred briefly with Ahra and the captains. "Well, Tobin, you're in charge here with your guard. Nik, Lutha, Quirion, you're with them." Quirion started to protest but Korin ignored him. "You'll hold our flank. I'll send a runner back for you if we need you."

"You two stay with them," Ahra told her brothers. "You know the lay of the land up here, in case they need a guide."

Korin pulled at his new amulet, then glanced at Porion, who gave him a nod. "That's it, then. Swords out, and follow me."

"The lookouts, my prince. Shouldn't we wait to hear back from them?" Ahra asked.

"We're already later than I meant to be." Korin cast an eye up at the brightening sky. "If they've gotten themselves lost, we'll give up any chance we had of surprise. Come on."

He waved his sword in a great circle and the rest of the company fell in behind him.

"Well, you heard him," whispered Tobin as the sound of their horses faded away through the trees.

The squires and Tharin's men strung tether lines between several trees and set about securing their horses.

"Running knots, boys," Tharin called softly, undoing a tight knot Ruan had made. "We want to be able to get loose in a hurry if we have to."

Then there was nothing to do but wait. And listen. There was no real reason to stand at attention, but no one sat. Hands on their sword hilts or tucked into their belts, the Companions stood in a loose circle, watching the path. Some of Tharin's men spread out, patrolling the edges of the clearing.

"It's the waiting gets under your skin," Amin muttered.

"How many raids have you been on?" asked Lutha.

Amin's cocksure demeanor gave way to a sheepish grin. "Well, only two with real fighting, but we done a lot of waiting!"

The sun was just showing over the tops of the trees when they heard the first distant shouts.

Tharin climbed onto a large boulder by the trail mouth and listened for a moment, then smiled. "From the sound of it, I'd say they caught them by surprise after all."

"Be all over 'fore we get anywhere near it," Amin grumbled. "Why don't the runner come?"

The distant shouting continued, but a breeze came up and the sigh of it in the branches drowned it out. Tharin stayed on his rock, watching the path like a hound waiting for its master's return.

He was the first to fall.

Chapter 34

The first moments of the ambush were eerily quiet. One minute Tobin was standing with the others, listening to the wind in the trees. Then, without warning, Tharin let out a choked cry and spun off his rock with an arrow protruding from his left thigh, just where the split in his hauberk hung a little open.

A good shot, or a lucky one, Tobin thought, heading for him. Then he was falling, knocked sideways.

"Stay down, Tob!" Ki seemed determined to remain on top of him.

"Tharin's hit!"

"I know that. Stay down!"

Crushed into the long grass, Tobin couldn't see past Amin, who was sprawled close beside him.

The air over their heads was filled with the dragonfly buzz of arrows now. Arrows thudded into the ground on both sides of Tobin and Ki. He could hear shouting in the trees. Somewhere nearby a man cried out in pain—Sefus was it? A horse screamed, then the whole tether line began to rear and kick. The ropes snapped and the horses scattered.

The arrow storm stopped as suddenly as it had started. Heaving Ki off, Tobin was the first on his feet. Everyone had scattered. Some were still down in the grass. Others had made it to the edge of the trees. Koni and some of the others were trying to calm the remaining horses.

"To me! To me!" Tobin shouted, drawing his sword and pointing to the cover of the trees to his right. "Come on, quickly!"

No sooner had he spoken than the arrow assault resumed, but the others had heard. Some ran with their shields up, others trusted to speed.

Ki shielded him as best he could without getting underfoot. Nikides and Ruan made it to them, and Ki's brothers were there, too, shields up to catch the flying shafts.

But too many of them had been caught out in the open. Some weren't moving; at least three of Tobin's guard lay too still. The only one he could make out was Sefus, staring up at the sky with an arrow through one eye. Beyond him, Tobin saw someone else on the ground wearing the bright surcoat of a noble; from the colors, it was either Lutha or Barieus.

"Tobin, come on!" Ki urged, trying to pull him deeper into the trees. Tobin looked back at the boulder where Tharin had been, but there was no sign of the man. Praying his friend had made it to cover, Tobin ran to join the others hunkered down behind tree trunks and stones. Strangely, that empty feeling under his heart had disappeared; he didn't feel much of anything. Looking out through the trees, he saw more bodies in the meadow, arrows sticking up like thistles around them.

Ki grasped Tobin's arm again and pointed off to the right. "Do you hear that?"

Branches were crackling under someone's boots nearby; whoever it was was headed their way. Tobin quickly took stock. Nikides and Ruan were the only other Companions with him. Quirion was nowhere to be seen. Besides Amin and Dimias, he had Koni and five other guardsmen. By now they could make out enemy sounds to their left, as well.

Damn, they caught us and split us, Tobin thought grimly. It was the worst possible start, especially since they had no idea how many men they were facing. Everyone was watching him.

"Nik, you take Koni, Amin, and those four and go to

the left," he said. It sounded like there were fewer people that way. "The rest of you, with me."

Koni shrugged off his shield and gave it to him. "Take this, Tobin."

Tobin accepted it gratefully. "Sakor's luck, everyone." Slipping his left arm through the straps, he set off, leading his little force deeper into the woods on the right.

They'd gone less than twenty yards when a pack of burly men broke cover and rushed them with axes, cudgels, and swords. There was no time to think after that. Tobin ran at them with Ki at his side, dimly aware of others running with them to meet the attack.

The two lead bandits bore down on Tobin like hounds on a rabbit; a noble was worth a ransom, and they probably took him for an easy catch. Ki blocked their way and got his sword up in time to keep the taller of the two from splitting his skull. The other man darted around and made a grab for Tobin. He wore a short mail shirt and helmet, but it was clear from the way he lunged in that he wasn't a trained warrior. Tobin jumped back, then caught the fellow across the thigh with his sword. The man dropped his axe and went down, howling and clutching at the spurting wound.

Before Tobin could finish him, a blur of motion on his left made him turn and he nearly fell over a dead swordsman just behind him, close enough to have killed him. Silently thanking whoever had stopped him, Tobin turned to face another man charging him with an upraised cudgel. It was a foolish stance to take and Tobin was able to sidestep and strike him across the belly. The fellow staggered. Ki leaped in and finished him off with a stab to the neck.

More of the brigands appeared and rushed them. Shouts, screams, and curses rang out on all sides, punctuated by the clash of steel on steel. Tobin saw Dimias battling someone twice his weight and ran to help him but Amin leaped from behind a tree and caught the man across the throat.

Ki had been knocked down and Tobin turned to help him, only to find his path barred by another axe man. Years of training seemed to fall effortlessly into place. Almost before he knew what he was doing, he'd hacked at the man's right shoulder, then followed through with a killing swing to the neck. He'd practiced the move a thousand times before, but it had never come so easily. The bandit wore no coif; Tobin's blade sliced skin and muscle, then fetched up against bone. The man tumbled sideways, blood spurting from the deep gash in his neck as he fell. A gout hit Tobin in the face; the taste of hot copper and salt on his tongue made his own blood burn for more.

The distraction nearly cost him his life. Ki yelled and Tobin turned. For an instant he saw nothing but the blade coming at his head. Then he was falling backward, knocked off his feet by a blast of icy air. He hit a tree and fell awkwardly over on his side as his attacker bore him to the ground. Tobin struggled, trying to get away, then realized that the man wasn't moving. His head lolled limply as Ki and Amin hauled him off Tobin, dead as a trout.

Tobin caught sight of Brother leering at him over Ki's shoulder, his pale face twisted into that same animal snarl he'd worn when he'd killed Orun.

"Thank you," Tobin whispered, but Brother was already gone.

"Bilairy's balls!" Amin exclaimed, gawking down at the dead man. "What'd you do? Scare him to death?"

"I—I don't know," Tobin said, as Ki helped him up. How had Brother found him? Ki's quick glance said he'd guessed, or perhaps even seen Brother.

It wasn't until Dimias looked around, and said, "By the Flame! We done all right, didn't we?" that Tobin realized the fighting was over.

Half a dozen men came running toward them through the trees, with Tharin in the lead. The arrow was gone, but a dark stain had spread down from the rent in his trousers.

Tharin seemed untroubled by it. He was hardly limping, and his blade was dripping blood.

"Here you are!" he panted. "Thank the Light you're safe! I didn't see which way you ran—" Looking around at the dead, his eyes widened. "By the Flame!"

"What about you?" Ki demanded.

"It was a glancing hit and pulled out clean," Tharin told him, still looking around, counting the dead.

"You should have seen our prince!" Koni exclaimed. "At least three of these are his. How many, Tobin?"

"I don't know," Tobin admitted. It was already a blur in his mind.

"First time out and all these," Amin said, clapping Ki proudly on the shoulder. "You done yourself proud, little brother. You, too, Yer Highness. Which 'uns your first?"

Tobin looked back and was dismayed to see his first man, the one he'd cut in the leg, alive and trying to crawl away into the trees.

"Best finish the bastard," Koni said.

"Yes, see to him, Tobin," Tharin said quietly.

Tobin knew what he had to do, but that empty space below his heart was back as he walked slowly toward the man. Killing in battle had been easy, just a reflex. But the idea of finishing a wounded man on the ground, even an enemy, made his stomach lurch. Even so, he knew better than to hesitate with all the others watching him. He wouldn't shame himself by showing weakness now.

He sheathed his sword and drew the long knife at his belt. Blood was still flowing from the gash on the man's leg; he'd left a trail on the rust-colored pine needles.

He'll probably die of that, if I don't finish him, Tobin thought, moving in fast. The man's head was bare, and his filthy hair was long enough for a good grip. One of Porion's lessons came back to him. *Pull the head back. Slice deep, hard, and quick.*

As he bent to do it, however, the man rolled onto his

back and threw his arms over his face. "Mercy, lord. I cry mercy!" he screeched.

"He ain't no lord to claim it!" scoffed Dimias. "Go on, finish him."

But the plea froze Tobin where he stood. He could see exactly where to aim the blow; the thick vein was pulsing in the man's throat. It wasn't fear that stayed his hand, or weakness; it was the memory of the king stabbing the bound wizard.

"He asked for mercy," Tobin said, lowering his knife.

The man stared at Tobin over his upraised hands. "Thank you, m'lord. Bless you, m'lord!" He struggled to reach Tobin's boot, trying to kiss it, but Tobin pulled away in disgust.

"Go on, get out of here. If I see you again, I will kill you."

Dimias snorted as the wounded man scuttled off into the trees. "There's one more we'll have to fight again. He's all 'bless you, lord' now, but he'll stick a knife in you next chance he gets."

"You may be right, boy, but that was nobly done, all the same," said Tharin. Then, lowering his voice so only Tobin could hear, "Next time, strike quickly, before they have time to beg."

Tobin swallowed and nodded. His sword hand was sticky; the blood on it felt like cold molasses and made him queasy.

Others of their company straggled in to join them as the boys found their kills. Tharin painted vertical lines on their cheeks with the blood and put a bit on their tongues, too.

"To keep the ghosts of all you kill in battle from haunting you," he explained when Tobin grimaced.

"Where are the others?" Tobin asked, looking around. More soldiers had gathered around them by now, but Nik hadn't returned yet. "Did you see Lutha or Quirion?" By his count more than a dozen of his guard were missing, and they could still hear scattered sounds of fighting.

"Arius was hit," Tharin told him. "I saw Lord Nikides fighting on the far side as I came across to you. There are still a few archers at work, and I counted ten bandits trying to make off with horses."

Amin spat on the ground. "They knew we was coming, the bastards."

"That, or they backtracked Korin," said Tharin.

"Then we've got to get to him!" Ki exclaimed. "If there are enough of them to come after us—"

"No, our post is here," said Tobin. "Korin said he'd send for us if he needs us."

Tharin saluted him. "With your permission, I'll send men out to scout the surrounding woods."

Reaching the clearing, they found Barieus still shooting at two enemy archers. The fallen Companion in the meadow was Lutha. The boy lay facedown in the grass with an arrow in his back. He was alive, though, and trying to crawl to safety. As Tobin watched, another shaft thudded into the ground near Lutha's outstretched hand.

Barieus cried out and ran into the open for a better shot. His arrows sped true, but even at this distance Tobin could see that he was weeping.

Tobin marked the enemy archers' position and set off to flank them.

"Follow the prince!" Tharin called.

Tharin and Ki caught up with him just as they surprised four more swordsmen skirting the clearing. Tharin ran one through and the others fled. They found one archer dead; the other was gone by the time they reached the tree he'd been sheltering behind.

Ignoring Tharin's warning, Tobin ran out to Lutha. Barieus was already with him.

"I'm sorry," he sobbed. "I tried to get to him, but I couldn't get out!"

Lutha pushed himself up, trying to rise, but a coughing fit took him. Bloody foam flew from his lips and he collapsed, clawing at the grass.

"When it started, we were caught out here," Barieus told them. "He said to run and I thought he was with me, but—"

"Hush, Barieus. Stay still, Lutha," Tobin said, clasping Lutha's cold hand.

Tharin knelt to inspect the wound.

"Struck a lung, by the looks," said Dimias.

Tharin nodded. "It'll leave a sucking wound when it comes out. We'd better leave it where it is for now."

Lutha squeezed Tobin's hand, trying to speak, but he couldn't. Blood bubbled from his mouth with every breath.

Tobin kept his head down to hide his own tears. Lutha had been his first friend among the Companions.

"Let me have a look, my lords," said Manies, who acted as leech for Tharin's men when a drysian wasn't around. He probed gently around the base of the shaft. "We ought to get him back to Rilmar, Prince Tobin. This will take more healing than anyone can give him here." He turned to Amin. "Any drysians about?"

"Yes, in the village south of the keep."

"Good, then let's get him back."

"How?" Tobin asked. He'd been prepared for battle, but not for a friend dying at his feet.

"Manies can take him," said Tharin. "Amin, you ride for the healer." He paused, looking down at Tobin. "By your leave."

"Yes, go," Tobin said, realizing they were waiting for his order. "Go on. Hurry!"

Some of the horses had been found. Amin leaped onto the closest one and thundered off down the trail. Manies mounted another and Tharin lifted Lutha into his arms, positioning the boy sideways so that the arrow stood free of the rider's chest. Lutha was silent, except for his wet, labored breathing.

"Let me go with him, Tobin," Barieus pleaded, and ran to find a horse.

Tobin's legs felt too weak to hold him as he rose and

surveyed the other bodies lying in the long grass—Arius, Sefus, and three other guardsmen—Gyrin, Haimus, and their old sergeant, Laris. Tears blurred his eyes again. He'd known these men his whole life. Laris had carried him around on his shoulders when Tobin was small.

It was too much to take in. Tobin turned away as the others began the task of wrapping the corpses for transport. Ki was tending to Arius; Quirion was nowhere to be seen.

Nikides and his party wandered back into the clearing. Nikides looked a bit green, but he and Ruan both had the warrior marks on their cheeks.

No word came from Korin. There was nothing to do but wait.

The sun was high by then and it was growing warm in the clearing. Flies had already found the dead. Several of the guardsmen had wounds, but they were minor. Koni tended to them while Tharin and the others combed the woods for missing horses, whistling and clucking their tongues. The Companions and Ki's brothers kept watch in case the bandits regrouped and came back for a second raid.

Standing watch with Tobin, Ki stole a look at his friend's pale, solemn face and sighed. He'd never admit it, but he was a little relieved to stay here. He'd had enough of killing for one day. Proud as he was to have fought for Tobin, he'd taken no pleasure in the slaughter. It had been nothing like the ballads made it out to be, just something that had had to be done, like picking weevils out of the flour barrel. Perhaps it would be different against real soldiers, he thought.

And the sight of people he'd known lying dead? And poor Lutha coughing up blood—that wasn't like the ballads, either. Ki wondered guiltily if there was something wrong with him.

There'd be more wrong than that, if it wasn't for

Brother. He had to swallow hard to keep from retching. He hadn't let himself think of that, but now with things so quiet, he couldn't help it. He'd seen the swordsman coming at Tobin from behind. He'd tried to get to him but two others had blocked his way. Trying to dodge, he'd stumbled and fallen. By the time he got up it would have been too late, if not for Brother.

Tobin had seen him, too, knew it was Brother and not Ki who'd saved him at the critical moment. Ki had done the one thing no squire must ever do; let himself get separated from his lord in a pitched battle.

Was that why Tobin was being so quiet?

Quirion straggled in at last with some yarn about chasing off horse thieves. But everyone saw that his blade was clean, and how he couldn't look anyone in the eye. He sat down by Arius' body and pulled his cloak over his head, crying softly.

At least I didn't run away, thought Ki.

An hour or so later Dimias let out a whoop from his post in a tall tree overlooking the trail.

"More bandits?" called Tobin, drawing his sword.

"Nah, it's our folk. Coming in slow, too." Dimias slumped glumly against the trunk. "Guess they didn't need us after all."

Korin rode into sight with Ahra and Porion. The others began cheering, but one look at Ahra told Ki something was amiss. Korin didn't look right, despite the crusted warrior marks on his cheeks.

"What happened?" Nikides asked.

"We got them," Korin replied, but even as he grinned, there was something in his eyes that wasn't right. The other Companions were bloodied, too, and bragging, but Ki could have sworn that some of them were stealing odd looks at Korin behind his back. Caliel's right arm was in a sling and Tanil was riding double behind Lynx, looking pale.

Ki tried to catch Porion's eye, but Porion gave him a warning look, then shouted, "Prince Korin is blooded. He is a warrior today!"

There was more cheering after that. Everyone bore the coveted marks except Quirion, who crept off sniveling. Caliel's squire, Mylirin, had taken an arrow in the shoulder, but his hauberk had stopped the point, though it left a nasty abraded bruise. Zusthra was proudly displaying a sword cut on his left cheek and Chylnir was limping, but the rest of the Companions seemed more or less whole. The guard and Ahra's riders hadn't been so fortunate. There were at least a dozen carrying shrouded bundles, and others were wounded.

They had the stolen women with them, too, or at least those who'd survived. They were a ravaged, empty-eyed lot, some of them wearing little more than rags and blankets. Ahra's women were tending to them, but looking into those faces, Ki couldn't help wondering if Innis had been right, after all.

Tobin had told him about Una earlier and he looked for her anxiously among them. It took a while to recognize her. Dirty and wild-haired as any lowborn fighter, she was busy bandaging the arm of one of her cohorts.

"Hullo," she said, giving him a half smile as he joined her. "I've thanked Tobin already and I'll thank you now. You were good teachers."

"I'm glad to hear it."

She nodded, then went back to her work.

"It was a hard fight, but we cleaned out that nest of vermin," Korin was saying. His bravado faltered when Tobin showed him Arius and told him what had happened to Lutha, but when Tobin mentioned the friends they lost among his guard, Korin just shrugged. "Well, that's their lot, isn't it?"

Korin had ordered the bandits and their camp burned. As they came out of the forest, Ki looked back and saw a distant pillar of smoke rising over the trees.

His spirits rose at the sight. They'd succeeded. He and Tobin had done their part and both lived to fight again. Ki even managed a silent thanks to Brother. But he kept an eye on Korin as they rode back. The prince was too quiet, his laughter forced.

They rode at ease now, and it was easy enough for Ki to drop back among his sister's riders. He found Una again, riding near the end of the column.

"What happened?" he whispered.

Una's silent, warning look told him nothing except that he was right to wonder.

Chapter 35

As soon as they came in sight of Rilmar, Tobin, Ki, and Nikides galloped ahead to learn if Lutha had survived the journey. Sekora was grave when she met them in the hall. Larenth sat by the main hearth with Barieus. The squire had his face in his hands, shaking his head slowly as Larenth spoke to him in a low, surprisingly gentle voice.

"How is Lutha?" Tobin asked.

"Drysian's with 'im." Sekora pointed to the sitting room where they'd met Larenth the previous day. "He stopped hollerin' a while back. The healers ain't let no one in 'cept my woman Arla, who brings the water an' all."

They joined Barieus, but no one could sit still. Presently Korin and the others came in downstairs; Tobin could hear some of them laughing. Even the wounded men were in good spirits, having done a good day's work.

The remaining Companions came upstairs and Lynx sat down by Barieus, offering silent comfort.

"Your bandits are dealt with, Sir Larenth," Korin told him.

Tobin couldn't read the old man's face as he turned his good eye on the prince. "Lost a few of yer own, I hear?"

"Yes, I'm afraid we did."

"Brandywine, Sekora!" Larenth called. "Let's drink to the dead, and to the ones who come back."

A servant brought them tarnished silver cups and Sekora filled them. Tobin sprinkled his libation on the rushes, then downed the rest. He'd never cared for the strong spirit, but he was grateful now for its burning heat. After a few gulps he felt sleepy and warm; the clatter from the kitchens and the homely chatter of the servingwomen all seemed far away. Korin and some of the older boys drifted outside, but Tobin stayed with Barieus and their friends, waiting.

"I failed him," Barieus moaned. "I should never have gotten ahead of him!"

"I heard him tell you to go," said Lynx.

But the squire was inconsolable. Sliding off the bench, he sat on the rushes, head buried in his arms.

The evening meal came and went uneaten before an old man in a brown robe emerged, wiping his hands on a bloody cloth.

"How is he?" Korin demanded.

"Surprisingly well," the drysian replied. "He's tough as a weasel, that one."

"He'll live?" cried Barieus, leaping up with hope in his reddened eyes.

"That's still on the knees of the Maker, but the arrow caught only the edge of one lung. Two finger's span to the left and he'd be lying with the dead. The other lung's got breath enough to bring him through the night. If the wound doesn't fester, he could mend." He turned to Sekora. "You've honey enough, my lady? There's nothing much better for quick healing than a honey poultice. If that doesn't work, have the dogs lick the wound to clear the pus. Have someone keep watch with him through the night to see he's breathing. If he makes it to morning, he has a chance."

Barieus was gone before the man finished speaking.

Tobin followed. Lutha lay gasping in a trundle bed by the fire. His eyes were closed, and his face was grey as an old bone except for the blue cast of his lips and the dark circles under his sunken eyes. Barieus knelt beside him and wiped at his eyes as Tobin joined him. "Can you make a Dalna charm?" he asked without looking up.

Tobin looked at the bloodstained horse charm Lutha still wore; this one hadn't done him much good. But he nodded anyway, for the squire's sake. "I'll ask the drysian what to use."

When they had all burned their handfuls of earth, grain, and incense on the house altar, the Companions gathered around the kitchen hearth, waiting for their watches with Lutha. Quirion sat a little apart, too ashamed to look at any of them. Tobin had said nothing, but everyone knew he'd broken and run.

Exhaustion crept up on Tobin and, without meaning to, he fell asleep. He woke with a start sometime later to find the fire burned to embers and the house silent. He was lying on his side, head pillowed on Ki's leg. Ki snored softly above him, slumped against the woodbin. Across the hearth Tobin could just make out Nikides asleep against Ruan's shoulder. Korin, Caliel, and Lynx were gone.

Tobin found a candle on the mantelpiece and lit it in the embers, then threaded his way through the maze of cupboards and storage hulks toward the stairs. He was nearly there when a dark figure resolved from the shadows and touched his arm. It was Ahra.

"If you're looking for your cousin, he's sitting with that boy who was struck down," she whispered. "Best leave him be, I'd say."

"What happened, Ahra?"

She held a finger to her lips, then blew out his candle and led him through a dank passage to a moonlit side yard with a mossy stone well. Ahra pushed the wooden cover back and drew up the bucket, then took a dipper from a nail and offered it to Tobin. The water was cold and sweet. He drank deeply and handed the dipper back.

"What happened?" he asked again.

"Here, close by me," she said, sitting on the stone rim. Tobin sat down beside her and she put her head close to his, speaking softly. "We're not supposed to talk of it, but the others saw, so you might as well know." She pressed her clenched fists to her knees, and Tobin realized she was furious.

"The camp lay in a little valley about a quarter mile from where we left you. We met the scouts and they said the place looked deserted; no sign of armed men there at all. I knew right then something was wrong and tried to tell the prince. So did his own captain and old Porion, too, but he was all for going on.

"We came to the edge of the trees and had a clear view. There was a line of tents and cabins along a stream. There were some women at the fires, but no sign of the men. The land around was meadow, open ground with no cover. 'It's late for them to be abed,' I told the prince, but he comes back with 'They're probably drunk. It's a rabble there, not an army.'

"A good many bandits were trained soldiers before they went freebooter. I tried to tell him that, too, but he wouldn't listen. It was then Porion points out there's two big corrals, but only a few horses in them. Anyone could see the men had scarpered, but nothing would do for the prince but we make a charge. He wouldn't even wait for a reconnoiter. So off we went, hell-bent for leather, yelling all the way. The Companions were keen, I'll give them that. Their battle cries would've scared the enemy to death in their beds, if they had been in 'em.

"We rode right into the camp and not a soul to greet us but those poor women. They didn't know where the men were, but we weren't long in finding out. They waited for us to dismount and break ranks to search the camp, then down they came out of the woods not a quarter mile from where we'd been, fifty strong on horseback and sweeping down on us like a hurricane."

She paused and sighed. "And the prince just stood there, staring. Everyone waited, then Porion says, respectful as you please, 'What orders, my lord?' He come around then, but it was too late. It was too late the minute we charged down into that camp.

"We didn't have time to get mounted again or send word to you. The Companions and some of us closed 'round the prince and took what cover we could behind a hayrick next to the corrals. Everyone else scattered. By then their archers were in range and sent a storm of arrows at us." She shook her head. "The prince fought well enough once he got started, but there are empty saddles in my group just because he wanted a grand charge. Well, you heard him after, didn't you? It's their *lot*."

The bitterness in her voice left little to say. She took another sip from the dipper. "But Tharin and some of the others told me how you rallied your men and fought. Sakor-touched, you are. I was proud to hear it, but not surprised. My father saw it in you, though he didn't think much of your cousin. He's not often wrong, that old rascal."

"Thank you for telling me," Tobin said. "I—I guess I'll go sit with Lutha now."

She caught his arm. "Don't say I said anything, will you? I just thought you should know."

"I won't. Thank you."

He felt sick to his stomach as he groped his way back to the kitchen. It was worse than he'd imagined. He lit the candle again and crept upstairs.

Lutha's door was open a few inches, and a thin band of light fell across the hall floor and the children and dogs sleeping there. Tobin made his way around them and peered in.

A candle burned on a stand next to Larenth's armchair. It was turned half-away from the door, but he could see Korin's profile as he sat there, watching the labored rise and fall of Lutha's chest.

"Where is everyone?" Tobin whispered, closing the door and coming to join him. He caught the reek of wine halfway across the room. As he came around the front of the chair, he saw that Korin was cradling a clay wine jar in his arms and that he was very drunk.

"I had Lynx and Caliel put Barieus to bed. Took both of 'em to drag him away." His voice was thick, the words slurred. Korin let out a soft, derisive laugh. "Best order I gave today, eh?"

He tipped the jar up again and swallowed noisily. Wine ran down his neck, staining the front of his filthy shirt. He hadn't changed or bathed since their return. His hands were filthy, the nails rimmed with dried blood.

He wiped his mouth on his sleeve and gave Tobin a bitter smile. "You did all right, I hear. And Ki, too. All of you, 'cept Quirion. He's out, soon's we get back!"

"Softly, Kor. You're going to wake Lutha."

But Korin went on, his face bleak. "I was never meant to be king, you know. I was fourth, Tob. And there was a sister ahead of me, too. That would have done for the Illiorans. They could have had their queen. Gherian and my oldest brother Tadir were groomed from the cradle. By the Four, you should have seen them! *They* were born to it. They'd never have—" He took another long swig and swayed to his feet. Tobin tried to help him but Korin pushed him away. "S'all right, coz. This is what I'm good at, isn't it? Where's Tanil?"

"Here." The squire emerged from a shadowed corner and got an arm around him. The look in his eyes might have been pity or disgust. Perhaps it was both.

"G'night, coz." Korin attempted a bow as Tanil led him away.

Tobin heard them stumble and a child's sleepy protest, then the sound of unsteady steps fading away upstairs.

Tobin sat down and watched Lutha, trying to rein in his thoughts. Poor judgment—and surely that was Korin's sin today—was harshly judged in any commander. The king's son, it seemed, was judged more harshly, rather than less.

But everyone thinks I'm a hero. Tobin certainly didn't feel like one. Not with Lutha gasping for life in front of him and all those corpses in the courtyard out front.

On the heels of this came another thought, however. For years he'd resisted thinking about what Lhel's revelation really meant. All the same, the knowledge had taken root, and just like the witchgrass pushing up between the cracked flagstones outside, it had been stubbornly growing all this while, forcing its way to daylight.

If I'm to be queen, then Korin will have to step aside. But maybe that would be for the best?

But it didn't feel that way. Tobin had spent the first twelve years of his life living a lie, and the last two trying to ignore the truth. He loved Korin, and most of the others, too. What would happen when they learned the truth, not just that he was a girl, but that she was to supplant the king's own son?

Time passed, measured in the rise and fall of Lutha's thin chest. Did his breathing sound better, or worse? It was hard to tell. It didn't sound quite so wet as it had, and he wasn't bleeding at the mouth. That must be a good thing, surely? But it was loud and harsh, and every now and then it would seem to catch in his throat, then give way. After a while Tobin noticed that he was matching breaths with Lutha's, as if it would help him along. When Lutha's breath caught, his own stopped as he waited for the next rattling inhalation. It was exhausting to listen to.

By the time Nikides and Ruan came in Tobin was glad to give over the vigil. There was someone else he had to talk to.

He didn't need a candle to find his way back to the deserted well yard. Satisfied that he was alone, he whispered the summoning words. Brother emerged from the shadows and stood in front of him, brooding and silent.

"You saved my life today. Thank you."

Brother just stared.

"How—how could you find me, without the doll?"

Brother touched Tobin on the chest. "The binding is strong."

"Like that day Orun was hurting me. I didn't call you then, either."

"He was going to kill you."

Even after all this time, the words sent a chill through him; neither of them had spoken of it. "He wouldn't have. He'd have been tortured to death."

"I saw his thoughts. They were murder. That man today was the same."

"But why do you care? You've never had any love for me. You used to hurt me every chance you got. If I died, you'd be free."

Brother actually grimaced at this, a stiff, unnatural play of features on that face. "If you die with the binding still in you, then we will *never* be free, either of us."

Tobin hugged himself as waves of cold rolled off Brother. "What will happen when I take the binding out?"

"I don't know. The witch promises I will be free."

Tobin couldn't remember the last time he'd gotten a plain answer from his twin. "Then—whenever I'm in battle, you'll be there?"

"Until I'm free."

Tobin pondered this, torn between wonder and dismay. How could he ever really prove himself if he always had supernatural help?

Brother read his thoughts and let out a sound Tobin guessed was meant to be a laugh; it sounded more like rats running through dead leaves. "I am your first squire."

"First?" Tobin began, then, by some trick of memory, or Brother's, he was back in his mother's tower, her dying scream loud in his ears. "Did you push her out?"

"I pulled you in."

"But why not save her, too?" It came out too loud and he clapped a hand over his mouth. "Why didn't you?" he whispered.

"Her mind was filled with your death, too."

The scuff of feet on stone froze Tobin where he stood. Ki stepped out into the moonlight and his eyes widened.

"I see into his mind, too," whispered Brother, and this time he leered as he faded away.

"What's he doing here?" asked Ki.

Tobin explained as much as he could, and was surprised to see Ki look uneasy when he told him what Brother had said about him. "Tobin, I'd never hurt you!"

"I know that. I don't think that's what he meant. Besides, if I was in any danger, he'd have killed you by now, I guess. Don't mind him. When it comes to you, he usually lies, just to make me feel bad."

"If I ever turn on you, I hope he does kill me!" Ki exclaimed, more shaken than Tobin had guessed. "I wouldn't, Tob. I swear it by the Flame!"

"I know that," Tobin said, taking his friend by the hand. "Let's go in. I'm cold to the bone. Forget about him."

But as they settled down by the kitchen hearth again, he fingered the lump under his skin, wondering if he'd be glad to be free of Brother at last, or not.

Chapter 36

Tobin never learned what the king had said to Korin after their return from Rilmar. In private, Ki wondered what Melnoth and the others had actually reported. The mission had been a success, after all, and that had been the joyous announcement at court when they'd returned to Ero, with the dried blood on their faces.

Life did change, however. They were all full warriors now, in the eyes of the world, and two days after the Sakor festival, they once again donned their finest garments for Korin's wedding.

Royal weddings were rare and portentous events, so there'd been considerable speculation as to why Prince Korin's was so hastily thrown together. There had been little time for the proclamation to be carried through the land, and attendance was a bit scanty because of it. Nonetheless, when the great day came the entire city was decked and garlanded, and every temple sent clouds of rose-scented incense up into the cold winter air with prayers for the couple's happy future.

The ceremony was before the great shrine inside the New Palace and was witnessed by a great crowd of family and nobles. Crowned and regal, King Erius wore a red robe of state heavily embroidered with gold and bright jewels. Korin wore a long tunic of similar design, and a coronet. Tobin stood with them in his best surcoat and the rest of the Companions flanked them on the left. Tobin keenly felt the gap in their numbers. Arius was dead, Quirion banished for cowardice, and Barieus was with

Lutha, who was still recovering at his father's estate near Volchi.

The arrow wound had been slow to heal, but a bout of pneumonia had come closer to killing him than the shaft. Fortunately, the drysian at Rilmar had been right; Lutha stubbornly clung to life and was strong enough now to write to his friends, complaining bitterly of boredom. No one spoke of it openly, but it remained to be seen whether he would recover sufficiently to rejoin them.

In the outer courtyard of the shrine, a chorus of young girls tossed pearls and silver coins into the air and burst into song, announcing the arrival of the bridal party. The crowd parted as they entered.

Aliya looked like a queen already. She wore a gold coronet fashioned to look like a wreath of flowers, and strands of pearls and golden beads were braided into her shining auburn hair. More pearls, citrines, and amber beads crusted her shimmering gown of bronze silk. Some clever seamstress had arranged the waistline to hide any telltale rounding of the bride's belly.

Standing with his father and the high priests of the Four, Korin received her from her father's arm and they knelt before Erius.

"Father, I present to you the Lady Aliya, daughter of Duke Cygna and his lady, the Duchess Virysia," Korin said solemnly, but loud enough for all to hear. "Before the gods and these witnesses, I humbly ask your blessing on our union."

"Do you give your daughter freely to my son?" Erius asked her parents, who stood just behind the couple.

The duke laid his sword reverently at the king's feet. "We do, Your Majesty."

"May the blood of our houses be mingled forever," Duchess Virysia said, giving the king the symbolic dower gift of a caged dove.

Erius smiled down at Korin and Aliya. "Then my blessing is given. Rise, my son, and present my new daughter."

Aliya rose, blushing happily. Erius took her hands and kissed her on both cheeks, then whispered something in her ear that made her blush even more. Eyes sparkling, she kissed his hands.

Turning them to face the assembly, Erius joined their hands and covered them with his own. "See, people of Ero, your future king and queen. Send runners through the kingdom!"

Everyone cheered and threw millet in the air to ensure that the union would be fertile. Tobin caught Ki laughing as he did so and couldn't help chuckling himself.

The proclamation was repeated again before the people of the city later that morning. Following Skalan custom, the king threw a lavish public feast afterward that lasted until dawn the following morning. Bonfires burned all over the city, and long banquet tables were set up in the same square where the execution platform had stood. Some whispered that the tables had been made from the same timbers.

The principal guild masters and merchants were seated; others crowded along the edges of the square or watched from windows and rooftops. Food arrived by the cartload, wine flowed in rivers, and when night fell, Zengati fireworks lit the skies for hours.

Tobin and the other Companions watched from the snowy roof gardens of the New Palace. Somewhere downstairs, Korin and his princess had taken possession of their new chambers. Zusthra and Alben were speculating gleefully on what was currently going on.

Tobin and the others ignored them, excitedly discussing what was to come tomorrow. At midday they were to set sail with the future king and his consort on a royal progress of the coastal cities. They'd spent weeks watching the ships being prepared. In addition to the royal bark, there was a veritable flotilla of other vessels carrying Korin's guard, entertainers, horses, a small army of servants and craftsmen, and one vessel devoted solely to feeding the whole entourage. They'd be gone for nearly a year.

"Well, it's not going off to war," Ki observed, "but at least it gets us out of town."

The fireworks were still blazing overhead when they heard someone running up the balcony stairs toward them.

"Prince Tobin! Where are you, Master?" a thin, panicked voice cried out.

"Here, Baldus! What's the matter?"

A brilliant white burst in the sky illuminated the page's pale face as he reached them. "Oh please, come down at once. It's terrible!"

Tobin caught him by the shoulders. "What is it? Is someone hurt?"

"Aliya!" Baldus panted, out of breath and clearly upset. "She's sick, her woman says. Prince Korin is frantic!"

Tobin dashed for the stairs. Only when he'd reached the lighted corridor below did he realize that Caliel had followed. Neither spoke as they ran on together through the endless hallways and courtyards to Korin's rooms. Rounding a final corner, they nearly collided with a man in the livery of Duke Cygna. Beyond him, a knot of nobles hovered around the prince's door.

"Talmus, what's happened?" Caliel demanded.

The servant was pale. "My lady—The princess, my lord. She's ill. Bleeding."

Caliel clutched at Tobin's arm. "Bleeding?"

Tobin went cold. "It's not plague?"

Talmus shook his head. "No, Highness, not plague. The drysians say she's losing the child."

Tobin slumped down onto one of the chairs that lined the corridor, too stunned and sorrowful to speak.

Caliel joined him and they listened to the weeping of the women down the corridor. Now and then a muffled cry could be heard inside.

The king soon joined them. His face was flushed with

wine, but his eyes were clear. He swept past Tobin and the crowd at the door parted for him as he went inside. As the door opened, Tobin thought he could hear Korin weeping, too.

It was dawn before it was over. Aliya survived, but the child did not. That was the Maker's blessing, the drysians murmured afterward. The tiny child, no bigger than a newt, had neither face nor arms.

PART III

The origins of Skala's so-called Third Orëska remain shrouded in mystery, though there is little doubt that it had its roots in a loose confederation formed sometime during the reign of Erius the Priest Killer, son of Agnalain the Mad.

Wizardry was already common among the Skalans—the unforeseen and, in the minds of many, unfortunate result of the mingling of our two races. But the powers of Skalan wizards were for the most part inferior to our own, and had been further debased with the loss of so many of their more powerful mages during the Necromancers' War.

Some scholars postulate the hand of Aura at work among the Skalans. How else to explain the rise of a generation of hedge wizards and conjurers not only to unity but to genuine power? Yet I question why these newfound powers should have taken such an alarmingly different form over the resulting centuries. The Third Orëska vehemently denounces all forms of necromancy, and the stated precepts of their great school proscribe such studies, yet I have myself witnessed their use of blood magic, and instances of communion with the dead are not unknown. As Adin í Solun of Lhapnos observed in the third volume of his Histories, "Despite the ties of trade and history between our two lands, one must never forget that throughout her early history, Skala faced Plenimar, not Aurënen."

Since my sojourn in that capital, I can vouch for the famed hospitality of the Orëska House, but the veil of secrecy remains; the names of the Founders are not taught or spoken of now, and the few accounts made by earlier scholars all conflict, confounding any attempt to decipher the truth from them.

—excerpt from Oriena ä Danus of Khatme's
Treatise on Foreign Magiks

Chapter 37

It was Tharin who sent word to Arkoniel of the princess' miscarriage. Tobin and Ki had been closest to the events, but didn't have the heart to write of it.

"*It was just as well,*" Tharin wrote, touching on the child's deformities.

"It's Illior's will," Nari muttered. It was a bitter midwinter night and the two of them sat by the kitchen fire bundled in cloaks with their feet on the hearth bricks. "The king never sired a healthy child after his little ones died. Now the curse has fallen on his son. Before Iya brought me to Rhius' house, I never thought of the Lightbearer as cruel."

Arkoniel stared into the flames. Even after all these years, the memories had not dimmed. "Knowledge and madness."

"How's that?"

"Iya once told me that only wizards see the true face of Illior; that only we feel the full touch of the god's power. The same power that gives knowledge can also bring madness. There's a purpose in all that's happened, all that will happen, but it does seem cruel at times."

Nari sighed and pulled her cloak closer around her. "Still, no crueler than the king and his Harriers killing all those girls, eh? I still see the duke's face in my dreams, the look in his eyes as they stood over poor Ariani, with all those soldiers downstairs. That witch did her job well that night. What do you suppose ever happened to her?"

Arkoniel shook his head slightly, and kept his gaze on the flames.

"Just between you and me, I always wondered if Iya didn't do away with her. She's my kin and I mean no disrespect, but I wouldn't have put anything past her that night."

"She didn't kill her. Even if she'd wanted to, I doubt she could have."

"You don't say? Well, I'm glad to hear it. One less death on her conscience, anyway."

"And mine," Arkoniel said softly.

"You're a different sort than Iya."

"Am I?"

"Of course. I saw it from the start. And has it ever occurred to you that the demon never touched you after that first time when he broke your wrist?"

"He scared my horse and it threw me. He never touched me."

"Well, there you go. Yet he attacks Iya every time she shows her face near him."

"He spoke to me once. He said he tasted my tears." Nari gave him a questioning look and he shrugged. "I wept as I buried him. My tears fell on the body. That meant something to him, apparently."

Nari was quiet a moment. "Except for his poor mother, I think you were the only one who did weep for him. Rhius' tears were all for his wife. You're the one who came back to care for Tobin, too. And now you've got all these others to look after. You don't see her doing that, do you?"

"They wouldn't be here at all if it wasn't for her," he reminded her. "This vision she and the rest of them had? I never saw it. I never have."

More wizards found their way to the keep, arriving by ones and pairs. By the time word came of Korin's marriage and Aliya's miscarriage, six new refugees had arrived, together with a handful of servants. A small herd of horses and donkeys grazed in a forest clearing, hidden from the prying eyes of tradesmen.

Cerana, an old friend of Iya's, was the first to come that autumn. Lyan and Vornus rode in together soon after, a grey old pair in their fourth age, accompanied only by a burly manservant named Cymeus. The wizards spoke as fondly to one another as if they were husband and wife; Arkoniel suspected they had not been bothered with celibacy in their youth, either.

Melissandra, a southern sorceress, soon followed, arriving like a storm-battered bird one night. Dark-eyed and quiet, fear made her seem younger than her hundred-odd years. She'd been wealthy before the Harriers had come for her; her servingwoman, Dar, had charge of a money chest.

Hain arrived with the first snowfall. A thickset, ordinary youth with a patchy beard, he'd been an apprentice when last Arkoniel had seen him. But, like the old wizards, he gave off the aura of real power, despite his poverty and inexperience.

Lord Malkanus and his small entourage made it to the keep just before snow closed the roads. Only a few decades older than Arkoniel, his talents were middling, but he'd enjoyed the patronage and bed of a wealthy widow in Ylani, and arrived with three manservants, a chest of gold, and a very high opinion of himself. Arkoniel could have done without this one. Malkanus had always been disdainful, holding him and probably Iya, too, as little better than scruffy wanderers. Neither time nor circumstance had done much to mend his manners. Arkoniel was sorry to see Iya leave him one of her tokens, and still couldn't fathom why the Lightbearer would speak to such a man.

Rooms were dusted out, bedsteads found, and soon everyone was settled in, more or less comfortably. Malkanus had made a fuss over sharing rooms, so Arkoniel gave him his old bedchamber on the third floor, neglecting to mention the other occupant of that part of the house. Much to his disappointment, Ariani paid no attention to the new lodger.

* * *

Cook and Nari were delighted to have more people in the house, and the servants fell in willingly with the household chores. The keep began to feel like a real home again, despite the odd nature of its occupants.

Arkoniel had never seen so many wizards in one place before, and it took some getting used to. He never knew when he'd bump into someone practicing invisibility or levitation spells in the hall, but he was grateful for their company. Lyan and Vornus were powerful, and Hain had potential. Melissandra, though more limited, was a master of wards, and soon had the meadow and roads ringed with signals. Arkoniel breathed a bit easier after that. She was kind with the children, too, and joined with Lyan and Vornus to help Arkoniel with their lessons. Little Wythnir fell in love with her at once and Arkoniel began to fear he'd lose his first apprentice.

At his insistence, all the wizards took a hand with the children, testing their abilities and offering their own special talents. Kaulin and Cerana practiced charms and simple household magic. Lyan, on the other hand, could send messages in colored points of light, a rare skill indeed. Vornus and Melissandra shared an interest in transformational spells and she had some skill with wards and locks. Eyoli's mind-clouding skills, though simple in nature, were of considerable practical use but, as it soon proved, nearly impossible to teach. It was a natural ability, like being able to carry a tune or roll your tongue into a tube. Wythnir and Arkoniel could hold an illusion for a few seconds, but the rest had no luck with it.

These were all useful skills, but it was proud, foppish Malkanus who surprised them all with a dangerous talent for manipulating fire and lightning. The younger children were not allowed to learn these spells, but Arkoniel had him work closely with Ethni and the adults, telling them, "If the Harriers do decide to pay us a visit sometime, I'd like to give them a proper welcome."

As the winter wore on, however, it became clear that many spells, especially the more difficult ones, could not be universally taught or learned.

As he'd expected, Virishan's orphans were unable to learn more than the simplest of spells. But Wythnir's potential showed itself. The boy thrived, having so many teachers, and by midwinter he could transform a chestnut into a silver thimble and had managed to set the stables on fire while trying to duplicate a spell he'd picked up from Malkanus when Arkoniel wasn't looking. Arkoniel lectured him sternly but was secretly pleased.

The servants proved as useful as their masters. Noril and Semion, two who'd come in with Malkanus, had a knack with horses, and the third, Kiran, fashioned toys for the children from wood and scraps of rags. Vornus' man Cymeus was a skilled carpenter and made it his business to keep the house in repair. Not content to fix where he could improve, he rigged a weighted wooden arm over the well so that even little Totmus could draw water with ease simply by pressing on the far end of the pole. He showed Cook how to irrigate her ever-expanding garden by means of a roof cistern and clay pipes, and installed a similar apparatus in the wooden washing tub in the kitchen, so that instead of dipping out the dirty water, she could simply remove a plug and let the water drain away through a pipe he'd laid into the garden.

"Isn't that the cleverest thing!" she exclaimed as they all gathered to watch the water swirl away down the drain.

Cymeus, a tall, bearded bear of a man, blushed like a girl, and said gruffly, "Just something I picked up in our travels, is all."

"You're too modest as always, my friend," Vornus said with a chuckle. "He's a wizard, even without magic, this one is."

Arkoniel was careful in revealing his own magic, for it was irrevocably mingled with Lhel's. Spells he'd come to take for granted would have revealed his secret teacher. Yet it was she, rather than Arkoniel, who insisted on secrecy.

"How would you explain my presence here, eh?" she asked as he lay with her one winter night.

"I don't know. Couldn't we just say that you came down from the hills and settled here?"

She stroked his cheek fondly. "You've been with me so long, you've forgotten the ways of your own people. And speaking of your people, have you taken the pretty little bird caller to your bed?"

"Once," he admitted, guessing she already knew.

"Only once? And what did you learn?"

"The reason for the vow wizards take." Lhel might not be beautiful, or young, but her power had drawn him as nothing else did, both to her hearth and her bed. Joining with her was like being filled with lightning. With Ethni, he was dark inside. His power flowed away into her but there was no return except a little affection. The physical spasm was nothing, compared to the joining of power. He'd tried to hide his feelings, but Ethni had sensed it and not come to his bed again.

"Your Lightbearer sets you a narrow path," Lhel said when he tried to explain.

"Is it different with your people? You can bear children, even with your magic."

"Our people are very different. You've forgotten, knowing me as you have. I'll be no better than a necromancer in the eyes of your new friends. That haughty young fire thrower would burn me to a cinder as soon as look at me."

"He'd have to go through me first," Arkoniel assured her, but he knew she was right. "It won't always be so," he promised. "Because of you, Skala will have her queen again."

Lhel gazed up into the shadows above them. "Yes, it will be soon. It's time I kept my promise."

"What promise?" he asked.

"I must show you how to separate Tobin from Brother."

Arkoniel sat up. He'd waited years for this. "Is it difficult? Will it take long to learn?"

Lhel leaned over and whispered in his ear.

Arkoniel stared at her. "That's it? That's all? But—why all the mystery? You could have told us that years ago and spared yourself this exile!"

"It is not only for that that the Mother bade me stay. The unbinding may be simple, but who would have woven the new binding when it was needed? And perhaps you'd still have your entire finger, for not creating the magic you have. The Mother foresaw and I have been where I must be."

"Forgive me. I spoke without thinking."

"As for the simplicity of the unbinding, all the more reason to keep it secret. Would you trust that unhappy child with such knowledge?"

"No."

"And do not be deceived," she said, settling down in the blankets. "The deed may be simple, but the doing of it will take all the courage she possesses."

Lhel's words haunted Arkoniel, but there were other concerns closer to home.

"Only the other day the butcher's boy remarked on how much more meat I'm ordering," Cook warned one night as they sat down to a noisy supper in the hall. "And with the snow so deep in the meadow, we'll soon have to buy fodder for the horses. I don't think your mistress foresaw that; it's only going to get worse if more arrive. And that's not even thinking of spies, if there are any."

Arkoniel sighed. "What can we do?"

"Good thing for you I was a soldier before I was a cook," she replied, shaking her head. "First off, we have to stop buying so much in Alestun. The men can hunt, but that won't do for vegetables. I didn't have enough of a garden this year, so we'll have to go farther afield. Two Crow Ford is only a day's journey by wagon, and none of us are known there. Send a couple of the men this time, posing as traders or traveling merchants, and different ones the next. Tobin's grandfather used that strategy one winter when we had to go into winter camp near Plenimar."

"There's the difference between wizards and soldiers. I'd never think of such things. Consider yourself our quartermaster." As she turned to go back to the kitchen, a thought struck him and he laid a hand on her chapped red forearm. "All these years I've known you, but never asked your true name."

She laughed. "You mean to tell me you don't know what every tradesman in Alestun knows?" She raised an eyebrow at him, but she was smiling. "It's Catilan. I was Sergeant Cat in my day, of the Queen's Archers. I'm a bit past it for swordplay, but I can still pull a bow. I keep in practice when I can find the time."

"How did you ever end up a cook?" he asked without thinking.

She snorted. "How d'you suppose?"

Chapter 38

Aliya's miscarriage delayed the royal progress for nearly a month and it was whispered around the Palatine that some of the king's advisors wanted Korin to put her aside; the details of the miscarriage could not be entirely suppressed. But a divorce would have brought far too much attention to the reasons and, moreover, Korin did seem genuinely to love her, though Tobin and the other Companions could not fathom why, as marriage had not tempered her manner toward them.

"Guess she must be sweeter in private," Ki groused, after she'd slighted him in the hall one day.

"It would be worth her while to be, given what she has to lose," Nikides agreed. "And she's smart enough to know it. Look how she's got the king doting on her. She knows who cuts the loaf."

Erius had grown immensely fond of her and had visited her daily with gifts during the weeks of her seclusion.

She recovered quickly under her mother's care and that of half the drysians of the grove. By the time she was well enough to sail the sorrow had passed and people were speaking hopefully behind their hands of the good effect fresh sea air might have on a young bride.

After cooling their heels for so long, Tobin and the others greeted the departure announcement with jubilation. Bored beyond measure with city life, the prospect of a voyage, even in the dead of winter, was a welcome escape.

Tobin had reasons of his own to look forward to it. A

week before they were to leave, Iya made another of her unexpected visits.

"This is a rare opportunity for you," she told him as they sat alone in his mother's house. "Never forget that you are meant to rule this land. Learn as much about it as you can. See with the eyes your teacher Raven has given you."

"Because I'll have to protect Skala from Plenimar?" said Tobin.

"No, because you may have to win it from your uncle or cousin."

"A war, you mean? But I thought the Lightbearer would—I don't know—"

"Smooth your way?" Iya gave him a grim smile. "In my experience, the gods create opportunities; it's left to us to grasp them. Nothing is assured."

That night she told him of the vision she'd had at Afra before his birth. "I've visited the Oracle since then, but Illior has shown me nothing different. The future is a frayed rope and we must twist up the strands as best we can."

"Then I could fail?" The thought sent a chill over Tobin.

Iya clasped his hands in hers. "Yes. But you must not."

*T*hey set sail on the twelfth of Dostin, the masts of their ships gay with banners and garlands. Korin took his Companions and guard, and a small household of servants. Aliya was accompanied by her mother and several aunts, servants, two drysians, masters of her hounds and hawks, and a portable Dalnan fertility shrine.

The weather was frigid but calm enough for coastal sailing, and the little fleet made first landfall at Cirna five days later. Tobin was delighted to see this holding at last, important in its way as Atyion; but coming here also meant traveling with its current Protector. Lord Niryn would sail with them, and play host when they arrived at the fortress.

Niryn met them on board the morning of their departure, looking more noble than wizard. Under a cloak lined with winter fox, he wore robes of thick silver silk trimmed with pearls.

"Welcome, my princes!" he cried as heartily as if he were the captain of the venture.

Tobin studied the skillful stitching on the wizard's sleeve, carefully not thinking of anything but that.

The village at Cirna was nothing but a cluster of rude cottages above the sheltered harbor on the east side of the isthmus. Their welcome was jubilant, however, and set the pattern for the rest of the journey. A handsome, dashing young future king with a beautiful wife on his arm was a happy sight; no one outside the Palatine knew of his first showing as a warrior.

Korin made a short speech, then Niryn led them up a frozen switchback road to the fortress that commanded the isthmus road. It was an imposing pile and Tobin blushed, thinking of how he'd so casually tried to give it away. Sir Larenth might have been a poor choice to rule such a stronghold, but Tobin would have preferred him to its current Protector.

The fortress keep was nothing like Atyion. Ancient, damp, and cheerless, it was less a noble residence than a barracks. Disliking both it and their host, Tobin spent as much time as he could exploring with his friends.

The parapets all faced north. The high curtain wall had three levels, with wooden walkways and loopholes for shooting. The top of the wall was open, with a broad allure to stand on and merlons with arrow loops. The boys stood at the crenels between, imagining an enemy force bearing down on them along the isthmus road. The fortress had been built at the narrowest point of the land bridge and the sheer fall of the cliffs on either side offered little purchase, except for the steep track down to the village.

From the walls they could look east over the Inner Sea,

then turn and, less than a mile away, see the distant expanse of the Osiat.

"Look at that!" Ki exclaimed. "The Inner Sea is the color of turquoise today, but the Osiat is like ink."

"Is that Aurënen over there?" Ruan asked, pointing at peaks visible far off in the west across the water.

"No, that lies much farther south," Tobin replied, recalling the maps he and Ki had studied in the palace library. "If you keep going west from there, you'd end up in Zengat, I think."

Riding along the headlands, they peered over the sheer, dizzying cliffs on the western side. Far below they could see the backs of circling gulls, and below that, the white curl of surf against the sheer stone face.

"The isthmus is like a fortress wall," said Tobin. "To get to that little point of land down there, you'd have to sail back all the way around Skala."

"That's why there are hardly any settlements on the west side," said Nikides. "The land is steeper on that side of the mountains, and there aren't many good harbors. And Grandfather says the Three Lands all face Kouros because it's the heart of the world."

"Good. That means we don't have to sail all the way 'round, at least," said Ruan, who was prone to seasickness.

But Tobin was still looking at that tantalizing jut of land in the distance. It thrust out against the unexpected blue of the Osiat Sea and was covered by what looked like oak trees. What would it be like to walk there? He'd probably never know and the thought made him oddly sad. This windswept ribbon of land, and the rugged mountains, which ran like a spine down the middle of the Skalan peninsula, effectively cut the country in half.

Ｔhey left Cirna and began a halting progress along the jagged northern coast. Sometimes they stayed in castles, and sometimes in cities, meeting the same acclaim, the same blessings and speeches and toasts at each port of call. By spring, they'd only gotten as far as Volchi, but Tobin had already filled two journals with military observations. Thoughts of other sorts he knew better than to commit to paper.

Chapter 39

Iya arrived at the keep at midsummer with three more wizards for Arkoniel's little band. She was delighted with his progress, especially when she learned that he and Eyoli had mastered Lyan's message-sending spell.

The nights were warm and they spent the second evening walking along the cool riverbank. Behind them, the windows of the keep were warm with candlelight. A large log had washed up after the spring floods and they sat on it and dangled their bare feet in the water. Iya watched him send a trifling message off to Lyan in a tiny globe of bluish light. A moment later the woman's laughing reply sped back in a firefly spark of green.

"Amazing!" Iya exclaimed.

"Actually it's not a difficult spell at all, if you can perceive the pattern."

"That's not what I meant. You're young, Arkoniel, and you've spent the better part of your life caught up in this scheme of mine. Don't you remember how it was before? Wizards don't live in groups, and they seldom share their knowledge. Remember how frustrated and hurt you'd be if someone showed you a pretty spell but wouldn't tell you how it worked?"

"Yes. And you'd tell me it was rude to ask."

"So it was, but these are different times. Adversity is binding us closer—both this lot of yours, and that group I told you of in Ero."

"Your Wormhole wizards?" Arkoniel chuckled.

"Yes. How many other little cabals do you suppose there are, out there?"

"There are the Harriers. They were the first."

Iya's lips tightened in distaste. "I suppose you're right. When I first heard of them I thought it couldn't last. Yet here we are." She shook her head. "Yes, different times, indeed."

Arkoniel glanced back at the warm glow in the windows. "I like it, Iya. I enjoy seeing so many children together, and teaching them. I like sharing magics with the others, too."

She patted his hand and rose to go. "It's what you're meant for, my dear."

"How do you mean? As soon as we've accomplished your task, it will all go back to the way it was before."

"I'm not so sure. Do you recall what I told you of my vision at Afra?"

"Of course."

"I didn't tell you everything. I saw you."

"Me?"

"Yes, standing in a great, shining white palace filled with wizards, with an apprentice by your side."

"Wythnir?"

"No, you were a very old man in my vision. It must have been centuries from now and the child was still very young. I didn't understand at the time but now I think I begin to see the significance."

Arkoniel looked up at the keep again and shook his head. "It's no shining palace."

"Ah, but you're not old yet, either. No, I think we are seeing the very beginning of a path that will shape your life."

"Both our lives."

"I suspect not."

The words sent a stab of dread through him. "I don't know what you mean, Iya, but believe me, you'll be welcome anywhere I go. It will probably be you who builds that white palace. You just saw too far, that's all."

Iya tucked her hand under his arm as they walked

back up the hill. "Perhaps you're right. Whatever it means, I know what I was shown, and I am content."

Neither of them said anything for a while. As they reached the bridge, she asked, "How are you coming along with that doorway spell of yours? You still have most of your fingers, I see."

"Actually, I have some exciting news. I showed it to Vornus and he saw something similar practiced by a centaur mage in the Nimra Mountains. He calls it translocation magic. I think that describes it better than doorway. It isn't anything as simple as that, but rather a vortex that sucks objects away like a whirlwind. The problem is that the vortex spins too fast. If I can slow it somehow, I might even be able to transport people."

"Be careful, dear boy! That's a dangerous path you're on. I've thought so since you first showed it to me."

"Don't worry, we're using rats and mice for now." He smiled wryly. "Given our latest attempts, I suspect the keep will be free of vermin before we're through. All the same, I have hope."

"That's not the only danger I was thinking of. You must always consider the consequences of such power. Promise me that you'll keep this a secret for now."

"I will. I trust Vornus and Lyan, but I'm not so sure about Malkanus. He has power enough as it is, and seems to enjoy it for it's own sake."

"You have a discerning heart, Arkoniel. I've always thought so. If you don't let yourself be blinded by pity, it will serve you well."

Arkoniel flinched at the hint of reproach behind her words. Though she'd never said as much, he knew that she'd never entirely forgiven him for sparing Ki.

Chapter 40

Korin and the Companions returned to Ero with the autumn rains and were overjoyed to find Lutha and Barieus waiting on the quay to greet them when they'd sailed in. Lutha was not only well again, but had grown a full three inches.

"Almost dying agreed with me," he said, laughing as everyone exclaimed over him. "I still can't seem to catch up with you, though, Tobin."

Tobin grinned shyly. He'd grown so quickly over the past year that he'd needed new clothes made. He stood as tall as Korin, now, but even though he was nearly fifteen, he was still slender and beardless, a fact the others chafed him about unmercifully.

Tobin did his best to laugh, but inwardly he was increasingly dismayed. All of his friends were filling out like men. Ki was broader through the shoulders and now sported a sparse moustache and narrow chin beard, a fashion Korin had set in the spring. Nik and Lutha both boasted "double arrows," respectable points of silky hair above the corners of their mouths.

Even Brother had changed. They'd always been nearly identical, but over the past year Brother had taken on a more man-grown look, with shoulders as broad as Ki's. Soft black hair shadowed his upper lip and the middle of his chest, while Tobin's remained smooth as a girl's.

Over the summer he'd even found himself making excuses not to go bathing with the others; in spite of his new height Tobin still looked like a child compared to most of them.

Worse yet, he had a hard time not staring at their well-muscled bodies and privates. Wrestling matches, a favorite sport since he'd joined the Companions, evoked unsettling feelings, too, especially with Ki.

Tharin had guessed part of the problem as Tobin sulked around the ship's deck one hot day in Lenthin. Everyone else was ashore, swimming in a cove, but Tobin had stayed behind, pleading a headache. Even Ki had abandoned him.

"I was a skinny thing at your age, too," Tharin said kindly, sitting with him in the shade of the sail. "Any day now you'll have hair on your lip and muscles like a wrestler."

"Was it that way with my father?" Tobin asked.

"Well, Rhius grew faster, but you may take after your mother's side. Her father was a slim man, but strong like you." He gave Tobin's upper arm an appraising pinch. "You're all whipcord and wire, just like he was. And quick as a cat, too. I saw you get under Zusthra's guard yesterday. Quickness can overcome bulk any day if you're smart. And you are."

None of this made Tobin feel much better. He couldn't tell Tharin about the moonflow pains that plagued him more often now. Even knowing the truth, he felt left behind. No wonder the girls had all stopped flirting with him.

That's not why, a small secret voice whispered deep in his heart. *They know. They can tell.*

He knew what was whispered about Ki and him, whispers they both ignored for their own reasons. But sometime over the summer when he wasn't even looking, something had changed; something he didn't dare let himself think about when Ki was around, for fear it would show in his face.

Ki loved him as much as ever, but there was no question how his fancies ran. A few of the servant girls had given him a tumble back in Ero, and there'd been more opportunities on the voyage. Ki was handsome and easy-going; girls were drawn to him like cats to cream. He wasn't above bragging about his exploits to the other boys, either.

Tobin was always silent during these conversations, tongue locked to the roof of his mouth. *Just Tobin being shy, as usual,* everyone thought, and Ki saw no further than that. In his mind they were brothers, as they'd always been. He never said a word to Tobin about the whispers or treated him any differently. In return, Tobin swallowed the confused yearnings that assailed him at odd moments and did the same.

It was always worst on the full moon, when the moontide pangs tugged at his belly, reminding Tobin who he really was. Sometimes he even caught himself watching young women with envy wondering what it felt like to stride about in flowing skirts, with strands of beads woven into your hair and scent at your wrists—and to have the boys look at you that way.

Someday, Tobin thought, hiding his burning face in the pillow on such nights, trying not to think about Ki lying so close beside him, close enough to touch. *Someday he'll know, and then we'll see.*

Other times, alone and naked he looked down at his narrow hips and flat bony chest, took in the plain face reflected in his mirror, and wondered if he'd ever be a proper woman, either? Cupping his small penis in his hand, he tried to imagine the loss of it and shuddered, more confused than ever.

As they turned toward home at last, he vowed he'd find some way to visit Lhel.

Back in Ero at last, Tobin and Ki found themselves masters of a new suite of rooms in Korin's wing of the new palace. The other boys were assigned quarters nearby.

There was the usual round of balls and salons, and the pleasure of returning to their old haunts in the city. They'd only been home for a few weeks, however, when the king announced another execution in the square. Tobin had nearly forgotten the incident with the young priest, and the way people had looked at Korin that day, but now they rode out under double guard.

There were three wizards burned this time; Tobin kept as far from the platform as he could, fearful of being recognized; but, unlike before, the condemned went passively, silent behind their ugly iron masks.

Tobin wanted to look away when they burned, but he knew the others were watching him, and wondering. No doubt a few of them still hoping that he'd make a spectacle of himself again. So he kept his eyes open and his face turned to the blinding white fires, trying not to see the dark figures writhing within.

There was no dissent this time. The crowd roared its approval and the Companions cheered. Tobin blinked his smarting eyes and looked over at Korin. As he suspected, his cousin was watching him and gave Tobin a proud grin. Tobin's stomach lurched, and he had to swallow hard as bile rose in his throat.

Tobin could only pretend to eat during the banquet that followed. The nausea had passed, but he felt the stir of the pains deep in his belly, like a reminder. They grew stronger as the evening went on, as bad as they'd been that day he'd bled. Lhel had promised him that wouldn't happen again, but every new pain sent his heart racing. What if there was blood again? What if someone saw?

Niryn was at the king's side, as always, and more than once Tobin was certain he felt the man's cold gaze on him. Serving with the squires, Ki gave him a questioning look. Tobin hastily busied himself with the slab of lamb going cold on his trencher, forcing down a few mouthfuls.

As soon as they were released from the feast, he fled to the nearest privy and checked his trousers for blood. There wasn't any, of course, but it was still hard to meet Ki's worried gaze as he emerged.

"You sick, Tob?"

Tobin shrugged. "Executions still don't agree with me, I guess."

Ki put an arm around him as they made their way back to their chambers. "Me neither. And I hope they never do."

Your nephew still has no stomach for the just execution of your law, my king," Niryn remarked, as they sat smoking in Erius' gardens that night.

Erius shrugged. "He looked a little green, but he held up well."

"Indeed. Yet it is curious that a boy who has proven himself so well in battle would be unsettled by the death of a criminal, don't you think?" *But not merely unsettled.* The boy had been angry. It had rather amused the wizard, even as he'd stored the knowledge away. The prince was of no consequence, and circumstance might yet take care of any impediment he'd impose. Another battle, perhaps, or a touch of plague.

"Oh, I don't know about that." Erius watched a smoke ring he'd blown drift away on the evening breeze. "I knew a fine general, a true lion in battle, who would go white with fear if a cat came into the room. And I shouldn't tell you this, but I've seen General Rheynaris himself faint at the sight of his own blood. We all have our little quirks. It's no wonder a boy should blanch at the sight of a man being burned alive. Took me a while to get used to it."

"I suppose, Majesty."

"And what does it matter, anyway?" Erius chuckled. "I've no need of him as an heir anymore. Aliya's pregnant again, you know, and ripening nicely."

"You're very fond of her, Majesty."

"She's pretty, she's strong and has spirit—more than a match for that son of mine—and she dotes on me like a true daughter. And what a queen she'll make, if only she can throw an heir this time."

Niryn smiled and blew a smoke ring of his own.

Chapter 41

Arkoniel didn't realize how comfortable he'd grown until the false peace they'd enjoyed was shattered.

He'd been working with the children in the simples garden, harvesting the last of the season's herbs. There would be a full moon that night and he expected a frost. Suddenly a little point of light appeared a few feet from his nose. Wythrin and the others watched apprehensively as Arkoniel touched a finger to the message sphere. He felt the tingle of Lyan's excitement as the light disappeared and he heard her excited voice saying, "Hide at once! A herald is coming."

"Come, children, into the woods," he ordered. "Bring your tools and baskets. Hurry now!"

As soon as they were safely hidden in a thicket, he summoned a message spell of his own and sent it speeding to Eyoli in the workroom.

"Are the Harriers coming to get us?" Totmus whimpered, crouched close beside him. The others clung to Ethni and she hugged them close, but she was just as frightened.

"No, just a messenger. But we've got to be very quiet, all the same. Eyoli will come get us when it's safe."

A rider came up the hill at a gallop, and they heard the hollow report of hooves across the bridge. Arkoniel wondered if Nari would offer the rider the customary hospitality—a meal and a night's lodging. He didn't fancy the idea of sleeping under the stars that night. As if to underscore the thought, Totmus clapped his hands across his mouth to stifle a cough. Despite good food and Nari's care, he was still a pallid, sickly child and was showing signs of an autumn cold.

The sun crawled down the sky and the shadows cooled around them. The stars were pricking the purple sky when they heard the rider again. Arkoniel heaved a sigh of relief as the sound faded away on the Alestun road but still waited for Eyoli's point of light to tell them it was safe to come back.

Nari and Catilan met him in the hall. The other wizards were still hiding upstairs.

"It's from Tobin." Nari told him, handing him a parchment scroll bearing the Atyion seal.

Arkoniel's heart sank as he read it, though the message was jubilant: the Companions were home, the royal progress had been a success, and the king had granted Tobin permission to celebrate his birthday with a few weeks of hunting at his old home. Soon wagonloads of servants and provisions would be rumbling up the road to begin preparations.

"I suppose it had to happen, sooner or later." Nari sighed. "This is still his home, after all. But how in the world can we hide everyone with a pack of hunters racketing about the place?"

"It's no good sending them into the forest," said Catilan. "Someone is bound to stumble across any camp we make there."

"And what about you, Arkoniel?" added Nari. "What are we going to do with you? Not to mention the extra beds set up. And the gardens!"

Arkoniel tucked the letter away. "Well, General, what do you suggest?"

"The house is easily set to rights. The beds will be needed and the garden can be explained. But the rest of you will have to go away someplace," Catilan replied. "The question is, where? Winter's coming on fast." She drew

Totmus to her side and gave Arkoniel a meaningful look. "There'll be snow on the ground soon."

Eyoli had been listening from the stairs and came down to join them. "We can't travel in a group, like wandering players. Others have tried that. The Harriers make a point of stopping any they meet on the road claiming to be actors and the like. We'll have to scatter."

"No!" said Arkoniel. "Nari, you see to the children. Eyoli, come with me."

The older wizards were waiting anxiously for him in the workroom. Arkoniel had hardly finished explaining the situation before they erupted in panic, all talking at once. Melissandra bolted for the door, calling for Dara to pack, and Hain rose to follow. Malkanus was already planning defenses for the road. Even the older ones looked ready to run.

"Listen to me, please!" Arkoniel cried. "Melissandra, Hain, come back."

When they ignored him, he muttered a spell Lhel had taught him and clapped his hands. A peal of thunder shook the room, startling the others to silence.

"Have you forgotten already why you're here?" he demanded. "Look around you." His heart beat faster as the words poured out. "The Third Orëska Iya talks of isn't some far-off dream. It's here. Now. In this room. *We* are the Third Orëska, the first fruits of her vision. The Lightbearer brought us together. Whatever purpose there may be in that, we can't scatter now."

"He's right," said Eyoli. "Mistress Virishan always said our safety lay in unity. Those children downstairs? They wouldn't be alive now except for her. If we stay together, then perhaps we can stand against the Harriers. I know I can't do it alone."

"None of us can," old Vornus agreed, looking grim.

"I managed well enough," Kaulin retorted, dour as ever.

"By running away. And you came here," Arkoniel reminded him.

"I came only for safety, not to lose my freedom!"

"Would you rather wear one of their silver badges?" Cerana demanded. "How free will you be once the Harriers number you and write your name in their book? I'll fight for your queen, Arkoniel, but more than that, I want to drive those white-robed monsters out. Why does Illior allow such a travesty?"

"Perhaps we're proof that the Lightbearer does not," Malkanus offered, leaning against the wall by the window.

Arkoniel looked at him in surprise. The other man shrugged, fingering the fine silk embroidery on his sleeve. "I saw the vision and believed. I'll fight, if need be. I say we stay together."

"So we stay together," said Lyan. "But we can't stay here."

"We could go deeper into the mountains," Kaulin said. "I've been quite a ways up. There's game enough, if any of you know how to earn your food."

"But for how long?" asked Melissandra. "And what about the children? The higher we go, the sooner the winter will find us."

"Lyan, can you send one of your message lights to Iya?"

"Not without knowing something of where she is. It must be directed."

"All right, then. We make our own way. We'll pack the wagon and your horses with all the supplies they can carry, and see where the road takes us. Be ready by dawn."

It wasn't much of a plan, but it was a start.

Nari and the servants took charge of provisioning. With the help of the men, Arkoniel moved his meager belongings back up to his abandoned bedchamber on the third floor. When they'd finished he sent them to help in the kitchen yard, and found himself alone upstairs for the first time in months. Gooseflesh prickled up his arms. It was already dark.

He packed hurriedly, throwing a few days' clothing into a pack. He wouldn't be gone long; as soon as he had the others settled somewhere, he'd come back and try to speak with the boys. He tried not to think of the locked door down the corridor, yet all the while he had the growing sense that Ariani was watching him.

"This is for your child. All for her," he whispered. Grabbing up the lopsided pack, he was halfway to the stairs when he realized he'd forgotten the bag containing the bowl. It had been months since he'd thought about that, too.

Turning slowly, he searched the darkness beyond his lamp. Was that a white shape hovering by the tower door, or just a trick of the light? With an effort, he started back for the workroom. The air against his face grew colder with every step, but he couldn't run away. Not without the bowl.

He dashed to the table and snagged the dusty leather bag from its hiding place underneath. Shoving it into the pack, he looked around fearfully, expecting any moment to see Ariani's blood-streaked face in the shadows. But there was no sign of her, only the chill, and perhaps that was just the night breeze through the shutters. With shaking hands, he added a few more simples and a jar of firechips to his collection.

He was halfway down the corridor again when another realization halted him in his tracks.

In a few days' time this house would be filled with young nobles, huntsmen, and servants. Every room would be needed.

"Bilairy's balls!" Dropping the pack at the top of the stairs, he drew out his wand and hurried back to his rooms.

Obscuration was not difficult magic, but it took time and concentration. By the time he'd hidden the doors to his chambers, making them appear to be bricked up, he was shaking and drenched with sweat. That still left two guest chambers on the other side of the corridor in use.

Only then did he realize he'd forgotten about the windows, which were visible from the road. With a snarl of frustration he swept aside the carefully crafted spells and began again, this time creating the illusion that there had been a fire; from outside people would see blackened stonework around the windows and charred shutters. As he obscured the last doorway again his lamp guttered out and he heard an unmistakable sigh.

Ariani was standing by the tower door, bright as a candle in the darkness. Water and blood streamed from her black hair, soaking the front of her gown and pooling on the floor around her feet. Silent as smoke, she glided to the workroom door, one hand pressed to her mouth, the other held at a strange angle against her side, as if she were carrying something. She stared at the illusion for a long moment, looking lost and confused.

"I'm protecting your child," he told her.

She held him with her eyes a moment, then faded away without a word.

Arkoniel hadn't expected to sleep that night, but he fell into a restless doze the second he lay down across the unmade bed in Tobin's room, and dreamed of riders hunting him through the forest, led by Ariani's ghost.

The touch of a cold hand on his brow brought him awake with a strangled cry. It was no dream; a hand was touching him. Flailing wildly, he tumbled off the wrong side the bed and found himself wedged helplessly between the mattress and the wall.

A woman stood on the other side of the bed, silhouetted against the light spilling in at the open window. Ariani had followed him here. His flesh crawled at the thought of her touching him as he slept.

"Arkoniel?"

That wasn't Ariani's voice.

"Lhel?" He heard a soft chuckle, then felt the mattress shift as she sat down. "By the Four!" Scrambling across the bed, he hugged her, then rested his head in her lap. Deer tooth beads pressed into his cheek. Dark against darkness, Lhel stroked his hair.

"Did you miss me, little man?"

Embarrassed, he sat up and pulled her close, burying his fingers in her coarse black curls. There were dead leaves and twigs tangled there, and the taste of salt on her lips. "I haven't seen you in weeks. Where have you been?"

"The Mother sent me over the mountains to a place my people once lived. It's only a few days' journey from here. Tomorrow I'll guide your wizards there. You must go quickly, though, and make what houses you can before the snows come."

Arkoniel pulled back a little, trying to make out her face. "Your goddess brought you back today, just when I most needed you?"

When she said nothing, he guessed she'd been back for some time. Before he could press the matter, however, she surprised him by shoving him back on the bed and kissing him hungrily. Fire shot through his belly as she climbed on top of him, lifting her skirt and fumbling at the front of his tunic. He felt rough wool against his belly, then warm skin. It was the first time she'd ever offered sex inside the keep and she was as desperate for it as he was. Holding his hands against her breasts, she rode him wildly, then lurched forward to smother their cries as they came. Lightning flashed behind Arkoniel's closed eyelids as he thrashed and moaned under her, then the world exploded into red light.

When his mind cleared, she was lying beside him, cupping his balls in one hot, wet hand.

"Your pack is too small for the journey," she murmured.

"It was full enough until you emptied it for me," he

chuckled, thinking it some joking slight against his manhood.

She rose on one elbow and traced his lips with one finger. "No, your traveling pack. You'll be no good to Tobin dead. You must go with the others and stay away."

"But you're here now! You could take them to your oak and hide them there."

"Too many, and too many strangers coming, perhaps with wizards who have enough sight to see through my magic."

"But I want to see the boys again. Teach me how you hid yourself for so long!" He grasped her hand and kissed her rough palm. "Please, Lhel. I ask in the name of the Mother—"

Lhel snatched her hand away and slid off the bed. He couldn't see her face as she pulled her clothes back into place, but he could feel her anger.

"What is it? What did I say?"

"You have no right!" she hissed. She crossed the room to retrieve her discarded shawl and the moonlight fell across her face, turning it into an ugly mask. The pallid light filled every crease and wrinkle with shadow and robbed her hair of color. The symbols of power blazed on her face and breasts, stark as ink on alabaster. The lover of a moment ago stood before him as he'd never seen her before—a vengeful hag.

Arkoniel shrank back; this was the side of her Iya had tried so often to warn him of. Before he could stop himself, he'd raised a hand in a warding sign against her.

Lhel froze, eyes lost in shadowed sockets, but the harsh mask softened to sorrow. "Against me you make that sign?" She came back to the bed and sat down. "You must never call on my goddess. She does not forgive what your people and your Orëska did to us."

"Then why did she have you help us at all?"

Lhel passed her hands over her face, smoothing away the symbols from her skin. "It is the will of the Mother that

I helped you, and Her will that I stayed to care for the un-
quiet spirit we made that night. All those long lonely days
I pondered the mystery of that. And then, when you came
to me and were willing to become my pupil—" She sighed.
"If the Mother did not favor it, you would not have learned
so much from me, so easily." She took his hand and her
fingers found the shiny stump of his severed finger. "You
cannot make a baby for me with your seed, but your magic
and mine made something new. Perhaps one day, our
people will create more together, but we still follow different gods. Your Illior is not my Mother, no matter how you
try to tell yourself it is so. Be true to your own gods, my
friend, and have a care not to offend those of others."

"I meant no—"

She brushed his mouth with cold fingertips. "No, you
meant to sway me by invoking Her name. Don't ever do
that again. As for the other wizards here, they won't be
pleased to see me. You recall our first meeting? Your fear
and repugnance, and how you called me 'little trickster' in
your mind?"

Arkoniel nodded, ashamed. He and Iya had treated
Lhel like some lowly tradesman, offering no respect even
after she'd done all they'd asked.

"I will not win them as I did you." Lhel ran a finger play-
fully down his belly to the thatch of hair below. "Just see to
it that the strong ones don't attack me." She pulled back a
little, looking hard into his eyes. "For their sake, yes?"

"Yes." He frowned. "I wonder what Tobin and Ki will
think, not finding me here?"

"They're smart boys. They'll guess." She thought a moment. "Leave that mind clouder."

"Eyoli?"

"Yes. He's very clever, and can keep himself unnoticed. Who will think twice about a stableboy? If Tobin
needs us, he can send word." She stood again. "Look for
me along the road tomorrow. Bring as many supplies as
you can carry. And more clothes. You will listen to me,

won't you, and stay away? There's nothing to be gained by going back."

Before he could answer she was gone, fading into the darkness as swiftly as a ghost. Perhaps one day she would teach him that trick, too.

There was no hope of sleep now. Going down to the kitchen yard, he checked the supplies in the wagon again, counting blankets, coils of rope, and sacks of flour, salt, and apples. Thank the Light the king had appointed no steward or Royal Protector here. Wandering through the yards, he gathered every tool he could find—handsaws, hammers, two rusted axes left behind in the barracks, a small anvil he found at the back of the farriers' shop. He felt better, doing something useful, and all the while he felt the growing conviction that a corner of some sort had been turned. After years of wandering with Iya, here he was with a handful of fugitive wizards and a cart—his new Orëska.

It was a humble beginning, he thought, but a beginning all the same.

Chapter 42

The stars were fading when Arkoniel and the others set out. Hain drove the children in the cart; the rest rode. Wythnir clung behind Arkoniel's saddle, his meager bundle wedged between them.

"Where does this road go, Master?" he asked.

"To the mining towns north of here, and finally to the coast, west of the isthmus," Arkoniel replied. Iron, tin, silver, and lead had drawn Skalan settlers into the mountains centuries earlier. Some of the mines still produced enough to keep people there.

He said nothing of the history Lhel had taught him; how Skalan soldiers—Tobin's ancestors among them—had used this road to make war against Lhel's people. The *Retha'noi* had been great raiders and warriors, but their magic had been even stronger and more feared. Those who'd survived had been branded necromancers and driven deep into the mountains. They were no longer hunted; but they remained exiles, driven from the fertile coastal lands that had been theirs. When Arkoniel and Iya ventured into the mountains in search of a witch, they'd felt the sullen animosity that still smoldered in the hearts of that small, dark race.

He'd done as Lhel asked, told them nothing of her, only that they were to meet a guide who would lead them to safety. They came upon her just after dawn. She stood waiting atop a boulder by the road.

The others reined in sharply. Malkanus reached into his pouch, readying some magic against her, but Arkoniel rode between them.

"No, wait. Don't!" he said. "This is our guide."

"This?" Malkanus exclaimed. "A filthy hill witch?"

Lhel folded her arms and scowled down at him.

"This is Lhel, an honored friend well-known to me and to Iya. I expect you all to treat her as such. Illior brought her to us years ago. She shares the vision."

"Iya approves of this?" asked Lyan, who was old enough to remember the raids.

"Of course. Please, my friends, Lhel has offered her help, and we need it. I can vouch for her goodwill."

Despite Arkoniel's assurances, tensions remained high on both sides. Lhel rode grudgingly on the cart beside Hain, who leaned away, avoiding her touch as if she had the Red and Black Death.

They reached the first pass that day and toiled up through the steep valley beyond as the air grew colder and snow crept down the sides of the peaks to edge the road. The trees were sparse and stunted, leaving them at the mercy of the wind. Wolves howled nearby at night, and several times they heard the screech of catamounts echoing between the peaks.

The children slept together under blankets in the back of the cart while the older wizards tended the fires and kept watch. Totmus' cough grew worse. Huddled among the others, he coughed and dozed but could not rest. Under the suspicious stares of the Orëska wizards, Lhel brewed a tea for him and gently coaxed it into him. The child brought up alarming gobbets of green phlegm and seemed the better for it. By the third night he was laughing with the others again.

The wizards remained wary, but the children were more easily won over. During the long, weary hours in the cart, Lhel told them stories in her broken Skalan and showed them pretty little spells. When they stopped each night she disappeared into the darkness, returning with mushrooms and herbs for the stewpot.

*   *   *

𝒯he third day they descended along the edge of a gorge, and the forest rose up to meet them again. Hundreds of feet below, a blue-green river tumbled between the echoing walls. Just beyond the ruins of an abandoned village, they turned west along a tributary stream and followed it into a small, densely wooded valley.

There was no road. Lhel led them along the riverbank, and into towering hemlock. Soon the forest was too dense to take the cart any farther, and she led them on foot along a smaller brook to an overgrown clearing among the trees.

There had been a village here, but not one built by Skalan hands. Small, round roofless stone huts stood along the riverbank, none of them larger than an apple cellar. Many had fallen in and been reclaimed by moss and creepers, but a few were still sound.

A few weathered logs still leaned at disparate angles around the edge of the clearing, marking where a palisade had kept out wolves and catamounts, and perhaps Skalan invaders, as well.

"This good place," Lhel told them. "Water, wood, and food. But you must build soon." She pointed up at the sky, which was slowly filling with grey clouds. They could see their breath on the air today. "Snow soon. Little ones must have warm place to sleep, yes?"

She walked to one of the huts and showed them holes drilled in some of the top stones. "For roof poles."

"Will you stay with us, Mistress?" Danil asked, holding the witch's hand tight. The day before Lhel had shown him how to call field mice to his knee, something even Arkoniel had not thought the child capable of. The little boy had followed the witch around like a puppy ever since.

"For a time," Lhel replied, patting his hand. "Maybe learn you more magic?"

"Can I learn, too?" asked Totmus, wiping his snotty nose on his sleeve.

"And me!" the twins cried eagerly.

Lhel ignored the glares from the older wizards. "Yes, little ones. All you learn." She smiled at Arkoniel and he felt another surge of that strange assurance that things were falling into place as they were meant to.

Under Lhel's direction, the servants made several of the old foundations habitable for the night, building makeshift roofs of saplings and boughs.

Meanwhile, Malkanus, Lyan, and Vornus took Arkoniel aside.

"Is this your Third Orëska?" Malkanus demanded angrily, jerking his thumb at the children tagging along after Lhel. "Are we all going to be necromancers now?"

"You know it's forbidden," Vornus warned. "She can't be allowed to go on teaching them."

"I know the histories, but I'm telling you, they're not entirely correct," Arkoniel maintained. "I've studied for years with this woman, and learned the true roots of her magic. Please, just let me show you, and you'll see that it's true. Illior would never have guided us to her if we weren't meant to learn from her. How can that not be a sign?"

"But the magic we practice is pure!" said Lyan.

"We like to think so, but I've seen Aurënfaie shake their heads at some of our work. And remember, our magic is no less unnatural to our kind than Lhel's. We had to mix our blood with the 'faie before we had any wizards in the Three Lands. Perhaps it's time to mingle with a new blood, one native to Skala. The hill folk were here long before our ancestors arrived."

"Yes, and they killed hundreds of our people," Malkanus snapped.

Arkoniel shrugged. "They fought off the invaders. Would any of us have done differently? I believe that we're meant to make peace with them now, somehow. But for now, believe me when I say that we need Lhel's help, her kind of magic. Talk with her. Listen with an open heart to what she tells you, as I have. She has great power."

"I can feel that," muttered Cerana. "That's what troubles me."

Despite Arkoniel's assurances, the others went away shaking their heads.

Lhel came to him, and said, "Come, I'll teach you something new." Walking back to the wagon, she searched through the baggage and pulled out a copper basin, then set off along the stream, leading him deeper into the forest. The ground was steep here, and the banks tiered with mossy ledges and shaggy frost-burned clumps of fern and caneberry. Thick stands of cattail rushes waved at the water's edge. She pulled up one and peeled the fleshy white root. It was fibrous and dry so late in the year, but still edible.

"There's plenty to eat here," Lhel said, as they moved on. Pausing again, she plucked a large yellow mushroom from a rotting tree trunk and offered him a bite. "You must hunt before the snow comes, and smoke the meat. And collect wood. I don't know if all the children will see springtime. Totmus won't, I think."

"But you healed him!" Arkoniel cried, dismayed. He'd already grown found of the boy.

Lhel shrugged. "I did what I could for him, but the sickness is deep in his lungs. It will come back." She paused again. "I know what they said about me. You spoke for me, and I thank you, but the older ones are right. You don't know the depth of my power."

"Will I ever?"

"Pray you don't, my friend. But now I'll show you something new, but only you. Give me your word you'll keep this to yourself."

"By my hands, heart, and eyes, you have it."

"All right then. We begin." Cupping her hands around her mouth, Lhel let out a harsh, bleating call, then listened. Arkoniel heard nothing but the wind in the trees and the gurgling of the stream.

Lhel turned and gave the call across the stream. This time a faint reply came, then another, already closer. A large stag emerged from the trees on the far bank, sniffing the air suspiciously. It was as large as a palfrey, and had ten sharp prongs on each curving antler.

"It's the rutting season," Arkoniel reminded her. A stag in his prime was a dangerous thing to meet this time of year.

But Lhel was unconcerned. Raising a hand in greeting, she began to sing in that high, tuneless voice she sometimes used. The stag let out a loud snort and shook its head. A few shreds of antler velvet fluttered from the prongs. Arkoniel saw a piece fly loose and noted where it landed; if he survived this encounter, he knew of a concoction that called for it.

Lhel sang on, drawing the stag across the stream. It splashed up onto the bank and stood swinging its head slowly from side to side. Lhel smiled at Arkoniel as she scratched the beast between the antlers, calming it like a tame milk cow. Still humming, she drew her silver knife with her free hand and deftly nicked the large vein just under the stag's jaw. A freshet of blood spurted out, and she caught it in her basin. The stag snorted softly, but remained still. When an inch or so of blood had collected in the basin, Lhel passed it to Arkoniel and laid her hands on the wound, stopping the flow with a touch.

"Stand back," she murmured. When they were safely out of reach, she clapped her hands and shouted, "I release you!"

The stag lowered its head, slashing the air, then sprang away into the trees.

"Now what?" he asked. A thick, gamy odor rose from the basin, and he could feel the lingering heat and the strength of the blood through the metal.

She grinned. "Now I show you what you've wanted so long to know. Set the basin down."

She squatted beside it and motioned for Arkoniel to do

the same. Drawing a leather pouch from the neck of her ragged dress, she passed it to him. Inside he found several small herb bundles wrapped in yarn, and some smaller bags. Under her direction, he crumbled in a handful of bindweed flowers and some tamarack needles. From the small bags came pinches of powdered sulfur, bone, and ochre that stained his fingers like rust.

"Stir it with the first twig you find within reach," Lhel instructed.

Arkoniel found a short, bleached stick and stirred the mix. The blood was still steaming, but it smelled different now.

Lhel unwrapped one of the firechips he'd made for her and used it to light a hank of sweet hay. As she blew the pungent smoke gently across the surface, the blood swirled and turned black.

"Now, sing as I do." Lhel let out a string of strange syllables, and Arkoniel struggled to copy them. She would not translate the spell, but corrected his pronunciation and made him sing it over until he had it right.

"Good. Now we weave the protection. Bring the basin."

"This is how you hid your camp, isn't it?"

She answered with a wink.

Leading him to a gnarled old birch that overhung the brook, she showed him how to coat his palm with the blood and mark the tree, singing the spell as he did so.

Arkoniel winced a little; the blood felt thick and oily on his fingers. Singing, he pressed his hand to the peeling white bark. The blood stood out starkly against it for a moment, then disappeared completely. There wasn't even a trace of moisture left.

"Amazing!"

"We've only just started. It does no good, just one." Lhel led him to a large boulder and had him repeat the process. The blood disappeared just as readily into the stone.

As the sun sank behind the peaks and the shadows went cold, they made a wide circuit around the camp, creating a ring of magic that would confound the senses of any stranger who happened to stray near it. Only those who knew the password—*alaka*, "passage"—could pass through it.

"I used to watch you and the boys trying to find me." Lhel chuckled. "Sometimes you looked right at me and never guessed."

"Would this work for a town? Or for an army on the field?" he asked, but she only shrugged.

They finished their work under a rising full moon and followed the flickering glow of the campfires back to the others, who'd been busy in their absence. Two of the stone circles were snugly capped and some of the supplies had been carried up from the cart. Dry wood lay stacked by a newly dug fire pit and Eyoli was chopping more, mostly large fallen branches the children had dragged from the woods. At the stream's edge, Noril and Semion were busy butchering a fat doe.

"It's a good omen," Noril said as he worked the hide free of the carcass. "The Maker sent her right into the camp while we were putting on the second roof."

Dar and Ethni soon had chunks of venison spitted over a crackling fire along with the heart, liver, and sweetbreads. While the meat cooked, Arkoniel explained about the protection spell and the password. Cerana and Malkanus exchanged suspicious glances, but Eyoli and the children ran off to test it.

It seemed like a lucky start. There was plenty of meat for everyone that night, and bread to go with it. After supper, Kaulin and Vornus produced pipes and shared them around the circle as they listened to the night sounds. The crickets and frogs were silenced for the year, but they could hear small creatures pattering in the woods. A large white owl swooped across the clearing, greeting them with a mournful hoot.

"Another good omen," Lyan said. "Illior sends his messenger to bless our new home."

"Home," Malkanus grumbled, pulling a second cloak around his shoulders. "Out in the wilderness with no proper food and drafty chimneys to live in."

Melissandra took a long pull from one of the pipes and blew out a glowing red horse that flew twice around the fire before bursting with a bright pop over Ethni's head. "Some of us have made do with a great deal less," she said, and smoked out a pair of blue birds for Rala and Ylina. "We've got water, good hunting, and shelter." She gave Lhel a nod. "Thank you. It's a good place."

"How long will we be here?" Vornus asked Arkoniel.

"I don't know yet. We'd better get some proper cabins built before the snow flies."

"Are we carpenters now?" Malkanus groaned. "What do I know about making cabins?"

"We can see to that, Master," Cymeus assured him.

"Some wizards know how to do an honest day's work," Kaulin threw in. "More hands make less work, as they say."

"Thank you, Kaulin, and you." Arkoniel stood and bowed to Dar and the other servants. "You've followed your masters and mistresses without complaint, and made us comfortable here in the wilderness. You've heard us talk of the Third Orëska. It occurs to me now that you are as much a part of it as the wizards. For now we'll build with logs and mud in exile, but I promise you, if we keep faith with Illior and accomplish the task we've been set, we'll have a palace of our own one day, as grand as any in Ero."

Kaulin gave Malkanus a jab with his thumb. "You hear that? Take heart, boy. You'll be living soft again before you know it!"

Dozing in Ethni's arms, Totmus let out a ropy cough.

Chapter 43

Tobin rode the last mile to the keep at a gallop, over-joyed to come home again at last. Emerging from the trees at the bottom of the meadow, he reined in and looked around in surprise.

"Damn!" Ki exclaimed, coming up beside him with the others. "Looks like the king's brought half of Ero out with us!"

Across the river, the yellowed meadow had been transformed into a village of tents and makeshift stalls. Tobin hadn't wanted any fuss, but this looked like a country fair. Scanning the tradesmen's banners fluttering on poles, he saw every sort from bakers to jess makers. There were hosts of performers, of course, including the troupe from the Golden Foot Theater.

"We're a long way from the city here," Erius said laughing, having overheard. "I wanted to be sure you boys have suitable entertainment while you're here."

"Thank you, Uncle," Tobin replied. He'd already counted five minstrel banners and six pastry makers. He wondered what Cook would do if they tried to invade her kitchen. She had been a warrior, after all, and didn't take kindly to interference with her cooking.

"Look there!" Ki exclaimed, pointing up the hill. Nari had sent word of the fire, but it was still a shock to see those blackened windows where Arkoniel's rooms had been. What had the wizard been doing? Tobin wondered, though he knew better than to say that aloud. Arkoniel's presence here was still a secret; the wizard was probably hiding at Lhel's camp.

Nari and Cook came out to greet them and made a great fuss over Korin, welcoming him to the house.

"And just look at you two!" Nari exclaimed, standing on tiptoe to kiss Tobin and Ki. "You're all grown since we saw you last."

Tobin was surprised at how short she seemed. As a child he'd always thought her tall.

Later, as he gave the Companions a tour of the place, he noticed other changes, things apparent only to someone who'd lived here before. The larger herb garden below the barracks, for instance, and the fact that the kitchen garden had been spaded up to three times its old size. Except for one new squint-eyed stableboy, the household had not grown.

The house was brighter than he remembered, too, more homelike, but that was Nari's doing. She'd furnished every room and brought out all the best linen, plate, and tapestries. Even the third floor was cheery in daylight, the rooms on the left side of the corridor lined with cots for the small army of servants that had accompanied them. Arkoniel's old rooms across the hall were bricked up until repairs could be made.

Slipping away as the others prepared for supper that night, he climbed the stairs again and walked slowly to the far end of the hallway. The tower door was locked, the brass handle tarnished with neglect. He rattled the latch, wondering if Nari still had the key. Standing there, he remembered how frightened he used to be, imagining his mother's angry ghost staring at him through the wood. Now it was just a door.

A wave of longing swept over him. Tobin rested his forehead against the smooth wood, and whispered, "Are you there, Mother?"

"Tobin?"

He jumped, but it was only Ki at the top of the stairs.

"There you are. Cook wants you to taste the soup, and here you are not even dressed yet—Say, what's wrong?"

"Nothing. I was just looking around."

Ki saw through that, of course. Coming closer, he cautiously brushed the wood with his fingers. "I'd forgotten. Is she in there?"

"I don't think so."

Ki leaned against the wall beside him. "Do you miss her?"

Tobin shrugged. "I didn't think so, but just now I remembered her the way she was on her good days before— Well, before that last day. Almost like a real mother." He pulled out the ring and showed Ki his mother's serene profile. "That's what she was like, before Brother and I were born."

Ki said nothing, but leaned his shoulder against Tobin's.

Tobin sighed. "I've been thinking. I'm going to leave the doll up there."

"But *she* said to keep it, didn't she?"

"I don't need it anymore. He finds me anyway, whether I have it or not. I'm tired, Ki. Tired of hiding it, hiding him." *Hiding myself, too,* he thought, but bit back the words. Looking around, he let out a halfhearted laugh. "It's been a long time since we've been here, hasn't it? It's not how I remembered it. It all seemed so big and dark then, even after you came to live here."

"We got bigger." Grinning, Ki tugged Tobin away. "Come on, I'll prove it."

Nari had kept their old bedchamber just as they'd left it, and next door the toy city and a few childish sculptures were gathering dust in their places. In the bedchamber, the suit of mail Tobin's father had given him still hung on its rack in the corner.

"Go on," Ki urged. "You haven't tried it in ages."

Tobin pulled the hauberk over his head, then scowled at their paired reflections in the glass.

"Father said when this fit, I'd be old enough to ride off to war with him."

"Well, you're tall enough," said Ki.

He was, but still too slender. The shoulders of the hauberk shirt slumped halfway to his elbows, and the sleeves hung well past his fingertips. The coif kept sliding down over his eyes.

"You just haven't filled out yet." Ki clapped the old helmet on Tobin's head and rapped his knuckles against it. "That's a fit, at least. Cheer up, for hell's sake! The king said he'd let us ride coast patrol when we get back. Better pirates and bandits than no fighting at all, eh?"

"I guess so." Tobin caught movement out of the corner of his eye and turned to find Brother watching him from the shadows. He had on the same sort of mail, but his fit. Tobin tugged the hauberk off and slung it over the stand. When he looked again, the ghost was gone.

For the first time in Tobin's life, the great hall was filled with comrades and huntsmen, music and laughter. A fire crackled warmly on the hearth, illuminating the tables set up around it and throwing shadows on the painted walls. Players strutted between the tables and the minstrel gallery across the hall was packed with musicians. The whole house rang with the sounds of celebration.

Cook had evidently come to some sort of agreement with the city folk, and proudly helped serve the lavish feast. Dressed in a new gown of brown wool, Nari served as their steward. The only other women present were servants and entertainers. Pregnant again, Aliya had remained at her mother's house under the watchful eye of the drysians.

Seated in a place of honor beside Tobin, Tharin looked around wistfully. "I haven't seen the place like this since we were boys."

"We had some fine times here!" the king said, clinking his mazer against Tobin's. "Your grandfather led a fine hunt—stag, bear, even catamounts! I look forward to tomorrow's ride!"

"We have something special planned for your name day, too," Korin said, sharing a wink with his father.

The warmth and company raised Tobin's spirits and he joined in gladly with the songs and drinking games. By midnight he was almost as drunk as Korin. Surrounded by friends and music, he could let himself forget prophecies and past sorrows for a little while; he was master of this house at last.

"We'll always be friends, won't we?" he said, leaning on Korin's shoulder.

"Friends?" Korin laughed. "Brothers, more like. A toast to my little brother!"

Everyone cheered, waving their mazers about. Tobin joined in, but the laughter died in his throat as he caught sight of two dark figures lurking in a shadowed corner of the minstrel's gallery. They stepped forward, oblivious to the fiddlers sawing away beside them; it was Brother and their mother. Tobin went cold at the sight of her. This was not the kind woman who'd taught him to write and draw. Bloody-faced, eyes burning with hatred, she pointed an accusing finger. Then both ghosts faded away, but not before Tobin saw what she held under her arm.

He scarcely remembered anything of the banquet after that. When the last dessert was finished he pleaded weariness and hurried upstairs. His traveling chest was still locked, but when he burrowed down through the tunics and shirts the doll was gone, just as he'd feared.

"Fine. I'm glad!" Tobin raged at the empty room. "Stay here together, like you always did!" He meant it, and couldn't understand why tears welled up to blind him.

Chapter 44

The weather held fair and the hunting was good. They rode out at dawn each day and combed the hills and brakes, returning with enough stags, bear, grouse, and conies to feed a regiment. The king was in good spirits, though Tobin knew better than to take this for granted. It was easier to relax and trust a little, without Niryn there to read his every thought and gesture.

Every night they drank and feasted, entertained by an ever-changing troupe of players. Tobin avoided the third floor and did not see the ghosts again.

"Maybe we should look for the doll," Ki said, when Tobin finally told him what had happened.

"Where? In the tower?" Tobin asked. "It's locked and the key is missing; I already asked Nari. And even if it wasn't, I wouldn't go up there again."

He'd thought about it, even dreamed about it, but nothing in the world would make him go near that room or that window again.

He put the doll out of his mind and Ki didn't mention it again. He was more concerned about Lhel. They'd slipped away and ridden up the mountain road several times, but found no sign of Lhel or Arkoniel.

"Probably safer for them, with this great crowd wandering everywhere," Ki said, but he sounded as disappointed as Tobin felt.

On his name day morning Tobin saw that a new pavilion had been erected just beyond the barracks. It was nearly as large, and made of brightly painted canvas hung with silk banners and gaily colored ribbons. When he asked about it, Korin replied with a wink and a smirk.

At the feast that night it was clear some conspiracy was afoot. Korin and the others spent the meal whispering and laughing among themselves. When the last of the honey cakes had been eaten, they rose and surrounded him.

"I've got a special birthday present for you, coz," said Korin. "Now that you're old enough."

"Old enough for what?" asked Tobin uneasily.

"Easier to show than tell!" Korin and Zusthra picked Tobin up and hoisted him on their shoulders. Looking back in alarm as they bore him away, he saw the squires blocking Ki from following. He didn't seem upset, though. Far from it, in fact.

"Happy birthday, Tob!" he called after him, laughing and waving with the others.

Tobin's worst fears were realized as they carried him down to the gaudy pavilion. It was a brothel, of course, run by one of the king's favorites in Ero. Inside, heavy tapestry curtains divided the tent into different rooms around a central receiving area. Braziers and polished brass lamps burned there, and it was furnished like a fine villa, with rich carpets and fancy wine tables. Girls in sheer silk chemises greeted the guests and guided them to velvet couches there.

"I chose for you," Korin announced proudly. "Here's your present!"

A pretty blond woman emerged from behind one of the tapestry walls and joined Tobin on his couch. The other Companions had girls of their own, and from the looks of things, they were far more at home with all this than he was. Even Nikides and Lutha appeared to be pleased with this development.

"You're a man now, and a warrior," said Korin, toasting him with a golden mazer. "It's time you tasted a man's pleasures!"

Caught in a nightmare, Tobin fought to hide his dismay. Alben was already smirking with Urmanis and Zusthra.

"I'm honored, my prince," the girl said, settling close beside him and offering him sweetmeats from a gilded plate. She was perhaps eighteen, but her eyes were as old as Lhel's as she looked him over. Her manner was demure, but there was hardness just behind her smile that curdled the dinner in Tobin's belly.

He let her fill his cup again and drank deeply, wishing he could just vanish or sink through the ground. He could do neither, unfortunately, and at last the girls rose and took their chosen paramours by the hand, leading them off to the rooms at the back of the pavilion.

Tobin's legs would hardly support him as the girl parted a curtain and drew him into a tapestry-walled inner chamber. A silver lamp hung from a chain overhead, and incense burned in a censer on a carved stand. Patterned carpets gave softly under his boots as she led him to a curtained bed. Still smiling her false smile, she began to unlace his tunic.

Caught between mortification and despair, Tobin kept his head down, praying she wouldn't see him blush. To run away would make him the laughingstock of the Companions, but the alternative was unthinkable.

Tobin's heart was hammering so hard in his ears that he hardly heard her when she stopped and whispered, "Would you rather not undress, my prince?"

She was waiting, but no words would come. He stared miserably at the floor and shook his head.

"Just this, then," she murmured, reaching for the lacings of his trousers. He flinched away and she stopped. They stood like that for some time, until he suddenly felt the soft brush of lips against his cheek.

"You don't want this, do you?" she whispered close to his ear. "I saw it the minute they dragged you in."

Tobin shuddered, imagining what she'd tell Korin

later. He'd cast Quirion out for cowardice in battle; would this amount to the same thing?

To his astonishment, she hugged him. "That's all right, then. You don't have to."

"I—I don't?" he quavered, and looked up to find her smiling, a real smile. The hardness had left her face; she looked very kind.

"Come, sit with me."

There was nowhere to sit but on the bed. She curled up against the bolsters and patted the place beside her. "Come on," she coaxed. "I won't do anything."

Hesitantly, Tobin joined her and pulled his knees up under his chin. By that time soft cries and louder grunting were coming from the other enclosures. Tobin resisted the urge to plug his ears; he recognized some of those voices and thanked the Four that the squires hadn't come along, too. He couldn't have stood hearing Ki going on like that. It sounded almost like they were in pain, yet it was strangely exciting, too. He felt his body responding and blushed more hotly than ever.

"The prince means well, I'm sure," the girl whispered, not sounding as if she meant it. "He's been quite the stag since he was younger than you, but he's a different sort of fellow, isn't he? Some boys aren't ready so young."

Tobin nodded. It was true enough, in its way.

"But you have your reputation among your friends to consider, I think?" she went on, and chuckled at Tobin's groan of agreement. "That's easily dealt with. Move over to the edge, if you please."

Still wary, Tobin did as she asked and watched in amazement as she knelt in the middle of the bed and began to make those alarming sounds, moaning, laughing deep in her throat, and letting out little yelps very much like those that were echoing around them now. Then, to his complete consternation, she began to bounce on the bed like a child. Without breaking off her cries, she grinned and held out her hands to Tobin.

Understanding at last, he joined her and started bouncing on his knees with her. The bed ropes creaked and the rails rattled. She raised her voice in an impressive crescendo, then collapsed on the bed with a breathy sigh. Burying her face in the coverlet, she smothered a fit of giggling.

"Well done, coz!" Korin called drunkenly.

Tobin covered his mouth with both hands to stifle his own sudden laughter. His companion looked up at him, eyes bright with shared merriment, and whispered gleefully, "I believe your reputation is safe, my prince."

Tobin lay down close beside her so he could keep his voice low. "But why?"

She rested her chin in her hands and gave him a sly look. "My task is to bring my customers pleasure. Did that please you?"

Tobin stifled another laugh. "Very much!"

"Then that's what I shall report to your cousin and the king when they ask me. Which they will." She gave him a sisterly kiss on the cheek. "You're not the first, my dear. A few of your friends out there share the same secret."

"Who?" Tobin asked. She clucked her tongue at him and he blushed again. "How can I thank you? I don't even have my purse with me."

She stroked his cheek fondly. "You are an innocent, aren't you? A prince never pays, my dear, not among my sort. I only ask that you remember me kindly and treat my sisters well when you're older."

"Your sisters—? Oh, I see. Yes, I will. But I don't even know your name."

She considered this, as if weighing the question. At last she smiled again, and said, "It's Yrena."

"Thank you, Yrena. I won't forget your kindness, not ever."

He could hear people moving around, the rustle of clothing and the rattle of belts.

"We'd better put on the finishing touches." Grinning,

she pulled the lacings of his tunic awry, tousled his hair, and pinched color into his cheeks with her fingers. Then, like an artist, she pulled back to inspect her work. "Nearly there, I think." Going to a small side table, she took up an alabaster rouge pot and painted her lips, then kissed him several times on the face and neck. When she was done she wiped her mouth on the sheet and pressed a last kiss to his brow. "There now, don't you look the proper wastrel? If your friends ask for details, just smile. That should be answer enough for them. If they insist on dragging you back, say you'll have only me."

"Do you think they might?" Tobin whispered, alarmed.

Laughing silently, Yrena kissed him again and sent him on his way.

Yrena's ruse worked. The Companions carried him back to the keep in triumph and the squires listened enviously as the other boys bragged about their evening's conquests. Tobin felt Ki's eyes on him every time he avoided answering questions.

Alone in their room later, Tobin could hardly look him in the face.

Ki hiked himself up onto the windowsill, grinning expectantly. "Well?"

After a moment's hesitation, Tobin told him the truth. Ki might laugh at him, but they could laugh together.

But his friend's reaction wasn't quite what he'd hoped. "You mean, you—couldn't?" he asked, frowning. "You said she was pretty!"

Every time he'd lied to Ki, it had been because of the same secret, and every time it had felt like a betrayal.

Tobin struggled with himself a moment longer, then shrugged. "I just didn't want to."

"You should have said something. Korin would have let you pick another—"

"No! I didn't want any of them."

Ki stared down at his dangling feet for a long time, then sighed. "So it *is* true."

"What's true?"

"That you—" It was Ki blushing now, and he still wouldn't look at Tobin. "That you don't—you know—fancy girls. I mean, I thought when you got older and all—"

The panic Tobin had felt in the brothel tent crept back. "I don't fancy anyone!" he shot back. Fear and guilt made the words come out angry.

"I'm sorry! I didn't mean—" Ki slid off the sill and took him by the shoulders. "That is, well—Oh, never mind. I didn't mean anything by it, all right?"

"Yes, you did!"

"It doesn't matter, Tob. It doesn't matter to me."

Tobin knew that wasn't true, but that Ki wanted it to be.

If only I could tell him, Tobin thought. *If he knew the truth. How would he look at me then?* The urge to blurt it all out was so strong that he had to turn away and press his lips together to stop the words.

Somewhere nearby, he could hear Brother laughing.

Neither of them spoke of it again, but Ki didn't join in with the others' good-natured teasing when Tobin found excuses not to go back to the painted tent.

Tobin rode out alone more often after that, searching for Lhel and Arkoniel, but they were still nowhere to be found.

Chapter 45

The king kept his promise and at mid-Kemmin, the Companions rode out to hunt bandits in the hill country north of Ero. Korin talked as brashly as ever, but Tobin could tell that he was anxious to redeem himself in their eyes. According to Tharin, whispers about his previous falter had found their way around the Palatine.

The night before the Companions left, the king hosted a feast in their honor. Princess Aliya sat at her father-in-law's right and played hostess. In spite of early fears, this pregnancy had progressed well. The birth was expected soon after the Sakor festival and her belly filled out the front of her gown like a great round loaf.

The king continued to dote on her, and she was all sweetness with him, and with everyone in public. In private, however, Ki's prediction had proven true. She was still the same harridan she'd always been, and the discomforts of her state had not improved her temper. Tobin escaped her sharp tongue most days, though only because he was Kin. Korin wasn't so fortunate; already exiled from his lady's bed for months, he'd quietly gone back to his old ways. Aliya had learned of it, of course, and the ensuing rows had become legendary. According to her lady-in-waiting, the princess had a strong throwing arm and excellent aim.

None of this made Tobin like her any better, but he found himself fascinated by her all the same, for she was the first pregnant woman he'd known. Lhel said this was part of a woman's secret power and he began to see what she meant, especially after Aliya insisted that he put his hand on her belly to feel the child move. Mortified at first, his embarrassment gave way to wonder as something hard and slippery skittered fleetingly against his palm. After that he often caught himself staring at her belly, watching for that mysterious play of movement. That was Korin's child, and his own kin.

That winter started wet and unseasonably warm. The Companions and their men set out in drizzle and didn't see the sun again for weeks. The roads were churned mud under their horses' hooves. Inns and forts were sparse in this part of the country, so they spent most nights in waxed canvas tents—damp, cheerless encampments.

The first pack of bandits they found was a paltry one, just a few ragged men and boys who'd been stealing cattle. They surrendered without a fight and Korin hanged the lot.

A week later they found a stronger band entrenched in a hillside cave. They captured their horses, but the men were well armed and held out for four days before hunger forced them out. Even then, they fought fiercely. Korin killed the leader in the midst of a bloody melee. Tobin added three more to his score, and without any help from Brother. He hadn't tried summoning the ghost or seen any sign of him since leaving the keep.

The soldiers stripped the bodies before burning them, and only then was it discovered that eight were women, including Ki's second kill. She had grey in her hair and old scars on her arms.

"I didn't know," he said, troubled.

"She was a bandit, Ki, same as the others," Tobin told him, but it gave him an odd feeling in his stomach, too.

Tharin and Koni had paused over another body. Tobin recognized the stained green tunic in Koni's hands; this had been one of his own kills. This woman was older than the other. Her sagging breasts and the thick streaks of white in her hair made him think of Cook.

"I knew her," Tharin said, draping a ragged cloak over the body. "She was a captain in the White Hawk Regiment."

"I can't believe I fought a woman!" Alben cried, rolling one of his kills over with his foot. He spat in disgust.

"There's no shame in it. They were warriors in their day." Tharin spoke quietly, but everyone heard the angry edge behind the words.

Porion shook his head. "No true warrior goes freebooter."

Tharin turned away.

Korin spat on the dead captain. "Renegade trash and traitors, all of them. Burn them with the others."

Tobin had no sympathy for lawbreakers—Una and Ahra had both found ways to serve without turning renegade and the women of Atyion were content to wait. But Tharin's unspoken anger stayed with him, unsettling as the smell of burned flesh that clung to their clothing as they rode away.

The dead captain haunted Tobin's dreams for weeks after, but she was not a vengeful spirit. Naked and bloody, she knelt weeping to lay her sword at his feet.

Chapter 46

The rains held steady through Cinrin. On Mourning Night high winds blew in off the sea, tearing the black shrouds from the bronze festival gongs and scattering them like funeral offerings through the rain-lashed streets. The gongs clashed against their posts, sounding a midnight alarm instead of the dawn triumph.

There were bad omens during ritual, as well. The Sakor bull resisted, tossing its head, and it took the king three strokes to make the critical gash. When Korin delivered the entrails and liver to the waiting priests, they found them riddled with worms. Propitiatory sacrifices were carried out at once, but a week later the portent was realized, or so it seemed.

Tobin was dining with Korin in his chambers that evening, a small affair in Aliya's honor. Rain drummed hard on the roof, all but drowning out the harp player.

It was an informal meal, and everyone was reclining on couches. Aliya laughed as Erius endeavored to make her comfortable with extra cushions.

"You're a carrack filled with treasure, my dear," he said, patting the great swell of her belly. "Ah, there he is, the fine fellow, kicking at his grandfather. And again! Are you certain you only have one baby in there?"

"I've felt so many pokes and jabs, you'd think I'm bearing a whole regiment!" She cradled her swollen middle. "But it's to be expected with a boy child, or so the drysians tell me."

"Another boy." Erius nodded. "The gods must favor a

Skalan king, or the Maker would not send us so many. First Korin, then young Tobin here for my sister. And all the girls gone. A libation for my grandson, and a toast! To the kings of Skala!"

Tobin had no choice but to join in, and did so with mixed emotions. He wished the child no harm.

"That was a rather paltry libation, Tobin," Erius chided, and Tobin realized with a start that he'd been watched.

"My apologies, Uncle," he said, hastily pouring out half his cup on the floor. "Blessings on Korin and his family."

"You mustn't be jealous, coz," Korin said.

"It's not like anyone ever expected you to be the true second heir, is it?" Aliya said, and Tobin went sick all over, wondering if anyone else saw the flash of naked malice in her eyes. "You'll always be Korin's right hand, of course. And what greater honor could there be?"

"Of course." Tobin forced a smile, wondering how she'd treat him once the child was born. "I never thought any differently."

The feast went on, but Tobin felt as if the whole world had suddenly shifted out from under his feet. He was sure he saw Aliya's father stealing hard looks at him, and the king's smiles seemed false. Even Korin ignored him. The food was tasteless in his mouth, but he forced himself to eat, in case someone was still watching him, judging his demeanor.

The first dessert had just been served when Aliya let out a sharp cry and gripped her belly. "The pains," she gasped, white with fear. "Oh Mother, the pains have come, just like last time!"

"It's all right, poppet. It's close enough to your time," the duchess said, beaming. "Come, let's get you to your bed. Korin, send for the midwives and drysians!"

Korin took Aliya's hands and kissed them. "I'll be with you soon, my love. Tobin, call the Companions and have them keep the vigil for us. My heir is coming!"

* * *

By custom, the Companions kept watch outside the birthing room. They milled nervously among the other courtiers, listening nervously to the shrill cries that came with increasing frequency from within.

"Is that how she's supposed to sound?" Tobin whispered to Ki. "It sounds like she's dying!"

Ki shrugged. "Some holler more than others, especially the first time." But as the night dragged on and the cries turned to screams, even he grew uneasy.

The midwives came and went with basins and grim faces. Just before dawn one of them summoned Tobin inside. As Royal Kin, he was required to be among the witnesses.

A crowd stood around the curtained bed, but a place was made for him by the king and Korin. His cousin was sweating and pale. Chancellor Hylus, Lord Niryn, and at least a dozen other ministers were there, together with priests of all four gods.

Aliya had stopped screaming; he could her ragged panting from the bed. Through a gap in the hangings Tobin caught sight of one bare leg, streaked with blood. He looked away quickly, feeling like he'd seen something shameful. Lhel had spoken of magic and power; this was more like torture.

"Soon now, I think," the king murmured, looking pleased.

As if in answer, Aliya let out a shrill scream that raised the hair on Tobin's neck. It was followed by several others, but the voices were not hers. Aliya's mother tumbled out from between the bed hangings in a dead faint and he heard women weeping.

"No!" Korin cried, tearing the curtains aside. "Aliya!"

Aliya sprawled like a broken doll in the middle of the blood-soaked bed, white as the linen nightgown rucked up around her hips. A midwife still knelt between her splayed legs, weeping over a swaddled bundle.

"The child," Korin demanded, holding out his arms for it.

"Oh my prince!" the woman sobbed. "It was no child!"

"Show it, woman!" Erius ordered.

Keeping her face averted, the midwife turned back the wrappings. It had no arms, and the face—or what should have been the face—was featureless below the bulging, misshapen brow except for slitted eyes and nostrils.

"Cursed," Korin whispered. "I am cursed!"

"No," rasped Erius. "Never say that!"

"Father, look at it—!"

Erius whirled and struck Korin across the face, knocking the prince off his feet. Tobin tried to catch him, but ended up sprawled under him instead.

Grasping Korin by the front of his tunic, Erius shook him violently, shouting, "Never say that! Never! Never, do you hear me?" He let go of Korin and rounded on the others. "Anyone who carries this tale will be burned alive, do you hear me?" He slammed out of the room, shouting for the room to be put under guard.

Korin staggered back to the bed. His nose was bleeding; it trickled down over his mouth and into his beard as he clasped her limp hand. "Aliya? Can you hear me? Wake up, damn you, and see what we've done!"

Tobin scrambled away, desperate to escape. As he turned for the door, however, he caught sight of Niryn calmly examining the dead child. He'd turned away from the others; Tobin could see only the side of his face, but a lifetime of reading faces made him catch his breath. The wizard looked pleased—triumphant, even. Shocked, Tobin did not have time to retreat before the wizard looked up and caught him staring.

And Tobin felt it; that nauseating feeling of cold fingers tickling through his bowels. He couldn't move or even look away. For a moment he was certain his heart had stopped in his chest.

Then he was released and Niryn was speaking to Korin as if the last few moments had not happened. The midwife had the little bundle now, though Tobin had not seen him pass it to her.

"It is undoubtedly necromancy," Niryn was saying. He stood close to Korin, a fatherly hand on his shoulder. "Rest assured, my prince, I will find the traitors and burn them." He glanced at Tobin again, eyes cold and soulless as a snake's.

Korin was weeping, but his fists were clenched and the muscles in his jaw worked furiously as he cried out, "Burn them. Burn them all!"

Standing outside with the others, Ki heard Erius shouting, and ducked out of the way when the king stormed out.

"Summon my Guard!" Erius roared, then rounded on the boys. "Go on, get out of here, all of you! Not a word, any of you. Swear it!"

They did, and scattered, all but Ki. Keeping watch from a doorway down the corridor, he waited until Tobin came out. One look at his friend's white, dazed face was enough to make him glad he'd stayed. He hurried Tobin back to their rooms, bundled him into an armchair by the fire with blankets and a mazer of strong wine, and sent Baldus to find Nik and Lutha.

Tobin downed a full mazer before he could speak, then told them only what they already knew; that the baby was stillborn. Ki saw how his hand shook and knew there was more to the tale than that, but Tobin wouldn't say. He just pulled his knees up under his chin and sat silent and shivering until Tanil arrived with news that Aliya was dead. Then Tobin put his head down and wept.

"Korin won't leave her," Mylirin told them as Ki tried to comfort Tobin. "Tanil and Caliel tried everything short of carrying him, until he ordered us out. He wouldn't even let Caliel stay. Niryn is still there with him, talking of nothing but burning wizards! I'm going back now and staying outside that door until they come out. Can I send for you, Prince Tobin, if Korin wants you?"

"Of course," Tobin whispered dully, wiping his cheeks with his sleeve.

Mylirin gave him a grateful look and went out.

Nikides shook his head. "What wizard could hurt an unborn child? If you ask me, it's Illior's—"

"No!" Tobin lurched up in his chair. "Don't say that. No one is to say that. Not ever."

That was no stillbirth, thought Ki.

Nikides was sharp and caught it, too. "You heard the prince," he told the others. "We never speak of it again."

Chapter 47

Lhel stayed with Arkoniel and the others at the mountain camp, but slept alone in her own hut. Her abrupt withdrawal hurt Arkoniel, she knew, but it was as it must be. The other wizards would not follow him if they saw him as her fancy man. As for Lhel, the Mother was not done with her.

As she'd foreseen, little Totmus died within a few weeks of their arrival. She joined the others in mourning him, but knew that the winter would be hard enough without a sickly one to tend. The others were strong.

With Cymeus to guide them, they strove to build a larger shelter before the storms hit. The children spent every spare minute gathering wood, and Lhel showed them how to forage for the year's last roots and mushrooms, and how to smoke the meat Noril and Kaulin brought in. Wythnir and the girls added to their stores hunting rabbits and grouse with their slings. Malkanus made himself unexpectedly useful one day by spell-slaying a fat sow bear that wandered into the camp.

Lhel showed the town dwellers how to make use of every bone, tooth, and shred of sinew, and how to suck the rich marrow from the long bones. She taught them how to tan every hide, stretching the raw skins on cedar branch racks and rubbing them with a mash of ashes and brains to cure them. Despite all this, the older wizards still did not trust her or she them, and she was careful to keep her spellcraft hidden. Let Arkoniel teach them what he would. That was the thread the Mother had spun.

The provisions they'd brought and what little they

could forage would not be enough and they all knew it. With a long winter staring them in the face, food, hay, clothing, and livestock would have to be carted in. Vornus and Lyan took the cart and set off along the north road to trade in the mining towns.

Snow found them soon after, sifting down from the grey sky in huge feathery flakes. Gentle but steady, it silently built up in mounds on the boughs and capped every stone and stump. By the time the wind was cold enough to make small, sharp flakes the Skalans had managed to construct a lean-to byre and one long, low-roofed cabin. It was crude, but large enough for them all to crowd into at night. They didn't have enough rope or mud to chink the walls, but Cerana wove a spell against drafts and Arkoniel set another on the bough-thatched roof, knitting the green branches tight against the weather.

On the night of the winter solstice Lhel brought Arkoniel into her hut. He had no thought of the Mother or Her rituals as they coupled, but he was hot and eager, and the sacrifice was well made. The Mother granted Lhel visions that night, and for the first time since she'd taken the young wizard to her bed, she was glad that his seed could not fill her belly with a child.

By the time dawn came, she was miles away, leaving not so much as a footprint in the snow for a farewell.

PART IV

The Plenimarans' first attack was not launched with armies or ships, or with the necromancers and their demons, but with a scattering of children abandoned along the Skalan coast.

—Ylania ë Sydani, Royal Historian

Chapter 48

A farmer driving his cart home after the day's trading in Ero noticed the little girl crying beside the road. He asked after her people, but she was too shy or too scared to tell him. Judging by her muddy wooden clogs and drab, rough-spun dress, she wasn't from the city. Perhaps she'd fallen off the back of another farm wagon. He stood up and scanned the road ahead, but it was empty.

He was a kind man and, with night coming on and no help in sight, there seemed nothing to do but carry her home to his wife. The child stopped crying when he lifted her onto the seat, but she was shivering. He wrapped his cloak around her and gave her a bit of the sugar candy he'd bought for his own little daughters.

"We'll tuck you in between my girls tonight and you'll be warm as a weevil in porridge," he promised, and clucked to his horse to walk on.

The little girl sneezed, then happily went on sucking the sugar lump. Born mute, she couldn't tell the man that she didn't understand his words. She knew he was kind, though, from the sound of his voice and the way he handled her. He was nothing like the strangers who'd carried her away from her village in a boat full of sad people and abandoned her on the roadside in the night.

She couldn't thank him for the sugar either, and that made her sad, for it eased the hot, swollen feeling in her throat.

Chapter 49

The dreary winter dragged on in Ero. Mourning banners for Aliya hung wet and tattered on every house and shop. Inside the Palatine walls everyone from the king to the lowest kitchen scullion wore black or dun and would for a year and a day. And the rains continued to fall.

The palace servants grumbled and burned censers of acrid herbs in the hallways. In the new Companions' mess, the cooks brewed bitter drysian teas to purify their blood.

"It's this open winter," Molay explained, when Tobin and Ki complained of it. "When the ground doesn't freeze, the foul humors breed thick, especially in the cities. No good will come of it."

He was soon proven right. The Red and Black Death erupted with renewed fury all along the eastern coast.

Niyrn quietly moved Nalia, now nearly twenty, to Cirna. Thanks to their remote location and lack of shipping trade, the fortress and village had been untouched by disease. The girl and her nurse were dismayed by this grim, lonely new home, but Niryn vowed to visit more often.

By Dostin the deathbirds had burned more than twenty houses in Ero harbor, with their plague-ridden occupants nailed up inside.

But that did not stop the spread of it. A plague house was discovered near the corn dealer's market, and the contagion spread through the surrounding neighborhood. Seven tenements and a temple of Sakor were burned there, but not before some of the terrified inhabitants escaped to spread the pestilence.

In mid-Dostin the Companions' favorite theater, the Golden Foot, was struck, and the whole company of actors, along with their dressers, wigmakers, and all the servants were condemned by quarantine.

Tobin and Ki wept at the news. These were the same players who'd entertained them at the keep during the name day hunt; they'd made friends among the actors.

The Foot lay just five streets down from the Palatine gate and the loss was compounded when the king canceled all audiences and sent word forbidding any Companion to leave the palace until further notice. With all entertainments forbidden for the first month of mourning, the boys found themselves trapped.

Master Porion urged them to continue with their training, but Korin was too despondent and often too drunk. Dressed in black, he moped alone in his rooms or walked in the rooftop gardens, hardly answering when anyone spoke to him. The only companionship he seemed able to tolerate was that of his father or Niryn.

The winds shifted at month's end and the drysians predicted that the shift would cleanse the air. Instead, a new and more devastating sickness struck. By all reports it had started in the countryside, with outbreaks reported from Ylani to Greyhead. In Ero the first cases were seen around the lower markets, and before any ban could be imposed it had already swept up to the citadel.

It was a pox, and began with soreness in the throat, followed within a day by the spread of small black pustules over the torso. If it stopped at the neck, the patient survived, but more often than not the spots spread to the face, then into the eyes, mouth, and finally, the throat. It reached its crisis within five days, at the end of which the sufferer was either dead, or hideously scarred and often blind. The Aurënfaie had seen such illnesses before and within days of the first outbreak there were few 'faie to be found in the city.

Niryn declared this the work of traitorous wizards turned necromancer. The Harriers redoubled their hunt despite more open dissent, especially against the burning of priests. Riots broke out around the Lightbearer's temples. The king's soldiers quelled such uprisings without mercy, but the burnings were once more held outside the city walls.

Illior's crescent began to appear everywhere—scrawled on walls, painted on lintels, even crudely drawn in white trailor's chalk on the mourning banners. People slipped into the Lightbearer's temples under cover of dark to make offerings and seek guidance.

Wizards proved strangely immune to the pox, but Iya did not dare risk a visit to Tobin for fear of carrying the infection to him. Instead, she used Arkoniel's translocation spell to send small ivory amulets inscribed with sigils of Illior to him, Ki, and Tharin.

As the outbreak worsened, piles of pox-ridden corpses mounted in the streets, abandoned by their frightened families at the first sign of illness, or perhaps simply dying where they'd fallen after blindly seeking help that never came. Anyone who even appeared infirm risked being stoned in the streets. The king gave orders for the sick to remain inside under pain of execution by the city guard.

Soon, however, there were few to enforce the order. Strong men—especially soldiers, seemed to be the most susceptible and the least likely to recover, while many who were old and infirm escaped with nothing worse than scars.

As the city sank into despair, Iya and her Wormhole compatriots grew bolder. It was they who drew the first crescents on city walls, and they who whispered to any who would listen: " 'So long as a daughter of Thelátimos'

line defends and rules, Skala shall never be subjugated.'
She is coming!"

Twenty-two wizards now lived in secret below the
abandoned Aurënfaie shops. Arkoniel's young shape
changer, Eyoli, had joined them there when snow cut him
off from Arkoniel's camp in the mountains.

Cut off from their customary entertainments, the Companions soon grew restless. Tobin went back to his sculpting and gave lessons to any who wanted to learn. Ki
showed a knack for it, and Lutha, too. Lynx could draw
and paint, and they began to collaborate on designs for
breastplates and helmets. Nikides shyly revealed a talent
for juggling.

Caliel attempted to organize a company of players
from available talent among the nobles, but after a few
weeks everyone was thoroughly bored with each other.
Cut off from the ladies of the town, most of the older boys
made do with serving girls again. Zusthra was betrothed to
a young duchess, but no marriages could be celebrated
during the first months of official mourning.

The female pains troubled Tobin more often now, no
matter what the moon's phase was. Usually it came on as a
fleeting ache, but other times, especially when the moon
was new or full, he could almost feel something moving in
his belly, the way Aliya's child had. It was a frightening
feeling and worse for having no one to talk to about it. He
began to have new dreams, too, or rather one dream, repeated night after night with variations.

It began in the tower at the keep. He was standing in
the middle of his mother's old room there, surrounded by
broken furniture and piles of moldy cloth and wool.
Brother stepped from the shadows and led him by the
hand down the stairs. It was too dark to see; Tobin had to
trust the ghost and the feel of the worn stone steps under
his feet.

It was all very clear, just as he remembered it, but when they reached the bottom of the stairs the door swung open and suddenly they were standing at the edge of a high precipice above the sea. It seemed like the cliffs at Cirna at first, but when he looked behind him, he saw green rolling hills marching into the distance and jagged stone peaks beyond. An old man watched him from the top of one of the hills. He was too far away to make out his features, but he wore the robes of a wizard and waved to Tobin as if he knew him.

Brother was still with him, and drew him away to the very edge of the cliff until Tobin's toes hung over the edge. Far below, a broad harbor shone like a mirror between two long arms of land. By some trick of the dream, he could see their faces reflected there but his was the face of a woman and Brother had turned into Ki. In the way of dreams, it surprised him every time.

Still teetering precariously on the brink, the woman she'd become turned to kiss Ki. She could hear the stranger on the hill shouting to her, but the wind carried his words away. Just as her lips met Ki's the wind pushed her over the edge and she fell—

It always ended that way and Tobin would wake to find himself sitting bolt upright in bed, heart pounding and an erection throbbing between his legs. He had no illusions about that anymore. On those nights when Ki stirred in his sleep and reached out to him, Tobin fled and spent the rest of the night wandering the palace corridors. Yearning for things he dared not hope for, he pressed his fingers to his lips, trying to recall the feel of that kiss.

The dream always left him low-spirited and a little scatterbrained the next day. More than once he caught himself staring at Ki, wondering what it would feel like actually to kiss him. He was quick to squelch such thoughts and Ki remained oblivious, distracted by the more tangible affections of several welcoming servant girls.

Ki slipped away with them more often now and sometimes didn't come back until dawn. By unspoken agreement, Tobin did not complain of these sorties and Ki did not brag of them, at least not to him.

One windy night in Klesin, Tobin was alone once again, pondering designs for a set of jeweled brooches for Korin's mourning cloak. It was a stormy night and the wind made lonely sounds in the eaves outside. Nik and Lutha had come by looking for him earlier, but Tobin was in no mood for company. Ki was off with Ranar, the girl in charge of the linens.

The work allowed him to escape his racing thoughts for a while. He was good at sculpting, even famous for it. During the previous year's royal progress, pieces he'd made for his friends had caught the fancies of their hosts. Many had since sent gifts, along with precious metals and jewels, requesting a bit of jewelry to remember him by. The exchange of gifts was not only acceptable, Nikides had observed, but held the possibility of connections of other sorts being made later on. Who wouldn't want to be thought well of by the future king's beloved cousin? Tobin had read enough history to appreciate the wisdom of this advice and accepted most commissions.

Nonetheless, it was the work itself he really cared for. To bring an image in his head to reality in his hands pleased him in a way nothing else did.

He was nearly finished with the first wax carving when Baldus brought word of a visitor.

"I'm busy. Who is it?" Tobin grumbled.

"It's me, Tobin," Tharin said, looking in over the page's head. His cloak was rain spattered and his long, pale hair windblown. "Thought you might like a game of bakshi."

"Come in!" Tobin exclaimed, his dark mood falling away. It had been weeks since the two of them had had a quiet moment alone. "Baldus, take Sir Tharin's cloak and fetch us wine. And send for something to eat—a dark loaf and some cold beef and cheese. And a pot of mustard, too! Never mind the wine. Bring us ale."

Tharin chuckled as the boy ran off. "That's barracks fare, my prince."

"And I still prefer it and the company that goes with it."

Tharin joined him at the workbench and examined the sketches and half-finished carvings. "Your mother would be proud. I remember when she gave you that first lump of wax."

Tobin glanced up in surprise; Tharin seldom spoke of her.

"Your father, too," he added. "But she was the artist of the pair. You should have seen him working on that toy city of yours. You'd have thought he was rebuilding Ero full scale, the way he labored over it."

"I wish I could have shown him these." Tobin pointed at three miniature wood-and-clay structures on a shelf over the bench. "Remember the Old Palace he made?"

Tharin grinned. "Oh, yes. Out of a fish-salting box, as I recall."

"I never noticed! Well, these aren't much better. As soon as the plague bans are lifted, I'm going to talk to real builders and ask to learn their craft. I see houses in my head, and temples with white columns and domes even, bigger than anything in Ero."

"You'll do it, too. You've a maker's soul, as much a warrior's."

Tobin looked up in surprise. "Someone else told me that."

"Who was that?"

"An Aurënfaie goldsmith named Tyral. He said Illior and Dalna put the skill in my hands, and that I'd be happier making things than fighting."

Tharin nodded slowly, then asked, "And what do you think, now that you've done both?"

"I'm a good warrior, aren't I?" he asked, knowing that

Tharin was probably the only person who'd ever give him an honest answer.

"Of course you are! But that's not what I asked."

Tobin picked up a slender triangular file and twirled it between his fingers. "I guess the Aurënfaie was right. I'm proud to fight, and I'm not afraid. But I am happiest messing about with all this."

"That's nothing to be ashamed of, you know."

"Would my father say the same?"

Baldus and two servers bustled in with bottles and trays and laid a table for them by the hearth. Tobin sent them out again, and poured the ale while Tharin cut slices of meat and cheese and set them to warm on thick slices of bread by the fire.

"This is almost as good as being home," Tobin said, watching him work. "It's been a long time since you and I have sat alone by a hearth. What made you think of it tonight?"

"Oh, I've been meaning to. But as it happens, I've had rather an odd visitor today. A woman named Lhel, who claims to be a friend of yours. Yes, I can see by your face you know the name."

"Lhel? But how did she get here?" Tobin's heart turned to lead in his chest as Iya's warning echoed in his memory. What would she do if Lhel had told Tharin his secret?

Tharin scratched his head. "Well now, that's the odd part. She didn't so much come to me as appear. I was reading in my room and heard someone call my name. When I looked up, there was this little hill woman, floating in the middle of the room in a circle of light. I could see the keep behind her, clear as I see you now. To be honest, I thought maybe I'd dreamed it all until just now."

"Why did she come to you?"

"We had quite a chat, she and I." Tharin's eyes grew sad. "I'm not a brilliant man like your father and Arkoniel, but I'm no fool, either. She didn't tell me much I hadn't guessed at already."

Tobin had longed to speak the truth to Tharin, but now he could only sit dumbstruck, waiting to hear how much Lhel had actually revealed.

"I wasn't there when you were born," Tharin said, bending down to turn the bread on the hearthstones. "It always struck me odd, Rhius sending me off just then on an errand his steward could have taken care of. I'd always thought it was your mother's doing."

"My mother?"

"She was jealous of me, Tobin, though Illior knows I never gave her any cause to be."

Tobin shifted uneasily in his chair. "Ki told me—That is, about you and my father."

"Did he? Well, that was all in the past by the time he married her, but it was no secret, either. More than once I offered to take some other post, but Rhius wouldn't hear of it.

"So that night I thought it was her decision, me not being there. I didn't think much of it until the day your father died. I told you how his last words were of you, didn't I? But I never told you what he said. He knew he was dying—" Tharin stopped and cleared his throat. "I'm sorry. You'd think after all this time—But it's always like it was yesterday. With his last breath he whispered to me, 'Protect my child with your life. Tobin must rule Skala.' Illior forgive me, I thought his mind was wandering. But later, when I told Arkoniel about it, the look in his eyes said otherwise. He couldn't tell me more and asked me if I could keep my vow to your father, knowing no more than I did. You can guess the answer to that."

Tobin blinked back tears. "I've always trusted you."

Tharin raised his fist to his breast in salute. "I pray you always do, Tobin. As I said before, I'm not clever, and I came to think that with all the wars and plagues, maybe you'd be the last heir left to take the throne. But there were other things I'd wondered about. Like why you and Ki called that demon twin of yours 'Brother' rather than 'Sister.' "

"You heard that? And you never asked."

"I gave Arkoniel my word I wouldn't."

"But Lhel came and told you about him?"

"She didn't have to. I saw him."

"Where?"

"At Lord Orun's house the day he died."

"He killed Orun," Tobin blurted out.

"I thought as much. He was still crouched over the body when I kicked the door in. I thought it was you at first, until the thing looked around at me. By the Light, I don't know how you've stood it all these years. The one glimpse I had turned my blood cold."

"But you never told Iya what he did."

"I thought you would."

"What else did Lhel tell you? About me?"

"That you must claim the throne someday. And that I should keep myself ready and never doubt you."

"That's all?"

"That's all, except that she'd had her eye on me for a long time and thought well of me." He shook his head. "I knew what she was the minute I saw the witch marks on her face. But even so, I was glad of her good opinion."

"She always said Iya and Father should have told you. Arkoniel thought so, too. It was Iya who said no. I know Father would have, if it hadn't been for her."

"It doesn't matter, Tobin. He did tell me in his own way when it mattered the most."

"It was to protect you," Tobin admitted, though he still held it against the wizard. "She says Niryn can read minds. I had to learn how to cover my thoughts. That's why Ki doesn't know, either. You won't tell him, will you?"

Tharin handed Tobin some of the warm bread and cheese. "Of course I won't. But I imagine it's been hard on you, keeping so much to yourself all this time. Especially from him."

"You don't know how many times I almost said something! And now—"

"Yes, and now." Tharin took a bite of bread and chewed it slowly before going on. At last he sighed, and said, "Ki knows how you feel about him, Tobin. Anyone can see it, the way you look at him. He loves you in his way, too, but it's as much as you can expect from him."

Tobin felt his face go hot. "I know that. He's got half a dozen girls in love with him. He's with one of them now."

"He's his father's son, Tobin, and can't help wanting to play the tomcat." He gave Tobin a wry look. "There are those who'd welcome a warm look from you, you know."

"I don't care about that!" But even as he said it, a little voice in the back of his mind whispered *Who?*

"Well, it might be wise to at least consider it. Lhel said as much. A fellow your age ought to be showing some interest, especially a prince who can have his choice."

"What does it matter to anyone?"

"It matters. And it would be easier on Ki if you seemed happier."

"Lhel told you this?"

"No, Ki did."

"Ki?" Tobin wished the chair would swallow him.

"He can't feel what you want him to feel, and it hurts him. You know he would if he could."

There was no answer for that. "Everyone's always said I'm odd. I guess they can just go on thinking it."

"You have good friends, Tobin. One of these days you'll find out just how good. I know this is hard for you—"

"You know? How could you know?" All the years of fear and secrets and pain caved in around him. "How could you know what it's like to always have to lie, and be lied to? To not even know what your real face looks like until someone shows it to you? And Ki? At least my father knew how you really felt!"

Tharin busied himself with the bread again. "And you think that made it easier, do you? It didn't."

Tobin's anger dissolved to shame. How could he rail at Tharin, of all people, especially after he'd revealed so much? Sliding from his chair, he clung to him, hiding his face against Tharin's shoulder. "I'm sorry. I had no right to say that!"

Tharin patted his back as if Tobin was still the little boy he'd carried on his shoulders. "It's all right. You're just starting to see what the world's really like."

"I've seen it. It's ugly and hateful."

Tharin tilted Tobin's chin up with one finger and looked him sternly in the eye. "It can be. But the way I see it, you're here to change that, make it better. A lot of folks have gone to a lot of trouble for you. Your father died for it, and so did your poor mother. But you're not alone as long as I'm alive. Whenever the time comes, I promise you, I won't let you be alone."

"I know." Tobin sat back and wiped at his nose. "When the time comes, I'm going to make you a great, rich lord, and no one can stop me."

"Not if I have anything to say about it!" Tharin's faded blue eyes were bright with amusement and affection as he handed Tobin another slice of bread. "I'm right where I want to be, Tobin. I always have been."

Chapter 50

No one saw them coming, not even those of us who'd sworn our lives as guardians. Who would have thought to look for an attack by sea on such a night? What captain would cross the Inner Sea that time of year?

The winds piled the waves like haystacks beyond the harbor's mouth that night, and shredded the clouds across the moon. The lookouts could hardly be blamed for missing them; you couldn't see your neighbor's house.

The great striped-sailed fleet of Plenimar sailed out of the very jaws of the gale and took Ero unawares. They'd sailed the last miles with lanterns doused—a feat that cost them ships and men but gained them the crucial element of surprise. Nineteen wrecks would eventually be cataloged; the number that made anchor just north of Ero was never known but the force that disembarked numbered in the thousands. Taking the outposts by surprise, they slaughtered every Skalan they found regardless of age and were at the city gates before the alarm went up.

Half the city was dead or dying of that winter pox; there were scarcely enough soldiers left to hold the gates.

—Lyman the Younger,
First Chronicler of the Orëska House.

*　　*　　*

$\mathcal{T}$he storm that night was so loud that the Palatine guards did not hear the first alarms in the lower city. Runners brought word, spreading panic up to the citadel like wildfire.

The sound of gongs and shouting woke Ki. He thought at first that he was dreaming of the Sakor festival. He was about to pull the pillows over his head when Tobin lurched out of bed, taking the covers with him.

"It's an alarm, Ki. Get up!" he cried, fumbling about in the dim glow of the night lamp. Ki sprang from bed and pulled on the first tunic his hands found.

Molay burst in still wearing his nightshirt. "It's an attack, my lords! Arm yourselves! The king wants every man to the audience chamber!"

"Is it Plenimar?" asked Tobin.

"That's what I heard, my prince. The messenger claims the districts outside the walls are in flames from Beacon Head to Beggar's Bridge."

"Go wake Lutha and Nik—"

"We're here!" Lutha cried, as they rushed in with their squires.

"Get dressed. Arm yourselves and meet me here," Tobin ordered. "Molay, where's Korin?"

"I don't—"

"Never mind! Send for Tharin and my guard!"

Ki's hands shook as he helped Tobin into his padded shirt and hauberk. "This is no bandit raid, eh?" he muttered, trying to make light of it. "Tobin?" For a moment he thought his friend hadn't heard.

"I'm all right. This just isn't quite how I pictured our first real battle." Tobin took Ki's hand in the warrior clasp. "You'll stand by me, won't you? No matter what?"

"Of course I will!" Ki searched Tobin's face again. "Are you sure you're all right?"

Tobin squeezed Ki's hand. "I'm sure. Come on."

*　　*　　*

Iya stood on the roof of the tenement above the Wormhole, cursing furiously against the wind. It blew in from the sea, carrying the stench of burning. The harbor wards were in flames and beyond that enemy warships blocked the harbor mouth. Skalan ships in dry dock had been set aflame, and those at anchor had been cut loose to run aground.

The enemy hadn't breached the walls yet, but they would. She'd already scryed their positions and found sappers and necromancers at work. They'd set up catapults, as well, and were lobbing some sort of fire over the eastern wall. Smoke was already billowing in the dyers' ward.

The streets below were impassable. Throngs of people were running downhill with any implement they could find. Others were trying to drive cartloads of household goods through the crowds, not realizing that there was no escape. The enemy had men before every gate.

None of that was her concern. She'd cast seeking spells for the boys already, only to find that they'd left the amulets she'd sent them in their room. Bracing herself against the wind, she closed her eyes and summoned another spell, though she already feared where they must be. Her eyes burned behind her lids; pain throbbed in her temples, but she found them at last.

"Damnation!" she screamed, shaking her fists at the sky.

There was no question of the Companions being left behind. With half the city garrison already dead of plague and Plenimaran rams pounding at every gate, no warrior could be spared. Armed with bows and swords, the boys took their place at the head of the column massed on the practice grounds. The king mounted his black charger and held up the Sword of Ghërilain. Raising his voice to be heard over the wind, he shouted, "There's no time for long speeches. I've just gotten word that there are necromancers at the east gate. May Sakor judge the enemy for the cowards they are and give the victory to us today. Stand together, warriors of Skala, and drive the marauders from our shores! Every gate must be held, and every foot of wall. They must not enter!" Wheeling his horse, he led them out.

The rest of them followed on foot. Looking over his shoulder, Tobin could see Tharin and his men just behind him, bearing the royal standard of Atyion. Ki walked grimly at his side, their extra quivers rattling against his back.

They cleared the gates and Tobin caught his breath. In the grey light of dawn, he could see the banks of smoke rolling up from the ruins outside the city walls. There were defenders already on the walls, but too few and too sparsely deployed.

The reason for this soon became horrifyingly clear. The Companions had not been allowed down into the city since the pox struck, and none of the reports had prepared them for the reality of the situation. Erǫ was a charnel house.

Bodies lay rotting in every street, too many for the dead carriers to deal with. Perhaps they were all dead, too. Tobin shuddered as they passed a sow and her young pulling the body of a young girl to pieces. Everywhere he looked, the living stepped around the dead as if they were piles of garbage. Even with the cold wind, the stench was sickening.

"If the Plenimarans don't get us, the pox will!" Ki muttered, clapping a hand across his mouth.

A ragged woman knelt keening over the body of her pox-raddled child, but looked up as they passed. "You are cursed, Erius son of Agnalain, and all your house! You've brought Illior's curse down on this land!"

Tobin looked away quickly as a soldier raised a club to silence her. Erius gave no sign that he'd heard, but Tobin saw Korin flinch.

The streets near the east gate were nearly impassable,

choked with panicked people, carts, and crazed animals of all sorts. Erius' guard swept ahead with truncheons to clear the way.

At the walls, however, they found men, women, even children ready to repel the invaders. The tops of the walls and towers were lined with men, but there too they were thinly spread. As Tobin watched, a few enemy soldiers gained the top and were savagely repelled. Arrows hissed overhead, and some found their mark. Skalan warriors tumbled down to join the heaps of dead and dying below.

"Look," said Ki, pointing to a pile of bodies. Two dead Plenimarans lay tangled with the others. They both wore black tunics over their mail, and had long black hair and braided beards. It was the first time either of them had actually seen a Plenimaran.

"To the walls!" Erius shouted, dismounting and brandishing his sword again.

"With me, Companions!" Korin cried, and Tobin and the others followed him up the shuddering wooden stairs to the hoardings above.

From here, Tobin could look down through the arrow slits and murder holes at the seething mass of fighters below. The Skalan defenders hurled stones down at them and dumped buckets of hot oil and tar, but it did no more than create a temporary gap in the press. The Plenimarans had already set up hundreds of square wooden mantlets to shelter their archers, and they kept up a steady hail of arrows from there. At the gate below, a sappers' shed had been moved up against the doors and Tobin heard the dull, steady rhythm of a battering ram crew at work.

Shoulder to shoulder with Ki and Tharin, Tobin raised his bow and took aim at the forces swarming below. When their arrows were spent, they helped dump stones through the murder holes and push off scaling ladders. Some still made it up, however, and they found themselves running endlessly to beat them back. Ki was still beside him, and Tobin caught glimpses of some of the other boys, but as the battle went on they got separated from them among the other defenders. Tobin lost sight of Korin but even in the worst of it, Tharin and Ki were there at his back.

It all seemed to go on forever. They gathered what arrows they could and shot back, and used long poles to push off more scaling ladders. Tobin and Ki had just finished with another one, sending half a dozen men falling back onto their comrades, when an arrow struck the cheek guard of Tobin's helm. He staggered and a second hit his right shoulder, bruising him through the mail and padding. Ki and Tharin pulled him to cover in a hoarding.

"How bad is it?" Tharin asked, ripping back the torn sleeve of Tobin's surcoat.

Before Tobin could tell him that it was nothing, a catapult stone shattered the wooden wall a few feet from where they stood and they were all thrown to their knees.

An instant later a huge roar erupted to their left and the stone parapet shuddered beneath them. Screams rang out and men came stampeding past, shouting, "They've broken through!"

Leaping up, Tobin looked out through an arrow slit and saw a heap of shattered stone and wood where the gates had been. Enemy soldiers were pouring through.

"That's necromancers' work," Tharin gasped. "The ramming crew was only a decoy!"

Caliel and Korin ran past. "Zusthra's dead, and Chylnir!" Caliel cried, as Tobin and his men followed.

A few yards on they found Lynx crouched over Orneus, trying to shield his fallen friend from being trampled. Both of them were bloody. A black-fletched arrow had struck Orneus in the throat. His head lolled and his eyes were blank and fixed. Lynx threw his own helmet aside and tried to lift him.

"Leave him, he's dead!" Korin ordered as he passed.

"No!" Lynx cried.

"You can't help him!" yelled Tharin. Hauling the sobbing squire to his feet, he clapped the helmet back on his head and shoved him into a trot in front of him.

Fighting their way through another mass of men, they found General Rheynaris kneeling beside the king. Erius' helm was gone and blood flowed from a gash across his brow, but he was alive and furious. As Korin reached him he staggered to his feet and pushed the others away. "It's nothing, damn you! Get away from me and do your duty. They've broken through! Korin, take your men down the stair near Water Street and outflank the bastards. Get down there, all of you, and drive them back!"

Water Street was empty when they reached it and they stopped to take stock of who was left. Tobin saw with alarm that Lutha and Nikides weren't with them.

"I lost sight of them about an hour ago," Urmanis told them, leaning on Garol. His right arm hung useless in a makeshift sling.

"I saw them just before the gates went down," said Alben. "They were with Zusthra."

"Oh hell! Caliel, did you see them?" Ki asked.

"No, but if they were anywhere beyond where I last saw him—" Caliel trailed off hoarsely.

Tharin, Melnoth, and Porion took count and found they had fewer than forty men accounted for. Tobin looked anxiously around at his guardsmen and was glad to find most of them still with him. Koni gave him a weary salute.

"There's no time to worry about the missing now," Captain Melnoth said. "What are your orders, Prince Korin?"

"Don't worry," Tharin murmured to Tobin. "If Nikides and Lutha are alive, they'll find us."

"Prince Korin, what are your orders?" Melnoth asked again.

Korin stared toward the sound of fighting, saying nothing.

Porion moved to the prince's side. "Your orders, my prince."

Korin turned and Tobin read fear plain in his cousin's

eyes. This must be what Ahra had seen during that first raid. Korin looked imploringly at Porion. Melnoth turned away to hide his look of dismay.

"Prince Korin, I know this part of the city," Tharin told him. "We'd do best to go through that alley over there to Broad Street and see if we can pick off any scouting parties they send our way."

Korin nodded slowly. "Yes—yes, we'll do that."

Ki shot Tobin a worried look as they drew their swords and followed.

They encountered two small scouting groups and managed to kill most of them, but as they headed back toward the gates they were nearly overrun by a huge force running through the streets with torches, setting everything in their path ablaze. There was no choice but to run.

"This way!" Korin yelled, dashing up a side street.

"No, not that way!" shouted Tharin, but the prince was already gone. They had no choice but to follow.

Rounding a corner, they found themselves cornered in a small market square. No other streets let out from it, and several of the surrounding buildings were already in flames. Dashing through the nearest doorway, they took cover in an inn, only to find that more flames blocked the sole exit in the back.

Tobin ran to the front of the house and peered out through a broken shutter. "Oh hell, Kor, we're trapped!"

The enemy had followed them. There were at least sixty men outside, talking among themselves in their coarse, guttural tongue. Several were advancing with torches to set the inn afire; as Tobin and the others watched, they threw the brands onto the roof. Archers stood ready to shoot anyone who tried to escape out the front.

"We'll have to fight our way through," said Ki.

"There are too many!" Korin snapped. "It's madness to go out there."

"And it's death if we stay here," Porion told him. "If we

LYNN FLEWELLING

put your guard in the forefront and Prince Tobin's behind, we might be able to rush them." He gave them a grim smile. "This is what I trained you for, boys."

There was little hope and they all knew it, but they formed up quickly, with the Companions massed around Korin. Everyone looked scared, except Lynx, who hadn't spoken since they'd come off the walls. Clutching his sword, he saw Tobin watching him and made him a slight bow, as if to say farewell.

Tobin caught Ki's eye and did the same, but Ki just set his jaw stubbornly and shook his head. Behind them, Tharin muttered what sounded like, "I'm sorry," as he rubbed the smoke from his eyes.

"On your order, Prince Korin," whispered Melnoth.

Tobin was proud to see that Korin did not falter as he raised his hand to give the signal.

Before they could throw the doors open, however, they heard an outcry in the yard, then screams of pain.

Rushing back to the windows, they saw Plenimaran soldiers writhing on the ground, engulfed by blue-white flame. It spread to any who tried to help them, and the rest were already scattering in panic.

"The Harriers!" Korin exclaimed.

Tobin had guessed the same but saw only a few ragged-looking people running away down the alley. Then a lone figure stepped from the shadows into the red light. "Prince Tobin, are you there?"

It was Iya.

"I'm here!" he called back.

"It's safe for the moment, but we'd best hurry," she called.

Melnoth grabbed his arm as he started for the door. "You know her?"

"Yes. She was a friend of my father. She's a wizard," he added, as if it needed any explanation.

Iya bowed low to Korin as they came out. "Are you hurt, Highness?"

"No, thank you."

Tobin stared down at the charred, twisted corpses around the yard. "I—I didn't know you could do—"

"I had a bit of help. They've gone on to see what else they can do to halt the invaders. I fear there's little hope, though. Prince Korin, your father was wounded and carried back to the Palatine. I suggest you join him there at once. Come, I know a safe route. The Plenimarans haven't broken through to the upper wards yet."

Night was coming on and a cold drizzle soaked them as they trudged toward the Palatine. A heavy lethargy stole over Tobin, and the other boys were silent, too. It went beyond exhaustion or hunger. They'd all looked Bilairy in the face at that inn; if it hadn't been for Iya and her mysterious helpers, they'd all be roasting in the embers.

Their way was blocked here and there by rough barricades—carts, furniture, chicken coops, scraps of lumber—anything the panicked defenders had been able to lay their hands on. In one street they were forced to crawl under a cartload of pox victims.

It was quiet here, but there had been fighting. Men of both armies lay dead in the streets, and Tobin saw several Harrier wizards and guards among the dead.

"I didn't think you could kill them!" Alben exclaimed, giving a dead wizard a wide berth.

"You can kill most wizards easily enough." Iya paused and held her hand over what remained of the dead man's face. After a moment she shook her head contemptuously. "Most of these white-robes are just bullies who've learned to hunt in packs. They intimidate and torture those weaker than themselves like wolves chasing down a sick deer. They're good for little else."

"You're speaking treason, Mistress," Korin warned. "I tell you that as someone who owes you his life, but you must be careful."

"Forgive me, my prince." Iya tapped the numbered

brooch at her throat. "I know better than you how danger-ous it is to speak against your father's wizards. I'll presume once more, though, and tell you that his fears are mis-placed. The wizards and priests who've died were as loyal to Skala as you or I. We're fighting for Ero even now. I hope you'll remember that later on."

Korin gave her a curt nod, but said nothing.

The upper wards were untouched, but from their van-tage point Tobin could see that much of the lower city was burning, the flames spread by the marauders and the wind.

As the Palatine gate came into sight ahead of them Iya motioned for Ki to go on ahead and drew Tobin aside. "Keep close to your friends," she whispered. "Your hour is coming and this is the sign. The Afran Oracle showed me, though I did not understand at the time. Keep the doll with you. Don't be parted from it!"

Tobin swallowed hard. "It's at the keep."

"What? Tobin, what possessed you—"

"My mother took it back."

Iya shook her head. "I see. I'll do what I can, then." She looked around quickly, then whispered, "Keep Koni by you at all costs. Don't let him out of your sight, do you hear?"

"Koni?" The young fletcher was one of Tobin's fa-vorites among his guard, but Iya had never shown any in-terest in the man before.

"I have to leave you now. Remember all I've said." And she was gone, as if the earth had swallowed her.

"Iya?" Tobin whispered, looking around in alarm. "Iya, I don't know if I'm ready. I don't know what to do!"

But she was gone and some of the others were looking back at him, wondering why he'd lagged behind. Tobin ran to catch up.

"Funny, her showing up like that just when she was needed, and gone just as fast, eh?" said Ki.

"There you are!" Koni exclaimed, falling in beside them. Tobin wanted to ask if Iya had spoken to him, too, but didn't dare with so many others listening. "I lost you once down there on the walls. I don't mean to again."

"Or me," said Tharin, looking more haggard than Tobin had ever seen him. "That was a bad moment, back there." He shot a quick look at Korin and lowered his voice. "Keep your eye on me during the next fight."

"I will." It still hurt to think ill of Korin, but he'd seen it for himself this time, the hesitation Ahra had spoken of. It had nearly cost them their lives.

Chapter 51

"How is my father?" Korin demanded of the guards at the Palatine gate.

"Wounded, my prince," the sergeant told him. "He sent word to tell you that he's in the summer pavilion near the temple. You're to go to him at once."

The Palatine was crowded with the wounded and refugees from the lower wards, and with livestock driven there in case of siege. Goats and sheep bleated at them from villa gardens, and pigs were rooting along the elm-lined avenue beyond the gate.

Scattered cheers greeted the Companions as they hurried on. The palaces and most of the villas were dark as Mourning Night, but watch fires burned everywhere. The open grounds and gardens where they'd trained now looked like a battlefield. People huddled around fires, cloaks pulled over their heads against the rain. The smells of smoke and cooking were heavy on the air. Tobin could hear children crying in the dark, horses nickering, and, on all sides, the steady murmur of worried talk.

The pavilion was brightly lit. Inside, officers and nobles milled about nervously, keeping a hushed watch.

A smaller group was gathered around a table at the center of the enclosure. The other Companions hung back as Tobin and Korin went to join them.

"My princes, thank the Four!" Hylus called, as they approached. "We feared you were lost."

Erius lay on a table, his face white, eyes closed. He was naked from the waist up and Tobin saw that his right side was badly bruised, and his arm splinted. The Sword of Ghërilain lay at his left side, the blade black with blood.

General Rheynaris was with him, and Niryn stood at the foot of the table, looking grave. Officers and servants stood close by and Tobin saw Moriel among them. He was dressed for battle and his surcoat was stained with soot and blood. He met Tobin's eye and saluted him. Surprised, Tobin nodded at him, then turned back to the king.

Korin's face was pale in the firelight as he leaned over his father. "What happened?"

"A necromancer's spell struck the wall near us soon after we last saw you, my prince," Rheynaris replied. His face was bloody and his left eye was swollen shut. "It shattered the wall and fragments struck your father down."

Korin clasped the king's good hand. "Will he live?"

"Yes, my prince," a grey-haired drysian replied.

"Of course I will," Erius rumbled, opening his eyes. "Korin—What news in the city?"

Rheynaris caught the prince's eye and shook his head.

"The fight goes on, Father," Korin told him.

Erius nodded and closed his eyes again.

Tobin stood with them for a while, then went back to join the others around one of the braziers near the stairs.

They'd been there for some time when a familiar voice cried out, "There they are. They're alive!"

Nikides and Lutha emerged from the crowd below and ran to embrace Tobin and Ki. Barieus was with them, but there was no sign of Ruan. They were as filthy as everyone else, but appeared to be unhurt.

"We thought you'd died with Zusthra at the gates!" Tobin replied, relieved beyond words to see his friends alive.

"Where's Ruan?" asked Ki.

"Dead," Nikides said, and his voice was hoarse with emotion. "A Plenimaran came at me from behind and Ruan got between us. He saved my life."

Ki sat down heavily on the steps beside Lynx. Barieus sat with him and pulled his cloak over his head.

"Oh Nik, I'm sorry. He died a hero," Tobin said, but the words were hollow. "Orneus is dead, too."

"Poor Lynx." Lutha shook his head. "That's three more of us gone."

The drysians must have done their work well, for when they'd finished the king refused to be carried to the palace, but instead demanded a chair be brought. Moriel and Rheynaris helped him into it and Korin placed the Sword of Ghërilain across his father's knees. Niryn and Hylus stood behind the makeshift throne like sentinels.

Erius leaned heavily on the arm of the chair, fighting for breath. Erius gestured for Korin to kneel by his side and they spoke for a while in low voices. The king gestured to Niryn, Rheynaris, and Hylus to join them, and the debate went on.

"What's going on?" Tobin whispered to Nikides. "Your grandfather looks worried."

"The reports are bad. Our warriors managed to block the east gate again, but there are still Plenimarans loose in the lower wards, and word came in a while ago that another group has broken through at the south gate. Their necromancers are worse than any of the stories. The Harriers are all but useless against them."

Lutha glanced over at Niryn. "Seems all they're good for is burning wizards and hanging priests."

"Careful," Tobin warned.

"What it comes down to is that we can't hold them off," Lutha said, keeping his voice down. "We just don't have enough men."

Nikides nodded. "No one wants to say it yet, but Ero is lost."

The rain had stopped at last and the clouds were breaking up and scudding west. Patches of stars showed through, so bright they cast shadows. Illior's crescent hung over the city like a sharp, white claw.

Food was brought out from the palaces and temples, but the Companions had little appetite. Wrapped in their cloaks against the cold spring night, they sat on the stairs and sharpened their swords, awaiting orders.

*T*ired beyond words, Ki finally gave up and put his back against Tobin's, resting his head on his knees. Caliel and the remaining Companions sat with them, but no one felt like talking.

We wanted battle, and we got it, Ki thought dully.

Lynx had moved off by himself and sat staring at a nearby fire. Nikides was grieving silently for Ruan, too, but Ki knew it wasn't the same. A squire was pledged to die for his lord. To fail in that was to fail in everything. But it wasn't Lynx's fault; it had been madness on the walls.

How much comfort would that be for me, if I'd lost Tobin? he thought bitterly. *What if that arrow had hit him in the throat instead of the shoulder? What if Iya hadn't shown up when she did? At least then we'd all be dead together.*

As Ki watched, Tharin emerged from the darkness and went to Lynx, draping a blanket over the younger man's shoulders. He spoke quietly to him, too soft for Ki to hear. Lynx drew his knees up and hid his face in his arms.

Ki swallowed hard and rubbed at the sudden stinging behind his eyelids. Tharin understood better than any of them how Lynx felt right now.

"What will happen to him?" Tobin whispered, and Ki realized he'd been watching, too. "Do you think Korin will let him stay a Companion?"

Ki hadn't thought of that. Lynx was one of them, and one of the best. "Not much for him to go home to. His father's a lord, but Lynx is the fourth son."

"Maybe he could be Nikides' squire?"

"Maybe." But Ki doubted Lynx would welcome such

an offer just yet. He hadn't just been loyal to Orneus; he'd loved the drunken braggart, though Ki had never understood why.

In the pavilion behind them the generals were still talking with the king. The Palatine was eerily quiet, and Ki could hear the steady drone of prayer in the Temple of the Four; the smell of incense and burnt offerings seemed to permeate the air. Ki looked up at the cold sliver moon, wondering where the gods had been today.

The wind shifted soon after, carrying the smell of smoke and death up from the harbor, and the faint sound of enemy voices singing.

Victory songs, thought Ki.

A touch on his shoulder startled Tobin out of a doze.

It was Moriel. "The king is asking for you, Prince Tobin."

Ki and Tharin followed silently, and Tobin was glad of their company.

Tobin could smell brandywine and healing herbs on the king from ten feet away, but his uncle's eyes were sharp as he motioned for Tobin to take a stool at his feet. Hylus, Rheynaris, and Niryn were still there, and Korin, too. All of them looked grim.

Erius extended his left hand for Tobin's and looked into his face so intently Tobin suddenly felt afraid. He said nothing, listening to the rasp and hitch of the king's breathing.

After a moment Erius released him and sank back in his chair. "Pigeons were sent out this morning to the coastal cities," he whispered hoarsely. "Volchi has been worse hit by this pox. They have no one to send. Ylani can raise some men, but the garrison there is small to begin with."

"What about Atyion? Solari must be on his way by now."

"There's been no reply," Hylus told him. "Several birds were sent, but none has returned. Perhaps the enemy intercepted them. Whatever the case, we must assume Solari has not heard the news."

"You must go, Tobin," the king rasped. "We must have Atyion's might! With the standing garrison, Solari's men, and the surrounding towns, you might be able to raise three thousand. You must bring them, and quickly!"

"Of course, Uncle. But how will I get there? The city's surrounded."

"The enemy doesn't have enough men to completely hem us in," Rheynaris told him. "They've concentrated their main force along the eastern wall and at the gates. But they're stretched thin between, especially on the north and west sides. A small group could get out. My scouts found a likely spot near the northwest wagon gate. We'll lower you through a murder hole. You'll have to find horses once you get outside."

"What do you say, Tharin?" the king asked.

"Assuming we can find fresh mounts along the way, we could be there by midday tomorrow. But the trip back will be slower, with so many marching. It might be three days before we get back."

"Too long!" Erius growled. "Force march, Tharin, as we did at Caloford. If you don't, there'll be no city left to save. Ero is the heart of Skala. If it falls, Skala falls."

"How many should I take with me?" asked Tobin.

"The fewer the better," Rheynaris advised. "You'll be less likely to be seen."

"Even less so if they go dressed as common soldiers," Niryn said.

Tobin gave the wizard a grudging nod. "Tharin and Ki will go with me." He paused, then added quickly, "And my guardsman, Koni. He's one of my best riders."

"And me! Take me!" his other men clamored from the shadows outside the pillars.

"I'll go." Lynx shouldered his way past the others and strode over to kneel at Korin's feet. "Please, let me go with him."

Korin whispered to his father and Erius nodded. "Very well."

"And me!" Lutha cried, struggling through the press.

"No," Erius said sternly. "Korin must take my place in the field tomorrow and needs his Companions around him. There are too few of you left as it is."

Abashed, Lutha bowed low, fist to his chest.

"That's it, then. You four accompany Prince Tobin," Rheynaris said. "I'll see that you have plain garments and an escort to the wall."

Erius raised his hand as they turned to go. "A moment, nephew."

Tobin sat down again. Motioning him to lean closer, Erius whispered, "You're your father's son, Tobin. I know you won't fail me."

Tobin caught his breath, unable to look up.

"No false modesty now," Erius croaked, misreading him. "I'm going to say something now that I shouldn't, and you're not to repeat it, you hear?"

"Yes, Uncle."

"My son—" Erius leaned closer, grimacing in pain. "My son is not the warrior you are."

"No, Uncle—"

Erius shook his head sadly. "It's true, and you know it. But he will be king, and tomorrow he faces the enemy in my place. Hurry back with those reinforcements, then stay close to him, now and always. It will be you standing in Rheynaris' place when he wears the crown, won't it? Promise me, Tobin."

"Yes, Uncle." The memory of his mother's face the day she'd died made the lie come easier. But as he hurried away to change clothes, he could not meet Korin's eye.

Korin couldn't hear what his father was saying to Tobin, but something in his father's expression troubled him. His unease deepened when Tobin would not look at him.

"What's the matter, Father?" he asked, going back to

the king. "Don't worry, Tobin won't fail. And I won't either." Kneeling, he held out his hands for the sword. "Give me your blessing, Father, that I may lead as wisely as you."

Erius' grip tightened on the hilt and his eyes hardened. "You're overly hasty, my son. Only one hand wields the Sword of Ghërilain. While I have breath in my body, I am still king. Be content with proving yourself worthy of it."

Only Niryn was close enough to hear the rebuff. Korin saw the wizard's faint smile and swore revenge. "By the Four and the Flame, Father, I won't fail you."

Erius placed his left hand on Korin's head. "By the Four and the Flame, I bless you. Keep Rheynaris with you and listen to his counsel."

Korin bowed to the king and strode away. Rheynaris followed, but, still stinging from his father's harsh words, Korin stubbornly refused to acknowledge him.

With Rheynaris' scouts to guide them, Tobin and his small force hurried on foot through the deserted streets. His own guard and a dozen of the king's armed men came with them to the north wall, but they met no resistance. The houses were shuttered on all sides. No light showed.

Climbing to the hoarding, they looked out through the arrow slits and noted the scattered watch fires below. The main concentration was along the harbor, but Tobin could see a chain of such fires scattered up the coastline, as well.

The land beyond the walls was flat, with little cover. The moon was down, but the stars gave enough light to make out the pale line of the high road.

In order to move quickly, Tobin and the others had left their heavy armor and shields behind. Clad in plain coats of studded leather, they wore their scabbards strapped on their backs and carried their bows in their hands.

"Here, Prince Tobin," one of the scouts whispered, lifting a trapdoor over a murder hole. It was a dizzying drop, fifty feet or so. Rheynaris' men readied the ropes they'd brought.

"I'll go first," Tharin whispered. Passing a knotted loop over his head, he tugged it securely up under his arms and sat down with his legs over the edge of the hole. He gave Tobin a wink as three brawny soldiers lowered him through.

Tobin lay on his belly and watched as Tharin reached the ground and melted quickly into the shadow of a nearby hedge.

Lynx went next, then Koni and Ki. Ki gave him a sickly grin as he slid off the edge and disappeared with his eyes squeezed shut.

Tobin went quickly, not giving himself time to think of the open space below his boots. Reaching the ground, he cast off the rope and ran to join the others.

Tharin had already taken stock. "We'll have to stay clear of the road. They'll be watching that and it's bright enough for them to see us moving. There's nothing to do but run for it and hope we find horses soon. Make sure your arrows are tamped."

Tobin and the others checked the wadded wool stockings they'd stuffed into their quivers to keep the shafts from rattling.

"Ready," said Ki.

"All right, then. Here we go."

The first few miles were harrowing. The starlight seemed bright as noon and cast their shadows across the ground.

The steadings closest to the city had been overrun. They were not burned, but the livestock had been taken and the inhabitants slaughtered. Men, women, and children lay where they'd fallen, hacked to death. Tharin didn't let them linger there, but hurried on to the next, and the next. It was several miles before they got north of the Plenimarans' path of destruction. The steadings beyond were deserted, their byres empty. The farmland between was open fields, with only a few hedges and walls to shelter behind.

At last they spotted a sizable copse and ran for it, only to be greeted by the unmistakable twang of bowstrings as they neared the trees. A shaft sang by Tobin's cheek, close enough for him to hear the buzz of the fletching as it passed.

"Ambush!" Tharin cried. "To the right! Get to cover."

But as they ran that way swordsmen leaped out to meet them. There was no time to count, but they were outnumbered. Tobin was still reaching for his sword when Lynx let out his war cry and hurtled past him to charge the nearest swordsman. Men closed in around him as his blade found steel.

Then the others were on them. Tobin dodged the first man who reached him and swung a crushing blow across the back of his neck just below his helmet. He went down and two more leaped at Tobin. "Blood, my blood," Tobin whispered without thinking, but Brother did not come.

Tobin fought on, flanked by Tharin and Ki. He could hear Koni shouting behind him, and the clash of steel off to his right told him Lynx was still standing.

The blood sang in Tobin's ears as he met each attacker and drove him back. They were strong, but he held his own until there was no one left to fight. Bodies littered the ground around them and he saw others running away.

"Let them go," Tharin panted, leaning on his sword.

"You all right, Tob?" Ki gasped.

"They never touched me. Where are the others?"

"Here." Lynx strode out from the shadows under the trees, his blade black to the hilt in the starlight.

"That was a damn fool thing to do!" Tharin shouted, grabbing him by the arm and shaking him angrily. "You stay close next time!"

Lynx yanked free and turned away.

"Leave him alone," said Tobin. "He acted bravely."

"That wasn't bravery," Tharin snapped, glaring at the sullen squire. "If you want to throw your life away, you wait until we have the prince safe in Atyion! Your duty is to Prince Tobin now. Do you hear me, boy? Do you?"

Lynx hung his head and nodded.

Tobin looked around. "Where's Koni?" No one else was standing.

"Oh, hell!" Tharin began searching through the bodies. The others did the same, calling Koni's name. The fallen men all wore the black of Plenimar and Tobin didn't think twice about sticking a knife in the few still moving.

"Koni!" he called, wiping his blade on his leg. "Koni, where are you?"

A low moan came from somewhere to his left. Turning, he saw a dark figure crawling slowly in his direction.

Running to him, Tobin knelt to examine his wounds. "How badly are you hurt?"

The young guardsman collapsed with a groan. The others reached them as Tobin gently turned him over. A broken arrow shaft protruded from his chest just below his right shoulder.

"By the Light!" Tharin leaned in for a closer look. "Who the hell is that?"

Tobin stared down in dismay at the fair-haired youth wearing Koni's clothes. His chest was soaked with blood and his breath came in short, painful gasps. "I don't know."

The young man's eyes flickered open. "Eyoli. I'm— Eyoli. Iya sent me. I'm—mind clouder."

"A what?" Ki drew his sword.

"No, wait." Tharin knelt by him. "You say Iya sent you. How do we know that's true?"

"She told me to tell Prince Tobin—" He grimaced, clutching at his chest. "To tell you that the witch is in the oak. She said—you'd understand."

"It's all right," Tobin said. "Back in Ero, she told me to keep Koni with me. He must be a wizard."

"Not—not much of one." The stranger let out a weak chuckle. "And even less of a fighter. She told me to stay close to you, my prince. To protect you."

"Where's Koni, then?" Tharin demanded.

"Killed, before the gates went down. I took his place and caught up with you before you were cornered at that inn."

"He's dead?" Grief-stricken, Tobin turned away.

"I'm sorry. It was the only way to stay with you. She said stay close," Eyoli gasped. "That's how she knew we were trapped. I sent word."

"Does she know where we are now?" asked Tobin.

"I think so. She must not have been able to get out."

Tobin looked back at the burning city. There was no question of waiting for Iya now.

"How badly is he hurt?" asked Ki.

"The arrow and a sword cut to his side," Tharin replied. "We'll have to leave him."

"No!" cried Tobin. "He'll die out here alone."

"Go, please!" Eyoli struggled to sit up. "Iya will find me. You must go on."

"He's right, Tobin," said Tharin.

"We're not leaving him to die. That's an order, do you hear me? He helped save all of us today. I won't leave until we've done what we can for him."

Tharin let out a frustrated growl. "Lynx, go find something for bandages. Ki, water bottles and cloaks. We'll wrap him well and leave him in the trees. I'm sorry, Tobin, but we can't do better than that."

"I'm sorry to leave you a man short," the wizard whispered, closing his eyes. "I should have told you—"

"You did your duty," Tobin said, taking his hand. "I won't forget that."

Ki came back with the cloaks and bottles, as well as several bows. Dropping them beside Tharin, he said, "What do you make of these?"

Tharin picked one up, then another. "They're Skalan made."

"They all were, every one I saw. Swords, too, as much as I could make out."

"Indeed?" Tharin set about cutting the arrow from Eyoli's shoulder. The wizard clutched Tobin's hand, trying not to cry out, but the pain was too much for him. Ki put a hand over his mouth and muffled the cries until Eyoli fainted. Tharin bandaged the wound, then picked up the bloody arrowhead and examined it closely for a moment. "Ki, Lynx, bundle him up as warm as you can and find a good hiding place for him in the trees. Leave him all the water you can find. Tobin, come with me."

Tharin went to the nearest body and began feeling over the dead man's chest and back with his hands. He let out a low grunt, then did the same with several other bodies. "By the Flame!"

"What is it?"

"Look at this," Tharin said, sticking a finger into a rent in the dead man's tunic. "Put your hand in it and tell me what you feel?"

"There's no wound. He died of this sword cut to his neck."

"The others were the same. And Ki's right about the weapons, too. These are Skalans in Plenimaran clothes."

"But why attack us?"

"Because they were ordered to, I'd say. And ordered to make it look like we were killed by the enemy." He got up and hunted around for a moment, returning with a handful of arrows. They had thick shafts, with four-vane fletching rather than three. "Skalan bows, but Plenimaran arrows. Easy enough to come by after the fighting we saw today."

"I still don't understand. If we don't get to Atyion, the city will fall!"

"It had to be someone who knew we were going to Atyion, by what route, and when. And know it in time to have this set up."

"Not the king! Even if he wanted me killed, he wouldn't sacrifice Ero."

"Then it would have to be someone with him tonight. Perhaps it wasn't Erius' idea to send you."

Tobin thought back. "Not Hylus!"

"No, I'd never believe that."

"That leaves General Rheynaris and Lord Niryn."

"And Prince Korin."

"No! Korin wouldn't do that. It had to be Niryn."

"It doesn't matter now. We've still got a long way to go and horses to find."

Ki and Lynx had made Eyoli as comfortable as they could in a nest of cloaks under an oak just inside the copse.

"I'll send someone for you," Tobin promised.

Eyoli freed one hand from his wrapping to touch his brow and breast. "Go, my prince. Save your city."

Just beyond the copse they came to a large steading. A low stone wall surrounded it and the gate hung open on its hinges.

"Careful, boys," Tharin murmured.

But the place had been abandoned. The barn doors were open, and the corrals empty.

"Bilairy's balls!" Ki panted, coming back from the barns empty-handed. "They must have driven the stock off rather than leave it for the enemy."

Tharin sighed. "Nothing to do but keep going."

They'd just reached the gate when they heard a strong, rushing wind.

Tobin looked around in surprise. The night was still, with hardly a breath of breeze.

The sound grew louder, then ended abruptly as a large, dark mass appeared out of thin air not ten feet from where they stood, tumbling and bouncing until it fetched up against a watering trough.

Tobin started toward it but Tharin held him back. Ki and Lynx advanced cautiously, swords drawn.

"I think it's a man!" Lynx called back.

"It is, and he's alive," said Ki.

"A wizard?" said Tobin.

"Or something worse," Tharin muttered, stepping in front of him.

The strange traveler rose slowly to his knees, holding up both hands to show that he was unarmed. Ki let out a yelp of surprise. "Tobin, it's Arkoniel!"

"By the Four, is it raining wizards today?" Tharin growled.

Tobin ran to help Arkoniel up. Instead of his usual hooded cloak, the wizard wore a shepherd's long fleece vest and a felt hat jammed down on his head and tied in place with a scarf. Leather gauntlets covered his arms almost to the elbow. He was breathless and shaking like a man with fever.

"How did you get here?" asked Tobin.

Arkoniel clutched Tobin's shoulder, still unsteady on his feet. "A spell I've been working on. Not quite perfected yet, but I seem to have arrived with all my arms and legs."

"Were you expecting bad weather?" Ki asked, eyeing the absurd hat.

"No, just a bad journey. As I said, the spell isn't quite right yet. I'm never sure if I'll arrive in one piece or not." Arkoniel pulled off the left gauntlet and showed them his splinted wrist. "Same one I broke that day I arrived at the keep, remember?" He pulled off the right glove with his teeth and undid the scarf holding his hat.

"How did *you* find us?" Tharin asked.

"You can thank Iya and Eyoli for that. They got word to me. Tobin, I believe you'll be needing this." Pulling off his hat, Arkoniel shook out Tobin's old rag doll. "Don't let go of it again."

Tobin stuffed it inside his studded coat as Lynx stared. "Can you walk?"

Arkoniel straightened his disordered clothing. "Yes, it's just a bit disorienting, traveling like that twice in one night. Can't say that I recommend it." He looked around. "No horses?"

"No," said Tharin. "I don't suppose you have a spell for that?"

Arkoniel gave him a wink. Taking out his crystal wand, he drew a figure in red light, then stuck two fingers in his mouth and let out a piercing whistle. "There, they'll be along."

Ki and Lynx went to the barn again. By the time they returned with the saddles, they could hear the sound of hooves on the road, approaching at a gallop. A few minutes later ten horses thundered into the yard and came to a stop around Arkoniel, nosing at his belt and tunic.

"You've become quite a useful fellow since I last saw you." Tharin laughed.

"Thank you. It's been an instructive few years."

Arkoniel drew Tobin aside as the others saddled the horses. "I suppose you know what all this signifies?"

Tobin nodded.

"Good. I think it might be best if your friends understood."

"Tharin already knows."

"You told him?"

"No, Lhel did."

Arkoniel grasped Tobin's shoulder with his good hand. "You've seen her! Where is she?"

"I didn't see her. She came to Tharin in some kind of vision."

Arkoniel sagged and Tobin saw the deep disappointment in his eyes. "She left us at Sakor-tide. I looked for her when I went back to the keep for the doll, but there was no sign of her anywhere."

"You mean it wasn't Lhel who got the doll back from my mother?"

"No. I found it in the tower. Someone had been up there before me. One of the tables had been righted, and a dozen or so of your mother's dolls were lined up there. You remember them? Boys with no mouths? Yours was with them. It was as if someone knew I was coming for it."

"Maybe Nari?"

The tower door is still locked and I threw the key in the river years ago. It could have been Lhel, but—Well, I think maybe your mother knew that you needed it back."

Tobin shook his head. "Or that Brother needed it."

"What do you mean?"

"She always loved him, not me." He clutched at the lump the doll made inside his coat. "She made this to keep him with her. She carried it everywhere, so he'd be there. She loved him."

"No, Tobin. Lhel told her to make the doll. It was the only way to control Brother after—after he died. Lhel helped her, and set the magic on it to hold him. It may have given your mother some comfort but it wasn't love."

"You weren't there! You didn't see how she was. It was always him. She never wanted me."

A look of genuine pain crossed Arkoniel's face. "Oh, Tobin. It wasn't your fault or hers, how things were."

"Whose, then? Why did she treat me like that, just because he was stillborn?"

Arkoniel started to speak, then turned away. Tobin caught him by the sleeve. "What is it?"

"Nothing. It's all in the past. Right now you must get to Atyion. It would be safest to reveal yourself there."

"But how? Lhel's not here to undo the binding."

"She taught me. It's actually quite simple. Cut the cord she made of your hair that's around the doll's neck, take Brother's bones out of it, then cut out the piece of bone she sewed into your skin."

"That's all?" Tobin exclaimed softly. "But I could have done that anytime!"

"Yes, and if you'd known, you might have too soon and brought us all to ruin."

"I wouldn't have! I never wanted to. I don't want to now." Tobin hugged himself unhappily. "I'm scared, Arkoniel. What if—" He looked back at Ki and the others. "What will they do?"

"We should be moving on," Tharin called.

"A moment, please," Arkoniel told him. "It's time you told Ki. It's only fair, and you need him steady at your side."

"Now?"

"I'll do it, if you like."

"No, he should hear it from me. And Lynx?"

"Yes, tell them both."

Tobin started slowly back to Ki. He'd been tempted a hundred times over to just blurt it all out, but now fear choked him.

What if Ki hated him? And what about Korin and the other Companions? What if the people of Atyion refused to believe, refused to follow him?

"Courage, Tobin," Arkoniel whispered. "Trust Illior's will. For Skala!"

"For Skala," Tobin mumbled.

"What's wrong?" Ki asked before Tobin had said a word. "Is there bad news?"

"There's something I have to say, and I don't know how, except to just say it."

Tobin took a deep breath, feeling like he was on that cliff in his dreams, about to fall. "I'm not what you think. When you look at me, it's not me you're seeing. It's Brother."

"Who?" asked Lynx, looking at Tobin as if he'd lost his mind. "Tobin, you don't have a brother."

"Yes, I do. Or I did. He's the demon you've heard about, only he's really just a ghost. It wasn't a girl child who died; it was him. I was the girl, and a witch changed me to look like him right after I was born."

"Lhel?" Ki's voice was barely a whisper.

Tobin nodded, trying to read his friend's expression in the starlight. He couldn't and that scared him even more.

"You all know the rumors about the king," said Arkoniel. "That he kills all female heirs to protect his own claim and line. They're not just rumors. It's the truth. The Oracle at Afra warned my mistress, and told her that we must protect Tobin until she's old enough to rule. This is how we did it."

"No!" Ki gasped. He backed away. "No, I don't believe it. I know you! I've seen you! You're no more a girl than I am!"

I didn't know either, not at first! Tobin wanted to tell him, but his mouth wouldn't form the words because Ki was still moving away from him.

"I was there that night, Ki," Arkoniel told him. "I've devoted my whole life to keeping the secret until now. None of us had any choice, especially not Tobin. But now it's time for her true form to be revealed. Skala must have a queen, one of the true line."

"Queen?" Ki turned and ran for the barn.

"I'll speak with him," said Tharin. "Please, Tobin, let me do this. For both your sakes."

Tobin nodded, miserable, and Tharin strode away after Ki.

Lynx came closer, looking into Tobin's face. "This is really true? I mean—I've seen you, too, in the baths and swimming."

Tobin shrugged.

"Tobin didn't know about any of this either, until a few years ago," Arkoniel explained. "It won't be easy, what's to come. It means going against Erius and Korin, too. Tobin will need true friends."

"You'll be queen?" Lynx said, as if he hadn't heard.

"Somehow. But Lynx, you're a Companion. You've known Korin longer than I have." The words felt like sand in Tobin's mouth. "If you can't do this—I'll understand."

"You're free to go back to Ero now, if you wish," said Arkoniel.

"Go back? I never meant to go back. Tharin was right about me before, Tobin, so I might as well stay." He let out a mirthless little laugh and held out his hand. "That's not much of an oath, is it?"

Tobin clasped hands with him. "It's enough for me."

* * *

$\mathcal{T}$harin found Ki standing just inside the barn door, arms limp at his sides. "Why didn't he tell me?" he asked, voice leaden with grief.

Tharin fought hard to rein in his anger. He'd expected better of Ki than this. "He had no idea when you first met him."

"When, then?"

"That time he ran away to the keep. Iya and that witch woman made him swear not to tell. It's a heavy burden he's had to bear, Ki; one you and I can't even imagine."

"You knew!"

"Not until a few weeks ago. Rhius didn't tell me, either, but it wasn't because he didn't trust me. It was for Tobin's sake, and safety. It has nothing to do with us."

"What happens to me now?"

"What do you mean? Are you telling me you'll serve a prince but not a queen?"

"Serve?" Ki whirled around to face him. "Tharin, he's my best friend. He—he's everything to me! We've grown up together, trained and fought together. *Together!* But queens don't have squires, do they? They have ministers, generals, consorts. I'm none of that." He threw up his hands. "I'm nothing! Just the grass knight son of a horse thief—"

Tharin backhanded him so hard Ki staggered. "Is that all you've learned, after all these years?" he growled, standing over the cowering boy. "Do you think a wizard like Iya would choose you for no reason? Would Rhius bind you to his son if you were no more than that? Would *I* trust you with that child's life? A man can't choose his father, Ki, but he chooses his path. I thought you'd let go of all that foolishness." It was an effort to not slap him again. "Is this what I taught you? To run off sniveling in the dark?"

"No." Ki's voice quavered but he straightened to attention. Blood ran down from his nose and caught in the sparse hair on his lip. "I'm sorry, Tharin."

"Listen to me, Ki. Tobin doesn't have the first notion of

what's ahead of him. All he can think of is that his friends will turn away from him. That *you'll* turn away. He fears that more than anything else. And that's precisely what you did just now, isn't it?"

Ki groaned aloud. "Bilairy's balls! He thinks—? Oh, hell, Tharin, that's not why I ran!"

"Then I guess you'd better get back there and tell him that." Tharin stepped aside and Ki bolted out, back to Tobin. Tharin stayed where he was, waiting for a sudden fit of trembling to pass. His hand stung where he'd hit Ki; he could feel the boy's blood on his fingers. He stifled an anguished curse as he wiped his hand on his coat. Divine will or not, it was a hard road that had been set for all of them, all those years ago.

Ki couldn't have been gone for more than a few minutes, but it seemed like forever to Tobin before he came striding back from the barn alone. Walking straight up to Tobin, Ki hugged him hard, then knelt and offered his sword.

"What are you doing, Ki? Get up! You're bleeding—"

Ki rose and grasped him by the shoulders. "I'm sorry for running off. You just took me by surprise, that's all. Nothing's changed between us." He hesitated, chin trembling now as he searched Tobin's face. "It hasn't, has it?"

Tobin's voice was none too steady as he hugged Ki again. "You're my best friend. Nothing can change that."

"That's all right, then!" Ki let out a shaky laugh as he stepped back and clasped hands with him.

Tobin caught the gleam of unshed tears in his eyes. "You won't leave me, will you, Ki?"

Ki tightened his grip and gave him a fierce smile. "Not while I've got breath in me!"

Tobin believed him, and was so relieved he hardly knew what to say. "All right then," he managed at last. "I guess we better move on."

Chapter 52

As they rode on Tobin tried not to think about what lay ahead. Ki's first reaction had scared him more than any battle could. He believed his friend's staunch pledge, but more than once during that long ride he caught Ki stealing puzzled looks at him, as if he was trying to see the stranger under Tobin's borrowed skin.

I don't want to change! he thought miserably. Looking off to the distant mountains looming black against the stars, he wondered what it would be like to just ride away from everything—from the battle, the city, his friends, his fate.

But it was only a fleeting thought. He was a Skalan warrior and a prince of the blood. Scared as he was, he would never shame himself, or betray those he loved.

His name and signet got them fresh horses along the road, and they spread word of the invasion at every stop. By dawn they were in sight of the sea again, and reached Atyion an hour past noon.

Reining in at the town gate, Tharin called up to the guards on the wall, "Open in the name of Prince Tobin, lord of Atyion. The prince has returned!"

"Ero is under siege by Plenimar," Tobin told the startled sentries as soon as they were inside. "Spread the word. Every warrior must prepare to march back with me. No, wait!" he called as the man was about to run off. "The women, too; any who wish to fight for Skala are welcome under the banner of Atyion. Do you understand?"

"Yes, my prince!"

"Tell everyone to assemble in the castle yard."

"Well done, Tobin!" Arkoniel murmured.

They raced on through the town, only to find the drawbridge still raised beyond the castle moat. Tharin cupped his hands around his mouth and hailed the guard, but there was no answer.

Ki shaded his eyes and squinted up at the men on the wall. "Those are Solari's men."

"Open in the name of the prince!" Tharin shouted again.

Presently a man leaned over the battlement by the gate head. "I have Duke Solari's orders not to admit anyone from Ero, on account of the pox."

"Son of a whore!" Ki gasped.

"Open at once for the prince or be hanged for a traitor!" Tharin bellowed back in a voice Tobin had never heard him use before.

Arkoniel was calmer. "These are serious matters, fellow. Fetch your master to the walls at once."

"Solari can't do this!" Ki exclaimed hotly as they sat waiting. "This is Tobin's land, whether he's of age or not."

"The man who commands the castle commands Atyion," Tharin muttered, glaring across the moat.

"Brother was right," Tobin told Arkoniel. "He told me a long time ago that Solari wanted Atyion for himself."

The sun sank another hour in its course as they fretted outside the gates. A crowd of armed townspeople gathered at their backs while they waited. Word of the situation had spread. Tharin found several sergeants among them and ordered runners sent to the outlying steadings to raise the knights. Arkoniel sent others for the town priests.

Two women emerged from the crowd and bowed deeply to Tobin. One was clad in old-fashioned armor. The other wore the white robes and silver mask of the Illioran temple.

Even with the mask, Tobin recognized her and bowed. "Honored One, Lady Kaliya."

The priestess bowed, and displayed the many-colored

dragons on her palms. "I've long dreamed of your coming, though I did not expect you so soon. Atyion will not forsake the rightful heir."

Tobin dismounted and kissed her hand. "I won't forsake Atyion. Did you know?"

"That it would be you? No, Highness, but I am most pleased." She bent her head close to his, and whispered, "Daughter of Thelátimos, welcome."

More priests arrived. Arkoniel and Kaliya took them aside, speaking quietly. Tobin shivered as he watched them. One by one, they all turned and silently saluted him, hands to their hearts.

Presently Solari appeared on the parapet, and called down, "Greetings, Prince Tobin. I regret the poor welcome you received."

"Don't you know what's happening in Ero?" Tobin shouted back. "They sent messenger birds yesterday. The city is under attack!"

Astonishment rippled through the crowd.

"Yes, I know," Solari shouted. "But Atyion must be protected from plague at all costs."

"That ain't right!" someone in the crowd yelled.

"Even at the cost of her rightful lord's life?" Tharin shouted back. "Solari, this is Rhius' son, and he's here by the king's order! Your own son is there in Ero with him."

"Other pigeons have outdistanced you, Tharin, and my news is fresher. Lower Ero is lost and the king is trapped on the Palatine. They'll all be dead before you can get back."

"Traitor!" Ki screamed, brandishing his sword.

Solari ignored him. "Skala must be defended and Atyion is the greatest stronghold left. She must be led by a seasoned general. Give over your claim, Prince Tobin, and I will adopt you as my heir. Let the priests witness my pledge."

"I will not!" the Illioran priestess cried, and was echoed by the others. "I send the traitor's curse upon you!"

"You have other sons, Solari," Arkoniel replied. "Even if we believed you, how long would Tobin survive among them with all this to gain?"

"Not a fortnight!" a woman cried out in the crowd behind them.

"Someone shoot that traitor!" someone else called out.

"Storm the walls!"

"Hang the bastards! We'll never bend knee to 'em!"

Ki dismounted and went to Tobin. "Could you send Brother after him, Tob?" he whispered.

Somehow, Arkoniel heard and hissed, "Never ask that again, Ki. You don't know what you're saying."

He rode to the edge of the moat and raised his right fist in the air, clutching his crystal wand. The failing daylight struck fire through it. "Hear me, all you in the castle, and you here behind us." His voice carried like a battle cry. "I am the wizard Arkoniel, once the pupil of Mistress Iya. You knew us as the hearth friends of Duke Rhius. By his own hand, we have also been the protectors of his only child and heir, who stands here like a beggar at his own gate!

"Solari claims he's shutting out the plague. Has he ever done such a thing before? No, only now that he believes Ero lost. Know this, people of Atyion. These years of plague and death are the curse of Illior that King Erius brought down on the land. With the complicity of the people, he usurped the throne from Skala's rightful heir. Princess Ariani, daughter of Agnalain, mother of Tobin—she should have been queen!"

"He speaks the truth," Kaliya cried, displaying both palms in official sanction of his words. "Her child stands before you now, untouched by plague or famine. Prince Tobin's holdings—Atyion, Cirna, Alestun, Middleford, Hawk's Lee—all of them and their people have been spared. Did you never wonder why? I tell you now; it's because Ariani's blood runs true in his veins! Unknowing,

Tobin has been your true protector, blessed by Illior and all the Four."

The rumble grew to a cheer, but there was no response from the castle. Tobin looked around nervously. Despite the goodwill of the crowd, he felt very exposed. Solari's archers could be looking down their shafts at them that very moment. "Now what?" he asked Tharin.

Kaliya stepped close and grasped his stirrup. "I promised you my help long ago. Do you recall?"

"Yes."

"Yet you've never come seeking it. I offer it again. Give your battle cry, Scion of Atyion. Good and loud, now!"

Something in her voice gave him hope. Tilting his head back, he shouted, "Atyion! Atyion for Skala and the Four!"

Ki and the others took up the cry, and the crowd joined in fiercely, waving kerchiefs, shawls, and weapons of every sort. The sound rolled over Tobin like thunder and sang in his ears like wine.

Kaliya held up her hands for silence. "There. Do you hear that?"

The cry had been taken up inside the castle walls. "Atyion for Skala! For the Four!" It swelled to a roar, and was soon punctuated by the unmistakable clash of steel against steel.

Tharin bowed to the priestess with a grim smile. "Well done, my lady. Atyion knows her master's voice. They're fighting for you, Tobin. Call to them."

"Open the gates!" Tobin cried, but there was no reply.

They mounted and sat their horses tensely, watching the drawbridge. The sun fell another hour before the sound of fighting ended and they saw a new flurry of activity above the gate.

Some sort of struggle appeared to be going on. It was brief, and ended when a man was tossed screaming and flailing from the battlements with a noose around his neck. His cries were cut short as the rope fetched taut and snapped his neck. The green silk robe he wore was as rich as a king's; costly embroidery caught the sun as the body spun slowly at the end of the hangman's rope.

It was Solari.

Moments later the drawbridge rattled down and soldiers surged out to greet Tobin. Some among them wore Solari's green, but they were chanting Tobin's name.

There were women with them, too, still in skirts and aprons, but armed with swords. One of the cooks ran to Tobin and fell on her knees before him. Offering her sword up to him with both hands, she cried out, "For Atyion and the Four!"

It was Tharin's cousin who'd greeted him on his first visit here. Dismounting, Tobin accepted the blade and gave it back to her. "Rise, Grannia. You're a captain again."

Another great cheer went up, echoing between the castle walls and the town. It seemed to lift Tobin back into the saddle on waves of sound, leaving him dizzy and elated. Then Arkoniel was beside him again.

"It's time, Tobin," he shouted over the noise.

"Yes, I know."

Flanked by his companions and the chief priests, Tobin rode across the bridge into the huge bailey beyond. The brief battle there had left scores of dead, mostly Solari's men. Others had been herded into several corrals and knelt there under the watchful eye of Atyion archers and swordsmen.

Tobin rode in a wide circle, taking in the situation. Most of Solari's men had sided with Atyion in the end.

"The castle is yours, Prince Tobin," said Tharin.

Duchess Savia and her children were waiting for him at the head of the castle steps. The duchess held her head up proudly, but he saw the fear in her eyes as she pulled her children closer to her. Tobin's heart turned over in his breast as he saw the same fear in the children's eyes. He'd feasted and played with them the last time he was here, and held little Rose on his knee. Now she clung to her mother's skirts, wailing with fear at his approach.

Savia fell to her knees. "Kill me if you will," she cried, holding her hands out to him in supplication. "But I pray you in the name of the Four, spare my children!"

"You are under my protection," Tobin assured her. "I swear by the Four and the law of Skala that no harm will come to you!" He looked around. "Is Lady Lytia here?"

"Here, my prince," she called, stepping out from the crowd below.

"Lady Lytia, I proclaim you Steward of Atyion. See to it that my order is made clear to the garrison. No harm or insult is to be offered to the duchess and her children. They can stay in their chambers under guard for now. When you've seen them safely there, give the order for my banners to be raised."

"I will, my prince." The approval in her pale eyes as she gently guided the weeping duchess away warmed Tobin even more than the cheering had.

"You'd better address the garrison now," Tharin advised.

Despite his success so far, Tobin's stomach tightened into a cold knot as he looked out across the sea of expectant faces.

"Warriors of Atyion," he began, and his voice sounded thin and reedy in the open air. "I thank you for your faithful service this day."

Arkoniel stepped closer and whispered in his ear as they waited for the cheering to subside. Tobin nodded and took a deep breath.

"Good people of Atyion, you have loved me for my father's sake, I know, and welcomed me as one of your own. Today—" He faltered, his mouth dry. "Today the warships of Plenimar fill the harbor before Ero. The city is in flames and the enemy is at the gates of the Palatine."

He paused again, gathering his thoughts as the angry outcry subsided. "Today, I stand before you not only as the child of Rhius, but of Ariani; she who should have been queen." He stopped again, so scared he thought he might be sick right there in front of everyone. Taking a deep breath, he forced himself on. "Skala must have a queen again, if she is to survive. I have—I have something very odd to tell you, but . . ."

He turned desperately to Arkoniel. "I don't know how to tell them. Help me, please!"

Arkoniel bowed, as if in answer to some stern order, and raised a hand to the crowd for their attention. Ki moved in beside Tobin and clasped his shoulder. Trembling, Tobin shot him a grateful look.

Arkoniel reached inside his plain tunic and pulled out a silver amulet of Illior. "Warriors of Atyion, some of you know me. I am Arkoniel, a free wizard of Skala, follower of Iya. My mistress and I are the chosen protectors of Prince Tobin, ordained by Illior Lightbearer through the Afran Oracle sixteen years ago. My mistress was granted a vision while Ariani's children were still in the womb. You've all heard that the princess bore twins, and that the girl perished and the boy lived. That's not completely true. My mistress and I witnessed the births that night, and have kept the truth of the matter a secret until today.

"I tell you now that it was the girl who lived, not the boy. By the will of Illior and for the sake of Skala, the girl child was by the most fearsome and difficult magics given the form of her dead brother in order to escape murder at the hands of the king and his minions. That girl child stands before you now as Prince Tobin!"

Silence. Tobin could hear ducks quacking on the moat beyond the wall, and dogs barking in the village. Then someone yelled, "That ain't no girl!"

"What manner of magic could do such things?" a bearded Dalnan priest demanded, and his words set off a greater outcry, as the soldiers and townspeople who'd crowded into the bailey all began talking at once.

Tharin, Ki, and Lynx closed in around Tobin, hands on

their sword hilts. Arkoniel's knuckles went white as he clutched his wand, but it was the Illioran high priestess who stilled the crowd.

Kaliya clapped her hands over her head and a crack of thunder echoed between the walls. "Let them finish!" she cried. "Would I be standing here with them, and these my brethren of the other temples, if we did not think there was some meaning in their words? Let the wizard speak!"

Arkoniel bowed to her and resumed. "For fifteen years you have known this brave young warrior as the son of Rhius. Today, by the will of Illior, you are privileged to see her revealed at last as the true heir of the Skalan throne. You are blessed, people of Atyion. It is you who will bear witness that a rightful heir ordained by Illior has returned to you. You proved your good faith when you overthrew the traitor Solari. Put the seal on it by bearing sacred witness now with these priests of the Four."

There were a few scattered exclamations and grumblings as Arkoniel motioned everyone away from Tobin.

"He's too exposed! Can't we do this inside the hall?" Tharin muttered.

"No, it must be seen. Please, Tharin, you must step back."

Tharin gave Tobin a last tense look, and Ki and the others grudgingly moved aside with him, but only to the far end of the stairs. The priests did the same on the other side.

Though his friends were no more than twenty feet away, Tobin suddenly felt very alone and exposed. No one was cheering or chanting his name now. The bailey seemed like a sea of skeptical eyes.

Kaliya smiled, as if she sensed Tobin's mounting fear and accepted it with compassion. The others watched with obvious unease.

Arkoniel came to Tobin and presented him with a thin silver knife; it had been Lhel's. "She gave me this sometime ago. Use it with courage," he whispered, kissing Tobin on both cheeks. He'd never done anything like that before. "Remember what I described to you. Begin with the doll. Be brave, Tobin. These are your people watching."

My people. The entire throng seemed to be holding its breath. Clutching the knife, Tobin felt his fear seep away, leaving him with the same inner stillness he felt before battle. Even so, his hands shook as he pulled out the doll and felt for the hair cord in the fold of its neck. Slipping the tip of the blade under it, he cut it and let it fall away. Then he sliced open the worn muslin and emptied the crumbling herbs, yellowed wool, and all those bits of delicate bone from the doll's body. Something small and shiny tumbled out, and bounced down the stone steps. It was the golden tablet bearing the Oracle's words. He'd forgotten he'd hidden it there. It landed at the feet of a bearded sergeant, who hesitantly picked it up. When Arkoniel motioned him to stay where he was, he held it up, and whispered, "I hold on to it for you, shall I, my prince?"

Then Brother was standing there beside him, watching him with hungry black eyes. Judging by the sudden cries and gasps, others could see him, too.

"Your clothes," Arkoniel called softly. "You must take them off. Ki, help him."

Brother hissed softly as Ki approached but did not try to stop him. Not letting himself hesitate or think, Tobin took off his sword belt, the studded coat, and shirt and handed them to Ki. Brother's presence raised gooseflesh along his arms. The ghost stood close beside him, barechested now. Tobin quickly shucked off his boots, socks, trousers, and, after another moment's doubt, his linen clout. Ki gave him a wan smile as he added them to his pile. He was scared, too, and trying not to show it.

"It's all right," Tobin whispered, pulling the chain over his head and holding it out to him. "Keep these for me."

Ki closed his fist around the ring and seal and raised his hand to his heart, saluting Tobin as he retreated to his place with Tharin.

Naked, Tobin faced the crowd and felt for the bone shard. There it was, just below the skin. The tiny ridges of Lhel's stitching were rough against his fingertips.

"Quickly!" Brother hissed.

Tobin looked into his brother's black eyes one last time as he raised the silver knife. "Yes."

Bracketing the lump with two fingers, he pressed the knife's sharp point to the taut skin. He couldn't see what he was doing, but his touch was deft. He grimaced as it broke the skin. Blood trickled down.

"Cut deeper!" Brother crooned.

Tobin cut again, twisting the knife, and searing fire shot through him as the tip found its target. He fell to his knees, and the knife clattered to the stone stairs beside him.

"Release me!" Brother screamed, crouching to show Tobin the bleeding wound on his own breast. Blood ran down his cheeks in scarlet tears. "It hurts! Finish it!"

Gasping, Tobin squeezed his eyes shut and shook his head. The pain was too much.

"Now!" a woman shouted. "It must be now, daughter!"

Opening his eyes, Tobin saw the ghosts.

They stood in a circle around him, all of them crowned and all holding the Sword of Ghërilain upright before them. He didn't recognize them—the tomb effigies had been too crude to capture their living features, but he knew who they were. Ghërilain the First stood there watching him, and his own blood-soaked grandmother. And that gaunt, sad-faced man beside them—he must be Thelátimos, the last rightful king.

Cool fingers brushed his brow. Tobin looked up into the one face he had seen before. It was Tamír, the murdered queen. It was she who'd called out to him, and she spoke again now. *Courage, daughter. It must be now, for Skala!*

Someone put the knife back in his hand. It was Ki. He wept as he knelt beside Tobin.

"You can do it," he whispered, and retreated. He looked like he was sending Tobin to his execution.

Tobin raised the knife. Pain pulled his lips back in a snarl as he gouged deeper. He'd always imagined that the tiny shard would slip out like a splinter, but the flesh had grown fast to it, like a tree bole healing around a nail. He twisted the blade again and heard someone screaming. It sounded like Brother but his own throat was raw with it.

The tiny fragment came free, still sheathed in a pulpy shred of raw flesh. He scarcely had time to feel it between his fingers before a new wave of pain engulfed him, beyond anything he'd ever imagined.

White fire engulfed him, so intense it was icy cold. Caught in that inferno, he couldn't breathe or think or scream or hear, but somehow he saw Brother, felt the spirit grappling with him, enfolding him, passing through him like a cold black shadow at the heart of that white fire.

And then the pain was gone and Tobin was curled in his side on hot, smooth stone in the sunlight. The ghosts were still around him, but fainter now, like shapes made of grey gauze. The stairs were scorched black in a great circle around him.

And Brother was gone.

Looking around, he did not see the shocked, silent onlookers, only that his twin was not there. He felt it, too; an aching emptiness filled him. There had been no farewell between them, no parting words. He had cut Brother from his body and the ghost had left him. Tobin could scarcely comprehend it.

"Tob?" A warm hand clasped his elbow, helping him sit up. It was Ki.

Tobin reached out to him, then froze in horror, staring down at the strange skin covering his arm. From fingertips to shoulder it hung in loose colorless shreds like a rotted glove. His whole body was the same; his skin was in tatters around him, flayed by the horrendous magic he'd unleashed. He rubbed gingerly at his left forearm and the skin fell away, exposing smooth, whole skin below. The wine-colored wisdom mark was still there, brighter than ever.

He flexed his fingers, brushed his hands together, and rubbed at his arms, shedding the old skin like a snake in spring. He rubbed at his face and felt a thin, dry mask pull away, leaving the crescent-shaped scar still visible on the chin. The fire had somehow spared his hair, but he could feel the old scalp pulling apart beneath it.

He ran his hands down over his chest and stopped, only beginning to fully comprehend what had happened. The old skin that covered his chest was pulled tight, bulging like—

Like a maiden's bodice.

Shivering, Tobin stripped the old husk away and stared down at her small breasts.

Tobin was dimly aware of a growing murmur as she stood and looked down. Her boy's genitals had wizened to dried husks. She pulled at the loose skin above them and they sloughed off and fell away.

Ki turned away, a hand clamped across his mouth, and she heard him retch.

The world was going slowly grey around her. She couldn't feel the stairs under her feet anymore. But Tharin was with her, wrapping a cloak around her, holding her upright. And Ki was back, too, his arm tight around her waist. "It's all right. I've got you."

The priests and Arkoniel were there, too, and the cloak had to be opened, an inspection made. Tobin kept her eyes on the sky above their heads, too numb to care.

"It's all right, Tob," Ki murmured.

"Not—Tobin," she whispered. Her lips were sore, and her throat was raw.

"Yes, she must take a woman's name now," Kaliya said.

Arkoniel let out a soft groan. "We never discussed that!"

"I know," Tobin whispered. The ghostly queens were with her again. "Tamír, the queen who was murdered and denied. She came to me—offered me the Sword. Her name—" The grey fog rolled away and tears stung her eyes. "And Ariani, for my mother who should have ruled. And Ghërilain, for Illior and Skala."

The ghostly queens bowed to her, then sheathed their swords and faded away.

The priestess nodded. "Tamír Ariani Ghërilain. May the name bring you strength and fortune." Turning to the crowd, which had fallen silent again, she cried out, "I bear sacred witness! She is a woman, and bears the same marks and scars."

"I bear witness," the priestess of Astellus echoed, and the others with her.

"I call on you all to bear witness," Arkoniel shouted to the crowd. "The true queen has returned to you! By the wisdom mark on her arm and this scar on her chin I verify that this is the same person standing before you now, but in her true form. Behold Tamír the Second!"

Won over at last, the people began to cheer, but even that could not drown out the rending crack that rang out behind Tobin. The ornate wooden panel over the castle door—the one carved with the sword of Sakor—split and fell away, revealing the original stonework below.

The Eye of Illior once more guarded Atyion.

Tobin raised her hand to make reverence. But the roar of the crowd caught her, swept her up into the air as the world went black around her.

In that same moment the Afran Oracle laughed aloud in the darkness of her cavern.

Hiding with half a dozen other wizards in the ruins of an Ero tavern, Iya staggered and covered her face as a brilliant burst of white light blinded her. Behind her closed lids the light slowly faded to reveal the face of a black-haired, blue-eyed young woman. "Thank the Lightbearer," she whispered, and her companions echoed the words with the same reverence and wonder. Then with one voice they shouted it aloud. "Thank the Lightbearer! The queen returns!"

In the mountains north of Alestun the wizards of Arkoniel's exiled Third Orëska saw that same vision and hurried to find one another, crying out the news.

All across Skala, wizards who'd accepted Iya's small tokens, and many who had been deemed unworthy, shared the vision and wept for joy or shame.

The vision struck Niryn a twofold blow as he paced the ramparts. He recognized that face despite the transformation and raised his fists at the sky, raging at the Lightbearer's betrayal and Solari's, and the failure of his own assassins to remove the Scion of Atyion from his path.

"Necromancy!" he cried, swelling like an adder in his rage. "A false face and a false skin! But the strands are not yet woven."

A Harrier guard unwise enough to approach his master just then was struck blind and died a day later.

Lhel woke in her lonely oak tree house and cast the window spell. Looking through, she saw Tharin bearing the girl down some passageway. Lhel gazed into that still, sleeping face. "Keesa," she whispered, and was certain she saw Tobin's eyelids flutter a little. "Keesa, remember me." She watched a moment longer, making certain that Ki was with them, then closed the portal.

It was winter yet in the mountains. Crusted snow crunched under her feet as she limped to the spring, and ice still ringed the dark pool.

But the center was clear. Leaning over the water, she saw her face in the gently rippling surface, saw how old she looked. She'd had no moonflow since the winter solstice and her hair was more white than black. Left to a normal life among her own people, she would have a husband, children, and honor. Yet her only regret as she crouched over the water was that she left no daughter to tend this sacred place—the mother oak and its sacred spring—lost for so long to her people.

She turned her palms up to the unseen moon and spread the seeing spell over the water. A single image rose in the dark water. She studied it for a moment, then walked slowly back to the hollow oak and lay down on her bed, palms upturned at her sides again—empty, accepting— and listened to the wind in the branches.

He came silently. The weathered deerskin flap over the door did not stir as he entered. She felt him stretch out beside her, cold as a snowbank, and wrap his arms around her neck.

I've come back to you at last.

"Welcome, child!" she whispered.

Icy lips found hers and she opened her mouth willingly, letting this demon they'd called Brother steal her last breath as she had stolen his first. The balance was restored.

They were both free.

Chapter 53

Erius sat at the window of the gatehouse tower, watching his city burn. Despite the healers' best efforts, gangrene had set in and was spreading. His shoulder and chest were already black, his sword arm swollen and useless. Unable to ride or fight, he must lay here on a couch like an invalid, surrounded by long-faced courtiers and whispering servants. There were few officers left to bring him reports. Still gripping the Sword of Ghërilain, he presided helplessly over the loss of his capital.

The Plenimarans had broken through again just after dawn the day before. By nightfall most of the lower city was lost. From here, he must watch as cartloads of plunder trundled toward the black ships in the harbor, and crowds of captives—his people—driven like cattle among them.

Korin had proven worthless in the field. Rheynaris had remained at his side, feeding him commands until an arrow felled him just after midday. With fewer than a thousand defenders left, Korin had retreated to the Palatine and was endeavoring to hold the gates. A few other regiments were still fighting somewhere below, but not enough to stem the tide. Enemy soldiers by the thousands hemmed the Palatine in, battering at the gates and hurling flaming sacks of oil-soaked hay over the walls with their catapults. Soldiers and refugees streamed back and forth from the springs and cisterns with buckets, trying to save what they could, but the fires were spreading. Erius could see smoke billowing up from the roof of his New Palace.

Niryn's Harriers had fought bravely, but even they were no match for the enemy. Decimated by necromancers, felled in the streets by sword or shaft, the survivors broke and scattered. There were also reports of rebel Skalan wizards, who had appeared mysteriously the day before. These were confusing; according to Niryn, the wizards attacked his own, rather than the enemy. Other witnesses insisted that these same traitors had fought for Skala. They were said to command fire, water, even great packs of rats. Niryn gave no credence to such tales. No Skalan wizard had such powers.

Erius had watched the northern roads all day. It was too soon to hope, even if Tobin had reached Atyion alive, but he couldn't help looking, all the same.

He couldn't help missing Rhius; his old friend seemed to haunt him now, mocking him. If his old Companion still lived, the might of Atyion would already be with Ero now, strong enough to turn the tide. But Rhius had failed him, turned traitor, and only a stripling boy was left to fetch Solari.

Dusk came, and darkness, and still there was no sign, no word by rider or pigeon. Refusing the drysian's draughts, Erius sent everyone away and kept his vigil alone.

He was dozing by the window when he heard the door open. The lamps had guttered out, but the fires below cast enough light for him to make out the slight figure standing just inside the door.

Erius' heart sank. "Tobin, how are you back so soon? Were you turned back on the road?"

"No, Uncle, I went to Atyion," Tobin whispered, walking slowly toward him

"But you couldn't have! There's been no time. And where are your troops?"

"They will come, Uncle." Tobin was standing over him now, face hidden by shadow, and suddenly Erius felt a terrible coldness.

The boy leaned down and touched his shoulder. The chill spread through Erius, numbing him like poison.

When Tobin leaned closer and the light caught his face at last, Erius could not move or cry out.

"Oh, they will come," Brother hissed, letting the horrified man see his true face. "But not for you, old man. They come for my sister's sake."

Paralyzed, Erius stared uncomprehendingly at the monstrous thing standing there. The air shimmered and the bloody specter of his sister appeared beside it, stroking the rotting head with motherly affection. Only then did he understand, and it was already too late. His fingers clenched convulsively around his sword hilt as Brother stopped his heart.

Later, Korin would have to break his father's fingers to free it from his dead hand.

Chapter 54

Swans. White swans flying in pairs against an impossibly blue sky.

Tobin sat up, heart pounding, unsure what room this was.

Atyion. My parents' room.

The bed hangings were pulled back, and a misty dawn was brightening outside the window. Curled up between Tobin's feet, Ringtail bared his teeth in a great yawn, then began to purr.

"Ki?"

The other side of the enormous bed was smooth, the pillows plump and undented.

Tobin climbed out and surveyed the large chamber with rising concern. There was no pallet or servant's alcove and no sign of Ki at all. Where could he be? Tobin headed for the door but a fleeting image in the tall looking glass caught and held him.

There she was at last, that stranger who'd looked at him from Lhel's spring. Tobin stepped closer, caught between shock and wonder. The stranger did the same, a tall, awkward, frightened-looking girl in a long linen night-dress. They shared the scar on their chins, and the pink wisdom mark on their left forearms.

Tobin slowly pulled the shirt up. The body wasn't so different, still all whipcord and angles, except for the small breasts that swelled just below the crusted wound. But lower down—

Some thoughtful servant had left the chamber pot in

plain sight by the bed. Tobin just made it and collapsed on hands and knees, retching dryly.

The spasm passed and she forced herself back to the mirror. Ringtail twined around her bare ankles. She picked him up, hugging him close.

"That's me. I'm Tamír now," she whispered to the cat. Her face was not so different, a little softer, perhaps, but still plain and unremarkable except for the intense blue eyes. Someone had washed away the last bits of ragged skin and brushed it from her hair. It hung in smooth black waves around her face; she tried to imagine it braided with ribbons and pearls.

"No!" Fleeing the mirror again, she looked in vain for her clothes. She went to the closest wardrobe and threw it open. Her mother's velvets and silks caught the morning light. Slamming the door, she went to the next wardrobe and pulled on one of her father's dusty tunics, but it was too large. Yanking it off, she took a black cloak from its peg and wrapped herself in that instead.

Her heart hammered in her chest as she rushed to the door to find Ki.

She nearly fell over him. He was dozing on a pallet just outside, sitting with his back to the wall and his chin on his chest. Her headlong rush woke him. Two soldiers standing guard snapped to attention and saluted, but she ignored them.

"What the hell are you doing out here?" she demanded, hating the unfamiliar timbre of her voice. Just now it sounded rather shrill.

"Tob!" Ki scrambled up. "I—That is, it didn't seem proper—"

"Where are my clothes?"

"We weren't sure what you'd want."

"What I'd want? *My* clothes, damn it. The ones I arrived in!"

Ki turned to the nearest guard and stammered out,

"Send word to Steward Lytia that Tob—that the princess—that Tamír wants the clothes that were washed."

Tobin pulled Ki into the chamber and slammed the door. "I'm Tobin, Ki! It's still me, isn't it?"

Ki managed a sickly grin. "Well, yes and no. I mean, I *know* it's still you, but—Well, Bilairy's balls, Tob! I don't know what to think."

The confusion in his eyes fed her growing fear. "Is that why you slept in the corridor?"

Ki shrugged. "How would it look, me crawling into bed with a princess?"

"Stop calling me that!"

"It's what you are."

Tobin turned away, but Ki caught her and clasped her by the shoulders. "It's who you have to be. Arkoniel had a long talk with Tharin and me while you slept. It's a lot to take in and I don't think it's fair the way everything happened, but here we are and there's no going back." He slid his hands down her arms to clasp her hands, and she shivered at the touch.

Ki didn't seem to notice. "It's worse for you than me, I know, but it's still damn hard," he told her, the anguish clear in his face. "I'm still your friend, Tob. You know I am. I'm just not so clear on what that's going to mean."

"It means the same as always," Tobin shot back, gripping his hands. "You're my first friend—my *best* friend—and my sworn squire. That doesn't change. I don't care what anyone thinks! They can call me anything they like, but I'm still Tobin to you, right?"

A soft knock interrupted them and Lytia came in with Tobin's clothes over her arm. "Tharin sends word that the first troops are assembled. I took the liberty of searching the castle treasury for suitable armor, since you had to leave yours behind. I'll send it up as soon as it's been cleaned, and some breakfast."

"I'm not hungry."

"None of that, now." Lytia shook a finger at her. "I'm

not to let you out of this room before you both have something to eat. And what about a bath? I washed you as well as I could while you slept, but if you'd like a tub carried up, I'll order it."

Tobin blushed. "No. Tell Tharin I need to speak with him, please. And Arkoniel, too."

"Very good, Highness."

As soon as she was gone Tobin pulled off the nightshirt and began to dress. She was in the midst of lacing her breeches when she noticed that Ki had turned away. His ears were scarlet.

Straightening up, she threw her shoulders back. "Look at me, Ki."

"No, I—"

"*Look* at me!"

He turned, and she could tell he was trying hard not to stare at her small, pointed breasts. "I didn't ask for this body, but if I have to live with it, then so do you."

He groaned. "Don't, Tob. Please don't do this to me."

"Do what?"

Ki looked away again. "You can't understand. Just— cover yourself, will you?"

Shaken, Tobin pulled on her tunic and looked around for her boots. The room blurred and she sank down on the bed, choking back tears. Ringtail jumped into her lap and bumped his head under her chin. Ki sat beside her and put an arm around her, but the embrace felt awkward, and that hurt, too.

"I'm your friend, Tob. I always will be. But it will be different and I'm just as scared as you are. Not being able to share a bed, or even be alone together anymore—I don't know how I'll stand it."

"It doesn't have to be like that!"

"Of course it does. I hate it, but it does." His voice was gentle now, and sad in a way she'd never heard before. "You're a girl, a princess, and I'm man-grown, not some little page who can sleep at your feet like—like this cat here."

It was true, and she knew it. Suddenly shy, she took his hand again and held it tight. Her own was still brown, but her palm had lost much of its roughness in the transformation. "I'll have to build up those calluses all over again," she said, her voice too high, too unsteady.

"That shouldn't take long. Ahra's always felt like old boot leather. Remember her, and all those women who met you yesterday. You're still a warrior, just like they are." He kneaded her upper arm and grinned. "Nothing lost there. You can still break Alben's fingers for him, if you need to."

Tobin gave him a grateful nod, then pushed Ringtail off and stood up. Offering him her hand, she said, "You're still my squire, Ki. I'm going to hold you to that. I need you with me."

Ki stood and clasped with her. "Close as your shadow."

With that, the world seemed to settle back into place, at least for the moment. Tobin glanced at the brightening window in annoyance. "Why did they let me sleep so long?"

"You didn't give us much choice. You hadn't slept in a couple of days, and then what with all that last night? It really knocked you over. Tharin said to let you rest while he mustered the garrison. We'd have had to wait anyway. I'm surprised you're on your feet at all."

Tobin bristled. "Because I'm a girl?"

"Oh, for hell's sake—If I'd had to cut myself open and then have the skin fried off me, I don't know that I'd be up and around so fast." He grew serious again. "Damn, Tobin! I don't know what that magic was, but for a minute there it looked like the sun had come down blazing right where you stood! Or Harriers fire." He grimaced. "Did it hurt?"

Tobin shrugged. "I don't remember much about it, except for the queens."

"What queens?"

"The ghosts. You didn't see them?"

"No, just Brother. For a minute there I thought you were both finished, the way you looked. He really is gone, isn't he?"

"Yes. I wonder where he went?"

"To Bilairy's gate, I hope. I tell you, Tob, I'm not sorry to see the last of him, even if he did help you now and then."

"I suppose," Tobin murmured. "Still, that's the last of my family, isn't it?"

When Lytia came back she wasn't alone. Tharin, Arkoniel, and several servants were with her, carrying bulky cloth-wrapped parcels.

"How do you feel?" asked Arkoniel, taking Tobin's chin in his hand and examining her face.

Tobin pulled away. "I don't know yet."

"She's hungry," Lytia said, laying a huge breakfast for them on a table by the hearth. "I think perhaps you should let the princess eat before anything else."

"I'm not, and don't call me that!" Tobin snapped.

Tharin folded his arms and gave her a stern look. "Nothing more, until you eat."

Tobin grabbed an oatcake and took a huge bite to satisfy him, then realized how hungry she really was. Still standing, she wolfed down a second, then speared a slice of fried liver with her knife. Ki joined her, just as famished.

Tharin chuckled. "You know, you don't look so different in daylight. A bit more like your mother, perhaps, but that's no bad thing. I bet you'll be a beauty when you fill out and get your growth."

Tobin snorted around a mouthful of cardamom bun; the mirror had told a different tale.

"Maybe this will cheer you up." Tharin went to the bed and opened one of the bundles the servants had left there. With a flourish, he held up a shimmering hauberk. The rings of the mail were so fine it felt like serpent skin under Tobin's admiring hand. It was chased with a little goldwork along the lower edge, neck, and sleeves, but the pattern was a clean, simple one, just intertwined lines, like vines. The other parcels yielded a steel cuirass and helm of similar design.

"That's Aurënfaie work," Lytia told her. "They were gifts to your father's grandmother."

The cuirass bore the Atyion oak chased in gold. Both it and the hauberk fit as if they'd been measured for her. The mail hung lightly and felt as supple as one of Nari's knitted sweaters.

"The women of the castle thought you'd be wanting this, too," Lytia said, holding up a new surcoat. "There's a padded undercoat, and banners in your colors, as well. We won't have the Scion of Atyion riding into battle like some nameless thane."

"Thank you!" Tobin exclaimed, pulling the surcoat on over her hauberk. Going to the mirror, she studied her reflection as Ki buckled on her sword. The face framed by the antique coif wasn't that of a frightened girl, but the one she'd always known.

A warrior's face.

Ki grinned at her in the glass. "See? Under all that, you don't look any different at all."

"That may be for the best," said Arkoniel. "I doubt Erius will be pleased to hear he has a niece rather than a nephew. Tharin, make certain word is passed among the troops that the name Tamír is not to be spoken in Ero until the order is given."

"I wonder what Korin will say?" asked Ki.

"That's a good question," Arkoniel mused.

Tobin frowned at her reflection. "I've wondered about that ever since you and Lhel told me the truth. He's not just my kinsman, Arkoniel; he's my friend. How can I hurt him after he's been so good to me? It wouldn't be right, but I can't think what to do. He isn't very likely to just step aside, is he?"

"No," said Tharin.

"That's best left on the knees of the gods," Arkoniel advised. "For now, perhaps it's best if it's Prince Tobin who returns to Ero's aid. The rest will have to be sorted out afterward."

"If there is an afterward," Ki put in. "The Plenimarans aren't going to just step aside, either, and they have necromancers and plenty of soldiers. Sakor only knows how many!"

"Actually, we were able to do a bit of spying for you," said Tharin, grinning at Tobin's look of surprise. "Some of these wizards can be quite useful when they choose."

"You recall that time I flew you to Ero?" asked Arkoniel.

"That was a vision."

"A sighting spell, it's called. I'm no general, but with a bit of help from Tharin here, we estimated that the enemy has perhaps eight thousand men."

"Eight thousand! How many do we have here?"

"There are five hundred horsemen in the garrison, and nearly twice that with the foot and archers," said Tharin. "Another few hundred should stay behind to hold the castle if it's attacked. My cousin Oril will act as your marshal here—"

"Fifteen hundred. That's not nearly enough!"

"That's only the standing garrison. Word was sent to the outlying barons and knights as soon as we got here. Another two thousand can follow by tomorrow with the baggage train." He paused and gave Tobin a grim smile. "We don't have much choice, except to make do with what we have."

"Grannia sent me to ask if the women warriors might ride in your vanguard," Lytia told her.

"Yes, of course." Tobin thought a moment, recalling something of Raven's lessons. "Tell her only the very best fighters are to be in the front. Keep the others back in the ranks until they get seasoned. There's no shame in it. Tell them Skala needs them alive and fighting. There are too few of them to waste foolishly." As Lytia turned to go, she asked, "Will you be coming with us?"

She laughed. "No, Highness, I'm no warrior. But old Hakone taught me how to provision an army. We saw your father and grandfather off to many a battle. You'll have all you need."

"Thank you all. Whatever happens after this, I'm glad to have such friends with me."

Chapter 55

Fifteen hundred warriors seemed like a great force to Tobin as they rode out from Atyion that day. Ki and Lynx rode at her left, resplendent in their borrowed armor. Arkoniel looked awkward and uncomfortable in his mail shirt and steel cap, but Tharin had insisted. The priests who'd seen her transformation rode with them to bear witness in Ero. Captain Grannia and forty of her warriors rode proudly in the vanguard in front of them. Most were Nari's age or Cook's and had grey braids down their backs. They sang war songs as they rode, and their brave, clear voices sent a thrill through Tobin.

Tharin was her war marshal now, and introduced the other captains as they rode. Tobin knew some of them from previous visits. These men had all fought for her father and readily pledged themselves to her a second time, despite the strangeness of the situation.

Before they left the borders of Atyion, hundreds more from the southern steadings streamed out to join them—grizzled knights, farmers' sons with polearms on their shoulders, and more women and girls, some still in skirts. Grannia sorted the women out, sending some back into the ranks and others home.

"I wish there'd been time to get word to Ahra," Ki said, nodding at the women. "She and Una would want to be with you."

"News of Ero must have traveled," said Tharin. "I expect we'll meet up with them sooner or later."

They overtook other groups of warriors on their way to the city, alerted by Tobin's northbound passage the previous day. They addressed her as Prince Tobin and no one disabused them of it.

Most of the bands were village militias, but just before sundown they were overtaken by Lord Kyman of Ilear, who had five hundred archers and two hundred mounted warriors at his command.

Kyman was a huge, red-bearded old lord, and his scabbard showed the scars of many campaigns. He dismounted and saluted Tobin. "I knew your father well, my prince. It's an honor to serve his son."

Tobin bowed, muttering her thanks. Arkoniel gave her a wink, then drew Kyman aside for a moment. Tharin and the priests joined them and Tobin saw the priestess of Illior display her palm, as if for emphasis.

"I thought we weren't going to tell anyone?" Tobin muttered nervously.

"It's no good lying to the lords," said Ki. "Looks like he and Tharin are old friends, though. That's a good start."

When Arkoniel and Tharin had finished Kyman turned and stared at Tobin a moment, then strode over and looked up into her face, which was somewhat obscured by her helmet. "Is this true?"

"It is, my lord," she replied. "But I'm still Scion of Atyion and my father's child. Will you fight with me for Skala's sake, though sooner or later it may mean opposing the king?"

The man's coppery brows shot up. "You haven't heard, then? The king is dead. Prince Korin holds the Sword."

Tobin's heart sank; she'd clung to the hope that she wouldn't have to oppose Korin and the other Companions directly. There was no escaping it now.

"Your claim to the throne is as good as his for those who remember the Oracle," Kyman told her. "We've heard of you, you know. There've been rumors for years among the country folk of a queen who'd come and lift the curse from the land. But I didn't think there were any girls of the blood left." He jerked a thumb at Arkoniel and the priests. "It's a strange tale they tell, but there's no mistaking you as your father's blood. And I don't imagine you'd have the might of Atyion behind you, or my old friend Tharin either, if they didn't have good reason to believe you are what they say."

He dropped to one knee and presented his sword. "So my answer is yes. Let Ilear be the first to rally to your banner, Majesty."

Tobin accepted the blade and touched him on the shoulders as Erius had with Ki. "I don't claim the title of queen yet, but I accept, for Skala's sake, and Illior's."

He kissed the blade and took it back. "Thank you, Highness. I pray you'll remember Ilear and the house of Kyman kindly when you do wear the crown."

They stopped at sundown to eat and rest the horses, then marched on. A waxing moon peered out from behind scudding clouds, turning the muddy high road into a ribbon of black before them.

By midnight they could see a faint red glow in the southern sky above the black outlines of the hills; the city was still burning. Tharin sent a scouting party ahead to find the enemy's outlying posts. Among the ranks people were singing softly to keep themselves awake.

Weary as she was, Tobin's mind grew clearer as the night wore on. With an odd, dreamlike sense of detachment, she felt herself settling into this strange new body. Her arms and legs were no different, except for the annoying softness of her hands. Lytia had given her gloves for that. Her breasts, though small, had grown tender, and she was aware of them rubbing against the padded shirt under her hauberk.

The different fit of the saddle beneath her was the most disturbing change, not to mention the inconvenience of both trousers and a newfound modesty when she had to relieve herself. She hadn't been able to bring herself to examine that part of her body too closely. She resented not being able to take a piss properly, but all the same, it should have felt more like something was—lacking, that empty space in her trousers. Yet it didn't.

Arkoniel and Tharin treated her no differently than they ever had, and Ki was trying, but Lynx was still stealing sidelong glances. It was unsettling, but a good sign, in its way. It was the first time since Orneus' death that she'd seen him show interest in anything except getting himself killed.

Motioning for Ki to stay behind, she drew Lynx away from the main column.

"If you've changed your mind— If you can't go against Korin, I'll understand," she told him again. "If you want to go back to him, I won't let anyone stop you."

Lynx shrugged. "I'll stay, if you'll have me. I wonder what Nik and Lutha will do?"

"I don't know." But inwardly she quailed at the thought of her friends turning away.

Niryn strode across the echoing audience chamber to the throne accompanied by half a dozen of his remaining wizards and a phalanx of his Guard. A pigeon had come from Atyion just before nightfall bringing news of support, and the defenders had rallied.

Niryn had received word from his own spies there and meant to undo that slight hope.

Defeat sat heavily on the prince. Drawn and unshaven, Korin sat uneasily on his father's throne. He held the great Sword, but the crown remained on a small stand beside him, veiled in black. Chancellor Hylus and the other remaining ministers were with him, together with the tattered remains of his personal guard and Companions.

Niryn counted only eight Companions where there had once been nineteen. Sheltered as they had been at court all these years, they were no longer boys. He scanned their faces, making a quick evaluation. Alben and

Urmanis would prove loyal. So would Lord Caliel, though this one was an unwelcome influence on the new king; Niryn marked him to be dealt with later. That left only Hylus' bookish grandson, the homely one called Lutha, and a handful of squires who could be counted on, for good or ill, to follow their lords.

And Master Porion, he amended. The old warrior had some influence over the prince, as well, and would bear watching.

Reaching the dais, he bowed to Korin. "I bring grave news, Majesty! You have been betrayed."

Hectic color rose in Korin's pale cheeks. "What's happened? Who's turned on us?"

"Your cousin, and by the foulest of means." Niryn watched the play of doubt and fear across the young man's face. Touching his mind, Niryn found it wine-tinged, weak, and receptive. Others among his Companions were not so ready to believe him, however.

"Tobin would never do that!" Lutha cried.

"Silence!" Hylus ordered. "Explain yourself, Lord Niryn. How can this be?"

"The Lightbearer granted me a vision. I could not bring myself to believe it at first, but I've just received word that I saw true. Prince Tobin raised the garrison at Atyion against your liegeman, Solari, and murdered him and his family. He then employed some sort of necromancy to put on woman's form and declared himself the true heir of Skala by right of the Afran Oracle. Even now he marches against Ero with a host of thousands."

"What lunacy is this?" Hylus gasped. "Even if the boy was capable of such treachery, the captains of Atyion would never believe such a story, much less side with the enemy! You must be mistaken, Niryn."

"I assure you, I'm not. Before sunset tomorrow you will see the proof for yourself."

"No wonder he and that grass knight of his were so anxious to go over the wall," Alben muttered.

"Shut your mouth!" Lutha flew at the older boy, knocking him sprawling.

"That's enough!" Porion roared.

Caliel and Nikides wrestled Lutha off Alben and dragged him back.

Alben wiped blood from his mouth, and snarled, "He probably had this planned all along, he and that wizard woman of his. She was always sneaking in and out of his house."

"Mistress Iya?" Nikides said. "She came and went openly. Besides, she was only a hedge wizard."

"A bit more than that, perhaps," said Hylus. "I know the woman, Prince Korin. She is a loyal Skalan, and I would swear by my own name that she is no necromancer."

"Perhaps Tobin only put on women's clothes," Urmanis offered.

"Don't be a fool!" Lutha cried, still furious. "Why would he do that?"

"Perhaps he went mad like his mother," one of the squires sneered. "He always has been odd."

"Korin, think!" Caliel pleaded. "You know as well as I do that Tobin isn't mad. And he'd never betray you."

Niryn let them argue, marking enemies and allies.

Korin had listened all this time in silence as Niryn's magic wormed its way deeper into his heart, seeking out all the buried doubts and fears. His faith in Tobin was still too strong, but that would change when he saw the truth.

Niryn bowed again. "I stand by my word, Majesty. Be on your guard."

*T*obin's scouts returned just before dawn with word of a Plenimaran presence at a horse breeder's steading a few miles north of the city on the coast road. It appeared to be a prisoner camp, with fewer than a hundred men guarding it.

"We should swing wide around them and cut them off

before we attack," Tharin advised. "The less notice the main force has of us coming, the better for us."

"Eat the beast in small pieces, eh?" Kyman chuckled.

The scouts outlined the position. The enemy had taken over a large farmstead and had pickets set all around. Tobin could imagine her old teacher Raven sketching it out on the stone floor of the lesson room.

"We don't need the whole force to take such a small group," she said. "A hundred mounted warriors in a surprise attack should be enough."

Captain Grannia had fallen back to hear the report. "Let my company go with them, Highness. It's been too long since we drew blood."

"Very well. But I'll lead the charge."

"Is that wise?" Arkoniel objected. "If we lost you in the first battle—"

"No, she's right," said Tharin. "We've asked these warriors to believe a miracle. They'll lose heart if they think they're following a hollow figurehead."

Tobin nodded. "Everyone expected the first Ghërilain to hang back after her father made her queen, let the generals do the fighting for her. But she didn't, and she won. I'm as much Illior's queen as she was, and I'm better trained."

"History repeating itself, eh?" Arkoniel considered this, then leveled a stern finger at Tharin, Ki, and Lynx. "Don't you leave her side, you hear me? A dead warrior is even less use than a figurehead."

They swept down on the steading with drawn swords. A low earthen wall surrounded the house, barns, and three stone-and-wattle corrals. Tobin and her warriors rode down the few outlying pickets and cleared the walls, hacking down any defenders who ran to meet them.

It was Tobin's first mounted fight, but she felt the same inner calm as she hacked down the swordsmen who tried to unhorse her. She fought in silence, but heard Ki and

Tharin shouting as they fought beside her, and Grannia's women screamed like demons. Pale hands waved and gestured over the top of a corral, and Tobin could hear the screams of the captives there.

Lynx rode into the thick of the fight and dismounted.

"No!" Tobin shouted after him, but he was already gone. If he was determined to court death, there was nothing she could do for him.

The Plenimarans fought fiercely, but were outnumbered. Not one was left alive when the battle ended.

Ignoring the dead, Tobin rode to the nearest corral. It was filled with women and children from Ero. They wept and blessed her as she helped tear down the palings of the gate, and crowded around her horse to touch her.

Every Skalan child had heard dark tales of people being carried off to Plenimar as slaves, a practice unheard of in the western lands. Those lucky enough to escape and find their way home brought dark tales of degradation and torment.

A woman clung to Tobin's ankle, sobbing and pointing toward the barn. "Never mind us! You must help them in the barn. Please, General, in the Maker's name, help them!"

Tobin dismounted and pushed through the crowd and ran to the open barn door with Ki at her heels. A fallen torch smoldered in a pile of hay, and what they saw in that smoky light froze them in their tracks.

Eighteen naked, bloody men stood against the far wall, arms held over their head as if in surrender. Most had had their bellies slashed open; intestines spilled down around their feet like ropes of grisly sausage.

"Tharin!" she shouted, picking up the torch and stamping out the burning hay. "Tharin, Grannia, get in here. Bring help!"

Lynx came up, then staggered back, retching.

Tobin and the others had heard dark tales of what Plenimarans did with captured warriors. Now they saw it for themselves. The men had been beaten, then stripped, and their hands pulled over their heads and nailed in place through the wrists. The Skalan attack must have interrupted the enemy at their sport, for three had not yet been disemboweled. To Tobin's horror, a number of those who had been were still alive, and began to struggle and cry out at her approach.

"Lynx, go for healers," Tobin ordered.

Tharin had come in, and caught Lynx by the arm as he turned to obey. "Wait a moment. Let me have a look first."

Tharin let go of Lynx and drew Tobin close, speaking low into her ear as other soldiers crowded in at the door. "These that are cut open? Not even a drysian could put them right and it can take days to die."

Tobin read the truth in his friend's pale eyes and nodded. "We'll speed them on."

"Leave it be. They understand, believe me."

"But not those three who aren't butchered. We've got to get them down. Send someone for tools."

"Already done."

One of the three lifted his head at their approach, and Ki groaned. "Oh hell, Tob. That's Tanil!" The man next to him was alive, as well, but had been castrated. The third was dead or unconscious.

Tobin and Ki went to Tanil and got their arms around him, lifting him to take the weight off his nailed wrists.

Tanil let out a hoarse sob. "Oh gods, it's you. Help me!"

Grannia and several of her women went to work with farriers' pliers while others held the wounded men upright. The one who'd been castrated let out a scream as the nails came loose, but Tanil gritted his teeth, lips curled in a silent snarl of pain. Tobin and Ki lowered him to the ground and Lynx threw his cloak over him and cut strips from it to bandage the wounds.

Tanil opened his eyes and looked up at Tobin. She tossed her helm aside and stroked the dark hair back from his brow. He'd been badly beaten, and his eyes were vague.

"Korin?" he panted, eyes wandering from face to face. "I lost him . . . Stupid! I turned and he was . . . I have to find him!"

"Korin is safe," Ki told him. "You're safe, too. We made it, Tanil. Tobin's brought Atyion back to save the city. It's all right, now. Stay still."

But Tanil didn't seem to understand. Throwing off the cloak, he struggled weakly to get up. "Korin. I lost him. Got to find . . ."

A red-haired woman who'd been among the captives knelt by Tobin and touched her arm. "I'll tend to him, Highness, and the others. This was my farm. I've got all I need for them."

"Thank you." Tobin stood up and wiped a hand across her mouth. Some of the disembowled men had been taken down and laid out in the hay with cloaks pulled over their faces.

Tharin was dealing with those who still lived. As Tobin watched, he stepped close to one still nailed. He spoke close to the man's ear and Tobin saw the dying man nod. Tharin kissed him on the brow, then quickly plunged his dagger up under his ribs, into his heart. The man shuddered and went limp. Tharin stepped to the next man.

Tobin turned away, not wanting to see more, and stumbled into a young woman who'd come up behind her. She was dressed in the tattered remains of a silk gown. Sinking to her knees at Tobin's feet, she mumbled, "Forgive me, Prince Tobin, I only wanted to thank—" She looked up and her eyes went wide.

"I know you, don't I?" Tobin asked, trying to place her. She seemed familiar, but she'd been beaten, too. Her face was too bruised and swollen to recognize. Someone had bitten her on the shoulder, and the wound was still bleeding.

"I'm Yrena, my—" She started to say "prince" and stopped, still staring.

"Yrena? Oh!" Tobin felt her face go scarlet. "You were—"

The courtesan bowed her head, confusion still plain on her face. "Your birthday gift, Highness."

Tobin was aware of Ki staring at her as she raised the woman by the hand. "I remember you, and your kindness, too."

"It's more than repaid, for the fate you spared me tonight." Yrena's eyes filled with tears. "Whatever else I can do, I will."

"You could help with the wounded," Tobin replied.

"Of course, Highness." Yrena took Tobin's hands in hers and kissed them, then went to help the red-haired woman. Sadly, there was little left to do. Only one other man lay beside Tanil. All the others were dead, and soldiers were singing the dirge.

Tharin was wiping his knife with a rag. "Come away, Tobin," he said softly. "There's nothing more to do here."

A scream rang out beyond the house, then another, followed by shrill Skalan hunting cries.

"We must have missed a few," said Tharin. "Do you want prisoners taken?"

Tobin looked back at the mutilated Skalans. "No. No prisoners."

Chapter 56

The Wormhole stronghold was lost during the fourth day of the siege. The Plenimarans were systematically burning the districts of the city and Iya watched from a distance as the stone buildings above the Wormhole blazed like furnaces. Old Lyman and the others too old or infirm had been sped on, passing their life force into friends or former apprentices. There had been no safe place to move them.

The city was unrecognizable. The last of the free wizards crept through the raddled landscape like ghosts. Even the enemy had forsaken the wasteland they'd created, massing instead around the smoke-blackened bastion of the Palatine.

Iya and Dylias gathered the survivors near the east gate that night, sheltering in the ruins of a granary. Of the thirty-eight wizards she'd known here, only nineteen were left, and eight were wounded. None were warriors, but they'd moved with stealth and attacked small forces by surprise, banding together to use their newfound strength against necromancer and soldiers alike.

Some of them had fallen by magic—Orgeus had been caught in a magical blast of some sort and died instantly. Saruel the Khatme, who'd been with him, had lost the hearing in one ear. Archers or swordsmen had killed others. None had been taken alive.

Too many precious lives lost, Iya thought, keeping watch through that long night. *And too much power gone already.*

As she'd suspected, wizards could draw strength from

one another if they chose and it was compounded, not diminished. The fewer of them there were, the less power they could muster. And yet they had fought well. As near as she could tell, they'd killed all but a few of the necromancers. Iya had killed three herself, slaying them with the same heat she'd used to melt the cup the night she'd first visited the Wormhole. She'd never turned that on a living being before; they'd fizzled and burst their skins like sausages. It had been a most satisfying sight.

"What do we do now?" a young wizard named Hariad asked, as they crouched with the others in the smoky granary, sharing what food they'd been able to scavenge.

All eyes turned to Iya. She'd never claimed to be their leader, but she had brought the vision. Setting aside the stale crust she'd been eating, she rubbed at her eyes and sighed. "We've done all we can, I think. We can't get into the Palatine, and we're no match for an army. But if we can get out, we might be of some use to Tobin when she arrives."

And so it was decided. Iya and her ragged defenders abandoned the city and fled under cover of darkness and magic, making their way through the scattered Plenimaran pickets beyond the ruins of the north gate.

Following the same route Tobin had taken three nights earlier, they found their way to the copse where Eyoli still lay hidden. She expected to find a corpse, for she'd had no word from him since the night he was wounded. He'd managed one message spell, telling her of the ambush, then nothing.

Instead, she was amazed to find him unconscious but alive. Tobin had left him bundled in Plenimaran cloaks beneath a large oak, with half a dozen canteens around him. The crows had been busy among the dead scattered on the open ground beyond the trees, but the young mind clouder was untouched.

It was a cold, clear night. They built a small fire and

made camp under the trees. Iya gave Eyoli what help she could and he came to at last.

"I dreamed—I saw her!" he croaked, reaching weakly for her hand.

Iya stroked his brow. "Yes, we all did."

"Then it's true? It was Prince Tobin all along?"

"Yes. And you helped her."

Eyoli smiled and closed his eyes. "That's all right, then. I don't mind about the rest."

Iya stripped the crusted bandage from his shoulder and wrinkled her nose at the smell. The wound was full of pus, but there was no sign of the spreading rot. She let out a sigh of relief. She'd grown fond of this fearless young man, and come to depend on him, too. She'd lost count of the times he'd passed through the Harriers' net, carrying messages. He'd mastered the message spell, too, which still eluded her.

"Saruel, bring what simples you have left," she called softly. Iya wrapped herself in her cloak and leaned back against the tree while the Aurënfaie cleaned the wound. Summoning what strength she had left, she sent out a seeing spell, skimming above the darkened countryside to the Palatine. They still fought there, but the dead lay everywhere and the three necromancers she'd been unable to hunt down or vanquish were busy before the gates.

Turning her mind north, she saw Tobin and her raiders bearing down on a Plenimaran outpost, and the army that followed close behind. "Come, my queen," she murmured as the vision faded. "Claim your birthright."

"She has claimed it," a cold voice whispered close to her ear.

Opening her eyes, Iya saw Brother crouched beside her, his pale thin lips curled in a sneer.

"Your work is done, old woman." He reached toward her, as if to take her hand.

Iya saw her own death in those bottomless black eyes,

but summoned a protection spell just in time. "No. Not yet. There's more left for me to do."

The spell held, rocking the demon back on his haunches. He bared his teeth at her. Freed from Tobin, he seemed even less human than before. He had the greenish cast of a corpse. "I don't forget," he whispered, slowly melting into the darkness. "Never forget . . ."

Iya shuddered. Sooner or latter this piper would demand his pay, but not yet. Not yet.

A sound like thunder woke them at dawn. The earth shook and twigs and dead leaves rained down around them. Iya eased the stiffness from her back and limped to the edge of the trees with the others.

Their little copse was about to become an island caught between two great opposing waves. A dark mass of horsemen was nearly upon them from the north and Iya made out the banners of Atyion and Ilear in the forefront. To the south, a host of Plenimaran infantry was marching to meet them. In minutes they'd be at the center of a battle.

And where are you in all that, Arkoniel? she wondered, but knew a sighting spell would be wasted energy. There was no way to help him, even if she knew where he was.

The attack on the farmstead was no more than a raid, and a bit of good luck in the dark. No ballad or lesson had prepared Ki for the reality of battle.

Somehow word of their coming had reached the city. They'd gone less than half a mile from the farm when they saw a large force advancing to meet them.

Ki had listened as well as he could to old Raven's strategy lessons and histories, but he was happy enough to leave such things to Tobin and the officers. His only thought was to do his duty and keep his friend alive.

"How many?" Tobin asked, reining in.

"Two thousand or so," Grannia called back. "And they're not stopping to set stakes."

Tobin conferred briefly with Tharin and Lord Kyman. "Put foot and archers in the fore," she ordered. "Atyion's horse will take right wing, Ilear on the left. I'll stay at the center with my guard and Grannia's company."

The Plenimarans did not stop to parlay or entrench, but came at them in ordered ranks, spears gleaming in the sunlight like a field of silvery oats. Banners of red, black, gold, and white tilted on standards at the front. The forward lines marched in tight squares and used tall rectangular shields to form a wall and roof against arrows.

The Skalan archers went forward first, in five ranks of a hundred each. Aiming high, they shot over the shield line and sent wave after whistling wave of feathered death into the ranks of infantry behind them. The Plenimarans answered with flights of their own and Ki wheeled his horse and threw his shield up to protect Tobin.

Orders flew up and down the front line, bellowed from sergeant to sergeant. Tobin raised her sword and the foot soldiers set off at a trot to meet the Plenimaran line.

Tobin watched for an opening, then gave the signal again and kicked her mount forward. Ki and Tharin flanked her as they went from trot to canter to full gallop. When he could make out the faces of the enemy Ki drew his sword with the others and joined in the war cries.

"Atyion for Skala and the Four!"

They crashed into the melee and very nearly came to grief. A pikeman caught Tobin's charger in the side and it reared. For one awful instant Ki saw Tobin's helmeted head framed against the cloudy blue sky above him. Then she was falling, tumbling backward into the maelstrom of surging horses and men.

"Tobin!" Tharin cried, trying to urge his horse through the press to get to her.

Ki leaped from the saddle, dodging and ducking as he

sought a flash of her surcoat. A horseman knocked him sprawling, then he was rolling to avoid the trampling hooves that seemed to come at him from every side.

It turned out to be the right direction, for suddenly she was there in front of him, laying about with her sword. Ki ducked another rearing horse and dashed to her, putting his back to hers just as a Plenimaran knight broke through and swung a saber at her head. Ki caught the blade with his own and felt the shock of it all the way to his shoulder.

Tharin rode free of the press and brought his blade down on the man's head, knocking him off his feet. Ki finished the job.

"Come on, Kadmen has your horses!" he shouted.

He and Tobin mounted, but were soon afoot again as the line ground to a halt. It was like scything an endless hayfield, this fighting. Their sword hands were blistered and numb and glued to their hilts with blood before the enemy finally broke and ran.

"What happened?" Tobin asked as they climbed back into the saddle.

"Colath!" the cry came down the line. "Colath has come to our aid."

"Colath?" Ki shouted. "That's Lord Jorvai. Ahra will be with him!"

The Plenimarans were on the run by then, with Jorvai's orange-and-green banner close behind.

"No quarter!" Tobin cried, raising her sword. "After them, riders, and give no quarter."

Eyoli was too sick to move, and there was nowhere to take him anyway with the two armies clashing around them. Iya cast an occlusion over him where he lay and set wards to keep him from being trampled. Arrows sang through the foliage and Iya heard a cry, then the dull thud of a body hitting the ground.

"Iya, here. Hurry!" Dylias called.

A party of Plenimaran archers was running toward the

trees. Iya joined hands with Saruel and Dylias, and they began the chant. Power surged through them and with the
others Iya pointed a hand at the enemy. A flash like lightning sizzled from the wizards' fingertips and twenty men
fell, struck dead in an instant. Those few who survived
turned tail and ran.

"Run, you dogs. For Skala!" Dylias cried, shaking his
fist at their backs.

The battle swirled back and forth across the plain all
morning and the wizards manned the copse like a fortress.
When the last of their useful magic was spent, they took to
the treetops and hid there.

The two sides were evenly matched in number, and
the Plenimarans were a formidable foe. Three times Iya
saw Tobin's banner falter and three times it was taken up
again. Helpless to do anything but watch, Iya clung to the
rough trunk and prayed that the Lightbearer would not let
so much pain and sacrifice be lost here in sight of the city.

As if in answer to her plea, a huge body of horsemen
appeared from the north just as the sun passed noon.

"It's Colath!" someone cried out.

"A thousand at least!" someone else shouted, and a
ragged cheer went up.

The forces of Colath struck on the Plenimarans' left
flank, and the enemy line faltered, then broke. Tobin's
cavalry fell on them like a pack of wolves. The Plenimaran
standards fell, and what followed was a massacre.

The rout drove the few survivors back to the city. Tobin
led her army straight on for the northern wall.

The Plenimaran defenders there were ready for them.
They'd set stakes across the road and fortified the broken
gates. Archers behind the stake line and along the walls
sent a hail of arrows down on the Skalans as they charged.

For one awful moment Ki was afraid Tobin would
keep right on going into the enemy line. She looked like a

demon herself, fierce and blood-soaked. But she stopped at last.

Oblivious to the shafts whining around them, she sat her horse and surveyed the gate ahead. Ki and Lynx rode to cover her. Behind them Tharin was shouting and swearing.

"Come on!" Ki shouted, catching two shafts with his shield.

Tobin cast a last glance at the gate, then wheeled her horse and brandished her sword, leading the way back out of range.

"Sakor-touched!" Ki hissed through his teeth, spurring after her.

They rode back a quarter mile or so and stopped to re-group. As Tobin conferred with Lord Kyman and Tharin, a grizzled lord and his escort rode up and hailed her. Ki recognized Jorvai and his eldest sons, but doubted they'd know him. He'd been a scrawny swineherd on Jorvai's land when they'd last seen him.

Jorvai was the same hale old warrior he remembered. Recognizing Tobin by her surcoat, he dismounted and knelt to present his sword. "My prince! Will the Scion of Atyion accept the aid of Colath?"

"Yes. Rise, with Atyion's thanks," Tobin replied.

But Jorvai remained on his knees, looking up at her from beneath his shaggy grey brows. "Is this the son of Rhius I bow to?"

Tobin pulled off her helm. "I am the daughter of Ariani and Rhius."

Arkoniel and the Illioran priestess who'd come with them from Atyion stepped out to join them. "This is the one who was foretold. She is as she says," the priestess told him.

"It's true," Arkoniel told him. "I've known Tobin since birth, and this is the same person."

"By the Light!" A look of pure wonder came over

Jorvai's face. He had heard the prophecies, and believed. "Will the daughter of Ariani accept the fealty of Colath?"

Tobin accepted his sword. "I do, and most gratefully. Rise, Lord Jorvai and clasp hands with me. My father spoke well of you."

"He was a great warrior, your father. It seems you take after him. And here's Captain Tharin!" He and Tharin embraced. "By the Light, I haven't seen you in years. It's good to find you still among the living."

Tobin smiled. "Tell me, my lord, does Ahra of Oakmount still serve you?"

"She's one of my best captains."

Tobin motioned Ki forward and clasped his shoulder. "Tell Captain Ahra that her brother and I asked after her, and that she should seek us out when Ero is safe."

Jorvai looked more closely at Ki. "Well now! One of old Larenth's boys, aren't you?"

"Yes, my lord. Kirothius of Oakmount. And Rilmar," he added.

Jorvai laughed outright at this. "I miss the old bandit and his brood. I don't doubt you're well pleased with this one, Highness, if he takes after his old dad."

"He does, my lord," Tobin replied, and Ki could tell she liked the plainspoken old man. *No wonder*, he thought fondly; *they're cut from the same cloth*.

*T*his had been well-tended farmland when Iya and the wizard had crossed it last night. Now, as if some great tide had come and gone, the churned soil was scattered with bodies, hundreds of men and horses abandoned like broken toys across acres of trampled mud.

Tobin had chased off the enemy, but soon returned and stopped half a mile off. Iya gathered the others, and they set off to meet her, with some of the younger men carrying Eyoli in a cloak.

As they left the cover of the trees a black war charger thundered past with rolling red eyes, dragging its entrails behind it. His dead master dangled and bounced along-side, one foot still caught in the iron loop of a stirrup.

The groans of the wounded came from all sides as the wizards made their way across the battlefield. Skalan men-at-arms were still busy dispatching the dying and stripping the enemy corpses.

Ero was wreathed in a sullen sunset haze. The Palatine was still under siege, but Iya could also make out a dark line of men before the lower gates. The enemy would not be taken unawares there.

Reaching the main body of Tobin's army, they were questioned briefly, then led to the center of the great throng where Tobin was conferring with a group of warriors. Jorvai and Kyman were foremost among them. Ki and Tharin were both still with her, and Arkoniel, too, Iya saw with a rush of relief. The young wizard saw her and touched Tobin's shoulder. Tobin turned, and Iya's breath caught in her throat.

This was the face the Oracle had shown her—weary, filthy, not beautiful, but indomitable. This was their warrior queen.

"Majesty," Iya said, hurrying forward and sinking to her knees. The others joined her. "I bring wizards loyal to you and to Skala."

"Iya! Thank the Four, but where did you come from?" The voice was different, and yet the same. Tobin drew her to her feet and gave Iya a wry grin. "You've never knelt to me before. And I'm not queen yet."

"You will be. You've come into your own at last."

"And your work is done."

A chill ran up Iya's spine. Had Tobin intentionally echoed Brother's words? But she saw only welcome in her eyes and a fierce resolve.

"And your work is just begun, it seems, but you'll have help," she told Tobin. "This is Master Dylias. He and these others stood against the Harriers and fought for Ero. They were with me when I found you and the Companions the other day."

"Thank you all," Tobin said, bowing to the ragtag group.

"And we'll fight for you again, if you'll have us," Dylias said, bowing low. "We bring fresh word of the enemy's movements inside the city. We were there until last night."

Tobin took him to consult with her captains and lords, but Ki and Arkoniel stayed with Iya.

Arkoniel embraced her, holding her tight. "By the Light!" he mumbled, and she realized he was weeping. "We did it," he whispered against her shoulder. "Can you believe it? We did it!"

"Indeed we did, my dear." She gave him a squeeze, and he stepped back, wiping his eyes. For a moment he looked like a boy again and her heart swelled.

"I'm glad to see you, too, Mistress," Ki told her shyly. "I didn't like leaving you back there."

Iya smiled. "And here you are, right where you belong. I knew I chose well that day."

"You might have told me a bit more," he replied softly. She caught a hint of accusation in those dark brown eyes, but it disappeared as he caught sight of Eyoli, who was being tended to by several healers now. "Eyoli, is that you?" he exclaimed, hurrying over. "Hey, Tobin, look! He's alive after all!"

Tobin came back and knelt by the young wizard. "Thank the Light! I just sent riders looking for you, but here you are!"

Eyoli raised his hand to his brow and heart. "As soon as I have my strength back, I'll fight for you again. Perhaps I'll get better at it, with practice."

Tobin laughed, a clear, good sound in the midst of such a day, then stood and called out, "All of you, this is the wizard Eyoli, who helped me escape from Ero. I declare him a hero and my friend!"

A cheer went up and the young man colored shyly.

Tobin moved to Iya's side. "And this is the seer you've heard of. It was Mistress Iya who the Lightbearer spoke to, and she and Master Arkoniel who protected me as a child. They're to be held in highest honor forever."

Iya and Arkoniel bowed in their turn and touched their hearts and brows to Tobin.

Mounting her horse again, Tobin addressed them again in a loud voice.

"I thank you all for your bravery, your faith, and your loyalty. Every man and woman who fought beside me today is a hero worthy of the name, but I must ask more of you."

She pointed to the smoking city. "For the first time in our long history, an enemy holds Ero. By all reports, there may still be as many as six thousand waiting for us there. We must go on. I will go on! Will you follow me?"

The response was deafening. Tobin's charger reared and she brandished her sword. The blade caught the sunset light, flashing like Sakor's fiery sword.

Gradually the cheering took on a rhythm. "The queen! The queen!"

Tobin motioned for silence. It took some time, but when she could be heard again, she cried out, "By the Lightbearer's moon rising in the east, I swear to you that I will be your queen, but I will not claim that title until it's the Sword of Ghërilain I lift in my right hand. I'm told my kinsman Prince Korin holds it now—"

She was drowned out by a swell of angry voices.

"Usurper!"

"The plague bringer's son!"

But Tobin wasn't finished. "Hear me, loyal Skalans, and pass this on to all you meet as my will!" Her voice was hoarse now, but it carried. "Prince Korin's blood is as true as my own! I will not have it spilled. Any man who harms my kinsman harms me and will be counted among my enemies! Look there." She pointed at the ruined city again. "Even as you curse him, the prince fights for Skala. We fight for Ero, not against Korin!" She paused and seemed to sag a bit. "Let us save our land. We'll sort out the rest after that. For Ero and Skala!"

Arkoniel heaved a sigh of relief as the throng took up the call, but Iya frowned. "Doesn't she realize he won't just step aside?"

"Perhaps not, and even if she does, this was the right thing to say," he replied. "Not every lord will be as easily won as Kyman or Jorvai. There are too many of Solari's ilk left, and Korin has a legitimate claim in the eyes of many others. Tobin can't be known first as a kin slayer or renegade. Whatever happens later on, I suspect this speech of hers just laid the foundation of her legend."

"I'm not so sure."

"Trust the Lightbearer, Iya. The fact that she came through that battle in one piece is a good omen. And the fact that we're both standing here with her, too." He hugged her again. "By the Light, I'm glad to see you. When Eyoli sent word of the attack the other day—Well, it sounded bad."

"I didn't expect to see you so soon, either! Have you learned to fly?" she asked. "And what happened to your wrist? Were you hurt in the battle?"

He laughed. "No, I kept out of that. But I did make good use of that spell I showed you. Remember the one I lost my finger to?"

Iya raised a disapproving eyebrow. "The translocation? By the Light, you used it on yourself?"

"I've made some improvements since we last spoke. It was the only way to get to her in time." He held up his broken wrist again. "Can't say that I recommend it for general use just yet, but think of it, Iya! A hundred miles crossed in the blink of an eye."

Iya shook her head. "I knew you'd be great, dear boy.

I just had no idea how quickly you'd achieve it. I'm so proud of you—" She broke off with a sudden look of alarm. "Where is it? You haven't let it out of your possession already?"

Arkoniel pulled back his cloak and showed her the battered old leather bag at his belt. "Here it is."

"And there *they* are, and their necromancers," Iya murmured, frowning back at Ero. "Keep away from them. Hang back if you must, or throw it through one of those black holes of yours, but don't let it be taken!"

"I thought of that after I got here," he admitted. "I could send it back. Wythnir is still—"

"No. Remember what Ranai told you. Only one Guardian can carry it, and that child is not the one. If the worst should come and I still live, send it to me."

"And if you're—gone?"

"Well, I guess we better keep an eye out for other successors, eh?" She sighed. "What it has to do with any of this, I don't know, but at least we've come this far. I saw Tobin revealed, Arkoniel, that night in Ero. The others did, too. It must have been when the binding spell was broken. I saw her face as clearly as I see yours now. Did you and Lhel see her, too?"

"I did, but I don't know about Lhel. I haven't seen her since midwinter. She's just—disappeared. There wasn't time to look for her when I was at the keep yesterday, but Nari hadn't seen her since we left for the mountains."

"You're worried for her."

Arkoniel nodded. "She left in the dead of winter and took almost nothing with her. If she didn't return to the keep or her oak—Well, perhaps she didn't make it back at all. She had nowhere else to go except to her own people, and I don't think she'd do that before Brother was free."

"No, I'm sure she wouldn't."

"Perhaps she'll come to Ero," he said without much hope.

"Perhaps. What about Brother? Have you seen him?"

"Not since Tobin undid the binding. He appeared for a moment then. Have you?"

"A glimpse. He's not finished with us yet, Arkoniel." Her fingers were cold as she clasped his hand. "Be on your guard."

Chapter 57

Tobin's attack had temporarily distracted the Plenimarans from their assault on the citadel.

Leaning wearily on the ramparts, Lutha and Nikides watched with mounting hope as Tobin's small army decimated the Plenimaran force and drove it back behind the walls. Tobin's banner was at the forefront of every charge.

Despite this initial defeat, the remaining Plenimaran host still held the city and the citadel. The remaining Palatine defenders were exhausted from pushing off scaling ladders and putting out fires.

The Plenimaran catapults had been moved up the hill two days earlier and rained a steady bombardment of stones and fire. Many of the outer villas and temples had been lost. The Companions' former quarters at the Old Palace were an infirmary, filled with the wounded and the homeless.

The Plenimaran commander, Lord General Harkol, had demanded their surrender twice the day before and twice Korin had refused. They had water and food enough for an extended siege, but had long since exhausted their supply of arrows. They'd been reduced to tossing anything they could find down on the enemy's heads—furniture, paving stones, chamber pots, logs cut from the trees of the Palatine gardens and the Grove of Dalna. They'd even thrown down the stone effigies from the royal tombs.

"I believe the queens would approve," Chancellor Hylus had said dryly when he'd suggested it. "They gave their lives for Skala. I'm sure they would not begrudge a bit of stone."

The old fellow must have been right, Lutha thought. They'd managed to crush several Plenimaran necromancers at a blow with Queen Markira.

Watching Tobin's forces regroup that afternoon, Lutha shook his head. "You don't believe that nonsense of Niryn's, do you, Nik?"

"About Tobin claiming to be a girl?" Nikides rolled his eyes.

"No, I mean about him turning traitor and trying to take the throne."

"I believe that even less, but Korin seems to. You saw him the other day. And I don't like the way Niryn keeps him shut away every night, pouring wine down his throat and poison in his ear. That scares me more than that army down there."

Tobin attacked twice again before nightfall, storming the walls and barricades. The Plenimaran line held, but the ground beyond was littered with their dead. Rain blew in off the sea just after sunset, and clouds sealed the sky.

As the last light faded, another host marched out of the gloom to the south. It was impossible to make out their banners but Nikides said it looked like knights and yeoman, probably from Ylani and the towns of the middle coast. There were at least two thousand, and suddenly the Plenimarans found themselves besieged in the burned waste they'd made between the harbor and the citadel. The forces around the citadel began to thin and the flickering movement of torches through the night showed that they were dividing themselves to fight on three fronts.

I won't do it!" Korin said, pacing back angrily around his private sitting room. The room stank of wine and fear.

Niryn glanced over at Chancellor Hylus. The old man sat by the fire, his mind filled with treason, but said nothing. Niryn's hold over Korin was nearly complete and they both knew it.

Niryn had convinced the prince to leave his remaining Companions outside the door on guard—all but Caliel, presently glowering at Niryn in the shadows near the door.

It was nearly midnight. The storm had risen steadily since sunset. Rain and sleet lashed against the windows in angry gusts. The night was impenetrable except for the occasional flash of lightning.

"For Skala's sake, Majesty, you must consider the possibility," Niryn urged as another gust of wind shook the windows. "This new force from the south is nothing but a peasant rabble! They won't turn the tide, any more than Tobin's army will. Not in this weather. They know they're outnumbered and they've withdrawn. But the enemy sappers haven't stopped at the Palatine gate. I can hear them when the wind drops! They could break through at any moment and what will we do? You have only a handful of warriors left."

"The Plenimarans are caught in the same storm," Caliel countered, voice trembling with thinly veiled anger. "Korin, you can't just run away!"

"Again, you mean?" Korin shot back, giving his friend a bitter smile.

"That's not what I said."

Niryn was pleased to see some hint of division at last. "It would not be running away, Lord Caliel," he said smoothly. "If the enemy breaches the gate, they will kill everyone they find, including our young king. They'll drag his body through the streets and display his head as a trophy in Benshâl. The Overlord will wear the crown and Ghërilain's Sword at their victory feast."

Korin paused in his pacing and gripped the hilt of the great sword hanging against his hip. "He's right, Caliel. They know they can't take the whole country with one assault, but if they destroy Ero, capture the treasury and the

Sword, kill the last of the line—how long will Skala stand after that?"

"But Tobin—"

"Is as great a threat!" Korin shot back. "You've heard the reports. Every Illioran left in the city is whispering about it, saying the true queen has come back to save the land. Three more priests were executed today, but the damage is done. How long until this rabble unbars the gate to the renegades? You saw the banners among Tobin's army; the countryside is already rising to join him—or her!" He threw his hands up with a snarl of disgust. "It doesn't matter what the truth is; the ignorant already believe. And if he does manage to break through, what then?" He drew the sword and held it up. "Better for the Overlord to have this than a traitor!"

"You're wrong, Kor! Why can't you see it?" Caliel cried. "If Tobin wanted the city to fall, why come to our defense? He could just as easily have delayed and let the invaders do his dirty work for him. You saw how he fought today. Wait, I beg you. Give it another day before you do this."

Alben burst in and gave Korin a hasty salute. "Korin, sappers have broken through under the wall and the main gate just fell. They're pouring in like rats!"

Korin's eyes were like a dead man's as he turned to Caliel. "Gather my guard and the Companions. Ero is lost."

Chapter 58

Caught in that torrential downpour, Tobin's army had no choice but to hunker down and wait for dawn.

Using pikes, cloaks, and a bit of hedge magic, the wizards managed to construct a few small tents for themselves, and for Tobin and her officers.

Tobin and Tharin spoke at length with the Wormhole survivors, learning what they could of the enemy's strength, but their report was old news by now.

Sometime near midnight a shout of dismay went up among the ranks as a red glow blossomed against the sky.

"The Palatine!" Ki exclaimed. "They must have broken through. It's burning!"

Tobin turned to Arkoniel. "Can you show me what's happening, like you did with Tharin?"

"Of course." They knelt together on a folded cloak and Arkoniel took her hands in his. "We haven't done this since you were a child. Do you remember what I taught you?"

Tobin nodded. "You had me imagine I was an eagle."

Arkoniel smiled. "Yes, that will do. Just close your eyes and let yourself rise."

Tobin felt a dizzying sensation of movement, then saw the dark, rainswept plain sliding away below her. The illusion was strong; she could feel her wings and the rain beating down on them. A large owl flew with her, and it had Arkoniel's eyes. He glided ahead and she followed, circling the Plenimaran position by the gate, then soaring up to the devastation of the Palatine.

The New Palace, the temple, and the sacred grove: they were all in flames. Everywhere she looked she saw hundreds of people locked in close combat. There were no banners to tell her where the Companions were. It was utter chaos. As she circled the burning grove, however, she looked to the south and saw with amazement that another small army was encamped there, facing the contingent of Plenimarans who held the Beggar's Bridge gate.

She was about to swoop down for a closer look when she found herself kneeling under the dripping tent again, the beginnings of a headache throbbing just behind her eyes. Arkoniel was holding his head in his hands.

"I'm sorry," he gasped. "With everything that's happened these last few days, I'm a bit used up."

"We all are," Iya said, pressing her hand to the back of his neck.

Tobin got up and turned to Tharin. "We must attack. Now."

"We can't!" said Jorvai.

"He's right, Highness," Kyman agreed. "A night attack is always risky, but with this rain the horses will be more likely to founder, or run themselves onto stakes."

"We'll take our chances then, but we must attack now! The Palatine has fallen. They're fighting for their lives. If we don't help them, there'll be no one left to save by morning. There's another army on the south side and the Plenimarans have had to divide up to face them. Iya, what can your wizards do? Can you help us break through at the lower walls?"

"We'll do what we can."

"Good. Ki, Lynx, find our horses and send runners to alert the others. Kyman, Jorvai, will your people fight?"

"Ilear is with you," Kyman replied, pressing his fist to his heart.

"And Colath," Jorvai swore. "If nothing else, we'll give the bastards a nasty surprise!"

* * *

Word of the Palatine breach spread through the Camp. Despite rain, mud, and exhaustion, Tobin's shivering army found its feet and within an hour they were marching under order of silence toward the enemy line once again. Jorvai sent a raiding party to dispatch the outlying pickets and they did their job well. No outcry gave them away and the rain became their friend, hiding their approach from the sentries.

Iya and eight of the wizards stole on ahead. They kept to the high road, letting the darkness cloak them, conserving their strength for the task ahead. Arkoniel had complained bitterly when she'd ordered him to stay behind with the rear guard, but finally agreed when she'd pointed out that it wouldn't do for the last Guardian to find himself and the precious bowl he carried in Plenimaran hands if it all went wrong.

Holding hands like children so as not to get separated, Iya and her small band of saboteurs plodded along, wading down wheel ruts flooded into small streams.

They stopped just outside the stake lines. Wizards saw better in the dark than ordinary folk, and from here they could easily make out the bearded faces of some of the guards standing around their watch fires. A few hundred yards beyond lay the broken black mouth of the north gate, blocked by makeshift wooden barricades.

They'd agreed in advance that Iya would direct the spell, for her powers were the strongest for this sort of work. The others stood just behind her, their hands pressed against her back and shoulders.

"Illior help us," she whispered, raising her wand in both hands. It was the first time so many had joined at once for such a destructive magic. Iya hoped her old body was strong enough to channel it. Stifling her doubts, she lowered the wand in her left hand and narrowed her eyes. The line of stakes and the watchmen's fires blurred before her as the other wizards willed their power into her.

The spell burst through her and Iya was certain it would shred her to bits. It was like wildfire and hurricanes and avalanches raging all at once. Her bones sang with the force of it.

Yet somehow she survived, and watched in astonishment as pale green fire engulfed the stake line and the barricades beyond. It didn't look like flames, but a mass of writhing forms—serpents or dragons, perhaps. It grew brighter, then exploded. The ground shook and a great gust of hot wind rocked her on her feet. The blast left a roiling cloud of steam in its wake.

Then the ground was shaking again, and this time it came from behind. Someone grabbed her and they tumbled together into the icy water of a ditch. Horsemen surged around and over them, charging the new opening. Iya watched the fleeting shapes as if they were a dream. Perhaps it was a dream, for she couldn't feel her body.

"We did it! We did it!" Saruel cried, holding Iya close to shield her. "Iya, do you see? Iya?"

Iya wanted to answer her, but darkness came and claimed her.

The flash of the wizards' attack left black spots dancing before Tobin's eyes, but that didn't slow her as she led the charge through the gap. As Kyman had predicted, they caught the enemy completely off guard.

Kyman and Jorvai attacked the walls while Tobin and the Atyion garrison stormed up to the Palatine.

Red fire lit their way. The heat of the burning palace seemed to drive off the rain and the flames lit the surrounding area like a beacon.

The battle was still raging and once again they took the Plenimarans by surprise. It was impossible to tell how many they were fighting; with her guard at her back and Tharin, Ki, and Lynx close beside her, Tobin plowed on into the fray.

It was all confusion after that. The broken pavement underfoot hampered them, and familiar landmarks seemed to loom up at odd moments or in the wrong place. At the Royal Tomb the portico was empty, as if the stone effigies had somehow joined the fray. They fought on past the temple, but the pillars and roof were missing.

Small groups of Skalan defenders joined them, but they were outnumbered. The blackened walls around them caught the clamor of battle and magnified it.

They fought for what seemed like hours as rage carried Tobin past exhaustion. Her arms were soaked to the elbow with blood, and her surcoat was black with it.

At last the enemy seemed to be thinning, and she heard a cry among them that sounded like, "There away, there away!"

"Are they calling a retreat?" she asked Tharin, as they paused in the shelter of the tombs.

He listened a moment, then let out a grim laugh. "That's *dyr'awai* they're saying. If I'm not mistaken, it means 'demon queen.' "

Ki chuckled as he wiped his blade on the hem of his sodden surcoat. "Guess word of you got around, after all."

Captain Grannia climbed up to join them. "Are you hurt, Highness?"

"No, just getting my bearings."

"We have them on the run. My lot just brought down what looks to be a general, and a good number of the others tried to run for the gate. We killed most of them."

"Well done! Has there been any sign of Prince Korin?"

"Not that I've seen, Highness."

The captain and her women set off again. Tobin stretched and yawned. "Well, let's have at it."

Just as they were about to set off again, however, she looked around at her remaining guard and her heart sank. "Where's Lynx?"

Ki shared a dark look with Tharin. "Perhaps he got his wish, after all."

There was no time to mourn him. A gang of Plenimarans found them, and the battle was joined again.

Chapter 59

The rain and the battle ended just before dawn. The last of the Plenimarans broke and ran, only to be cut down by the Skalan forces manning the lower city. Lord Jorvai later estimated that even with the southern troops, they'd been outnumbered nearly three to one, but fury had driven them to a bloody victory all the same. "No quarter" remained the standing order, and none was given. Dawn found the rotting plague dead overlaid with dead and dying Plenimarans. A handful of black ships had escaped to carry the news of their defeat back to Benshâl, but most of the raiding fleet had been burned. Smoking hulks drifted on the tide or blazed grounded against the rocky shore. The water was strewn with floating corpses and thick with sharks feasting on this bounty.

Messengers were already streaming in from the lower wards and surrounding countryside. The lands south and west of the city were untouched, but to the north and throughout the city the granaries had been destroyed and whole wards burned flat. Enemy soldiers were rumored to have escaped inland during the night, and Tobin sent Lord Kyman after them.

Refugees were trickling back in, as well, and those who'd somehow survived the siege emerged from their hiding places, weeping, laughing, cursing. Like filthy, vengeful ghosts, they roamed the streets, stripping the dead and mutilating the wounded.

The Palatine was scarcely recognizable. Resting for a moment at the head of the temple steps with Ki and Tharin,

Tobin wearily surveyed the grim scene before her. Just below, her guard and Grannia's fighters kept an uneasy watch; it was too soon to tell how many Skalans here remained loyal to Korin.

Smoke cast a dreary twilight pall over the citadel and the stench of death was already rising. Hundreds of bodies choked the narrow streets: soldier and citizen, Skalan and Plenimaran, thrown together like broken dolls.

The king's body had been found in a tower room above the gate. He was laid out in state, but the crown and the Sword of Ghërilain were gone. There'd been no sign of Korin or any of the Companions. Tobin had dispatched a company of men to look for them among the dead.

Lynx was still missing, too, and Chancellor Hylus had not been seen. There'd been no word of Iya and the other wizards, either, and Tobin had sent Arkoniel down to look for them by the gates. There was nothing more to do but wait for word.

Warriors and drysians were at work carrying the wounded to the Old Palace but the task was overwhelming. Flocks of ravens were descending for the feast, strutting among the dead and mingling their harsh triumphant cries with the cries of the wounded.

The New Palace was still burning and would for days. The Treasury had not been looted, but was lost for a time beneath the flames and rubble. Hundreds of fine houses—Tobin's among them—were only smoking foundations, and those that still stood were stained black. The fine elms that had lined the avenue beyond the Old Palace were gone; their stumps stood like uneven teeth along the road, and the Grove of Dalna had been decimated by axe and flame. The Old Palace had suffered some fire damage, but was still standing. The Companions' training ground, witness to a thousand mock battles, was strewn with genuine dead, and the reflecting pool was dyed red.

Ki shook his head. "Bilairy's balls! Did we save anything?"

"Just be thankful that it's us standing here now, and not the enemy," Tharin told him.

Exhaustion settled over Tobin like a fog, but she forced herself to her feet. "Let's go see who's left."

Near the Old Palace a passing general of the Palatine Guard recognized her surcoat and sank to one knee.

"General Skonis, Highness," he said, searching her face with wondering eyes as he saluted. "I congratulate you on your victory."

"You have my thanks, General. I'm sorry we were too late to prevent all this. Is there any news of my cousin?"

The man bowed his head. "The king is gone, Highness."

"King?" Tharin asked sharply. "They found time for a coronation?"

"No, my lord, but he has the Sword—"

"Never mind that," said Tobin. "You say he's gone?"

"He escaped, Highness. As soon as the gates went down, the Companions and Lord Niryn took him away."

"He ran away?" Ki said, incredulous.

"He was taken to safety, my lord," the general shot back, glaring up at him, and Tobin guessed where the man's true loyalties lay.

"Where did he go?" Tharin demanded.

"Lord Niryn said he would send word." He looked boldly back at Tobin again. "He has the Sword and the crown. He is the heir."

Ki stepped angrily toward him, but Tharin caught his arm, and said, "The true heir stands revealed before you, Skorus. Go and spread the word. No loyal Skalan has reason to fear her."

The man saluted again and strode away.

"I don't like the sound of that," Tharin growled. "You need to make yourself known quickly."

"Yes." Tobin glanced around. "The old audience chamber is still standing. Send out word that anyone who can still walk is to go there at once. I'll address the people there."

"You should have a larger guard, too. Grannia, assemble a guard of six hundred. Have them form up in the front courtyard at once."

Grannia saluted and hurried away.

As Tobin turned to go, however, she caught sight of two familiar, blood-grimed figures approaching out of the haze of the palace gardens. It was Lynx and Una.

"There you are!" Una called out. Walking up to Tobin, she looked closely at her, then looked away blushing. "Lynx tried to tell me, but I couldn't imagine—"

"I'm sorry," said Tobin, and meant it. The neck of Una's tunic was open and Tobin saw she still wore the golden sword pendant she'd made for her. "There was no way to tell you before. I never meant to lead you on."

Una managed a stiff smile. "I know. I just—Well, never mind."

"So this is the girl who caused all that uproar with the king?" said Tharin, holding his hand out to her. "It's good to see you again, Lady Una."

"It's Rider Una, now," she told him proudly. "Tobin and Ki did manage to make a warrior of me, after all." She paused and looked at the smoke rising from the far end of the Old Palace. "You haven't heard any word of my family, have you?"

"No," said Tobin. "Did you come up to look for them?"

Una nodded.

"Good luck, then. And Una? I need more people for my guard. Ask Ahra if she'd be willing, when you go back, and I'll speak to Jorvai."

"I will. And thank you." Una hurried off toward the smoke.

"What happened to you, Lynx?" Ki demanded.

"Nothing," the other squire replied dully. "After we got separated last night I ended up with Ahra's riders outside the gates."

"I'm glad to have you back. I was afraid we'd lost you," Tobin told him.

Lynx acknowledged this with a nod. "We burned the Harriers' headquarters."

"That's a good night's work!" Ki exclaimed. "Were any of them in it at the time?"

"Unfortunately, no," he replied. "We killed all the greybacks we could find, but the wizards were already gone. Ahra and her people found their money chests and let out the last of the prisoners, then put the place to the torch."

"Good riddance," said Ki, as they strode on to the Old Palace.

The corridors and chambers of their former home echoed with the wails of the wounded—cries for help, for water, for death. Tobin and the others had to pick their way carefully so as not to step on them, they lay so thick on the floors. Some rested on mattresses or pallets made of clothing or faded tapestries. Others lay on the bare floor.

An elderly drysian in stained robes knelt before Tobin. "You're the one the Lightbearer's priests promised, aren't you?"

"Yes, old mother, I am," Tobin replied. The woman's hands were as bloodstained as her own, she saw, but from healing rather than killing. Suddenly Tobin wanted very much to wash. "The fires may spread. All those who can be moved would be better off outside the city. I'll have wagons sent."

"Bless you, Majesty!" the woman said, and hurried off.

"You can't escape the title," Ki noted.

"No, but Korin's already claimed it."

As they entered the Companions' wing someone among the wounded called her name. She followed the weak voice and found Nikides lying on a filthy pallet near the messroom door. He'd been stripped to his trousers and his left side was bound with stained rags. His face was white, and his breath came in short, painful gasps.

"Tobin . . . Is it really you?"

"Nik! I thought we'd lost you." Tobin knelt and held her water bottle to his cracked lips. "Yes, it's me. Ki's here, too, and Lynx."

Nikides peered up at her for a moment, then closed his eyes. "By the Light, it's true. We thought old Fox Beard was lying for sure, but look at you! I'd never have guessed . . ."

She set the bottle aside and clasped his cold hand between hers. "I'm less changed than you think. But how are you? When were you hurt?"

"Korin ordered us . . ." He paused, gasping. "I was with them as far as the gate, but then we ran into a great . . ." He broke off again, then whispered, "I never was much of a warrior, was I?"

"You're alive. That's all that matters," Ki said, kneeling to cradle his friend's head. "Where are Lutha and the others?"

"He and Barieus brought me . . . I haven't seen them since. Went with Korin, I expect. He's gone."

"We heard," Tobin told him.

Nikides scowled. "That was Niryn's doing. Kept at him . . ." He drew another shuddering breath and grimaced. "Grandfather's dead. Caught in the New Palace when it burned." His grip on her hand tightened. "I'm sorry he didn't live to see . . . Are you really a girl?" Spots of color rose in his white cheeks. "Really, I mean?"

"Near as I can tell. Now what about you. Can you be moved?"

Nik nodded. "I took an arrow, but it went through clean. The drysians claim I'll heal."

"Of course you will. Ki, help me move him to our old room for now."

*T*he sheets and hangings were gone, but the bed was still usable. They put Nikides on it, and Tharin went for water.

"Prince Tobin?" a soft voice quavered from the shadows of the old dressing room. Baldus peered fearfully around the doorframe, then ran to her and threw himself into her arms, sobbing.

She ran her hands over him but found no sign of a wound. "It's all right now," she said, patting him awkwardly. "It's over. We won."

Baldus caught a hitching breath and turned his tear-stained face up to her. "Molay—he told me to hide. We let the hawks free and hid your jewels, and then he put me in the big clothes chest and told me not to come out until he came back for me. But he didn't. No one came. And then I heard you . . . Where can Molay be?"

"He must have gone to help fight. But it's over now, so he'll be back soon," she said, though she didn't have much hope of that. "Here, have a drink from my bottle. Good, take it all. You must be thirsty after hiding for so long. You can go look for Molay among the wounded, if you like. As soon as you find him or anyone else we know, come and tell me."

Baldus wiped his face and squared his shoulders. "Yes, my prince. I'm so glad you're back safe!"

Ki shook his head as the boy ran off. "He didn't even notice."

*T*he sound of a familiar voice woke Iya.

"Iya? Iya, can you hear me?"

Opening her eyes, she saw Arkoniel kneeling over her. It was daylight. She ached all over and was chilled to the bone, but it seemed she was still alive.

With his help she sat up and found herself by the side of the road not far from where they'd stormed the gates the night before. Someone had pulled her from the ditch and wrapped her in cloaks. Saruel and Dylias sat beside her, and she could see more wizards nearby, smiling at her in obvious relief.

"Good morning," Arkoniel said, but his smile was forced.

"What happened?" There was no sign of the enemy;

Skalan soldiers guarded the gate, and people seemed to be coming and going unchallenged.

"What happened?" Saruel laughed. "Well, we were successful, but nearly killed you in the process."

You shall not enter.

Why did Brother's words come back to haunt her now? She'd survived. "Tobin? Is she—?"

"Jorvai was by earlier and said she came through with a whole skin again. He's convinced she's divinely protected, and from the sound of it, he must be right."

Iya stood up gingerly. She was sore, but seemed to be whole, otherwise.

A mounted herald came through the gate and galloped down the road, shouting, "Go to the Old Palace throne room. All Skalans are summoned to the Old Palace throne room."

Dylias took her arm, smiling broadly. "Come, my dear. Your young queen summons us!"

"Never were sweeter words spoken." She laughed, and all her aches and pains seemed to fall away. "Come, my battered Third Orëska. Let us present ourselves."

Saruel caught Iya by the arm just then. "Look! There in the harbor!"

A small ship was skimming across the water toward the ruined quays. Its square sail was an unmistakable shade of dark red, and it bore the emblem of a large white eye over a supine crescent moon.

Iya touched her heart and eyelids in salute. "The Lightbearer has a new message for us, it seems, and an urgent one, if the Oracle herself comes to deliver it."

"But how? How did she know?" gasped Arkoniel.

Iya patted his arm. "Come now, dear boy. What sort of Oracle would she be if she didn't see this?"

At the throne room the lead seals had been cut and the golden doors thrown wide. Entering with her guard, Tobin found the great chamber beyond already crowded. Sol-

diers and citizens made way for her in near silence, and
Tobin felt all those hundreds of eyes fixed on her. The silence was different than it had been in Atyion. It seemed
filled with doubt and skepticism, and the hint of threat.
Tobin had ordered that her guards keep their weapons
sheathed and Tharin had agreed, but he and Ki looked
wary as they walked beside her.

Some of the shutters had been pulled down and slanting afternoon light streamed in through the tall dusty windows. Open braziers on either side of the high stone
throne cast a red glow over the white marble stairs. A knot
of priests awaited her there. She recognized those who'd
come from Atyion among them, Kaliya foremost among
them, maskless There was still no sign of the wizards.
Someone had cleaned the birds' nests from the stone seat
and lined it with dusty velvet cushions, as it must have
been in the time of her grandmothers. Tobin was too nervous to sit yet.

She stood tongue-tied for a moment, recalling the suspicion she'd seen in General Skonis' eyes. But there was
no turning back now.

"Ki, help me," she said at last, and began unbuckling
her sword belt. With his help, she pulled off her surcoat
and the hauberk and padded shirt underneath. Untying her
hair, she shook it out around her face, then summoned the
priests of Ero up to join her.

"Look at me, all of you. Touch me, so that you can at-
test to these people that I am a woman."

A priest of Dalna ran his hands over her shoulders and
chest, then pressed his palm to her heart. Tobin felt a sensation like a warm moist summer breeze rise through her.

"She is a woman, and of the true blood of the royal
house," he announced.

"So you say!" someone in the crowd called out, and
others echoed it.

"So says the Oracle of Afra!" a deep voice boomed

from the back of the chamber. Iya and Arkoniel stood at the doors, flanking a man in a stained traveling cloak.

The crowd parted as they strode to the foot of the dais. Iya bowed deeply, and Tobin saw that she was smiling.

The man threw off his cloak. Underneath he wore a dark red robe. He took a silver priest's mask from its folds and fixed it over his face. "I am Imonus, high priest of Afra and emissary of the Oracle," he announced.

The priests of Illior covered their own faces with their hands and fell to their knees.

"You have the mark and the scar?" he asked Tobin.

"Yes." Tobin pushed back her shirtsleeve. He climbed the stairs and examined her arm and chin.

"This is Tamír, the Lightbearer's queen, who was foretold to this wizard," he proclaimed.

Iya joined them and he rested a hand on her shoulder. "I was there the day the Oracle revealed this wizard's road. It was I who wrote down her vision in the sacred scrolls, and I am sent now with a gift for our new queen. Majesty, we have kept this for you, all these years."

He raised his hand and two more red-robed priests entered, bearing something on a long litter. A handful of dirty, bedraggled-looking people followed. "The Wizards of Ero," Iya told her.

The litter bearers brought their burden to the foot of the throne and set it down. Something large and flat as a tabletop lay on it, swathed in dark red cloth embroidered with a silver eye.

Imonus descended to fold back the wrappings. Polished gold caught the light of the braziers, and those standing closest gasped as a golden tablet as tall as a man and several inches thick was revealed. Words were engraved across it in square, old-fashioned script like a scroll, the letters tall enough to be read halfway across the great chamber as the litter bearers stood the tablet on its end for all to see.

So long as a daughter of Thelátimos' line defends and rules, Skala shall never be subjugated.

Tobin touched her heart and sword hilt reverently. "Ghërilain's tablet!"

The high priest nodded. "Erius ordered this destroyed, just as he destroyed the steles that once stood in every marketplace," he proclaimed in that same deep, carrying voice. "The priests of the Ero temple saved it and brought it in secret to Afra, where it was hidden until a true queen came to Ero again.

"Hear me, people of Ero, as you stand in the ruins of your city. This tablet is nothing. The words it bears are the very voice of Illior, set there by Illior's first queen. This prophecy was fulfilled, and lived on in the hearts of the faithful, who have failed in their duty for a time.

"Here me, people of Ero, as you look on the face of Tamír, daughter of Ariani and all the queens who came before her, even to Ghërilain herself. The Oracle does not sleep, or see falsely. She would not send this sign to a pretender. She foresaw this queen before she was conceived, before Erius usurped his sister's place, before their mother was lost to the darkness. Doubt my words, doubt this sign, and you doubt the Lightbearer, your protector. You have slept, people of Ero. Awake now and see clearly. The true queen has delivered you, and stands here now to reveal her true face and her true name."

Tobin felt the hair on her arms slowly rise as the misty figure of a woman took shape beside her on the dais. As it grew more solid, she saw that it was a girl about her own age, dressed in a long blue gown. Over it she wore a cuirass of gilded leather emblazoned with the ancient crescent moon and flame emblem of Skala. The Sword of Ghërilain, which she held upright before her face, looked newly forged. Her flowing hair was black, her eyes a dark, familiar blue.

"Ghërilain?" Tobin whispered.

The ghostly girl aged before Tobin's eyes to a woman with iron-grey hair and lines of care etched deep around her mouth and eyes.

Daughter.

The sword was notched and bloody now, but shone more brightly than before. She offered it to Tobin, just as Tamír's ghost had, and her eyes seemed to hold a challenge: *This is yours. Claim it.*

As Tobin reached to take it, the ghost disappeared and she found herself looking instead out through one of the tall windows. From here, she could see past the burned gardens to the smoking ruin of the city and the wreckage-strewn harbor beyond.

So long as a daughter of Thelátimos—

"Tob?" Ki's worried whisper jolted her back to the present.

Her friends were watching her with concern. The Afran priest's face was still masked, but she saw Ghërilain's challenge mirrored in his dark eyes.

"Tobin, are you all right?" Ki asked again.

Her own sword felt too light in her hand as she raised it to salute the crowd, and cried out, "By this tablet, and by the Sword that is not here, I pledge myself to Skala. I am Tamír!"

Chapter 60

The sound of her chamber door being thrown open startled Nalia out of her dreams. The room was still lost in darkness, except for the thin bar of star-flecked sky visible at the tower's two narrow windows.

"My lady, wake up. They've all gone mad!" It was her page, and the child sounded terrified. She felt his fear as keenly as the ever-present damp that permeated every room of this lonely fortress they'd been exiled to.

Her nurse rolled over in the bed with an angry grunt. "Gone mad? Who's gone mad? If this is another of your night terrors, Alin, I'll skin you!"

"No, Vena, listen." Nalia ran to the window that overlooked the bailey and pushed the leaded pane open. Far below she could see torches moving, and hear the clash of steel. "What's happening, Alin?"

"The grey guard has turned on the Cirna garrison. They're slaughtering them!"

"We must bar the door!" Vena lit a candle from the banked coals, then helped Alin set the heavy beam across the iron brackets. Leaving him at the door, she brought Nalia a shawl and stood listening to the inexplicable chaos below.

It died away at last and Nalia clung trembling to her nurse, fearful of what the quiet might mean. Outside there was nothing but the distant sigh of the waves against the cliffs.

"My lady, look there!" Alin pointed to the other window, the one that faced south over the isthmus road. A long line of torches was approaching quickly along it. As they drew closer, Nalia could make out the riders who carried them, and hear the jangle of harness and mail.

"It's an attack!" she whispered.

"The Plenimarans have come," Vena wailed. "O Maker, save us!"

"But why would the grey guard attack the others inside the walls? What can it mean?"

Nearly an hour passed before they heard footsteps on the tower stairs. Vena and Alin pushed Nalia into the far corner, shielding her with their bodies.

The latch rattled. "Nalia, my dear, it's only me. You're quite safe. Open the door."

"Niryn!" Nalia ran to the door and struggled to heave the bar aside. "That was you on the road? Oh, you gave us such a fright!" The bar clattered to the floor. She flung the door open and fell into her lover's arms, feeling safe again.

Two Harrier guardsmen stood just behind him. "What's happening?" she asked, fearful again. Niryn never allowed any other men in her tower; the red hawks on the front of their tunics looked black as ravens in the dim light. "Alin said the men were fighting each other."

Niryn's beard tickled her bare shoulder as he gently pushed her away. "Mutiny and treason, my dear, but it's over now and you have nothing to fear. In fact, I bring you wonderful news. Tell your servants to leave us."

Blushing but delighted, Nalia nodded at Vena and Alin and they hurried out as they always did. The guardsmen made way for them, but remained. "My lord, I've missed you so—"

She tried to embrace him again, but he held her at arm's length. As she gazed up at that beloved face, some trick of the candle made his eyes look hard. She took a step back, pulling the shawl closer around her. "Something *is* wrong. Tell me, please."

He smiled again, and the same ungenerous light stretched it into a leer. "This is a great day, Nalia. A very great day."

"What—what do you mean, my lord?"

"I have someone I want you to meet." He nodded to the guards and they stepped aside to let another man pass. Shocked, Nalia tugged at her shawl again.

This one was young and very handsome, but he was dirty and unshaven, too, and smelled appalling. Nonetheless, she recognized the arms on his filthy surcoat and sank to her knees before him. "Prince Korin?"

"King Korin," Niryn corrected gently. "I present Lady Nalia."

"This? This is the one?" The young king's look of disgust chilled her more than the night air.

"Her blood is true, I assure you," Niryn said, going to the door.

Nalia watched in growing alarm as he stepped from the room and began to slowly close it after him. "Nalia, allow me to present your new husband."

ABOUT THE AUTHOR

Lynn Flewelling was born in Presque Isle, Maine, in 1958. She received her BS from the University of Maine in 1981 and went on to study Veterinary Medicine. She has had a variety of jobs including house painter, sales clerk, teacher and copy writer. Among her favourite writers and influences are: Tom Stoppard, Mary Renault, Umberto Eco, Stephen King, Joyce Carol Oates, Ray Bradbury, and Arthur Conan Doyle.

Lynn Flewelling currently lives in western New York with her husband and their two sons, and creatures that shed too much.

A Sorcerer's Treason

Book One of the Isavalta Trilogy

Sarah Zettel

When lighthouse-keeper Bridget Lederle rescues an oddly dressed, tattooed stranger from the storm-tossed Lake Superior he tells her he is from another world, a world in which she is a great magical force. Only she can save the Dowager Empress, currently under threat from her poisonous daughter-in-law. For a woman with nothing to lose, it's an attractive offer. But when Bridget arrives in Isavalta she finds nothing is quite as he promised her . . .

'This engaging and vivid slice of fantasy will keep fans of Robin Hobb more than happy'   *SFX*

'A sumptuous tale of subtle magic, malevolent sorcery and twisted loyalties – you won't regret venturing into Sarah Zettel's world.'   SARA DOUGLASS

'Zettel's first fantasy novel is a triumph of storytelling. Rich, compelling and exciting, this could be the best fantasy debut in years.'   JONATHAN WEIR, *Amazon*

ISBN: 0-00-711400-1

Fool's Errand

The Tawny Man: Book One

Robin Hobb

We are here, you and I, Fitz, to change the world. Again.

Fifteen years have passed since the end of the Red Ship War, with the terrifying Outislanders. Since then, Fitz has wandered the world accompanied only by his wolf and Wit-partner, Nighteyes, finally settling in a tiny cottage as remote from Buckkeep and the Farseers as possible.

But lately the world has come crashing in again. The Witted are being persecuted because of their magical bonds with animals; and young Prince Dutiful has gone missing just before his crucial diplomatic wedding to an Outislander princess. Fitz's assignment to fetch Dutiful back in time for the ceremony seems very much like a fool's errand, but the dangers ahead could signal the end of the Farseer reign.

'In today's crowded fantasy market Robin Hobb's books are like diamonds in a sea of zircons' GEORGE R R MARTIN

ISBN 0-00-648601-0

The Lightstone
1: The Ninth Kingdom
Book One, part one of the Ea Cycle

David Zindell

On the island continent of Ea it is a dark time of chaos and war. Once again Morjin, the fallen angel, is seeking the Lightstone. Already his assassins haunt the forests of Mesh, intent upon the death of the seventh son of its King. He is Valashu Elahad, the champion prophesied to find the Lightstone and vanquish Morjin.

What dangerous pride they both display, the fallen angel and the seventh son, to think the power of the Lightstone can belong to any one man. But Morjin's ruthlessness may yet succeed, and with the Lightstone he will free the Lord of Lies, who has been imprisoned for a million years.

'Vividly imaginative and truly grand. There's a richness of description, and a canvas as broad and colourful as they come'   *Time Out*

ISBN: 0-00-648620-7

A Game of Thrones

Book One of A Song of Ice and Fire

George R R Martin

IN THE GAME OF THRONES,
YOU WIN OR YOU DIE

As Warden of the North, Lord Eddard Stark counts it as a curse when King Robert bestows on him the office of Hand. His honour weighs him down at court where a true man does what he will, not what he must . . . and a dead enemy is a thing of beauty.

The old gods have no power in the south, Stark's family is split, and there is treachery at court. Worse, a vengeance-mad boy has grown to maturity in exile in the Free Cities beyond the sea. Heir of the mad Dragon King deposed by Robert, he claims the Iron Throne.

'A Game of Thrones grabs hold and won't let go. It's brilliant'
ROBERT JORDAN

'Such a splendid tale. I couldn't stop till I'd finished and it was dawn.'
ANNE McCAFFREY

ISBN: 0-00-647988-X

To Ride Hell's Chasm

Janny Wurts

A compelling standalone tale on an epic scale, filled with intrigue, adventure and dark magic.

When Princess Anja fails to appear at her betrothal banquet, the tiny, peaceful kingdom of Sessalie is plunged into intrigue. Charged with recovering the distraught King's beloved daughter is Mykkael, the rough-hewn newcomer who has won the post of Captain of the Garrison. A scarred veteran with a deadly record of field warfare, his 'interesting' background and foreign breeding are held in contempt by court society.

As the princess's trail vanishes outside the citadel's gates, anxiety and tension escalate. Mykkael's investigations lead him to a radical explanation for the mystery, but he finds himself under suspicion from the court factions. Can he convince them in time of his dramatic theory: that the resourceful, high-spirited princess was not taken by force, but fled the palace to escape a demonic evil?

'Janny Wurts writes with an astonishing energy . . . it ought to be illegal for one person to have so much talent'
STEPHEN R DONALDSON

'One to skive off work for'   *Starburst*

'An absorbing read . . . set in a delightful world'
Dreamwatch

ISBN 0-00-710111-2

Snare

Katharine Kerr

The Snare of Secrets

In despair at the corruption of his ruler, the despotic Great Khan, Captain Idres Warkannon sets out on a perilous journey in search of a saviour: the Khan's long-lost younger brother. Despite the strictures of his religion, he depends on the guidance of a mysterious sorcerer to cross the vast plains of purple grass in safety.

But the sorcerer, Soutan, is shadowed by a loyal member of the Great Khan's deadly secret service: Zayn Hassan has infiltrated a tribe of peace-loving nomads in order to carry out his spying mission. He certainly hasn't bargained for the simple pleasure of life on the plains, or the attractions of Ammadin, the tribe's fiercely independent spirit rider.

Journeying across the grass, centuries-old falsehoods are gradually revealed and all of the factions discover more about their histories and identities than they could ever have envisaged.

'A fantastic plot which turns a simple story into something far more original ... a cracking read'   *SFX*

'Kerr traces complex emotional and intellectual relationships as they evolve amid the dangers and vivid wonders of a world you won't soon forget'   *Locus*

'A compelling standalone fantasy'   *Dreamwatch*

ISBN 0 00 648039 X